THE TONTINE MURDERS

MURDERS

Louisa McDonald

This book is dedicated to my wonderful family with especial thanks to my lovely son, Tom, whose life was absolutely not enriched by the Formatting War of September 2023. Thanks, Tom

How it all began

Spring 1990

A fortnight after Aunt Edna's death, her grieving nephews and nieces arrived at Gerald's Tudorbethan house, ready to set off for the ceremony of farewell. They were dressed in sombre black and long faces just as the occasion demanded.

After a cup of weak tea and a Garibaldi biscuit, the cousins filed out of the kitchen, donned coats, adjusted hats, blew noses and cleared throats, searched for dusty mints in the crevices of pockets and handbags, and declared themselves ready to follow their aunt's coffin in a procession of limousines.

The funeral was long and tiresome as the funerals of the unloved so often are. The mourners mouthed sad hymns while their gaze drifted to the sunbeams piercing the window panes. It was mesmerising to watch the dust motes floating up and down and, somehow, before they knew it, it was as if they were not there at all. The black clothes and sensible shoes, and the hands clutching hymn books were all still present but the minds of their owners were far away. With the exception of Pammie - who had never been quite right in the head since the accident - the cousins were wondering, with barely suppressed excitement, how much money their aunt had left them.

The old woman had known that her family was desperate to find out the terms of her will. Indeed, the chief delight of her waning years had been to watch them squirming under the alternating promise of riches and the threat of their being destined elsewhere. In the absence of certainty, the cousins had spent many, many hours fantasising about the wonderful things they would do when the money was theirs.

And, here it was at last - the moment had come. Finally, God willing, they could all start living the life they deserved.

The letter arrived one week later.

May I, first of all, offer my sympathy on the loss of your aunt, Miss Edna Benson. She was a lady of prodigious talent and immense character and she will, I am certain, be missed by many. That number includes me for I knew her as a friend for close to three quarters of a century.

Secondly, I am obliged to inform you that, in both my unofficial capacity of confidante, and also in my official one as her lawyer, Miss Benson honoured me with the details of her will. As you are named in that document, I would appreciate your acceptance of the invitation outlined below.

As a man long past retirement, I am no longer burdened with the trappings of an office. Therefore, I have reserved a private room for our meeting at the Regency Suite in The King's Head, central Cardiff, this coming Friday, that is, the 18th of May, commencing at half past one. Please be prompt.

Yours sincerely,
Jolyon Merryweather.
(late of Johnson, Johnson and Merryweather, Cardiff).

When the 18th of May arrived, those with jobs had not submitted time-off requests. They didn't expect it to be agreed to at such short notice and they were afraid to highlight the date. A coincidental absence would be immediately suspect.

Many and varied were the stories consequently told that morning.

Just before lunch, Gerald, the oldest of the cousins, announced to the office that he needed to leave straightaway because of a domestic crisis at his daughter's house. Once he got to the King's Head, he had an altercation in the car park when a plump blond man in a tracksuit refused to shift his Fiesta three inches to the left in order to safely accommodate Gerald's vintage Jaguar. Gerald ended up parking in the wide spaces of the disabled bay but reasoned that nobody in a wheelchair was going to be frittering away cash on a Friday lunchtime so there was no harm done.

His teacher brother, Arnold, advised his Head of Department that he was terribly sorry but his sciatica had unexpectedly returned. Consequently, he wouldn't be able to teach Form Five for the double lesson after the mid-morning break . Nor would he be available for any of the afternoon periods. Then he fretted because his bus went past school twice on its way into town. On both of these occasions he hid by pretending to tie his shoelaces. The ghastly rush of blood to his head as he ducked down made him so dizzy that he very nearly alerted the driver to his distress. He didn't, though, because he remembered how unsympathetic the company had been during his last medical emergency on public transport.

The men's cousin, Venetia, rang her boss at the pharmacy to say that her bus had been run off the road by a maniac and that she had taken to her bed, too shocked to function. Then she was late getting to the pub because she kept changing her dress. Somehow, nothing seemed to fit any more. To make it worse, the new foundation that she'd filched from work didn't cover up the acne scars as it promised on the box. She'd been forced to use her old faithful Panstick and she'd got it all over the dress she'd finally chosen which she'd then had to sponge off.

The fourth cousin, Karen, was lucky. She hadn't needed to ask for time off at the boutique because the date coincided with her regular day off. Unfortunately, though, she was forced to cancel a longstanding lunch arrangement with her new acquaintance, Mr Singh. This was a nuisance because the man seemed to be looking very favourably at her latest business proposal. Then she was delayed because, although he had very kindly driven her into town, he didn't want to let her out of his car. She'd had to sit in the passenger seat for what felt like an age while he'd told her - again - all about his elderly mother in Chandigarh and how much he wished he could bring her to Britain. Karen was, of course, sympathetic but she needed to get on and out, not least because sitting for too long in one position threatened to crease her linen trouser suit.

Meanwhile, the youngest two cousins, Alison and her twin, Pammie, had also experienced a disrupted morning. Alison had had to explain to her sister over breakfast that she wouldn't be dropping her off at the Day Centre because the weekly singalong session had been cancelled. To make up for the disappointment, she promised to pick her up at one o'clock to take her out for lunch with the cousins. Meanwhile, Alison told her assistant at the library that she had stomach-ache.

Which, as it happened, was true. When the sisters arrived in the city centre, there was nowhere to park at the King's Head so they had to use the multi-storey and that was a good ten minutes' hike from the pub.

They all arrived there at more or less the same time.

Gerald scowled when he saw his cousins approaching the pub's swing doors just as he was doing the same, and he began a kind of disguised trot, hoping they wouldn't notice his sudden spurt of speed and try and catch him up or, even worse, overtake him. He'd wanted to arrive early, knowing how important it was to get the seat at the head of the table. There was just a chance that they'd get in the room ahead of him, especially Karen, who had little respect for primogeniture.

As it turned out, he needn't have worried - her heels were too high to allow haste. His brother, Arnold, couldn't hurry either because he'd re-tied his laces so tightly on the bus that he'd lost all feeling in his little toes on both feet, a fact which he found most worrying. Venetia was slow in walking as a result of the tightness of her dress which was making breathing rather tough. And Alison couldn't hurry because she was shepherding her sister past the sunny tables outside the pub where sat a chap with two Doberman puppies that Pammie was desperate to fondle.

Once inside the pub, they followed the yellowing signs for The Regency Suite, elbowing and apologising their way past beer drinkers and crisp-munchers, their shoes sticking to the swirling carpet underfoot. As they approached the room, the left-hand door was opened from the inside by an ancient, tiny man sporting Prince of Wales check and pince-nez.

"Good afternoon," he said. "Jolyon Merryweather. Delighted to make your acquaintance. Do come in and make yourselves comfortable. There's water on the table. Please help yourselves. It's a warm afternoon, isn't it?"

There was some hesitation as the cousins stared at the table and seven chairs.

"Take a seat," said Mr Merryweather. "Any seat at all, anywhere you like. I find that round tables are so much pleasanter, don't you agree? I do so hate it when one is forced to jostle for position at square tables. It brings out the worst in people right from the start."

Gerald was paralysed by the dilemma of simultaneously wanting to sit down first - which was the best seat at a round table? - but also last - where would everyone else choose to sit? Arnold was perplexed because he had hoped for a discreet place in a corner so that he could

4

loosen his shoes. Venetia desperately required a supply of fresh air so that her breathing might be eased but every window in the room was closed. Karen grimaced at the hard bentwood chairs because she needed a soft seat which would not ruin the linen folds of her suit. Alison wanted Pammie to sit next to her, but also not where she could look out through a window because of the threat of distraction from outside - but the Regency Suite featured glass on three out of its four walls.

Sitting had to be done, however: chairs had to be chosen slowly or quickly, near windows or not. Each of the cousins briefly introduced themselves to the elderly solicitor, with Gerald, of course, going first.

The solicitor opened a leather briefcase and extracted from it a thin file. He placed this on the table in front of him.

"I would like to begin," he said, "by providing a little contextual information. I hope that this detail will help you to understand the will which your aunt has left. It is, as you will hear, somewhat unusual."

He looked around, waiting for a sign, a murmured comment, a raised hand. No-one ventured word nor glance, not even Gerald.

"I have spent my working life," the man continued, "dealing with the affairs of high-wealth individuals. In my estimation, this group generally comprises three kinds of people.

"Firstly, there are those who have made their fortune through the manufacture and provision of goods or services. Crucially, they continue to work long after their financial situation demands it. These are, in the main, happy and contented folk.

"Then there is the second group. This band of people have made their fortune in much the same way as did the first. The difference between them is that, their wealth having been amassed, this second group sells up in order to spend their lives on perpetual holiday. These people, in my experience, are deeply unhappy. They have lost the purpose, drive and vision which characterised their younger years and are forever unable to return to the passion for living that they once had, be they now ever so rich.

"But in my experience, the unhappiest group of all is those who *inherit* wealth. These folk are never satisfied. They are unhappy while they wait for legacies to arrive - yet once the bequest is there, the contentment they had hoped for never materialises. The dream of the money has sustained them - but its actuality disappoints. It is true that they can now spend as they have always longed to do - but once a man has two houses, why would he need three? If four cars, why buy five? Sad indeed is the man who achieves all of his dreams."

Six pairs of anxious eyes stared at him. What the old man was saying was nonsense. It was far from sad to achieve one's dreams - on the contrary, it was not much short of miraculous. They had fantasised for decades about becoming rich and not one of them was in a position to wait forever. They needed that money and they needed it now.

"This is a future," said Mr Merryweather, "that your aunt wished to avoid as long as possible for you, her beloved nephews and nieces."

The voices around the table were hushed.

"Is there to be no money?" murmured Venetia.

"I'm not sure I like the sound of this," said Arnold under his breath.

"Has the woman left us nothing?" whispered Karen.

"There will be money," said the solicitor, "and it will be enough to smooth the sharp edges of life - although not a fortune, admittedly." At this, he hesitated for a moment and looked down at the file as if he were reading from it. When he next spoke, it was without raising his gaze. "Or at least not immediately."

After a second or two had passed, he looked up again at the cousins, whose faces were drawn and wary.

"I think you'd better tell us more," said Gerald.

"Indeed, "said Mr Merryweather, regaining his earlier, brisk pace, "an excellent suggestion. To continue then, let me just ask - has anyone here ever heard of a tontine?"

From the baffled silence, the answer was clear.

A tontine, Mr Merryweather went on to explain, was a type of life assurance scheme. Where it differed from the standard policy was that it was not tied to any one individual person. Instead, it was based on the lives of those in a particular named group. He could now reveal that Aunt Edna had employed him to initiate such a scheme on her behalf - and that the lives on which the tontine was based were theirs.

"And for this," said Mr Merryweather, "as I have already explained, she had good reason. It may not, at this moment, look that way but, be assured, Miss Benson had your best interests at heart."

The cousins looked at each other uncertainly.

Mr Merryweather got down to specifics. Their aunt, he said, had initiated the tontine policy fifteen years earlier, when she had first moved into Spring Heights Care Home. She had used the cash from the sale of her house to finance it and had, ever since, enjoyed a substantial annual income based on the interest.

"And this," he said, "is your inheritance. Following your aunt's death, the tontine policy belongs to you."

He picked up a glass of water and sipped briefly from it.

"From now on," he continued, "the yearly interest payment will be divided equally between you all. This will not, at first, be a huge, life-troubling amount. However, in the fullness of time..." he paused for a moment and gazed into the middle distance. "As I say, in the fullness of time, as each cousin dies, the amount paid to those remaining will inevitably go up."

He looked down once more at the file. "At this point, I am obliged to inform you that, under the - rather woolly - Life Assurance Act of 1774, it is possible - but by no means certain - that this tontine might be judged illegal."

"Of course, it is," said Gerald, his face flushed. "It cannot possibly be legal. I intend to seek advice. *Professional* advice."

"Mr Benson, you are, of course, free to challenge the terms of your aunt's will through the courts. However, if just one of you sets foot on this path, I have been instructed to dissolve the policy with immediate effect and to distribute the entire fund to charity. As a result, none of you would receive so much as a penny."

The faces around the table shifted from incomprehension to distress. They'd waited for this money nearly all of their adult lives - they had spent literally years dreaming of the difference it would make. How could Aunt Edna have done this to them? All those visits to Spring Heights Care Home, all that kowtowing and miserable compliance. The insults they'd borne and the humiliation. And all that time, she had planned to bequeath them - not the money which she'd promised and which they deserved – but this preposterous scheme.

"The choice is yours," said the solicitor, "You must either accept the terms of the tontine or fight the will and risk total disinheritance."

"This simply cannot be right!" shouted Gerald, banging the table.

"What a ridiculous plan!" cried Karen.

"Monstrous!" was Arnold's desperate response.

"You cannot be serious!" said Venetia, incredulous.

"How could Aunt Edna have done this to us?" asked Alison.

And Pammie, looking around at all of the angry faces, leant across and took her sister's hand.

Mr Merryweather did not attempt to speak over their outrage. Instead, as the voices faltered and stopped, he began to speak in an even quieter tone than he had employed before.

"I must now explain the most important feature of the tontine," he said. "And it is this: once the final cousin is left – that is, when the other five of you have died – that remaining person will immediately inherit the entire capital sum of the tontine plus any accrued interest."

He coughed delicately.

"Currently, the account is in extremely good health. I can therefore predict with confidence that that lone survivor will, overnight, become a millionaire. In fact, probably several times over. I leave it to you to decide whether that person is to be considered blessed – or perhaps cursed."

And by this, the biggest news of all, the cousins were struck dumb. There was nothing they dared utter. Because the truth, in all its magnificent horror, was clear.

Each of them finally understood that they were not, after all, going to inherit their aunt's money as they had always expected and believed. On the other hand, there was a chance that they could inherit much, much more. More than they had ever dreamed of. The difficulty was that there was only one road that led to the fortune Mr Merryweather described.

The last one alive inherits everything.

Which meant that, if they wanted to be rich, rich beyond the imagining, then every single one of their cousins - and of their siblings - had to die first.

And soon.

Chapter One

Gerald Benson

Autumn 1991

G erald walked into the kitchen, frowned at the cat and grimaced at the dog. Then he sat down at the breakfast-bar with all the heaviness of a person who had been pushed there. He hadn't been, of course, because he was the only one up. He stared out of the French windows at the milky sky and considered the mystifying sloth of his wife and daughter. Time and again, he had explained that, by lying in bed, they were missing the best part of the day. His words remained unheard and unheeded. At weekends, Janet and Tamara refused to make an appearance before half past nine. And when they did come down, they rarely looked prepared to meet the morning but instead tended to appear in the kitchen still dressed for bed. His wife had taken to wearing a candlewick dressing gown until eleven and his daughter wandered around the house in pyjamas until lunchtime.

This was not what he had imagined would happen when Tamara left her philandering husband and moved back into the little pink bedroom under the eaves.

He felt a paw scratching at his shin and looked down to see Poppy, the wretched puppy that Tamara had brought with her. Its eyes were large and glossy like slick brown marbles. It put its head to one side and pawed at him again. He kicked it: not hard, of course - he wasn't a savage - but enough to make it slink away to its bed in front of the radiator where it rested its jaw on the toys that littered the basket. It was a mystery to him that Keith had managed to keep the three-piece suite and the dining table but not the dog and cat that the couple had bought in the final year of their marriage: both purchased, no doubt, as some kind of substitute for the baby that, sad though it was, had refused to arrive.

Half an hour later, reinvigorated by a bowl of porridge and two cups of coffee, he made a start on the cryptic crossword. To his dismay, he saw that the puzzle had been written by ChillPill, his least favourite setter. It was clear that the man was on his usual form because Gerald couldn't immediately see a single answer. He liked to solve the clues in order, beginning with 1 across because there was a rightness to that, but today he stared at the paper for a full ten minutes: "*First couple of children always bring happiness* (5)". He chewed the end of the pen and gazed at the clue, willing it to make sense but the words began to swim before his eyes. *Happiness. Happiness...* how long was it since *he* had been happy?

Was it when he had first met Janet at a Christian Union dance thirty years ago? Or was it during their first fumbled kiss, snatched in the Plaza cinema while they were watching, or pretending to watch, 'The Magnificent Seven'? Afterwards, Janet had said how much he looked like Steve McQueen. He didn't think that was entirely true but then Janet was no film star herself, if he was being honest. Which was a good virtue to have.

Or was the last happy moment when Tamara was born? He remembered the night they'd brought her home from the hospital and how he'd gazed down into the cradle, watching the scarlet wrinkled bundle that lay there, bawling. And how she'd done much the same for many, many of the nights that followed. Janet told him that colic happened to most babies but the knowledge of the suffering of others hadn't helped the burden of his own.

But Tamara was twenty eight years old. Surely there had been some happiness since then?

Yes. There had been. He had felt cheerful, ecstatic even, on that glorious spring day last year, when he'd received the call from Spring Heights Care Home. Aunt Edna was dead. The money was as good as his.

The rapture hadn't lasted long, of course: news of the tontine had seen to that. There had been huge disappointment but he wasn't so surprised. Experience had taught him that constancy in joy was something expected only by fools. Yet it didn't seem unreasonable to want more than these islands of happiness in the sea of gloom that was otherwise his life.

A lot had changed since Aunt Edna had died, the most traumatic being that his son-in-law, Keith, had managed to impregnate the barmaid at the local pub. In one way, it was a relief. Before this, Gerald had assumed that he was going to have to pay the man a small fortune to agree to leave Tamara . Indeed, to leave the area, or, even better, the entire country.

Aunt Edna's bizarre will had put paid to any such dreams.

However, as it happened, when the rumours and the barmaid's bulge had become impossible to ignore, Tamara had chosen of her own free – if unhappy – will to leave her husband, bringing all of her tears, debt and pets back to her parents' house. She'd kept her job at the estate agents, though, Recently, Gerald had started dropping hints about how ideally situated she was to find a nice little flat in town somewhere.

Meanwhile, Janet had left her three days a week at the cake shop on the corner, claiming that she wanted to spend more time as a mother and housewife. She still ate lots of pastries, however, a habit which could only add to the enthusiastic blossoming of her waistline. He lived in hope that one day she'd feed an iced bun to the dog and kill it but this was unlikely because Tamara had subjected the family to a lecture on what darling Poppy could and couldn't eat.

Gerald's own employment was not what it was. He still had a few years to go before retirement but, increasingly, he'd been made to feel rather surplus. He tried to ignore the big assignments that, these days, went to shiny-suited adolescents rather than to him, and he'd learnt to accommodate learning about important meetings via gossip. But still. Time was when he'd been the man to listen to, he'd been the chap for the major contracts, the delicate negotiations, the fondling of secretaries on faux-leather office chairs. Those days had long gone, sunk below the horizon forever, along with his hair and his libido.

But then, retirement not being far off might be a good thing. He could start a new hobby, improve his golf handicap, go on out-of-season holidays with Janet...he looked up from the crossword and caught a glimpse of the thin-faced old man gazing at him in the mirror and he swallowed hard.

There came the whisper of candlewick dressing gown on the parquet flooring of the hall and the delighted yelping of a dog about to be fed. Please God make it an iced bun.

He gazed back down at the crossword and at the 1 across clue: "*First couple of children always bring happiness*". Then he picked up his ballpoint and wrote "*Cheer*".

The following Sunday was his 63ʳᵈ birthday. Janet had booked a table at the Crazy Bear Steakhouse. It wouldn't have been his choice of venue but, as she had told him, if he refused to offer an opinion on where to go, then he had no right to moan about the outcome.

"The problem is, Gerald," she said on the morning of his special day, "you're in denial. You don't want to have any kind of celebration because you don't actually want to have a birthday. You don't want any kind of marker that says you're getting older."

He refused to look up from the copy of Ulysses that he'd bought four years earlier. He was trying to read a few pages of it every day in order to challenge his brain.

"I think you'll find, Janet," he said, turning to page 46, "that I am no more reluctant than anybody else to participate in the ageing process. As usual, you're exaggerating."

"Honestly, sometimes, Gerald, you're like a wet weekend in Wigan." She came and stood behind his chair, blocking out the light from the window. "We need to think of Tammy," she said, putting one hand on his shoulder. "She needs cheering up. She's been through a very difficult time."

"I would appreciate it if you didn't keep calling our daughter 'Tammy'," he said finally. "Her name is Tamara and she was named after the ancient goddess of rivers and streams - not after some ghastly American pop singer." He put down his book but did not look up at her. "I suggest you go and get some proper clothes on. I suspect that not even in the Crazy Bear Steakhouse will they serve a woman wearing a dressing gown."

"You're a pompous bastard, Gerald." She took her hand away from his shoulder and tightened the belt around her middle.

He frowned. "I think you'll find that, if we're thinking of helping Tamara, then bad language is hardly the way forward."

Janet walked away without a word until she reached the louvered door at which point, she stopped, hesitated and then turned. "And I think you'll find," she said, "that you've been stuck on page 46 for the last six months."

She flounced out of the room with a smile. But her lips were trembling.

The birthday meal was a disaster. The music was too loud, so loud that, even had he wanted to make conversation, he wouldn't have been able to do so. The noise was made worse by the people on the next table who had brought half a dozen unruly children with them. Nor was he pleased by several other aspects of the restaurant. The waitress, for instance, was over-familiar: he had no idea why the management of these places imagined that diners enjoyed it when waiting staff bent down to speak to them at eye-level. He wasn't in a wheelchair, for God's sake. And it was no surprise that the food proved uninspiring. He pushed his plate away.

"Considering the name of this place, I find it extraordinary that they can't manage a steak without ruining it."

"Gerald," said his wife, putting down her knife and fork, "you asked for 'well-done'. That's what you wanted and that's what you got."

"I asked for sirloin and I got shoe leather."

"Well, I think this is a great place," said Tamara. "It's lively and young and busy."

"My point exactly," said her father. "I think it's time we left." He waved a hand at the waitress who tipped a finger at her stetson to show that she had seen his message. "And goodness knows what the point is of these cowgirl costumes. Utterly ludicrous."

The buck-skinned waitress approached them with a bill and a grin. Six minutes later, she left them with a request that they should all have a nice day. Gerald groaned.

"Cheer up, Dad!" said Tamara. "It's your birthday, remember?"

At which point, a rogue balloon from the next table hit him straight in the face.

At home, and a cup of tea and a slice of birthday cake later, he was feeling mollified. It was time for the presents. Poppy the puppy and

Coco the kitten had apparently chosen, bought and wrapped a box of chocolates for him. Tamara had bought her father a book of crosswords. It didn't contain any cryptic ones but the girl had done her best and for that he was grateful. Janet had bought him a book called "A Year in Provence" written by a chap called Peter Mayle. It was an autobiographical account of the writer's move into a French farmhouse with his wife and two dogs. Gerald could hardly imagine anything worse.

"Richard and Judy were talking to Peter Mayle on This Morning and they were absolutely raving about this book," said Janet. "So I thought you'd like it."

"Thank you, Janet," he said. "That's very kind." He put the present on the table next to his chair.

"But you haven't even opened it. You might at least read the blurb on the back cover."

"I'll read it later."

"You know, we could do something like he did - just sell up, leave everything behind and start again."

"Start again?"

"Yes," she put her hand on his knee. "Just the two of us."

"The two of us?"

"Yes - just like it used to be." She bent down and kissed him on the lips. "It would be fun- exciting, even."

That night, as Janet snored beside him, he began reading the Peter Mayle book. After ten minutes, he put it away and read page 46 of Ulysses. Pretty soon, he, too, was snoring. And then, half an hour into a dream that he instantly forgot upon waking, Janet crashed him back into consciousness by sliding one soft hand into his pyjama bottoms.

After an excellent night's sleep, he woke up feeling refreshed. To his surprise, Janet got up early and came downstairs properly dressed. Once there, she almost ignored both pets and cooked him a full English breakfast. As an extra bonus, he finished the crossword in record time.

Bright and optimistic, he set off for work. The sky glowed above his head, the birds sang in the trees and the smell of autumn was in the air. The bus came promptly and he smiled at the driver and, ten minutes into the journey, he had the pleasure of giving up his seat to a pregnant woman who looked at him gratefully and thanked him.

He got off the bus and walked briskly down St Mary Street until he reached Avis Buildings. Once inside, he climbed the stairs instead of getting in the lift. He was going to do this every day until he could manage to get to the third floor without being out of breath. A person was never too old to get fit. At the double doors that led into Accounts, he paused and surveyed the scene through the glass. He liked to circumvent the newly-introduced hot-desk arrangement by arriving half an hour before anybody else so that he could take the desk by the window. This manoeuvre was not always successful but, just as he knew it would, the day's gleaming positivity had bagged that for him, too. The place was still empty.

Opening the doors, he strode across to the desk, took off his coat, pulled back the chair, sat down, opened his briefcase, took his sandwiches out for later, and glanced into the street below. A man in a beret and striped jersey was sitting on a bicycle, stopping passers-by with what looked like exhortations to buy one of the strings of onions that were draped around his neck.

Perhaps Janet was right, he mused. Perhaps starting afresh somewhere Continental would be just the tonic they needed, just the step to get their lives and their marriage back on track. France was fairly close, and it was sufficiently similar to Britain to soon seem like home. They were still happy to be together, still keen to find enjoyment in life, and not so old to have given up on new horizons.

There was their daughter to consider, of course - but how long did parental responsibility last? He and his brother Arnold had fended for themselves almost from the moment that they became teenagers. Tamara would just have to get herself and her animals a little flat somewhere. She wouldn't be alone for long. There must surely be a chap out there looking for a girl who could offer him security and comfort without the encumbrance of children. And Tamara had a pretty face. And she would always be welcome to visit her parents in France, especially as she had O Level French and would be able to converse with the natives.

He looked out at the window again and smiled to see the straggly queue at the Frenchman's bicycle. The man was nodding his head at them and making enthusiastic gestures with one stripey arm.

The sudden hand on his shoulder made him jump. He turned round to see Jack Reynolds, the new office manager, who was standing there grinning at him like some kind of fool.

"Hey, Gerry, how's things?" said Reynolds.

Gerald frowned. To answer the man or to correct him? That was the question. "I'm fine, thanks," he eventually said. "And how are things with you, Jack?"

"If I'm honest, Gerry, not so great. Look, old chap, I know you're busy but would you mind popping into my office for a mo? There's just a few things I'd like to discuss with you."

'There 'are' a few things', thought Gerald, contemptuously. The word is 'moment'. I'm not an 'old chap'. And I'm certainly not called 'Gerry'.

"Absolutely," he said.

Jack Reynolds ushered Gerald into a chair Then he sat down behind a gigantic desk gleaming with mahogany polish and lack of paper. Briefly, Gerald pondered the likely inadequacies of the man's private appendages but his attention was diverted to something altogether more concrete and even more horrible when Jack Reynolds began to speak. Much of it was a ragged, impossible-to-process blur but Gerald knew that the man had uttered the words 'restructuring' and 'redundancy' and that he was not going to be part of the former but was definitely expected to participate in the latter.

"But you can't just get rid of me!" he stammered. "Nobody knows as much as I do about discounted cash-flow analysis. And what about the asset accounts? No-one here has my experience!"

"I know, Gerry, I know," said Jack Reynolds. "And believe me, we're gonna miss you." His face was sombre. "The engineering world is going crazy right now. With all your wealth of experience ...well...," he gave a sad, wistful smile, "you more than anybody will know that times are hard and that we all have to tighten our belts." The man looked as if he'd just buried his grandma. "Gerry, we're just gonna have to let you go." He stood up. "We'll see you right, though, don't you worry. There'll be a great package coming your way."

Gerald put his head in his hands. What chance was there now of French farmhouses or new chances? He was finished. Life was finished. "I've been here since I was twenty two years old," he said to the air, to the carpet, to the chair beneath him. To nobody. Because nobody was listening. "I'll never work again - I'm too old. Who'll want me?"

"No sense in hanging around in the office, old chap," said Jack Reynolds. "Why not just call it a day now? You'll be paid until the end of the month anyway - take the wife away for a bit. Have a holiday in company time."

Gerald stood up and left the room without a word. At the desk in the corner, he put his sandwiches back in his bag, put his coat on and trudged towards the double doors. A few more people had arrived. None of them would meet his eye. They must know, he thought, all of them must know. Suddenly, he felt very old. Very old and very lonely.

He walked past the onion-seller and made his way to Sophia Gardens where he sat on a bench and ate his sandwiches, kicking out at the cooing pigeons that bob-headed near his ankles. Then he went to the museum for a bit. It was free to get in. After a while, when he couldn't think of what else to do or where else to go, he got on the bus and went home. Home to where the only people who thought well of him would be. And once he'd told them his news, they wouldn't think well of him, either.

"Hello, Gerald, dear," said Janet. "You're home early - is everything ok?"

"Bit of a headache," he said. "Best to sleep it off, I think."

"I'll bring you a nice cup of tea and a paracetamol," she said. "And then, when you feel a bit better, maybe we could talk a bit more about going to France. Just for a holiday, I mean. Just to get a feel for the place."

"That'll be lovely, Janet," he said. "Can you make it two paracetamol? And lots of sugar in my tea. I'm feeling a bit low.

And he carried on feeling low. He couldn't face going into the office the next day to pick up the few things of his that were still there. Faced with his wife's puzzlement, he snored under the duvet and pretended to be asleep. By the afternoon, he had to tell her something so that she stopped asking what was wrong. He didn't honestly explain what had happened. He couldn't bring himself to utter the words.

"Bit of a bug, I expect," he said. "Should be gone soon."

Midweek, Janet went out to the travel agents and came home laden with brochures. "These will cheer you up," she said. He knew it wasn't her fault but he almost had to sit on his hands to stop himself from pushing her over and from knocking all the glossy booklets out of her grasp.

By Saturday morning, he was desperate to get out of the house and away from the conversations that Janet kept trying to foist upon him about Provence and stone farmhouses.

After an almost completely sleepless night, he came down early, had a quick breakfast and attempted the crossword. He couldn't finish it. The dog and cat did not dare approach him. His wife and daughter were still in bed. The clock ticked on the mantelpiece and shadows glinted and danced on the dresser. He sat in the oak veneer chair next to the fire and drummed his fingers against the armrest. Above his head, there were stirrings. They were up.

He was going to have to tell them.

He couldn't do it.

He had to.

He couldn't.

He would go out for a drive instead. He'd get some fresh air to clear his head and he'd think about how to tell them. He put on his raincoat. It was sure to be pouring later on. He would have liked to have worn his cap, too, but it wasn't in its usual place on the rack. He couldn't understand why. He'd worn it last weekend and he was always assiduous in putting his belongings where they were supposed to be: there was a place for everything and everything in its place. He hoped he wasn't going the way of his father, who'd started off forgetting where he'd put things but eventually couldn't recall what he was supposed to be doing with them once they were found.

Suddenly, there were loud excited voices from the kitchen.

"Mummy, come and look at darling Poppy! Come and see how sweet she looks!"

"Oh, Tammy! Go and get a camera quickly before she throws it off! Gerald! Come and see what Poppy's doing - she looks adorable!"

Gerald walked slowly into the kitchen. At first, he couldn't see what the fuss was about because of the combined fleshy vastness of his wife and daughter but when Tamara turned around that left a gap.

"Daddy, quickly, where's your camera?" The light glinted on her glasses as she looked at him, her face wide and urgent.

As he looked through the space between mother's candlewick gown and daughter's cartoon pyjamas, he could see the puppy, that spoilt and malodorous animal, nestling into the fleece of its bed. Its head was held at that calculating angle designed purely for the manipulation of humans, its eyes fixed, wet and impish, on the idiots crowded around it. And balanced jauntily on its head and shoulders was his missing cap.

"Who's a lovely girl, then?" cooed his wife, bending down over the dog basket.

"Shall I look in the cupboard on the stairs for the camera?" asked his daughter, "And is there any film in it, do you know?"

Pushing past both of them, he grabbed the hat off the dog's head, turned on his heel and walked into the hall. Whereupon, in the gloom cast through the leaded lights of the front door, his left shoe squelched into the soft, warm corpse of a mouse, left there a little earlier by Coco the cat.

Chapter Two

Gerald prized his car, a dark green 1980 Jaguar XJ6. He polished it every Sunday. No-one but him was ever allowed to drive it. Janet had learnt on an automatic and Tamara had her own car, thank God. As he was walking towards the garage, he almost fell into a stagger because a realisation had suddenly hit him: he was going to have to sell the Jag. He opened the garage door and stared at the car. He hesitated for a moment longer and then ran his hand over the bonnet, his fingers caressing the shapes and curves. He'd saved up for this beauty, done without all manner of things for it, he'd literally dreamt of the moment when his fingers would wrap around the steering wheel for the first drive out ... and now? He'd already considered the horror of having to sell the house - and it was an awful prospect - but losing the car would be like losing a part of himself. They would always be able to find somewhere else to live, however humble and poky. But the Jaguar? The Jaguar represented his dreams.

But he hadn't sold it yet.

He put his raincoat and cap in the back and climbed into the driver's seat. The moment he began to drive away from the Tudorbethan house and his plump wife and unhappy daughter, he felt a slow lightning of his spirits.

Raindrops started to fall just as he left the cul-de-sac but the wipers made short work of them and, anyway, the rain didn't last. Soon, a limp sun began to gleam from behind thin clouds that were strung out like strands of poached egg-white. Gerald drove ponderously on damp black roads, out through the red-brick townhouses, past the weekend cars and the bag-laden pedestrians, out past the suburbs with their washing lines and kids on rusty bikes, and past the Saturday matches and the girls in their new clothes, their arms looped through those of their best chums, until eventually he reached the greenery of Oakfield Country Park.

In the car park, he manoeuvred the Jag into the end of the row, straddling the painted line so that nobody could park in the space next to him. As he shook out the creases from his raincoat, ready to put it on, a gust of wind wafted a piece of blue paper across the gravel and towards his shoe. It was a five pound note. Looking quickly around, he stuffed the money into his pocket and strode towards the cafe.

Ten minutes later, he sat at a table clasping a cup of coffee and a pasty. He munched the pasty slowly, his face full of gloomy concentration. The future was going to demand sacrifice and doing without. As he contemplated ways of saving money or of making it stretch further, he felt his face tighten. This wasn't fair. He'd worked hard all of his life, done his best by his wife and child, given loose change to charities and donated superannuated clothes to the Salvation Army. He didn't swear, didn't drink, and went to church at Christmas. He was a good man.

His cogitations were halted when he choked on a bit of black pepper. He coughed and spluttered and tears began to roll down his cheeks. His throat was on fire.

Suddenly, he felt a tremendous banging on his back.

"Are you okay?"

He opened his eyes to see a pretty, middle-aged woman whose face was framed by a silk headscarf. Mahogany curls escaped past the loose bow tied at her throat. Her brown eyes were full of concern. She placed a hand gently on his shoulder.

He tried to nod.

"Here, have a sip of water," she said, holding out a cup.

He took it from her and swallowed a mouthful. The torment in his throat was momentarily quenched but he couldn't stop the paroxysms of coughing. Again, she thumped him on the back. Somewhere in his head battled a pair of conflicting thoughts: that, one, it was kind of a stranger to intervene but also that, two, as there was nothing lodged in his throat, the gesture was both pointless and painful.

He drank a little more water and wiped his face with the back of his hand. "Sorry," he mumbled, "but thank you. It was the pasty... a bit of pepper... took me by surprise."

"Yes, fiendish things, pasties," she said, smiling down at him. "Never trust them. Still, no harm done, eh?"

"No," he said, "no harm done. I'm fine. A bit embarrassing but I'll live to tell the tale." He handed her back the cup but she shook her head.

"I don't want it," she said." I was just leaving anyway. Glad I could help."

How attractive she was, thought Gerald. There was a little black mark, almost in the shape of a heart, just on the ridge of her cheekbone. A blemish, obviously, but somehow, it made her look exotic. It emphasised how large and round her eyes were. He realised he was staring at her and looked away. She smiled as if amused and then turned and walked towards the trees that edged the picnic tables, the pale blue of her coat a shimmer amongst the waving branches. Gerald leaned forward and sniffed the air. Where she had been standing, so close he could have touched her hand, there lingered the sweet smell of violets.

He walked slowly back to his car. He was in no hurry. Waiting for him at home was only female chatter about France and all-inclusive holidays and farmhouses.

And a revelation he didn't want to share.

Money. Everything came down to money. Or lack of it. Aunt Edna's will: that was supposed to have sorted everything out. If she'd left him the inheritance he deserved, he could have resigned from work with his head held high, instead of being edged out of the back door like an old sofa that nobody wanted anymore. He could have moved to France with his wife. He could have kept his car. They could have lived the high life. Instead of which, all he had was this ludicrous tontine which boiled down to a paltry few thousand a year.

But then, with a heady jolt of excitement, he remembered the thunderbolt clause of the tontine. That distant dream could actually come true. Those millions could be his. All of them. Literally, all he had to do was to keep on living. Or longer than his brother and cousins anyway.

It was the first positive moment of the week, almost, perhaps, of the year.

He could well outlive the others - why not? He looked after himself better than they did - well, perhaps with the exception of that hypochondriac, Arnold, who was always trying out some crackers health scheme or other. On the other hand, his brother took no exercise because he'd read somewhere that athletes often died while running marathons or climbing high peaks. And the cousins were no better. Venetia was depressed by her looks and he'd heard, many times over, that poor mental health negatively affected life-expectancy. Karen drank and smoked and lived a racy existence and that was just asking for

22

trouble. Pammie was potty and was sure eventually to do something insane like put her fingers into a plug socket or drink hair-dye by mistake. But what about her twin, Alison? He hadn't seen her for a while but the last time they'd met, she'd looked worryingly well.

His mind was whirling, the ideas tumbling over and over each other. Things were going to be all right. He just needed to approach it as if it were an assignment - the kind of project that required preparation. The obvious things were that he should get fit, eat well, avoid stress and sleep eight hours a night. And stay alive. There was no point in sugaring the pill. This was *literally* a fight to the death. And he intended to win. There were to be no more moments of gratitude for wind-blown fivers.

So full of these wondrous thoughts was he, that he didn't hear the rumble of the car behind him. It was a complete surprise to find himself being thrown up into the air by the bonnet when it slammed into the back of his legs. He slithered over the top of the car, before tumbling off the end of the boot. For a second, he lay there stunned but then he realised that he couldn't move. There was not much pain: just a ghastly numbness. A flurry of leaves began to flutter down from the circle of copper beeches which ringed the car park. A leaf landed on his cheek but he couldn't move his arm to brush it away.

He felt a rising panic and tried to call out but all that he heard escaping from his lips was a whispered bubble of air and wetness - was it blood? Was it *his* blood? Suddenly, he became aware of crushing pain, an agony that was beginning to pulsate throughout his limbs. Breath whisped out of him in little burning spurts. There was a pounding so intense in his head that it felt as if it would burst. Was he dying? It was surely impossible! Not now, not just at that moment, not when he'd decided he was ready to live for years more, decades more! And that he was going to be rich! Surely someone would come and help?

Help! Someone, anyone!

Where was the driver of the car that had hit him? For goodness' sake, they must have known what they'd done! Why didn't they help him? Maybe, even now, they were calling an ambulance and he would be saved. A sob caught in his throat. He was afraid. He wished there was someone there to hold his hand. He wanted Janet.

A rush of air began to ring in his ears. A speckled mist distorted his vision. The pain and the fear and the panic gradually subsided into a dizzy calmness, almost like the time he'd had a hernia operation and the anaesthetist had counted him down into oblivion from ten.

Ten ... He stared up blindly at the sky and thought of Tamara as a baby and recalled how he had always eventually managed to calm her sobs, by walking her around and around the little pink bedroom below the eaves, her head nestled into his shoulder ... *nine* ... He remembered Janet as a young woman and how he'd loved the softness of her smile as she gazed with a secret tenderness into his eyes ... *eight...* and the feel of her waist below his hand when they'd had that first dance at the Christian Union ball ... *seven* ... As the world gradually turned brown and then to black, he felt such a terrible, aching sadness that he wouldn't ever see them again ... *six* ... as he was losing himself to the warm darkness, there was, for no more than a moment, the feel of a gentle hand on his shoulder and the hint, just the faintest hint, of violets. And ... *five...*

Chapter Three

At her husband's funeral, Janet's cardigan wasn't buttoned up properly which meant that the longer half hung down over her stomach. She kept fumbling with the shorter edge, trying to pull it down. Eventually she gave up. There were bigger problems to face. For instance, she wanted to walk down the aisle of the chapel with dignity but her legs seemed to be not quite in harmony with each other. She was grateful when her brother-in-law, Arnold, offered his arm. He let her go as she reached her seat at the front. She stood for a moment, staring at the gold velvet curtains which draped from the ceiling. They pooled on the floor around the legs of the trolley which held her husband's coffin. She gazed at the photograph of Gerald which stood on the top of the casket. "Sit down, Mum," whispered Tamara.

The vicar spoke kind words but Janet didn't hear them. The first hymn started and the congregation stood. She rose to her feet and opened her mouth to sing but, to her surprise, no words came out. Tamara gripped her mother's hand. Arnold put his arm around her. When it came to the moment for the curtains to glide around the coffin and cut it off from view, she heard sobs and she knew that, though she had no awareness of making them, they were her own.

Later, back at the house, knots of people stood about in the kitchen, nibbling sandwiches and trying to look at their watches without being seen doing so. Janet had gone to bed, unable to face the crowd. Tamara walked around and spoke a few words to each. 'Thank you for coming.' 'Yes, it is so sad.' 'You're right, he was a wonderful man.' 'It was a lovely service.' 'Do have more cake.'

She felt almost as if she were in a trance.

Some of her dad's ex-colleagues had been at the church but, thank goodness, they hadn't come back to the house even though courtesy had demanded that they be invited. Her father had been treated badly by work, that was for sure - although the death-in-service benefit was still going to come to them and that was a relief. And the redundancy package was secure. And his pension. She supposed they'd have to sell the house and the Jag. But that would probably have happened anyway, what with him losing his job and everything. Why hadn't he told them? Why hadn't he shared his burden? It made no sense. She could have helped even if only by listening to him. Listening was very valuable, she knew that: it's what the Marriage Guidance woman had said to her and Keith. And Tamara had listened and listened to her husband and, although it hadn't kept them together, it had made the loss easier to bear. Well, a bit, anyway.

Keith hadn't come back to the house, either. He'd been at the service and that was good of him but he'd brought along his new wife and the baby and that had been hard to see. And the baby had been good as gold and the woman had said sympathetic things and Keith had hugged her and he still smelt of Old Spice and that was weird because it made her feel sad and happy at the same time.

She pulled herself together. There were guests to look after. It didn't do to wallow. That helped nobody.

"Would you like a sandwich?" she said to no-one in particular.

Arnold refused all his niece's offers of food because he'd read recently about the proven links between longevity and calorie restriction. He was coming to terms with the occasional dizziness that accompanied this near-starvation and had begun to diary these episodes so that he could discuss them with his doctor. As he stood in the corner, shuffling slightly from foot to foot, he wondered - now that he was the oldest of the cousins - if he should say a few words to the mourners. He hesitated, partly because he was afraid he'd stammer but also because he couldn't think of anything meaningful to say. He practised and rejected the opening phrases in his head: 'thank you for coming' - but no, it wasn't his house; 'those of you who knew my brother' - but everybody here knew him otherwise they wouldn't have come to the funeral; 'how sad we all are' - but he wasn't in the least bit sad.

He thought back to their childhood bedroom and the way his brother had dictated exactly how the space would be shared and the punishments for any infraction, however small. He remembered how Gerald had mocked him for his stammer. How Gerald hadn't chosen him to be Best Man when he had married Janet. How he had decided on two godmothers for Tamara and no godfather. And then there was what Arnold had done to Pammie. He suddenly felt rather faint and sat down on the nearest chair.

Meanwhile, their cousin, Venetia, stood outside in the garden, trying to ignore how uncomfortable she felt. A menopausal volcano was surging through her pores. She didn't know what else to do to get cool. She had already taken off her jacket and would have liked to take off her new black sombrero, too. Not only would she be cooler but it could have been waggled like a fan. She didn't dare remove it, however, because she was certain that her hair would be stuck to her scalp and so would reveal her deepest, darkest secret - she was going bald. No amount of cream and spray seemed to have any effect. She back-combed her hair into a bouffant every morning and, at first, it didn't look too bad - but when the ghastly flushes arrived (as they did, daily), the dampness which beaded her hot skin always managed to flatten her hair, too. It was so sad, so unfair.

Venetia gazed at her cousin, Karen, who was lounging on a cushioned sun-chair, talking animatedly to a tall man in a turban. Karen's hair was thick and blonde - surely it was dyed? It curled in a lustrous wave around her cheekbones. Venetia shook her head, almost as if she could throw the anger out of her heart and into the air. Stress wasn't good for her. It would only make her hair thinner, her complexion worse and her flushes even hotter. And she needed to remember why she was here: she was here to mourn her cousin. She tried to feel sad for him. But she couldn't. Gerald had never been kind to her, never. In fact, he had delighted in belittling her. 'You've put on a bit of weight, I think, Venetia.' 'That's a nasty eruption you've got on your cheek, Venetia.' 'I'm sure Karen could give you some fashion advice, Venetia'. Bastard. After all she'd done for him. She took off her hat and began to fan herself.

In the opposite corner of the garden, Karen held up her empty glass to Mr Singh. "Be a darling, would you?" she said. "Do just see if there's any more vino in the kitchen."

He grinned as he took the glass from her hand. "My pleasure."

How white his teeth were, she thought. Simply gorgeous. She settled back into the softness of the cushions and gazed around the garden. She hated funerals. All these people pretending to be sad. And then the desperate few who were genuinely grieving. She could cope with neither, being unable to humour the pretence nor to negotiate the grief.

And the clothes! So few women knew how to wear black. Like dumpy Venetia, for instance, who was standing under a beech tree, puce of face, vigorously waving a hideous charcoal-coloured hat through the air. She'd arrived at the service wearing three different shades of black in three different items - hat, dress and jacket. Horrendous. Meanwhile, Pammie was plumped into some godawful trousers tied at the waist with a cotton cord. And Alison was wearing an anorak for God's sake. Where did she think she was? Kwik-Save? And why, oh, why, had no-one helped the grieving widow button up her cardigan that morning?

Karen looked down at her own outfit with satisfaction - a black silk jumpsuit with a fuchsia scarf tied loosely around her neck. Perfect. It had been an extravagant purchase but one that she hadn't regretted for a moment. Mr Singh had commented on it favourably and it was important that he was impressed by her fashion choices considering the future she had mapped out for their joint business venture. She frowned. She wouldn't have needed this dependence on a stranger if Aunt Edna hadn't been so bizarre with her will. Or, for that matter, if Gerald had agreed to her proposals of last year. He had laughed in her face, called her ludicrous. What an oaf he was. He had no idea of fashion - with a wife and daughter who dressed like refugees, why would he care about that? But she had expected him to realise the mutual profits in her business plan. Well, he'd got his comeuppance. He'd done stupid things all of his life - married a dull woman, sired a fat daughter and bought an ugly house. Yes, he'd been a mean boy and an awkward man. He would be barely mourned. She felt a cool hand on her shoulder.

"This was all I could find, I'm afraid," said Mr Singh, as he held out a tumbler of viscous orange. "I think it might be some kind of cordial. All the wine has gone."

In the dining room, her cousin Alison munched a tuna sandwich and wondered if she dared to have a secret rummage in the kitchen.

This curiosity about other people's lives had begun just after Aunt Edna's death – perhaps as a result of the realisation that, without the promised legacy, her dreams of escape could not happen.

Some two months after the old lady's passing, she had found herself repeatedly gazing through house windows as she walked past them. She would stand on the pavement and pretend to be rifling through her handbag while she was actually clocking sofas and fireplaces and wondering who sat on those cushions and who lit those fires. Now she found herself doing this most days on different streets. It was fun. And part of it was the fear that someone might suddenly walk in to the room and see her staring, or might throw open the front door and demand to know what she was doing. She knew that, should that happen, she would be mortified but she also loved the thrill of risking it. Almost like having illicit sex in the park or something. Not that she'd ever done that. She'd never had sex anywhere, illicit or otherwise.

Possibly, also, this new habit was a product of boredom. Although she loved Pammie, living with her didn't exactly provide scintillating discussion. Her sister used to be so much fun, always the first to see the funny side of everything. But that was before she became a shell of a person. That was before That Awful Day. And that was Gerald's fault.

"Have you seen Pammie?" Alison asked Tamara, as she walked into the room.

"She was in the garden, I think," Tamara held out a platter of vol-au-vents. "Can I tempt you?"

"They look interesting," said Alison, her hand reaching out. "What's in them?"

"Mushroom in these ones, shrimp paste in those and egg mayonnaise in the ones in the middle."

"Lovely," said Alison, "What a nice variety. Just the one for me, though." She hesitated and then plucked a single vol-au-vent, crammed high with egg. "You've done your dad proud, Tammy." She munched

29

while she spoke. "Well done, love." She licked her fingers. "Where did you say Pammie was?"

"Out by the pond," said Tamara, mesmerised by the lump of egg stuck to Alison's top lip. It waggled as the woman was speaking. She should tell her really but didn't because it would be embarrassing for both of them. Even after all these years, Tamara had never quite got over having Alison as Brown Owl. Sharp memories of Brownie badges and Brownie trips and other humiliations persisted. Somebody else would surely mention the egg. It would fall off soon on its own, anyway. But in the meantime, Alison looked ridiculous and that wouldn't do.

Then came a brainwave.

"Oh, I'm such a fool!" she said, putting down the vol-au-vents on the table. "I've forgotten to hand out paper napkins - I'll just get you one."

When she came back with a wodge of serviettes in her hand, Alison had gone. Looking out through the French windows, Tamara could see her in the garden, bobbing around the flower beds. Clearly, she was asking people about whether they'd seen Pammie because she kept stopping and speaking to various groups and then zipping off again. Now she was speaking to Mr Lynd from next door or rather, as was the way with Mr Lynd, she was listening to him. He was always difficult to get away from but, as Tamara was watching and wondering whether she should go out and try and rescue her, she saw Alison make apologetic gestures and move away.

Then Alison stopped and briefly talked to a woman that Tamara didn't recognise. She was wearing a blue coat and a pink headscarf which seemed an odd thing to wear to a funeral. Perhaps it was a neighbour that had recently moved in. Or someone from her dad's work. Or ex-work, she supposed she should call it. She sighed and took the sandwiches back into the kitchen. How much longer would people expect to stay?

It was at this point that she heard the screaming and saw that everyone outside had turned away from the house to face the bottom of the garden. She opened the doors, stepped out onto the patio and tried to see what they were looking at, her hands across her forehead, shielding her eyes from the glare of the low sun.

There was another scream. She threw down the serviettes and ran across the lawn, rushing past Mr Lynd, past Venetia and Arnold, past Karen and Mr Singh, past the people standing under the trees and past those huddled around the flower beds. Just as she got to the sunloungers, the woman in the pink headscarf strode past, going in the opposite direction. As they crossed each other, Tamara was suddenly aware of the sweet perfume of violets.

And then she pushed aside the cluster of people in the furthest corner of the garden and saw Alison sitting, legs splayed, on the grass. Her head was back and she was keening into the wind. Cradled in her arms was her sister, Pammie, whose long brown hair was wet and spotted with green algae from the ornamental pond that Gerald had dug to celebrate Tamara's birth and neglected ever since.

Pammie's eyes were open and staring upwards as if she were looking at the sky. But she wasn't. And she never would again.

Chapter Four

Alison

The following year, April 1992

Before Pammie's death, Alison had dreamed of abandoning this dull world. It made her feel ashamed but that had included her poor, damaged sister whom she'd loved very much but whose care had ruled her life. She'd dreamed, too, of leaving the Brownies. And she'd fantasised about leaving the library where she worked, a place where silence was the rule and where, though the shelves were laden with novels and biographies and dictionaries and colour supplements, oh, so empty were the shelves of her heart! She'd fantasised about abandoning her responsibilities and becoming reckless. She'd imagined buying a cafe in Lindos or perhaps opening a language school in Capri or maybe a bed and breakfast in Malaga. She would dye her hair and lose two stones in weight and learn to smoke without coughing. She would wear shorts and mascara and eat exotic foods like octopus and aubergine, and she would read racy books on top of the counter not below it. She would.. yes... she would make friends.

When she'd heard the terms of Aunt Edna's will, and realised that none of these dreams could ever happen, she had become utterly and totally depressed. She would never be free of any of it. She would never be free of Pammie.

And then her sister had died.

Since Pammie's death, the evenings had become even longer and duller. Her twin had been maddening sometimes but having to look after somebody had at least given Alison a purpose. Pammie had been good company in her own way. She'd liked to play simple card games, ate with enthusiasm no matter what food was put in front of her, and would readily agree to whatever plans were suggested. She'd always been happy, never seemed bored or irritated, and had been easily distracted from paths that were better left untrod.

Now that she was gone, somehow the escape that reading used to provide was not as easy to find as it used to be. Sometimes, sitting in the lounge, beneath the glow of the standard lamp, tea and custard cream biscuits on the side-table, book in hand, Alison would get to the end of a page and realise that she didn't know what had happened and would have to read it again.

Other things had changed, too. A month after Pammie's death, a letter had arrived from a man called Percival Merryweather telling them that his grandfather, the ancient solicitor who had explained Aunt Edna's wretched inheritance to them two years earlier, had also died. This, much younger, Merryweather informed the cousins that the rules and the system of the scheme were to remain the same, even though it was now under his administration, rather than his grandfather's.

He was also writing to tell them that - rather horribly - with Gerald and Pammie dead, the income from the tontine had gone up. In fact, it meant that Alison could use the 1992 cheque to buy one of the latest large screen TVs. She knew that her sister wouldn't have begrudged her that.

Her penchant for investigating other people's lives had become a well-established habit now. She'd become adept at hovering in supermarkets while eavesdropping on conversations in the aisles. That had provided some super titbits to feast on. And another trick: last week, she'd gone into a boutique and taken a bundle of clothes with her into the fitting rooms. With the curtain closed, she'd sat down on the stool in the cubicle and listened to all kinds of chat going on around her. What she'd most enjoyed had been the attempts of friends to advise against purchases. 'No, of course it doesn't make you look fat.' 'It's just not a great colour on you.' 'Hmmm...maybe the size 14 was better?' 'Yes, it's definitely been cut on the small side.' Hilarious.

She was still addicted to staring from pavements through house windows. In fact, she had increased her range by sitting on the top deck of buses on Sunday afternoons and staring into other people's bedrooms. On narrow roads, where the distance between the house and bus windows was small, and when sunshine didn't spoil her view by creating reflections, there were rich pickings. But still, gazing through glass was a poor substitute for the real thing.

So she'd recently upped her game by poking through rooms in real life.

She began visiting people whenever the opportunity arose so that she could explore unnoticed. There was something especially alluring about half-open doors off upstairs landings. The darkness of the room beyond was hard to resist. She'd been round to an old schoolfriend's house recently and been a bit shocked by her risqué underwear. A Brownie parent had asked her over for coffee and she'd discovered divorce papers on the dressing table. In the last month, she'd managed to have some really interesting investigations in Karen's and Venetia's houses. Karen must be very distressed by all those bills and why, oh why, did Venetia still have so much faith in all those boxes and tubes and pots of cream? None of them made any difference, poor dear. She'd also visited Arnold in his bungalow and enjoyed looking through his vast medicine cabinet.

And things were looking up in work, too.

Since Christmas, she'd become a lot closer to Gordon, her assistant librarian. Before this, sharing space with him hadn't been easy because, although Gordon was a lovely person, he was a bit pongy. Some people just were, she supposed. Maybe it was something to do with his glands or hormones or something. But then, at New Year, he'd found a girlfriend, Lucy, who had prevailed upon him to smell much sweeter.

Over the last few months, Alison and he had begun to spend much more time chatting. It became clear that they shared similar interests in reading and films and they had great discussions about, for instance, who was the better writer, Dickens or Hardy - the answer being the latter, obviously. It was particularly enjoyable because she'd almost forgotten what it was like to have an interesting conversation with someone who wasn't a Brownie, or a Library customer. They had been to the pictures a few times, too. With her sister, she had only ever been able to visit the cinema to see Disney films.

Just recently, though, Gordon hadn't been around quite so much for these trips out. That was down to Lucy, his new girlfriend. It was great that she'd made Gordon smell better but, on the downside, it seemed that she got rather jealous whenever he shared his company with Alison.

In fact, they'd only met twice socially in the last month. At Easter, they'd gone out for a curry and a drink after work and it had been fun. Last week, he'd invited her round to his flat for a meal. She'd taken ages to get ready. It had been a bit of a shock when the door opened to reveal blasted Lucy hanging onto Gordon's arm. The food was delicious but it had been a bit awkward, just the three of them. And she hadn't the courage to have a poke about, not only for fear of getting caught, but because, despite improvements, his flat still smelt distinctly Gordonish.

Heathgrove Library was housed in an ornate and draughty Victorian building. In 1891, not long after the last brick was put in the wall, the local History Society had convened its first monthly meeting there. And it was still carrying on with that tradition, in a spirit that had not been dimmed even during the challenge of two world wars. On the fourth Tuesday of every month, the Society booked the blue meeting room. Sometimes, there would be guest speakers. Occasionally, the current chair, Simon Jelifant, would bring along a box of shards or bones or metal, for discussion. Now and again, there would be intense study of maps and charts.

One Tuesday morning, Alison found Simon Jelifant waiting for her outside the library almost an hour before it was due to open. He looked a little agitated.

"Alison," he said, "can I have a word?"

He needed several words as it turned out.

Heathgrove Abbey, a local private school, was desperately in need of funds after years of non-investment. Consequently, the governors had decided to sell off a chunk of the grounds to a developer.

This much Alison knew, the argument having formed the substance of recent articles and angry letter pages in the South Wales Echo. The problem was that the Abbey fields mattered not only to the school. The residents of the adjoining housing estate had no wish to lose the meadows and woods which currently formed the view from their back gardens. This was not least because the view added significant monetary value to their properties.

Simon Jelifant was about to add more weight to the argument against the development.

At their last meeting, a member of the History Society had brought along the results of an aerial survey of the Abbey school grounds.

"And what it shows, Alison, shows beyond any reasonable doubt, is that hidden in these ancient fields - ones that are about to be sold off to the highest bidder - are centuries of human endeavour. Many centuries."

"Right...I see." She wondered if he'd mind if she put the kettle on. Would it seem frivolous in the light of this weighty news? But she wasn't sure if she could face the morning without a coffee. "What sort of thing are you talking about, Simon?"

"The survey confirms what I've always suspected. We've got prehistoric settlements and burial mounds there, for a start."

"Gosh how exciting!" Perhaps if she were to offer him a cup, too? "You must be thrilled."

"Absolutely. But it doesn't end there. The crop marks suggest that the Abbey fields contain buried remains of funerary monuments dating back possibly as far as 4,000 BC."

"How extraordinary!" All but one of the cups in the staff kitchen were chipped. Would she have to give the only perfect one to him? "Really old, then."

"We can see circles from ancient pits that haven't been visible literally for millennia."

"Millennia? Goodness! " Where the hell was Gordon? She could have done with some support because, clearly, this early-morning revelation was going to lead to some kind of request and she didn't savour the conflict that would inevitably follow. "Would you like a cup of coffee?"

"Thanks but no." He took hold of one of her hands. "You know what this means, don't you?"

She coughed and pulled her hand away. "Celebration?"

"We need to apply for Scheduled Monument status."

At that moment, with a slight pong of body odour, Gordon limped in, looking rather flustered. "Sorry," he said, "got a puncture again. Bloody flints on the path. Hello, Simon. What are you doing here? Is the kettle on yet, Alison? I'm parched. Had to push my bike for the last mile. My feet are killing me."

"Simon was just telling me that the History Society has found Bronze Age remains"

"-Neolithic remains, Alison, much older."

"Sorry, *Neolithic* remains in Heathgrove Fields."

"Doesn't your house back onto those fields, Simon?" said Gordon, picking up the kettle and filling it. The noise of the water partially covered his question but Simon clearly heard it.

"That's got nothing to do with it, Gordon. It's not personal. These finds are of national significance."

Gordon opened the cupboard door and took out three cups. "Still, you probably don't want to swap a view of lovely meadows for a view of new semis, do you?"

"Simon doesn't want coffee, thanks, Gordon," said Alison.

"You're here very early aren't you?" said Gordon, putting one cup back. "Your history bods aren't booked to kick-off for another hour."

"Well, I thought you and Alison would want to hear the news ahead of time."

"That's very kind of you," said Alison. "I'll have the mug without the chip, please, Gordon."

"And I wanted to give you the heads-up," said Simon, "before the journalist gets here."

"I think I've got a massive blister coming on," said Gordon. "It was pushing my bike that did it. Do you mind if I take my socks off to check?"

"Yes!" shouted Alison and Simon, speaking as one.

"What journalist?" asked Alison.

"The one who interviewed me yesterday to talk about the finds."

"What's that got to do with us?" said Gordon sitting down on one of the chairs beneath the window that overlooked the car park .

"Well, obviously, the connection between the History Society and the library goes back over a hundred years..."

"Indeed, it does." Alison picked up her coffee. It was a chipped mug. She knew he'd do that.

"And it goes without saying that Heathgrove Library - a place of learning and culture and respect for our past - would be just as keen as we are to defend this local treasure that is literally on our doorstep."

"What exactly have you said to this journo, matey?" Gordon stood up. Even though his blistered heel was stopping him from standing up quite as tall as usual, he was still a good six inches taller than the other man. Simon took a step back. Gordon could be quite menacing when he wanted to be, as Alison had seen for herself when books were brought back damaged, or when kids ran around unsupervised, knocking over displays willy-nilly. "Have you dropped us in it?"

"I simply said what I sincerely believe to be the truth - that the whole community will unite to protect our history from sordid commercial enterprise."

Looking through the window, Alison saw a battered Volkswagen Beetle pull into the car park.

"Did you say that this journalist is coming here, Simon?" said Alison.

"Look," said Simon. "The library is the heart of the town. All of us are represented by you. You stand for what we, the community, believe in. If you're with us, and speak for us, that's-"

"-that's cheap publicity for a campaign in which we cannot take sides," said Alison. She put her cup down and looked at her Assistant Librarian for support.

"Time you were leaving, matey," said Gordon. "Off you trot."

Thus began the brief, but unpleasant, Battle of Heathgrove Abbey. The South Wales Echo, sensing fresh life in the conflict, ran a story about the prospective development, but adding the new – though unsupported - detail that the town library, as represented by the chief librarian, Ms Alison Benson, was at the forefront of the fight to preserve this unique slice of local history.

Cue, on Monday morning, the arrival of a small but vocal group of Heathgrove school parents demonstrating outside the library. They brandished placards, blew whistles and rang bells and wore an assortment of outfits to further their cause, including some stalwarts who had donned their old school blazers as a stand of solidarity with their alma mater. There must have been a time, perhaps long ago, when these had been the right size.

Pushing past them was an embarrassment, one which Alison would not have managed had Gordon not met her at the bus stop and ushered her through.

But the next morning was even worse because that was when the History Society decided to confront the parent demonstrators who, despite the weather, had turned up for a second day. The historians were fewer in number than the school throng but they'd made up for it by bringing along a keyboard . 'Kumbaya' might have made an appearance, Alison wasn't sure.

On the third day, the Heathgrove parents brought crates of fresh eggs with them. They hurled them at the History Society and, when that palled, at the library windows.

This turned the conflict into a story beyond local boundaries. That weekend saw photographs of the library and its staff splashed over national newspapers. It was beyond humiliating.

However, having the story shared nationwide turned out to be a helpful event because it brought the plight of the school to the attention of a wealthy Old Boy. He got in touch with his alma mater, declaring himself so grateful for his education there that he had decided to include the Abbey school in his will. In fact, he promised them an enormous bequest. As he was without kin or friend, the will was unlikely to be challenged. Equally importantly, he was 92 years old with a dicky heart, and so, fingers crossed, the school might not have to wait too long before they could cash the cheque. The Headmistress could have new windows and the History Society could dig up its Neolithic remains.

"Although the archaeological investigations might not start immediately," said Simon, turning his mug of coffee around so that he could avoid drinking hot liquid over the chipped rim.

"Scared that all that digging might spoil your view?" said Gordon.

"You can't rush into these historical excavations, you know," said Simon with a frown.

"Not to worry," said Alison. "This stuff has been in the ground for 6,000 years. A few more decades won't do any harm."

"Let's treat ourselves shall we?" said Gordon, as he closed the door, half an hour later, on Simon's jolly wave and fatuous grin. "After work, I mean."

"A glorious celebration now that ordeal by placard is over?"

"Exactly. We deserve it."

"What have you got in mind?" she said, as she began to put returned books back onto the shelves. "A quick half-pint down The Wheatsheaf?"

"I think we can do better than that - I'm thinking Biryani. What do you say?"

"Sounds like an excellent plan."

"Right, that's a date."

"By the way, I've been meaning to say thanks for all your help." She carried on transferring books. She didn't want to stop and look at him in case she blushed or showed herself up in some other asinine way. "While all the madness was going on, I mean." She stared at the book in her hand as if she were trying to work out the words on the spine.

"My help?"

"You know, escorting me through the nutters and ... well, you know , just being ... there." She looked up at last, with a shy smile on her lips. But it didn't matter after all. He was busy rifling through the card index.

"No problem, Boss. This is my library, too." He took a card out of the drawer and looked up at her. "Fancy a cuppa before the Baby and Books gang arrive? "

"Don't even think of giving me a chipped mug."

Chapter Five

As they were locking up the library that evening, Gordon said, "Do you mind if Lucy joins us tonight? For our celebration, I mean."

Alison made sure that her expression didn't change. Much as she tried, she found Lucy hard work. She was grateful for her contribution to the sweeter air in the library but it didn't alter the fact that the woman always made her feel uncomfortable. Awkward. Surplus. Gauche.

"I don't mind at all, Gordon. I'm sure she'll be as delighted as we are."

"Takeaway? Or a restaurant?"

"Takeaway, I think. At yours? Would that be ok?" That would make it easier to leave if being a gooseberry got too much.

Lucy congratulated them both on the cessation of hostilities . "You must be so pleased that it's over."

"Oh, we are," said Alison. "It wasn't much fun pushing past that lot every day."

"Well, you had my Gordon to escort you through," said Lucy. She leaned across and ruffled her boyfriend's hair. "You are so gallant!"

Gordon blushed and grinned and put an extra-large forkful of rice in his mouth. His hair stood up as if it had been scythed by a breeze.

"I honestly felt quite abandoned," said Lucy. "Thought I was going to have to draw myself a placard that said '*Hi, remember me?*'"

"You dafty," said Gordon.

"And so now the History Society can have a splendid time digging up all these Bronze Age treasures-"

"-Neolithic," interrupted Alison and then bit the inside of her lip.

"They won't dig up a thing," said Gordon. "Except perhaps last year's begonias. More wine, Boss?"

Alison held up her glass. "Better make this my last and then I'll be making tracks."

"The last bus isn't for ages. You don't need to go yet."

"It's been a long day."

"Not as long as last Wednesday - your face! When that egg landed on the windows!"

"*Mine?* What about *yours?* I thought you were going to go out there and bash them."

"Not all of them - just Simon. What a git."

"*Prize* git"

"Who's Simon?" said Lucy.

"Chief Tosser of the History Society," said Gordon.

"Oh, him," she said and began to twist a tendril of her hair. "Of course, I remember now."

How dark her hair is, thought Alison. And how shiny.

Nobody said anything for a little while. Gordon put on some music. When he sat down again, Lucy leaned across and rubbed the back of his hand. He began to hum along to the Beatles.

Finally, Alison could stand it no more. "Wow! I'm stuffed." She lay her knife and fork straight across her plate and stood up. "Could I just...?"

"Oh, yes," said Gordon and he stood up, too. "Down the corridor, up to the half-landing and third door on the right. Do you want me to show you?"

"Oh, Gordy," said Lucy, "I'm sure Alison can track down the bathroom all on her own. You'll embarrass her. And anyway, I'd quite like a top-up." She smiled and held up an empty glass.

Alison walked out into the corridor, closing the dining room door behind her.

In the bathroom, she saw two toothbrushes, one pink and one blue. Also on the shelf was a bottle of aftershave and four cans of heavy-duty antiperspirant. In the cupboard below the sink was a bottle of perfume, a pretty hairbrush, make-up remover and moisturiser. The woman must have moved in, she thought. The idea made her tummy hurt.

Opening the door, she looked around. Once in the corridor, she pulled the door closed again behind her. From the outside, it looked like someone was still in the bathroom, a halo of light illuminating the jamb. Then she turned to the bedroom immediately next to it. The door was half-ajar. She crept in through the shadows. It was not completely dark because of the sodium glare of the streetlamp immediately outside the window.

She eased open the drawer next to the bed. Right at the top was a packet of condoms. She shut the drawer quickly. Then she tiptoed across to the dressing table. Two drawers. One side contained underpants and socks. The other, frilly knickers and lacy bras. She picked a handful up and buried her face in them: they were drenched in violet fragrance and the scent of it was intoxicating. She carefully put them back.

Next she pulled open the wardrobe door. Inside was a row of crisp shirts - had Lucy ironed them for him? At the other end of the rail was a clutch of dresses. She took one out and held it against herself, staring into the cheval mirror in front of the window and feeling the silky fabric cool against her bare arms.

Suddenly, she was aware of a cloud of perfume and she knew without turning round that she'd finally been caught. In the worst possible place and by the worst possible person.

"What do you think?" said Lucy, standing, arms crossed, in the pool of light in the doorway. "Think it would suit you?"

Alison turned around. "I'm sorry," she said. "I know this is unforgivable."

Lucy held out her hand. Alison passed her the dress and Lucy opened the wardrobe door and put the garment back inside.

"Please don't tell Gordon"

"I won't. I promise."

Pushing past Lucy, Alison hurried back to the bathroom where she looked at her face in the mirror. Her cheeks were scarlet. She emptied the toothbrushes out of the tumbler and filled it with water. She gulped mouthfuls of it and threw some over her face, trying to cool it down.

When she pushed open the lounge door, she saw that Gordon wasn't there. Lucy was, though, the gorgeous, fragrant beloved.

"Don't worry, Alison," she said. "I haven't told him."

"Where is he?"

"He's gone outside for a fag."

"Lucy, I-"

"We could be friends, you and I."

"Could we?"

43

"Yes, why not?"

"We've nothing in common. You're beautiful - I'm not. You're slim and elegant - I'm not."

"We have Gordon in common."

"What do you see in him, Lucy?"

"You have no idea what he makes possible for me."

"Really?"

"Really."

"You surprise me. He's not exactly a catch."

"Yet you seem very fond of him yourself, I think ... .or am I imagining that?"

Alison didn't reply. She suddenly felt very old and very tired. "We'll never be friends, Lucy," she said eventually. "If you want to tell him that you found me rooting around in his bedroom, just go ahead."

"Well I won't - that would ruin everything. But I mean it when I say I'd like to get to know you - to spend some time with you. I would, really."

"I think I'll just get my coat. It's late."

Just at that moment, Gordon came back into the room. He looked between them, rather uncertainly as if he knew that he had walked into something that he didn't quite understand.

"Is everything ok?" he said.

"Oh, yes," said Lucy. "Alison and I were just chatting. We were getting to know each other a bit better."

He looked at Alison and frowned. "You look beat."

"I am," she replied. "I just need to get home, I think." She could feel a prickling in her eyes. God, she was tired. God, she was a fool.

"I'll walk you to the bus stop."

"No," said Alison. "There's no need. I'll be fine."

"We insist," said Lucy. "We'll *both* walk you there. It's a nice evening for a walk."

"It's actually drizzling slightly," said Gordon.

"We won't drown."

The three of them walked in procession down the hall. Gordon locked the flat door behind them and they made their way along the corridor to the flight of stairs that led down to the ground floor.

Alison got there first and placed her hand on the banister. Just as she put her foot on the top step, she felt - or thought she felt - a hand in the small of her back pushing her down the stairs. As she began to fall, she yelped aloud in fear and surprise.

And then she felt herself being dragged back again, back to safety, as Gordon lunged down the steps after her. She was aware of him grabbing her arm and of being pulled into his chest. But somehow, she wasn't quite sure how it happened, Lucy seemed to slide right past her, as if she had got caught up in the momentum of Alison's fall.

She fell face first down the stairs, slithering down the last couple. And then she lay groaning at the bottom, her right leg bent at an impossible angle.

Chapter Six

Arnold

The following year, July 1993

Before his aunt's mad will, Arnold Benson had planned to give up teaching and concentrate on his health and the wonders of private medicine. He'd heard tremendous things, for instance, about doctors using leeches in South America - or was it Central? - and then, once he was well and a man of leisure, he wouldn't need to worry about whether the Head of Department thought he was up to the job. All of which, he was certain, would put an end to the nightmares, actual ones, not just metaphorical ones, in which feral children jumped on desks and called him names. And he would find time to write the book of poetry that he knew was in him, just waiting to be coaxed out.

He didn't really like teaching. He loved his subject and he enjoyed the holidays but the classroom did not bring him happiness.

In particular, he loathed the educational school trip.

The main trouble with trips, the really awful thing, was the way that children became somebody else when they were on a coach and out of uniform. He had a hard enough time of it when they were sitting, grey-jumpered, in classrooms, and when there were corridors to which thugs might be sent. But once they'd put on jeans and hoodies, and eaten their own body weight in sugar, mayhem was inevitable. The madness would generally begin even before the coach had reached Newport. Singing and chanting was always the first sign.

For Arnold, this was especially horrible because the opening ditty was traditionally:

"Mr B-Benson on the bus goes 'Stop that noise!
'Stop that noise! 'Stop that noise!'

Mr B-Benson on the bus goes 'Stop that noise!
All day long!"

The children would repeat this for a solid five minutes but, other than yelling at them to stop that noise, he wasn't sure what to do about it. His colleagues didn't seem keen to help. In fact, he was certain that they enjoyed his discomfiture. It was almost a relief when the kids turned to screaming tuneless versions of the charts instead.

And the school trip of summer 1993 was looking to be much the same as all the others which had preceded it. By the time Form Four had finished with *"If I Could Turn Back Time,"* and had made a start on *"The Final Countdown",* his brain was spinning. As the most senior person on the coach, Deirdre, his Head of Department, should have stepped in but, clearly, she preferred the pretence of fiddling with the zip on her anorak. He took a deep breath and stood up to remonstrate with them himself but, just as he cleared his throat to shout, a Murray Mint hit him on the forehead and he sat down again without saying a word.

They were going to Dorset, to visit places associated with the novelist,Thomas Hardy. The tour would begin at his birthplace in Bockhampton and then the coach would whisk them past Max Gate, where the author had died in 1928 of old age and bad temper. This was a private property but glimpses of the place were possible through the trees. Their final destination would be the museum in Dorchester, ostensibly to gawp at Hardy's original manuscripts and a mock-up of his study. What the trip more accurately represented, however, was an opportunity for the students to run riot, firstly around the birthplace flower-beds and then, later in the day, fortified by still more sugar, around the museum's glass cabinets.

Arnold had made this trip many times with many different bands of children but it always ended the same way, with apologies and headaches and letters of complaint.

When they arrived in the Bockhampton car park, the children pushed past him and raced across to the cottage entrance. A perfunctory visit around the downstairs rooms was followed by a shuffle around the bedroom where Hardy had penned 'Far from the Madding Crowd'. *I wish,* thought Arnold.

Immediately outside the cottage, there was little more than beaten mud and sparse grass, trodden into scattered blades by thousands of visitor boots. But beyond that were beds of purple acanthus and tall crimson hollyhocks. On the other side of a wicker fence flourished a vegetable garden of peas and broad beans, and lines of strawberries, gooseberries and cherries. Here, at last, there was safety and tranquillity. No child wanted to wander among food that was sprouting from the ground, as opposed to lying limply in cellophane where it was supposed to be.

Arnold was keen on the idea of growing your own because you could never be sure what had been sprayed on the stuff you bought at the supermarket. He had even wondered about investigating an allotment. But that was as far as it got because he was revolted by the thought of getting mud up his nails or contracting tetanus from thorns.

That afternoon, just as he got to the end of a tall and frothy line of pea plants, he bumped into a woman coming from the other direction. Both of them, in that delightfully polite British way, cried *sorry!* and smiled apologetically. Then they stepped aside to allow free passage but, by chance, both stepped in the same direction and blocked each other's path again.

"Shall we dance?" said the woman.

How pretty she was, thought Arnold. What gorgeous brown eyes. Melting. Large. Like hot chocolate.

He concentrated before he said anything, practising the sounds in his head in advance of saying them, desperate not to stammer. "Beautiful garden, isn't it?" he said eventually.

"Fabulous," she said, her head on one side, a smile on her lips. "I especially like these Green Arrow peas" She ran one hand through the fronds, the heavy pods resting against her fingers. She nestled them in one hand as if she were gauging their weight and then looked straight into his eyes. He felt a sudden tingle in his groin and shivered.

"Yes," he replied. "I th-think just the same. They're so ... well, they're just so green, aren't they?"

She began to walk along the row and he noticed she had the slightest of limps. Somehow, that seemed to make her even more attractive. In literature, he knew, perfect women were rarely to be trusted. As was obvious in, for instance, the character of that beast, Madame Bovary.

There seemed to be an easy, and a natural, inevitability to his walking along beside her. For a moment they said nothing to each other. He racked his brain for something scintillating to contribute. It was useless. He knew it couldn't last long anyway. It would only be a matter of minutes before Form Four created such chaos that he and the other teachers were forced to leave. So he would just enjoy this brief time with her. Perhaps he could pretend, in his mind, that they were together, that they were always together, the two of them walking side by side, him the gentle English teacher with a heart of poetry and sunsets, and her the dark-haired beauty with her fine eyes and violet perfume.

"Do you know anything about Thomas Hardy?" she asked.

And there it was. The doorway. For though he might not know a Green Arrow pea from any other sort of legume, he did know a lot about literature. Now he could shine. He talked about Hardy's birth and his mother, and about his architectural practice and his meeting with the woman who became his wife. He talked about the novels and the house Hardy had built and about his poetry. And the woman gazed at him as he spoke and she told him how impressed she was by his knowledge and how grateful she was to have met him there and how much better her visit had been as a result. And ten minutes into the conversation, Arnold's mind had married them and bestowed four children upon their union.

When they reached the gooseberry bushes and Arnold was just about to tell her the story of Hardy's falling wildly in love with a travelling actress, the woman began to cough. He was paralysed. Should he pat her on the back? Offer to get her some water? And then the ghastly thought flew unbidden into his mind - *what if she's got something infectious?*

Shaking and spluttering, she reached into her bag, took out a packet of mints and put one in her mouth.

"Sorry about that," she said." I must have been walking along with my mouth open. My throat just became too dry all of a sudden, that's the problem." She waved the packet of mints towards him. "Would you like one? They're extra strong - a particular weakness of mine. I crunch them all day long - they keep one's breath sweet, I think."

She means my breath smells, thought Arnold. She's being polite but that's what she's trying to say. He took a mint and put it in his mouth. He didn't normally eat sugar because he was afraid of tooth decay which he'd read could cause heart disease. On this occasion, however, he didn't think he could refuse. The mint was so strong that, momentarily, it took his breath away. He pushed it to the side of his mouth so that he could speak. The menthol was burning the inside of his cheek so that it was hard to swallow his own saliva.

In the distance, he could hear sudden shrieking and raised adult voices. He knew what that meant. It was over.

"Well, I'd best go," he said, trying desperately to stop drool from slopping over the top of his lips. "It's been so lovely to meet you - "

"Lucy," she said, "Lucy Garonne. Thank you so much for today. "

The shrieking on the other side of the wicker fence became rather desperate.

"And I'm Arnold, " he said, holding out his hand to shake hers before deciding that that was an utterly doltish thing to do. He put it back in his pocket, hoping that she hadn't noticed.

"I know this sounds foolish," she said, "but I almost feel as if we were destined to be here together, as if we were meant to bump into each other at the pea plants. Isn't that strange?"

Briefly, he wondered if the entire thing had been a dream. He did actually feel a bit odd, a little bit out of body and sort of through a glass darkly. Maybe he was imagining the whole thing?

The reverie was destroyed when an urgent hand pulled at his sleeve. "Arnold! For God's sake, where have you been?" He turned around to see Deirdre, his Head of Department. "The bastards are running riot out there. Come on, it's time to go."

"Goodbye, Lucy," he said. The words sounded distorted to his ears. He put a hand to his lips and found that they were sticky and that his fingers were trembling. This was not the image of him that he wanted her to remember. He tried to grin confidently and as if he were happy.

"Goodbye, Arnold," she said.

He wondered if there were violins playing somewhere. If not, there should have been. He was 56 years old and this was, without a doubt, the single most romantic moment of his entire life. To be more precise, it was the *only* romantic moment of his life. And it was over almost as soon as it had begun. He couldn't be the first to turn away. He wanted to have every last glimpse of her pocketed away in his heart forever, to keep it there waiting for him to take out and savour at difficult times like last period on a Friday with Form Five.

"Arnold!" said Deirdre. "Get a move on, will you? "

Lucy smiled gently at him. He was close enough to smell her violet perfume, close enough to see the fine down on her cheeks below the heart-shaped beauty spot just below her right eye. She put one hand on his arm. "It's been a pleasure," she said before she turned and limped away under an archway between two fruit trees.

My life is over, thought Arnold and then, once she was out of sight, he spat the mint into his hand and threw it into a bed of sprouting onions.

Just as he reached the end of the wicker fence, he had a sensation of rushing water in his head. He steadied himself by leaning on the fence which rewarded him by embedding a thick splinter of wood straight into his palm. He hardly felt it. His flesh felt strange, sort of numb but painful at the same time. He heard Deirdre shouting at him but he couldn't make out what she was saying. He looked up at her and realised that he couldn't see properly - everything seemed to be opaque, almost like looking at the world through a smear of vaseline. *Help,* he tried to say. Maybe no sound came out: he couldn't be sure. He felt sick, horribly, horribly sick. His legs began to wobble and fold and, somewhere out there, he knew that there was mocking laughter. *Look at old Benson - he's drunk!*

This was it. This was the moment he had been fending off with pills and exercise and clean living. It had arrived and he wasn't ready. God had kept him alive just long enough to fall in love. But he would rather have not fallen in love and stayed alive, thank You very much.

He was vaguely aware of Deirdre's impatient hand on his shoulder as he tumbled to the ground. He landed face forward into the lawn. Several strands of spiky grass stabbed him straight up the nostrils. It was agonising but he couldn't flinch. His body wasn't listening to him anymore. As the breath caught in his throat, he tried to tell them that he was dying but the words were trapped on his lips.

When he woke up, he didn't know where he was. He was in a bed but it was too hard to be his own. Also, he was lying on his back, something he avoided because it increased the risk of haemorrhoids. His eyelids were too heavy to open but they glowed orange so that he knew the light must be very bright. In addition, he didn't recognise the noises round him. There was a lot of beeping and people talking loudly; he could hear a swishing of curtains and the metal rumble of wheels on lino. It was all very confusing. He felt his mind becoming fuzzy and was just about to drift off again when a soft hand gripped his arm.

51

He opened his eyes and suspected instantly that he was experiencing some kind of mental delusion. Or worse, even, that he was perhaps dead.

Lucy Garonne was sitting at his bedside, leaning forward over the blankets. Standing behind her was a nurse, a tall redhead with beefy shoulders and biceps like Popeye. He suddenly recognised both her and the floral curtains. He wasn't dead. He was in Tudor Ward. Again. He stared down at his toes beneath the cellular blanket and tried not to shake.

"Arnold," said Lucy. "Thank goodness! You had us all so worried!"

He looked away from his feet and gazed in wonderment at her face. Her eyes were full of compassion and she rubbed his arm with gentle fingers. The motion rubbed the hair on his wrists the wrong way and was quite an uncomfortable sensation. He determined to stick it out. But what was she doing here? What was *he* doing here? A vague recollection of falling into the grass came to him. He touched his nostrils tentatively with his free hand and winced.

"Welcome back, Mr Benson," said the nurse. "You'd be better off applying for a hospital Season Ticket, so you would."

Arnold closed his eyes while he searched for something cutting to say. "N-n-n-nurse O' Halloran," he said. "I'll have you know that I'm very ... Well, that is to say -"

"Yes?"

"Can't you see that he's tired?" said Lucy.

Arnold opened his eyes.

Lucy let go of his arm, stood up, and took a step backwards. The nurse was forced into a hurried retreat in order to avoid a stiletto heel being plunged straight through her plastic clogs. Arnold smirked and then hid it quickly, hoping that O'Halloran hadn't noticed. He remembered her ferocity with a thermometer.

"He needs to sleep." Lucy smoothed the bed sheets down and turned around. "Nurse, I believe the gentleman in bed four is trying to attract your attention."

And then it was just the two of them.

Lucy leaned over him. "Arnold," she said. "My dear man."

Her dress snagged on the side of the bed so that the neckline was pulled right down. He swallowed. The top of her breasts, her wondrous breasts, where they swelled up, tanned and taut, were just inches away from his face. Her lips were very close to his.

Her breath whispered over his cheeks. "I knew we were destined to meet again. I just knew it."

"Hello, Uncle Arnold."

He wrenched his gaze away from Lucy.

His niece, Tamara, stood at the bottom of his bed.

"I've brought you some grapes," she said, holding out a brown paper bag towards him. She put the fruit down on the blankets and took off her raincoat. "I know you like healthy eating." She sat down in the chair next to the bed and gazed with undisguised curiosity at his visitor. "Be careful - they've got pips in".

Lucy stared for a second longer into Arnold's eyes, smiled, stood upright and smoothed down her dress. Then she turned to Tamara.

"Hello," she said. "How lovely to find that Arnold has family." She gazed down at him with affectionate eyes.

"Oh, he's got lots of family," said Tamara, "not just me." She looked at her uncle. He didn't seem too bad - a bit pale perhaps but that was hardly news. Then she surreptitiously studied the woman. She was attractive, that was for sure. Beautiful, dark hair, good skin, nice eyes. Pretty birth-mark. And then Tamara looked at her still more closely. "Do I know you?" she asked. "You look familiar somehow."

"Well, that's hardly likely, Tammy," said her uncle. "Wherever could the two of you have met? The lady's not even local." He turned his gaze to Lucy. "Are you?"

Lucy held out her hand. "Delighted to meet you - Tammy, is it? I'm Lucy Garonne."

Tamara clasped the outstretched fingers awkwardly. There wasn't an awful lot of room, what with the coat on her lap, and her handbag, too, and the bed only inches away from her knees.

"Hi," she said. "Sorry, have I taken your seat? Would you like to sit down?"

"Tammy, can I have a grape?" said Arnold. "I'm starved. Can't remember the last time I ate anything." He frowned as a memory came back to him. He'd eaten something, all right. A mint. Lucy had given him a mint. No, he'd spat it out. Full of sugar. Dangerously toxic. She was being kind. His breath had offended her and she hadn't liked to say. What a lovely woman.

"How long have I been here?" he asked. "Are they going to do any tests? Do they think it's something...something sinister?" He noticed then the splinter in his hand. He closed his eyes, took a deep breath and pulled it out.

"You've been here," said Lucy, looking at her watch, "just under five hours."

"Five hours?" said Arnold, sucking at the wound in his palm. It was bleeding slightly. He wondered if he should ask for some antiseptic and a plaster. You could never be too careful. Although his tetanus jabs were definitely up to date. "That's a long time. Sounds serious. I'm normally out by now. They discharge people far too fast these days. Very bad practice. It might save money but it costs lives in the end." He took a handful of grapes from the paper bag which Tamara was holding out to him. "Did they bring me by ambulance? Was it driven by a fat chap called Roy? Or was it Albie, the skinny one?"

"I'm afraid I didn't notice," said Lucy. "But I don't think they're going to keep you in. They think it's stress - exhaustion, perhaps."

"Can't remember the last good night's sleep I had," said Arnold. "It's tough being an academic - very punishing."

"How will you get home?" said Tamara. "Shall I drive you? I came by car."

"Oh, I can help out," said Lucy. "If you'd like? It wouldn't be a problem."

"That's so kind," said Arnold. "Both of you - so kind. Should we just wait, though, and see what the doctor says? I'd like to be reassured that there's nothing badly wrong with me - I mean, it's not normal is it, to just pass out like that?"

"You've done it a few times, though, Uncle," said Tamara. "This is the fourth bag of grapes I've brought you this year."

"Tamara! Really!" said Arnold. "You make me sound like some kind of hypochondriac." He closed his eyes and folded his hands over the blankets, in jarringly corpse-like fashion. "Obviously, I'd much rather be healthy and fit but the truth is ... I don't feel at all well." The last words were uttered almost in a whisper.

The two women looked at each other, concern etched in both faces. They leaned back from the bed and the man lying there, silent and grey.

"Your uncle has had a shock, Tamara," said Lucy in subdued tones, "or do you prefer to be called Tammy?"

"I don't mind," said the girl. "I'm happy with either. It's only my dad who insists - used to insist - on calling me Tamara. It's after the ancient goddess of streams and rivers. He was most particular about it." And it was at that point, thinking about her father and his funny ways, his silly hang-ups, his kindness and how much she'd loved him, that she suddenly remembered where it was she had seen this woman before.

But how strange...

She opened her mouth but before she could pose the question, Lucy spoke. Her tone was a little louder than before and it seemed to Tamara that it was slightly rushed, urgent, even. Maybe she was imagining it.

"Tammy," she said. "I think your uncle is looking tired. He needs some rest. Why don't you and I go for a coffee? There must be a cafeteria here somewhere. By the time we get back, hopefully the doctor will have seen him and announced the all-clear." She took Tamara's arm. "Shall we?"

And Tamara found herself being waltzed out almost before she could marshal her thoughts, let alone her bag and raincoat, both of which fell to the floor in a heap. There was a moment or two of fumbling and then they were in the corridor, Lucy, serene and beautiful and Tamara, a red and flustered mess. The control continued at the formica table in the hospital cafeteria where Tamara was supplied with a milky coffee although she preferred it black, and a bun when she was not even slightly hungry.

"You know, Tammy," said Lucy. "I think you're right. You look familiar to me, too. I think we *have* met before. Is there any possibility - it seems such a coincidence - but was your father Gerald Benson?"

"Yes," said Tamara. "He was."

"There!" cried Lucy. "I knew it! I used to work with him. I hadn't made the connection between him and Arnold. What an extraordinarily small world. We got on famously, Gerald and me. What a delightful person he was. I heard on the grapevine the sad news," she leaned forward and placed a brief hand on Tamara's arm, "and so I took the liberty of inviting myself to his funeral. That must have been where we met."

"I saw you," said Tamara. "I saw you in the garden." She looked down and stirred the coffee. It was the closest she could get to drinking it.

There was silence for a moment or two. Tamara picked at the bun. Lucy gazed out of the window at the building site opposite.

"And how did you meet Uncle Arnold?" said Tamara finally.

"I'm taking a sabbatical," said Lucy. "Nerves, mid-life crisis - call it what you will. But I'm using the break wisely. I visited Jane Austen's grave in Winchester last week and the Charles Dickens Museum the week before that. Simply marvellous! Have you ever been?"

"No," said Tamara. "I never have."

"And then I read Tess of the D'Urbervilles," said Lucy. "Cried my eyes out. And so I thought - Thomas Hardy - that's a writer to investigate. And goodness me ! What an extraordinary life he had! I was pretty clueless but Arnold - he knows so much, he's so learned! He told me all about him. I really admire knowledge in a man. It's such an attractive quality. Don't you think?"

"I suppose so," said Tamara, thinking back to her ex-husband who read The Sun, and Viz annuals, and not much else. "I've never really thought about it."

"That's because you're young," said Lucy. "Gosh, that sounded patronising didn't it! Sorry, I didn't mean it to be. It's just that once you get a bit older, all the stuff that used to matter - the broad chest, the slim hips - they get to be less important than the other things - intelligence, kindness, wisdom. They're the qualities that last, after all. Hair falls out, wrinkles appear, waistbands expand - Age! It's all too hideous!"

"But how did you actually meet him? Arnold, I mean."

Was there, just for a second, a furrowing of the brow? A tightening of the lips?

And then Lucy smiled. "Oh," she said, "I'm sorry - I didn't explain it very well, did I? It was at Bockhampton, Hardy's birthplace. I was there trying to find out more about him. And your uncle was there, too, with a school group. We bumped into each other amongst the pea plants - it was rather romantic, actually."

"But how did you end up at the hospital with him?"

"Just chance. I'm a strong believer in the hand of fate - aren't you?"

"Not especially," said Tamara. "I think that too much reliance on destiny is bad. It can mean you don't do anything useful to get the future you want." She took a hesitant sip of the coffee. She'd left it too long to try it and it had gone cold. "If you're not careful, you can end up with a future almost by accident. And it might be one that you'd rather not have."

"How wise you are. But you sound sad, too."

"Were you in the ambulance with him?"

"Well, it's rather astonishing but it appears that when Arnold's colleagues called for an ambulance, the wait was going to be upwards of an hour - some accident on the M4, apparently. So they decided it would be better to get him back to school on the coach. I followed them in my car. The headmaster had rung for a local ambulance and it arrived in the yard at the same time as the coach did. That's why Arnold's here rather than in the Dorset County Hospital."

"I see. But how is it that you're on the ward with him?"

"I couldn't bear the thought of him being all alone here, alone and afraid and unwell - so I decided I'd be at his bedside when he came round."

"But you'd only just met him!"

"But, Tammy, life's like that. You said yourself that sometimes you have to work with fate - not just allow it to arrange your future for you. I had to follow that coach and follow that ambulance - because that was me 'doing something useful' just like you suggested. I can't explain it - but I feel a connection to Arnold. I knew that that one meeting in Hardy's garden wasn't the end. It was just the beginning."

A woman in an apron and paper trilby approached the table "Can I take these?" she said, pointing to the cups and plates.

"Yes," said Tamara. "Yes, here you go," and she pushed the crockery to the edge of the table.

"But you've hardly touched any of it," said Lucy.

"Sorry, " said Tamara. "I guess I have no appetite right now." She stood up. "Shall we go back to the ward?"

"Yes, let's. Maybe Arnold will be feeling better after that nap."

"Did you know that my father's cousin died in our garden?"

"What?" Lucy stood up and grimaced as if sitting down had made her leg seize up. Then she piled the cups and plates onto the waiting woman's tray. "Thanks so much," she said with a smile.

"On the day of my father's funeral, his cousin, Pammie. She banged her head and drowned in our pond. You were there. Didn't you see it?"

"Good lord! No - I had no idea. I had to leave in a bit of a hurry. I had a train to catch." Lucy looked incredulous. "How astonishingly awful. I'm so sorry."

They walked silently down the maze of corridors, Lucy with the slightest of limps and Tamara, to accommodate it, slowing down as unobtrusively as she could. The air was thick with suspicion and violet perfume. At the ward doors, they became aware of raised voices.

"But how can you be sure that it's nothing serious?" Arnold's voice was strident. "Aren't you going to take my b-blood? What about tests? If you don't mind me saying, I think you're being rather irresponsible."

"Mr Benson," said Nurse O'Halloran, "Irresponsible is the last thing I'm being. I have a duty of care with NHS funds. You've already had," she looked down at the file in her hands," twelve blood tests this year. All normal. If I thought you needed a test today, believe me, you'd get it. But you don't. The narrative we're seeing here is that you're just run-down and a bit anxious. You need to remember that while these investigations are free of charge to you, they have a cost to the hospital."

"This is disgraceful."

Lucy pulled the curtains open around Arnold's bed.

"Ladies," said Nurse O'Halloran, continuing to glare at Arnold but acknowledging their presence with a nod. "I was just explaining to Mr Benson here that what's wrong with him is fatigue and anxiety - nothing more, nothing less. If he could just learn to relax now ..." Arnold crossed his arms and looked away. "You need to make an appointment at your local surgery, so you do. You can discuss with your doctor a range of options to manage your symptoms."

"Thank you, Nurse," said Lucy.

"You're welcome." O'Halloran closed the file.

"Can I take him home?" said Lucy, smiling at Arnold. "I have nothing else planned for the evening," she placed a hand on his shoulder, "so I'm free to dedicate myself to your care - if you'd like?"

Tamara frowned.

"Yes," said the nurse. "The doctor's been and is happy to discharge him." She strode out with a swish of curtain. "We'll be writing to his surgery," she said, the words coming to them from over her shoulder.

"I can take you home if you'd like, Uncle Arnold?"

Arnold looked at his niece and then at Lucy. Tamara couldn't be sure but it was as if something secret had passed between the man in the bed and the woman at his side, some message in the eye contact.

"That's kind of you, Tammy," he said, "but if I'm going to be forced out of the ward - and it looks as if I am - then I should cause as little inconvenience to other people as possible. I wouldn't dream of asking you to take more time off work than you already have."

"But I've finished for the day. It's nearly ten o'clock at night."

"Really? I had no idea. Time stands still when you're in hospital. But if it's so late then that's even more reason for you to go home. You don't want to end up getting back to your bed tired out because of an old man like me."

"Well...if you're sure..."

"I am - but, honestly, I'm very grateful " He started to fold back the blankets off his legs. "Lucy, can you see my shoes? Are they under the bed?"

Lucy pulled out a pair of leather slip-ons from under the bed, handed them to him and then threaded her arms into the sleeves of a soft blue coat.

"Give my love to your mum," said Arnold, while he was putting on his shoes. "How is she by the way?"

"She's fine," said Tamara. " A bit sad, a bit quieter than she used to be, but she's not doing too badly."

"That reminds me," said Lucy, "I'd better ring my own aged ma. I hadn't realised how late it was, either! I ring her every night for a quick chat - parenting never ends, it seems, however old the child. She'll be worried if she doesn't hear from me." She picked up the empty grape bag from the bed. "You've done well with these, Arnold - they're all gone." She crushed the bag into a ball and put it into her handbag. "Look, while you're getting ready, I'll just pop down to the concourse. I think I saw some telephone boxes there. I'll be two minutes. Lovely to meet you, Tammy. " She held out her hand.

"Yes, lovely to meet you," said Tamara, "*again.*"

Was there the briefest of panicked looks directed by those fine brown eyes at Arnold?

"I'm not sure I can quite remember the way out of here," said Lucy. "They're a maze of corridors, these hospitals, aren't they?"

"Tammy will take you, won't you love," said Arnold. "She knows the way to the concourse. Give your uncle a hug before you go. Thanks for the fruit."

"Shall I come by and see you tomorrow?" said Tamara." I take it you won't be going in to school."

"Not a chance," said Arnold. "You heard the nurse. I've got to rest and relax."

"I'll be there to make sure you do just that," said Lucy. "I'm not leaving you. I'm sure you've got a spare bed, or a sofa or something."

Arnold swallowed.

"Your jacket is in the locker next to the bed," said Lucy, with a smile. "Look, sorry to nag, Tammy, but do you think we could be making tracks? I don't want my mother to be ringing up the hospitals in a panic trying to find me - can you imagine? Oh, the irony!"

"Of course," said Tamara. She put on her raincoat and carefully, slowly, did up all the buttons. Then she took a scarf out of her bag and tied it loosely around her neck. She took her time. Then she undid it and re-tied it. She looked at Lucy - was that ever-ready smile just a little forced? Then Tamara began to rummage in her handbag.

"Lost something?" said Lucy. Her eyes weren't smiling whatever her mouth was doing.

"Just looking for my car keys - you should always have them ready before you approach your vehicle. It's a safety thing. It's always better to be prepared for danger - that way you've got a better chance of fending it off."

"Very wise," said Lucy.

"Goodbye, Uncle Arnold," said Tamara, bending down over her uncle. He was sitting on the edge of the bed, carefully feeling the sides of his neck, almost certainly for nodules and lumps. She'd seen him do it before.

"Goodbye, dear. Thanks for coming."

"I'll be right back, Arnold," said Lucy. "Get your jacket on and don't go anywhere without me!"

The two women walked silently down to the concourse. At the bank of telephone boxes, they turned to face each other.

"Bye, then, Tammy," said Lucy. "Thanks for guiding me here." She opened the door of the first box. " My mother will be relieved to hear from me."

"Bye," said Tamara. "Thanks for looking after my uncle. I'll pop in to check up on him tomorrow. You've been really kind - but you mustn't feel obliged to stay with him beyond then. I can always stay in his house for the next couple of days - or he can come and stay with us. My mum would be delighted to have him."

"Well, let's see, shall we?" said Lucy. "Take care, now. Got those keys ready? Did you manage to get into Car Park A? That's always the most convenient one, isn't it?"

"I didn't, as a matter of fact - I'm all the way over in D."

"That's quite a hike. Bad luck."

Tamara set off under the glare of the lights and through the throng of the anxious. Hospitals were always busy places, it seemed, even when visiting hours were over. Sporting fabulous beards and moustaches, a crowd of turbanned men sat at a table looking glumly into the middle distance. Just beyond them, she sidestepped out of the path of a woman in a pink dressing gown who was attached to a drip on wheels which rolled alongside her like a reluctant pet. At the door, a fat man in a wheelchair smiled at her and she smiled back, trying to disguise her revulsion at the space on the seat where his left leg should have been.

Outside, a light rain was beginning to fall. The street lamps threw shining splinters of orange against the night sky. Worried relatives, facing unnamed tragedies, trudged along the pavement beside her. She found herself exchanging meaningful glances with them and smiles of sympathy. Head down against the evening chill and the summer rain, she put her hands in her pockets and walked on, taking care not to trip over the occasional upended and uneven stone. A fur of moss made them even more slippery than usual in the drizzle. She reached Car Park A and then, beyond that, B and C. There were spaces there now, not that that was helpful any more. On the other side of the fence, a man sat at the wheel of a red Range Rover, doors closed, lights off, just staring out into the darkness. As she passed him, he put his head in his hands in a gesture of despair.

By the time she reached Car Park D, she was alone.

In the distance, she could hear the revving of an engine. It sounded very loud against the background of the softly falling rain and the thudding of her own footsteps on the damp stones. And then, as she reached the pavement edge, just at the moment when she stepped off the kerb and onto the wet crossing, the revving of the unseen car became much closer. It appeared suddenly from around the corner of the oncology block.

It was only because Tamara had the good fortune to slip sideways on a slimy white zebra stripe that the car wheels did not go over her head. They made a terrible mess of her handbag, though.

Chapter Seven

About half an hour later, in Car Park A, Lucy opened the door of her Mini and took Arnold's elbow to help him in. He sat down gingerly and did the seat belt up. The car smelt of violets and he closed his eyes and breathed the scent in deeply, wanting to savour the fragrance before she got in and saw him doing it.

The driver's door opened with a whoosh of cool air and she sat down, opened her handbag and took out a pair of glasses. "I don't always wear these," she said, "but you're someone I want to keep safe - no risks taken when you're in my car!"

Arnold gazed at her through the darkness. How caring she was. How beautiful were the contours of her face even when lit only by the orange sodium that washed through the windscreen. He imagined being brave enough to touch her leg, of having the courage to give the flesh a quick squeeze of affection and gratitude. A flash of electricity coursed through him that was so intense that he gasped aloud and had to pretend to cough.

They set off along the maze of rain-damp roads which ribboned around the hospital and then out through the sleeping houses, stopping at red lights and indicating even at empty junctions. Weird how habits become ingrained, thought Arnold. Odd how routines become part of you even when they're not needed. The familiar is so comforting and so safe.

"Well," said Lucy. "Here I am, it's late at night and I'm driving around a strange town, with a man I don't know and I'm taking him to a house I've never visited. I can hardly believe myself. I'm so shy, normally. Still, change is invigorating, isn't it?"

"Oh, yes," said Arnold. "I'd hate to get into a rut - same old, same old. Blah - boring!" He gazed out through the window at the grey pavements and greyer houses.

"I hope I'm going the right way?" she asked. "Sorry, I should have asked for your address before we set off."

"Well, as luck would have it, we're driving in exactly the right direction."

"Good news!"

"That's Tammy's house just there," he said, pointing towards the cul-de-sac as they drove past it. "Well, her parent's house. I hope she got home safely."

"I'm sure she did - she seems a sensible kind of girl."

"She is. Anyway, I'll give you better instructions for my place as we get nearer."

"Thanks," said Lucy, flashing him a smile before turning back to the windscreen and the empty streets ahead. "I just headed for the exit and imagined you'd tell me where to go from there."

"Not a problem," said Arnold," No U-turns necessary so far!"

And the journey, including its ending, remained lucky. There was rarely a space outside his bungalow. But tonight, magically - for, after all, he had just been discharged from hospital and couldn't be expected to walk long distances - there was a gap directly in front of his garden gate. He used the bus on schooldays and his car was still parked where he'd left it last weekend, three doors away.

Once inside the house, he led her into the lounge.

"Take a seat," he said, indicating the sofa. "Would you like a cup of tea ? I've got herbal if you like that sort of thing. Or coffee, perhaps? No, it's a bit late for caffeine, isn't it? Don't want to be kept up all night, do you? Hah-hah!" *Shut up!* shouted his brain. *Just shut up!* He began to feel rather sick. The tingling in his stomach reminded him of the time he had agreed, much against his will, to accompany his cousin, Pammie, on the Big Dipper at Barry Island.

She patted the sofa. "Come and sit down," she said. "There's a space here, right next to me, that needs you to fill it."

The sudden unicorn in his pants made the walk to the sofa an awkward one but he attempted a saunter nevertheless. He slid onto the seat and took Lucy firmly by the shoulders. She leaned forward and kissed him and the throbbing in his nether regions became volcanic.

He wasn't sure quite how it happened but the next thing he knew they were lying on the sofa and he was on top of her, leaning on his elbows and gazing down at her face. Lucy started to stroke the bulge in his trousers. With her other hand she guided his fingers to the top of her legs. She began to undo his belt. As she slipped her hand inside the waistband of his y-fronts, a sudden pulsating avalanche flooded his body in waves of electricity that were so intense the world spun round in rainbow colours. In an instant, a hideous, but fantastic, instant, far beyond anything he could control, he completely exploded.

"Oh!" he gasped. "My G-god! I'm so sorry! I...I...it must be the stress ..." For one ghastly moment, he thought he was about to cry. He rolled off her and sat on the floor, his head in his hands.

A moment later, he sensed, rather than saw, Lucy sliding off the sofa next to him.

"Sweetheart," she whispered. "Don't worry. These things happen. Not just to you but to everybody." Her fingers gripped his knee, just below the soggy bits of trouser. "It doesn't alter how I feel about you. Not one jot."

He took his hands away from his face and opened his eyes. Slowly, he turned his head to look at her. "You are so lovely," he said. "I just don't know what you're doing here. What do you see in me, Lucy? What on earth do you see?"

She smiled so tenderly at him that the humiliation, just for a moment, receded. "I see a good man, Arnold." She kissed her fingertips and then laid them gently against his lips. "And that is worth rubies to me."

His crotch felt cold and sensitive. His head ached. The day had been extraordinary. The night, still more so. And yet...and yet... wondrous though it was to have this beautiful woman here by his side, her chestnut eyes full of compassion, her voice telling him marvellous things, what he really wanted now was for her to go away and leave him alone. He couldn't explain it other than that it was all too strange, too foreign, too much, to take in. After all, he had been in an ambulance. He had been in hospital not many hours before. There had been a medical emergency. And he hadn't eaten anything all day except a half-sucked mint and a bag of grapes.

"I can see that you're tired," she said. "Let's get you to bed. I'll camp in the spare bedroom so you can call me if you need help." She stood up, smoothed her dress and extended a hand to him.

He declined it, leaning instead on the sofa to get up. She frowned for a moment that was so brief, it was almost not there at all and then folded her arms. "Would you like to show me to my room, kind sir?" she said, smiling at him.

He walked across the room, trying to ignore the cold cardboard wetness of his trousers. "Follow me," he said. And then at the door of the lounge he stopped and turned. "You don't need to stay, you know. It's very kind but, honestly, I'll be fine. I just need a good night's sleep and all will be well."

She opened the door and stepped out into the hall. "Actually, Arnold, it's you who would be doing me a favour," she said. "I'm pretty exhausted myself. I'm not sure I'm up to the drive home if I'm honest. But if you'd like me to go -"

"Not at all!" said Arnold. "That was selfish of me. I'm sorry. I'm not quite myself - as - er - as you've already seen for yourself." He felt his face flush. "Of course, you must stay. Giving you a bed for the night is the least I can do." I hope she doesn't use my toothbrush, he thought. I hope she's got one of her own in her bag.

"Would you mind if I just made myself a cup of hot chocolate or cocoa or something? Have you got any?" She started to walk in the direction of the kitchen. "I think it would help me sleep."

How does she know which door is the kitchen? he wondered briefly, before following her in there. He opened a cupboard door and gestured to the contents. "I've got some organic stuff," he said. "It's hardly been used. I don't usually eat sugary things. It's something Tammy bought me last year as part of a Christmas hamper."

"Ah, yes," said Lucy." The lovely Tammy. She does like to bring you food, doesn't she? Why on earth do fat people assume that everybody constantly wants to eat?"

"My niece isn't fat. She's just a bit plump."

"Of course. And she has a pretty face."

"Yes she does." He lifted down a green tin and put it on the unit. "Look, I'm going to have to leave you to it, I'm afraid." He handed her a china mug. "The spare room is the next door on the left. The bed is all made up." He yawned and tried to cover his mouth. "I'm just so beat." His head was beginning to swim. "If I don't get to sleep quickly, it'll bring on palpitations - and they're a beast to get rid of once they start. Sorry, I know I'm not being much of a host." He smiled weakly. "It's been a bit of a day."

"You dear man," she said, taking his hand and kissing the palm where the splinter had been. He was too tired to flinch. "You go straight to bed. I'll make myself this cocoa and then settle down for the night.

Don't worry - I'll turn out all the lights and lock the front door and everything. We'll be snug as a bug."

He took his hand from her grasp and walked awkwardly back out into the hall.

"See you in the morning," she called. "Missing you already!"

He stopped for a moment at her words. The morning. He knew he should be glad that she wanted to be here for longer than just an evening, especially after...well, after what had happened. But this was his home. Of course, he was being ungrateful and perverse. The problem was that he didn't like sharing space. He hadn't liked it ever, not even when he was a boy and was forced to share a bedroom with Gerald. In fact, it was probably because of having to share with Gerald that he felt like he did.

"Good night," he called over his shoulder.

In his room, he peeled off his trousers and pants, folded them and put them in the laundry basket. He took out his pyjamas from under the pillow and put them on, threw back the quilt and got into bed. A click of the lamp and there was blessed darkness.

Just as the ache in his head began to loosen its grip, there was a knock at the door. He groaned. Now what does she want? Is there never to be any peace?

"Yes?" he said, his voice quavery and thin.

The door opened and she came in. She was carrying a mug. "I've made you some cocoa," she said. She put it down on the bedside table. "I know you don't like sugar but you've had a shock."

"Thank you," he mumbled, half into his pillow.

"Now, you drink it all up. Doctor's orders." She kissed him on the side of his head and left him.

He ignored the drink and was almost instantly asleep.

He woke soon after, though, his eyes staring out into the darkness. There was a noise nearby and it had spoilt his sleep. What a pain. He had ears like a bat. The boys in school were always saying so. *Batty Benson*, they said. He'd heard them.

He lay there for a moment trying to work out where the sound was coming from. It was the lounge. Someone was speaking. Who was it ? Was it the radio? Or the television? For goodness sake! Was the woman an insomniac? How very selfish - she knew how tired he was. He sighed, closed his eyes again and tried to go back to sleep.

But the sound kept getting in his head, impossible to ignore. He didn't think it was the radio or the telly, after all. It was a female who was speaking. There were gaps after she'd spoken, gaps where she was listening to the other person, the person he couldn't hear. Lucy must be on the phone. His phone. He hoped she'd offer to pay for the call. He was sure she would - she was a decent sort. Maybe it was her mother worrying. Maybe Lucy had called her again. He glanced at the clock on his bedside table. What was she doing calling her mum - calling *anyone* - at half past two in the morning?

It was a bit of a cheek when you thought about it, using another person's telephone without asking.

Why would a woman call a person secretly in the middle of the night?

He tried to fight the idea but there it was, taunting him. It had to be faced: was she - could she possibly have misled him? - *was she calling her husband?* It was the easiest thing in the world to take off a wedding ring. Oh, God...what had he got himself mixed up in? What if the man turned up, here, at the bungalow? What if he tried to pick a fight? Perhaps he should call the police. Ask them to come, ask them to take Lucy away, and take away her husband, too, who was almost certainly a big bruiser of a man.

He couldn't call the police. Lucy was using the only telephone.

He would get up, get up very quietly, and stand in the hall and listen to what she was saying. If everything appeared calm, if it seemed like her husband was agreeing not to come and find her, then he was safe. In the morning, he would confront her.

No he wouldn't. He didn't care if she was married. It was all over. There would be no confrontation. He would just ask her to leave, to leave and never come back. He wasn't interested in romance, after all. He would explain that he was married to his work. He was a committed academic and had no time for relationships. That was it.

But he had to know the truth.

He got up, crept through the darkness, opened the bedroom door as quietly as he could, sidled along the wall until he got to the lounge and stopped to listen. He couldn't make out the words. He put his ear to the door. That was better.

"Oh, darling, don't worry. It's going to be all right," said Lucy.

Darling? thought Arnold. Going to be all right? Is the brute angry? Is he about to jump in his car?

"Look, it'll be second time lucky!" she said.

Second time at what? he wondered. Marriage? Is she finishing with the husband? Does she sound sad? No, she doesn't. She sounds...cheerful.

"No, don't come round," she said. "I'm fine. Honestly."

No! Definitely don't come round!

"What do you think?" she laughed. "He lasted about five seconds. I didn't take my shoes off, never mind my pants!"

What? His face was on fire. What kind of woman was she, to be saying these cruel things, these *intimate* things? Had he stumbled into some kind of weird sex ring? He'd heard of people like this before. Was she what they call a "swinger"? Oh, the depravity! And to be talked about so disrespectfully on his own telephone!

"He's fast asleep," said Lucy. "I put a pill in his cocoa - he went out like a light."

What?

"Look, he couldn't taste the stuff on the mint and he won't taste it in his coffee in the morning, either. We were just unlucky this morning, that's all. Don't panic."

Couldn't taste what? *What was she talking about?*

"I'll clear out of here by ten. Might take them a while to find him, mind. Poor bastard seems a bit short on friends. Although that fat niece of his might pop over tomorrow, I'm not sure. Pity you messed it up tonight. She could turn out to be a problem."

He felt vomit rise up into his throat and clasped his hand over his mouth. The wood against his ears felt strange, the darkness was suddenly full of sparkles, the air felt leaden...don't faint! *Don't faint!*

"It will all be worth it, in the end, sweetheart, I promise you," said Lucy. "Three down, three to go!"

Arnold reeled away from the door and stumbled back to his room where he collapsed on the bed. He stared at the closed door, imagining it being flung open. At the thought of it, he shrank back into the bedding, his heart beating so fast he felt as if it was going to burst out of his chest. What should he do? What *on earth* should he do? He was afraid to go back out into the hall. What if she heard him and came out? Especially as she might be armed with a kitchen knife taken from his Littlewoods knife rack.

Maybe he should open a window and call for help? He'd heard that the thing to do was to call *FIRE!* when you were being attacked because people were more likely to investigate if they thought the danger might spread to them. He got out of bed and tiptoed to the window and drew the curtains apart. Although he opened the sash as quietly as he could, it squeaked just as it got to the highest bit and he froze. He stared at the door of his bedroom, sure that it was about to open and that Lucy - *she was mad, mad, mad as a hatter!* - would leap in and knife him.

But the door stayed closed.

He opened his mouth and prepared to shout out of the open window. But he couldn't bring himself to do it. Even though there was a lunatic in his lounge who wanted to murder him, he felt stupid calling out into the night air. It just wasn't very British, somehow.

Despite the whirling panic in his head, a bit of him was still calm enough to know that this was rather like the beginning of his favourite book, The Thirty Nine Steps: the enemy was outside, intent on carnage. What would Richard Hannay do? He would outwit them, that's what.

He opened his wardrobe and pulled on a pair of trousers over his pyjama bottoms. This was followed by a thick jumper and a coat, all donned at breakneck speed. He rifled through the drawers and grabbed his wallet and car keys.

What if she comes in now? *Hurry up*, Arnold, for God's sake, *hurry up!*

He pulled out a bag from underneath the bed and threw in some clothes any old how. Then he got a bundle of jumpers and fashioned a pretend body under the quilt. He put some under the pillow as well so that, at first glance, she would think that he was one of those odd people who liked to sleep with their head covered.

Is she coming? His heart seemed to be beating, not in his chest where it should be, but in his throat, each pulse almost knocking against his tonsils. *Is that footsteps?* He picked up a letter-opener from the top of the chest of drawers. It was sharp and shiny. He stuffed it into his pocket. Then he climbed out of the open window and stepped into the flower bed outside. He put his bag down on the mud, turned round, grabbed at the curtains to pull them together again, and pushed the window closed, his fingers slipping down the panes. Then he paused to consider the rest of his escape.

The moon was full and bathed the garden with silver light. In the distance, he heard a dog barking. He dashed down the path to the brick wall that framed the end of the lawn, opened the tall gate that stood in the middle of it, closed it behind him, and stood in the lane. Looking left and right, he took a breath and paused for a while, some bit of his brain already hearing Lucy's car racing towards him, knocking over the dustbins in her fury. But she didn't come. No-one did.

He ran down the lane, turned the corner into his street and looked towards number 18 where his Polo was parked. Luckily, getting to it wouldn't entail going past his own front door. He approached the car, bag clutched under his arm, with his back bent at the waist and head low. His eyes were fixed on his lounge window. It was in darkness. Had Lucy discovered his flight? Was she about to burst out of the bungalow and shout his name?

He knelt down in the gutter next to the car and fumbled with the keys, trying desperately to fit one into the lock. Door opened, he flung his bag onto the passenger seat, sank his backside onto the driver's seat, and quickly locked all the doors. Raised voices suddenly blasted out from some nearby house and he instantly threw himself across the faux leather, trembling. He lay there for a few seconds, his breath bursting out of him in gasps. *Get a grip, Arnold!* Breathe properly ...short in-breaths, long out-breaths...short ... and long... that was it.

He turned his head and looked up at the windows, waiting for a looming figure to appear, their fingers splayed against the glass. Lucy. Or her partner, the other person who wanted him dead. Whoever that was.

Don't think about it. Yes, someone was trying to kill him and that was certainly worth worrying about, but he was nearly safe. Getting away. That's what he had to concentrate on. *Getting far away.*

But why would anyone want to kill him? He had nothing. He didn't even own his own house thanks to Aunt Edna's lunacy. In fact, the total sum of his expectations was that blasted tontine. And then he thought about the word again. *The tontine...*Six people united by a common need to see the other five dead.

But it wasn't six people any more, was it? A cold hand gripped his stomach so ferociously that he had to clench his buttocks. *Three down, three to go!* That was what she'd said. *Three down, three to go!*

Is it..? Can it be...? It has to be. The three must be Gerald. Pammie. *And Arnold.*

He sat up, thrust the key into the ignition and dared himself to turn it. Suddenly, he became convinced that there was someone sitting in the back of the car. He couldn't bring himself to look in the mirror. He knew there would be a face reflected in it, staring back into his eyes.

70

Breath stuck tight in his throat, he froze, waiting for a hand to grip his shoulder. Eventually, he turned his head and looked, not at the mirror, but directly at the back seats. Somehow that was less frightening.

No-one was there.

He took a deep breath, put his feet on the pedals, and turned the key. The engine sounded incredibly loud and he trembled. *Go!* Shouted his brain. *Go now!*

And Arnold Benson drove away and escaped the beautiful woman with the violet perfume and subtle poison. Despite it all, despite the fear and the panic, he had never been so exhilarated in his life.

Chapter Eight

Tamara,

That same night

Meanwhile, some hours earlier, back at the hospital car park, and unaware of the drama about to unfold at her uncle's house, Tamara had picked herself up from the kerb and was leaning against a lamp post for support. The car was gone, the driver, whoever it was, clearly happy to leave her, perhaps for dead, on the zebra crossing. There was an irony somewhere about nearly getting killed in the grounds of a hospital. At least it would be convenient. And then she saw her handbag. It was mashed, completely flattened. It was the last present that Keith had ever bought her but she didn't feel sad, she felt furious. He'd never bought her anything expensive except for this one thing, not even after the miscarriage. She loved the bag, despite knowing that it was a guilt present, bought just as he'd decided to leave her. And now it was ruined, never to be replaced and impossible to repair, destroyed by some stupid bastard in a Mondeo. Her tights were ripped, too, and the heel of one of her boots had come off. She could howl at the injustice of it and at her utter powerlessness.

She wondered if she should call the police and tell them ... tell them what? That she had nearly - but not *actually* - been killed by a lunatic driver? That her handbag had been destroyed? Oh, they'd certainly jump into action at that. Other options? She could always get into her own car and drive around the hospital looking for him. And what would she do if she found him? Giving him a piece of her mind was about the sum of it. She was not a violent person, not even when her dignity and her tights and her boots and her bag, her precious bag, had been ruined. She was pathetic, that's what she was. *Pathetic.*

She limped to her car, the corpse of her bag clasped under one arm. She dug out the key, got in, sat down and, without any warning, burst into tears. That little accident had brought together so many sad things. Keith. The miscarriage. Her dad. Her dad who had been killed by a car just like she had nearly been. She fished in the side pocket of the door for the box of hankies that she always kept stashed there. This wasn't the first time that she had sat and sobbed in here. Not by a long chalk.

She blew her nose and then turned on the ignition. As she flexed her leg, sudden pain made her shriek and pull her foot off the clutch, thereby causing the car to stall. Turning on the roof light, she saw that there was a cut on her knee. She dabbed at it with the paper hankie, hoping that the blood wouldn't stain the upholstery. What a hideous night.

She felt the tears welling up again and she shook her head angrily. *For God's sake, grow a pair, Tamara.* She should remember that she wasn't the only one suffering. Think of the starving children in Africa. Think of the homeless and the poor. And what about Uncle Arnold? He'd certainly had a rough time of it today, too.

And that woman, Lucy. There was definitely something strange about her, something that made Tamara feel uneasy and on her guard. It just didn't fit, not any of it, not her story, nor her passion for Arnold. Though Tamara loved him, she couldn't see why such an attractive woman would be interested in her uncle, who was, to be honest, a shrivelled, middle-aged hypochondriac with grey hair and a predilection for V-necked jumpers.

Anyway, she would visit him tomorrow in her lunch hour and if Lucy was still there, she would try and find out a little bit more - including how well she knew her dad. Another story that didn't quite sound real. What had she said? " *We got on famously".* Really? That wasn't something she was used to people saying about her father and as for " *What a delightful person he was"...* well, that was mystifying. But then, if the woman's taste ran to tall, skinny older men with little in the way of charm, cash or wit, then maybe...

She drove home, wincing with the gear changes that made her knee smart. Once there, she sat outside, waiting for the lounge light to go off. She didn't want to explain anything to her mother. There'd be a fuss made and the rogue car and its psychopathic driver would only bring back painful memories to her mum, just as they had done to her an hour earlier.

The next morning, her knee was swollen and purple as an aubergine. She wasn't sure that she'd last the day in work but neither could she face the alternative of taking a sickie. Explaining to her mother why she was staying home wouldn't be easy. And it wasn't as if she would be nursed and coddled - quite the opposite. Since her father's death, her mother had spent most days on the sofa, eating biscuits and watching endless soaps. She didn't want to leave the house, not even to take Poppy for walks. Both Tamara's dog and mother were getting fatter and unhealthier by the week. The woman stayed in her nightie all day long, even at meal times.

A day spent at home would be no fun at all.

Instead, straight after breakfast, she decided to wrap around her leg an ancient elastic bandage filched from the first aid kit. There were no painkillers in there so she had to make do with an out of date packet of LemSip but that contained paracetamol so that was fine. Driving was out of the question, though, so she hobbled out to the bus stop.

As soon as midday hit, Tamara limped out of the office and onto the number 43 that went right past her uncle's bungalow. She rang his doorbell three times. There was no answer. She peered through the lounge window but could see no-one there. Then she walked round to the lane where she opened the gate that led into her uncle's back garden. Looking at the house, she was surprised to see that all the curtains were closed, which was odd considering it was daytime. Even stranger was that, beneath her uncle's bedroom window, a set of footprints was implanted in the mud, the toes facing the house. Had he been burgled? Perhaps he was inside, injured, even now while she stood outside, helplessly. She rapped on the glass. No-one came.

Back in the street, she hunted for his car. It was nowhere to be seen. Surely, she thought, if he'd gone somewhere with the creepy Lucy, they would have used *her* car, wouldn't they? What with him only just having been discharged from hospital and all. This was strangeness piled upon strangeness... and yet ... maybe she was reading too much into it. It was just as likely that Lucy had gone back to wherever she was from, and her uncle, feeling much improved, had gone into work after all.

Yeah...like that was going to happen...

Back at her desk, she rang Coningsburgh High. Having been a student there herself, she knew Sharon, the school receptionist, well. Luckily, this made it possible for her to be told the otherwise confidential news that her uncle Arnold had rung in sick that morning. Apparently, his department wasn't surprised. Details of his illness and trip to the hospital had been shared at breaktime the day before in the Staff Room, over Digestives and cups of weak tea.

"And was it definitely him, Sharon? He didn't ... oh, I don't know ... get someone else... a woman, say ... to ring on his behalf?"

It was definitely him. "And between you and me," said the receptionist, "with only a few days left of the Summer term, I don't think we'll see him back in school until September. Lucky chap."

I hope he is being lucky, thought Tamara. I really do.

"Will you let me know?" said Tamara. "If you hear from him, I mean?"

"Will do, Tammy . But don't worry, love. He'll be in touch with you before us. You're family, after all."

A fortnight later, Sharon rang Tamara to let her know that the school had received Arnold's formal letter of resignation. In it, he thanked them for being supportive colleagues and apologised for not having given them more notice. He told them that he was moving on to new horizons, although he did not state what these were.

Tamara visited the police station but they showed only a lukewarm, pat-on-the-head concern. Her uncle was a grown man. He'd sent a letter to his employers who had confirmed that it was written in his handwriting. There was no evidence of foul play. He'd simply decided to go away. He had the right.

Arnold also sent a letter to Tamara. Unfortunately, she didn't receive it until much later: too late, in fact.

Chapter Nine

Venetia,

November the same year

Venetia Benson had spent much of her life waiting for things to go wrong. There had been pockets of happiness, such as when Aunt Edna had died three years ago. That had been a glorious time. The promised inheritance had conjured vistas of plastic surgery and health farms and dating sites and all the opportunities that being beautiful might bring. The excitement faded quickly once it became clear that there wasn't going to be a massive cash legacy. The annual dividend from the tontine was hardly life-changing. But then, hope followed by disappointment had been the overriding characteristic of her existence.

In childhood, she had been tubby. She was delighted to become thinner as a teenager but the arrival of spots, braces and glasses soon brought her back to earth. As an adult, smoother skin, straighter teeth and contact lenses improved things but her life remained a constant tussle between the body she wanted and the one she'd been given.

There were minor victories to be had, usually achieved through acne concealer and diet sheets, but the battle required unceasing vigilance. The defiance of eating a doughnut or pizza or, heaven forbid, a bar of chocolate, inevitably resulted in a fresh crop of pustules and an inch on her waist.

The menopause was the latest skirmish being waged against her by God who, if ever proof were needed, was clearly not a woman. Hot flushes burnt her from the inside out, sleep had become an item of longing, and her front lady-bits hurt like she'd been impaled on a cheese grater.

These atrocities, horrid though they were, she could live with. It was the way she looked that she really hated. Had always hated.

Working in a chemists helped a little. The pharmacy carried a range of beauty products, lots of them with free testers and samples, and she had boxes and boxes of these in her bathroom cabinet. Some soothed her complexion and glossed her hair but many were too perfumed for her skin and scalp. She kept them anyway.

The products designed for weight loss were even less successful. Despite knowing this, she squirrelled them away in her cupboard and fridge and, from time to time, tried them out. The cardboard-chewy diet pills made her retch. The meal replacements - insipid shakes and soups - were so insubstantial that she found herself supplementing them with bread, which kind of defeated the object.

Reminders of all that she wasn't, via the company of thin, pretty or married women, was generally avoided. Consequently, her circle of acquaintance was beige, single and dowdy. She had no expectation of that changing anytime soon, especially since Aunt Edna's will had robbed Venetia of the one chance to look like the women whose company she so loathed.

And yet, the future is often hard to predict.

One November evening, four months after her cousin Arnold had seemingly disappeared, she was feeling especially despondent. Dougie, the pharmacist, had been a bit harsh towards her that morning. He'd found her in the staff kitchen just about to drink a cuppa made with a newly-arrived box of "Weight-Ease" teabags that she had lifted from the shop floor. He couldn't seem to understand the importance of testing the stock in order to better serve the customers.

"I'm sorry, Venetia," he said. "I know you mean well but you can't keep taking things from the shelves. If there are no samples, and you can't persuade the rep to give you some, then they have to be bought."

His eyes, round and shiny as marbles, gazed at her through rimless glasses. He smiled gently. She didn't smile back and he looked sad.

"Look," he said, "I'll tell you what - I'll dip into the petty cash and buy a box and we'll *all* try them - what about that?"

And that's what he'd done. Nobody else had the same issues with weight, though, so it seemed only fair to stuff half the box into her handbag to drink at home. Perhaps with a nice biscuit to disguise the bitterness.

That night, sitting on the sofa, cup and plate in hand, TV and East Enders on, there was a sudden knock on the door. Then came another, slightly more impatient knock. She got up with an irritated sigh. It was going to be that Jehovah's Witness lot again, despite everything she'd said to them last time.

When she opened the door, a waft of violet perfume flooded the hall. Standing in the porch was an elegant brunette wearing an eau de nil coat. Venetia smiled uncertainly, the way you do when somebody extraordinary appears in your life but your brain is incapable of producing anything sensible to say, so leaves all the work to your face.

Hi," said the brunette. "I hope you don't mind but I've just moved in - round the corner." She pointed vaguely towards the hundreds of potential addresses behind her. "I was hoping to make some new friends in the neighbourhood." Her grin revealed a perfect set of sharp white teeth. "Gosh! I hope that doesn't make me sound too pathetic!"

"Not at all," said Venetia, "no, really, not at all!" She took a step backwards. "Come on in. I was just about to put the kettle on. Can I offer you a cup?"

Over a pot of tea (the real thing, not the ghastly Weight-Ease) plus a plate of fig rolls, Venetia learnt that her guest's name was Lucy Garonne and that, wonder of coincidental wonders, she, too, was a beautician, only she was a real one with qualifications, not just a keen amateur with aspirations. She was also childless and recently widowed. Oh, it was so sad - too sad, really to talk about - but Lucy said she really wished that she could, one day, find a good friend to share her story with. She was making a new start: that was why she had moved away from the marital home which was somewhere down south - Venetia didn't quite catch the name of the town. And, of course, like lots of newcomers to strange places, she was finding it all a bit much, a bit lonely, what with her having lost her husband and her old home, and with being forced to start a new job, as well. Or at least she *would* find a new job but, for the moment, she was very happy to work freelance from her house.

"Like an Avon Lady?" asked Venetia

"Yes," said Lucy. "Very much like an Avon Lady - but with superior products."

"Superior products?"

"They're mostly sourced in France."

"France?" breathed Venetia. "I've never been to France."

"Really? Oh, you must go! It's wonderful!"

"I've never been anywhere, really."

"Women from France are the most beautiful in the world. They have such elegance! Such ...."

"Style?"

"Exactly, Venetia. You are so right. Such style!" Lucy crossed her legs and gazed down at her ankles. "But that's not by chance."

"It isn't?"

"French women know that they're fighting a war!"

"A war? Who are they fighting with?"

"It's not *who*, Venetia - it's *what*! Like *all* women, they're fighting *time*. But unlike the poor stuff we Brits are left with, *their* weapons actually work. And it shows. They put expensive creams on their skin. They wear elegant, beautifully-cut clothes. They exercise. They eat healthy foods."

"Would you like another fig roll?"

Lucy shook her head. "You're a dear to be so kind - especially as I'm rattling on about nonsense. I'm sorry. This is what happens when you live alone. I've forgotten how to make conversation. I haven't talked like this to .. well, not to anyone, really, not in ages. You're such a good listener." She smiled. "I'm sure I'm not the first person to tell you that! "

Venetia's face produced the kind of hopeful smile that photographers demand of the unwilling.

Lucy glanced down at her watch. "Goodness, is that the time? I must be going. I'm sure you've got things to do tonight. You don't want me here, messing up all of your plans!"

Venetia had no plans. East Enders was finished, she'd already eaten her dinner, and nothing else beckoned apart from a cup of cocoa and bedtime.

But when she tried to suggest more tea or more biscuits, Lucy stood up and brushed the crumbs off her skirt. "No, I must be off - it would be awful to outstay my welcome. I know you're just being polite - I can tell already that that's the kind of person you are. Sometimes, you just *know*, don't you? When you meet a new person for the first time, I mean."

Venetia was nonplussed.

"But look," continued Lucy, "I've had such a nice time tonight... what do you say to the two of us meeting up on Saturday for a drink? Or maybe even a curry or something?"

What a dilemma. Lucy was younger than her and also pretty - exceptionally so. Venetia usually avoided women like that because they made her feel cross. But there was something about Lucy that didn't make Venetia angry - in fact, quite the contrary. Lucy made her feel better, cheerful even. The way that she seemed enthusiastic about seeing her again and the way that she hinted they could become special friends: it made her feel something she wasn't sure she ever remembered feeling before. For the first time in her life, Venetia felt valued.

But curry was out of the question. Spice played havoc with her skin.

Seeing her hesitation, Lucy said, "But, obviously, if you'd rather not, I totally understand. I expect you're already busy." She picked up her eau de nil coat from the back of the chair and began to put it on. "Thanks for a lovely evening."

"Do you like Italian food?" asked Venetia.

That Saturday, over lasagne and a bottle of Chianti, Lucy told Venetia all about her dead husband. They had been childhood sweethearts. His death had devastated her. She had no other family, no friends, no ties anywhere, no special people, no special places.

"But still," she said, "moaning never got a person anywhere, did it?" She picked up the bottle and re-filled Venetia's glass. "I've lots to be grateful for."

"I'm the same," blurted Venetia. "It's just the same for me."

"You mean that you've got lots to be grateful for? I'm sure you have."

"No, not that. I mean, yes, I suppose I have." She stared down at her plate. "But I don't have anybody special either."

"Darling girl," said Lucy, "You don't have to say these things just to make me feel better."

"I'm not. I mean - obviously, I do want you to feel better - but ..." she picked up the glass and sipped a mouthful. The more she drank of it the less she liked the taste. It was starting to leave a metallic tang in her mouth. She should stop really. She wasn't used to it. "I have no-one."

"You have your family."

"I have my cousins, I suppose, but I don't see them very often. And even when I do, we don't get on especially well." Visions of Karen came into her mind and she stabbed a baby tomato in the side salad.

"Well, there's work, isn't there? I expect you're popular there."

Venetia pushed bits of pasta around the edge of her plate. She was still hungry but wasn't sure if she should risk eating any more of the meal. She could feel a rash prickling around her lips. It was the cheese in the bechamel sauce; it was too rich.

"I'm not close to the people at work. I'm not close to anyone. I never have been." To her surprise she felt a sob rising in her throat and she coughed to damp it down. She was not an emotional person. She accepted the dullness and the empty spaces in her life. She often felt irritation and envy - but rarely sadness. What, after all, was the point in that? It was embarrassing. She clasped her napkin to her mouth.

Then she felt a smooth cool hand closing over her own. "Well, you're not alone any more, Venetia. Not now."

And that made her feel so special that she had a rum baba from the sweet trolley.

Over the winter, these evenings out became a regular event. They went to restaurants that, before this, Venetia had only ever walked past without so much as a glance at the menu or at the bright lights within. They went to the bistro in St Mary Street and the Greek taverna in Roath. A couple of times, they visited the BBQ Bar and Grill next to the Capitol Cinema. Venetia was even persuaded one night to attempt the Mahal Curry House.

The result of all this eating out together was mixed. On the plus side, it was wonderful to have, at last, a friend - a proper friend - one who liked her, listened to her and made her feel important. On the other hand, all the rich food, the heavy sauces, sugary cakes and the syrupy wines were causing havoc. Her skin was inflamed and sore and she was putting on half a pound a week in weight. She felt sluggish and heavy.

Work was difficult. She was exhausted but was sleeping badly and more than once had missed the bus in the morning and been late. Dougie had been sympathetic the first couple of times but was becoming increasingly mean about it. Really, someone with so little sympathy for those who were struggling shouldn't be working in a pharmacy. Couldn't he see that she wasn't well?

"You're not ill, Venetia," he said. "You're just not ..."

"Not what, Dougie?"

"Not looking after yourself like you should."

"I don't know what you mean."

"All this going out that you've been telling us about, all this food - you know there are bound to be repercussions."

"What are you trying to say? I'm sorry, but this intrusion into my private life? It's totally unprofessional."

"Oh, Venetia!"

"I shall be speaking to my union about it."

"You're not in a union."

"But I can join one. I can join one today. In fact, I will. That's exactly what I'm going to do - and then let's see what happens. You won't be able to bully me then, Dougie."

"Venetia - please. Just come to work on time, will you? It's not too much to ask, surely?"

"I don't have to stay here, you know. I've told you before, lots of times - I could just leave, find somewhere else to work and live. Somewhere where I'm treated like a professional - like an actual human being, not just a skivvy."

She turned away and walked into the staff kitchen. She needed a sit down and a cup of tea before she could face the customers. Dougie had made her feel so stressed. Couldn't he see how hard she was trying, how difficult it was to keep things together? What an oaf.

Chapter Ten

It was Venetia's 51st birthday in February and Lucy had insisted on taking her out to celebrate. She was due to arrive at eight o'clock. When the doorbell rang at half past seven, Venetia felt a mixture of excitement at seeing her friend and irritation at her early arrival. She wasn't ready. The curlers were still in her hair and, though her make-up was done, she had not yet attempted to put on her dress. It was her favourite dress, a blue silk number that she kept for special occasions. She hadn't worn it for a while and she couldn't be sure that it was going to do up. She'd missed lunch that day, hoping it was going to make a difference. The doorbell rang again. Scowling at the mirror, she put on a dressing gown, pulled out her curlers and ran her fingers through her hair.

When she answered the door, with a fixed and false smile on her face, it wasn't Lucy standing there - it was Tamara. The smile on Venetia's face stayed where it was but it didn't represent what was going on in her head.

Tamara had a bunch of flowers in her hand which she held out. "Happy birthday!"

For a moment, Venetia did nothing and Tamara, her arm still outstretched, blinked once or twice.

"Thank you," Venetia said at last. "That's really kind." She took the flowers and wedged them into the crook of her elbow.

Tamara took a step forward as if to walk into the hall but Venetia didn't move away so the girl was forced to step back again.

"I'd love to invite you in," said Venetia, "but I'm supposed to be going out in half an hour and, well, look at me." She laughed and pointed to her hair. "I'm nowhere near ready."

Oh," said Tamara. "That's nice. Where are you going? Somewhere fabulous?"

"The Marco Polo."

"Super. Well, I just thought I'd pop round with these flowers - you know, to wish you a lovely day and everything."

"So sweet of you." Venetia looked down at her watch.

"Have a great evening," said Tamara. "Let's have coffee sometime? You and me ... and Mum, maybe? She'd love to see you."

"Let's do that," said Venetia, closing the door. "Bye, dear. "

"Sorry, but, before you go ..." Tamara held out a hand. "It's just - well, I just wanted to ask you something about Uncle Arnold"

"What?"

"I know the police think it's nothing to worry about - he's an adult, etc - but I'm still a bit concerned about him. I mean, it's been seven months now and, well, I just wondered if we should be trying to *do* something - you know, as a family."

"Do something?" Venetia's head was poking past the half-closed door, her stubby pink fingernails gripping the edge of it.

"Well, maybe ...I just thought that perhaps we should try to find him."

"Can this chat wait, Tammy? I'm sorry, dear, but I'm in such a rush. I don't mean to be rude but....my friend will be here any minute."

"Sorry, you're right - you did say. Can I ring you?"

"You do that." Venetia smiled and closed the door.

The light in the porch went out and Tamara stood there in the darkness for a while. Then she turned and walked away. Once she was sitting in her car, she stared out through the windscreen, seemingly without focus. It was some time before she moved away from the kerb and headed for the T-junction at the end of the close. As she did so, the engine of a nearby Mondeo instantly revved up. The car had been hidden deep in the shadows. The passenger door opened and a woman in an eau de nil coat got out. The car drove away without her. It turned right at the T-junction just as Tamara had done.

Meanwhile, Venetia couldn't do up her dress. The gaping expanse at the back revealed a full three inches of blotchy spine. One elbow was crooked awkwardly, high in the air, her fingers tugging desperately at the zipper head. The other arm was bent low round her back, the fingers trying to pull taut the bottom end of the zip. It was useless. All she did was shear off the nail varnish on her index finger. She could have cried in frustration. Even once she'd given up, it took her another five minutes to pull the dress off because it was stuck around her shoulders. With one final heave, the silk tore and she was free.

She searched desperately through her wardrobe, hanger bashing against hanger. There was nothing in there that she could wear, nothing that would be suitable for such a big night, or at least nothing that would fit. In fury, she picked up the silk dress from the floor, ripped off one of the sleeves, and threw both parts into the bin.

Then she looked in the mirror. A red-faced, middle-aged woman with thin hair was staring back at her. Rolls of flab sagged over the waistband of her pants. White heavy breasts poked out from the top of her bra cups. A large suppurating pimple stood proud just below her collarbone.

It was hopeless, all of it. She was fat. Fat, ugly and old. And it wasn't fair. She folded her arms as if to hide her bosoms. Head bowed, chin resting on her chest, her top lip began to tremble with a ferocious anger.

And then the doorbell rang. She put on her robe.

"I'm not well," she said to Lucy. "I'm sorry. I can't go out after all"

"What kind of not well?"

"I have a headache. I'm sorry."

Lucy rummaged in her handbag. "Let me get you a paracetamol."

"I work in a chemist's - do you really think I don't have painkillers in the house?"

Lucy closed her handbag with a snap. "There's no need to be rude, Venetia. I'm just trying to help."

Venetia bit her lip and looked down at the floor. "I know you are." She did up the belt of her robe a bit tighter. "I just... I don't want to go out, that's all."

"Well, then, let's stay in! We'll get a takeaway. It will be great. I can pop down the off-licence and pick up a bottle - maybe even some fizz! We're celebrating a special day, after all."

Venetia sank down onto the sofa and - try as she might, she just couldn't stop herself - she began to cry.

Lucy sat next to her, for a moment saying nothing. Then she took a handkerchief out of her handbag and put it on Venetia's lap. "What's wrong, darling girl? What is it?"

"It's me!" cried Venetia. "That's what's wrong! I hate being me!"

"But why?"

"Just look at me!" Venetia gesticulated wildly and Lucy's handkerchief fell to the floor. "My skin's a mess - I'm full of spots - and my hair - just look at it!"

"But we can do something about that, Venetia - I can help you."

"And I'm so fat! I hate this -I hate being like this!" She began to poke herself in the stomach, her fingers vicious.

Lucy grabbed her hand. "No! That's enough!" She picked up the hanky and began to dab at Venetia's cheeks.

Venetia pushed Lucy's hands away and then she bent forwards over her own lap, grabbed a handful of gown, and buried her face in it. "I don't want you to see me."

"But I like looking at you, Venetia. You have a beautiful face."

"I don't, " she mumbled through the fabric covering her mouth. "I'm covered in spots."

"I can sort that out." Lucy went down onto her knees and gently pulled Venetia's hands away from her face. "My dear friend." She gazed into Venetia's eyes. Streaks of mascara had made rivulets down her cheeks, slicing through the pan-stick concealer. "Look, I may not have many skills but these things I can do - I can clear your skin. I can make your hair thick and shiny. I can help you lose weight. This is what I do - this is how I make my living. I know about this stuff. And then? Then you can look like the person you want to be."

"Can you, though? Can you *really*?"

"Yes. I promise you. I can make everything better" She held out the handkerchief, grimy now with beige foundation, and Venetia took it and blew her nose loudly.

"How?" Venetia sniffed.

"I can give you some fantastic creams - not those godawful pots of stuff that you've got at the chemists but things that really work"

"And my hair?"

"I'll give you a special hair-thickening shampoo. It's made with natural things like egg and orange, and avocado and aloe."

"I don't want to make a cake!" Venetia tried to laugh but it sounded feeble.

"That's better!" said Lucy. "That's more like my girl!"

"Will you help me get thinner, too? Those Weight-Ease things are useless."

"Leave everything to me, Venetia." She smiled. "I know exactly what I'm doing."

"I'm sorry about tonight. I'm sorry I was mean."

"Don't give it another thought."

"I know I'm a rude woman. I don't mean to be. I want to be nice. But somehow, I open my mouth and horrible stuff comes out. I don't know why I say half the things I do."

"It's because you're unhappy. But you don't have to be. And, anyway, you're never rude to me - well, just the once and that's totally forgivable! That's what friends do, Venetia - they forgive."

"I'm glad you're my friend, Lucy."

"And I'm glad you're mine." She leaned forward and kissed one hot ravaged cheek. "Now, here's the plan: we're going to find something for you to wear in that wardrobe of yours, I'm going to do your make-up and hair and then, darling girl - it's your birthday, remember? - we're going to paint the town red!"

Chapter Eleven

Venetia was delighted with the bag of skin-care that her friend gave her for her birthday. The creams all had French names and impenetrable instructions but it didn't matter - Lucy would show her how to use them. She hoped there would be an improvement soon. She wanted to wake up in the morning without wondering what new and hideous excrescence the night would have brought to her face. She yearned to have shiny hair. And the thought of standing on the scales and seeing the needle getting lower every week was the stuff of dreams, beautiful, beautiful, dreams.

And dreams it remained.

"I don't understand it," said Lucy. "I just don't."

"You promised!" said Venetia. "You *promised* it would all go away! And it hasn't, has it? Eight weeks I've been using this stuff and I look just the same. I look worse if anything. My hair's falling out even more than before - you must have noticed. I'm nearly bald, for God's sake! I'm still the same spotty, ugly, fat old woman I always was."

"You're not old."

Venetia sipped her tea and grimaced.

"Is that WeightEase?" said Lucy. "I thought you'd stopped drinking that rubbish."

"The stuff you've given me isn't working. What am I supposed to do? Rely on you? No - I'm doing what I've always done - I'm relying on me."

"You do realise it could be interfering with the diet pills I've been giving you? "

"What?" Venetia put the cup down.

"And are you using the face creams *exactly* as I said? Especially the green pot with the picture of violets on it? "

"Of course I am."

"This is important, Venetia."

"Do you think I don't know that?" Suddenly, Venetia clenched her stomach and put her hand over her mouth. She rushed out of the room.

Lucy picked up the cup of tea and poured the contents down the sink. She hummed while she did so. Then she went back to the lounge and picked up a newspaper from the rack and began to flick through it. Venetia came into the room, looking ashen. She sat down on the sofa, still holding her stomach.

"Are you ok?"

"I've just been sick. I feel dreadful."

"It's that tea. You've got to stop drinking it."

"This is the third time this week I've been sick." Venetia jumped up and dashed out of the room once more.

"I can't help you if you don't do as I say," said Lucy when Venetia returned, a damp flannel held to her lips.

"I'm going back to bed."

"I'll come and sit with you," said Lucy, getting to her feet.

"No - I want to be on my own."

"As you like, "said Lucy, sitting down on the sofa again. She picked up a magazine and read her horoscope.

Venetia put on her nightie and got into bed. She pulled the blankets up and pushed them away and then she began to shiver and pulled them up again and clenched them around her shoulders. She removed one of the pillows from under her head and, a few moments later, put it back.

Lucy came into the room. "Are you ok?"

"I can't get comfortable." Her eyes were closed and her breathing shallow. "Everything hurts."

Lucy sat on the edge of the bed and stroked her friend's hair. A tuft of it came away in her hand. She stared at it, thoughtfully. "There's one good thing," she said, letting the hair fall through her fingers and into the bin next to the bed, "all this being sick is good for weight loss. It's bound to make a difference soon."

Venetia didn't reply.

Lucy turned off the bedside lamp. From the street outside, came the sound of children playing in the twilight.

"Why do we never go to yours?" Venetia's voice sounded quavery in the shadows.

"What do you mean?"

"I've never once been to your house - not in six months of knowing you."

"It's because it's a mess. I don't want you seeing it."

"I wouldn't mind seeing the mess."

"But I would mind you seeing it. You'd think less of me."

"Don't be ridiculous."

Children's laughter rang out and then a woman's voice, calling them into tea.

"Will you hold my hand, Lucy?"

The woman reached across and gripped her friend's hand. It was cold and rather limp.

"I'm afraid," whispered Venetia.

"Darling girl! Why? What are you afraid of?"

"I don't know."

"I'm here," said Lucy. "You don't need to be afraid of anything, not ever again". She nestled into Venetia's body, laying one arm across her chest. "I'll take care of you."

Venetia began to snore loudly and unevenly.

"Bye, darling girl," whispered Lucy as she got up from the bed. "Sleep tight. See you tomorrow."

In the hall, she opened the drawer of the telephone table, took out a front door key, closed all the curtains and turned off all the lights. Just as she was about to open the front door, the telephone rang. She dashed back into the lounge, almost tripping in the darkness, afraid lest the ringing should wake Venetia up. Unlikely though that was.

She picked up the receiver, hesitated briefly and then said, "hello?" in a strong Welsh accent.

"Oh, hello, there. It's Douglas Conway here, at the pharmacy. I was just wondering if I could speak to Venetia?"

"Who'd you say you was?"

"Douglas Conway."

"And who'd you say you wanted?"

"Venetia? It's just that she hasn't been in work this week and I haven't heard from her so -"

"-There's no-one here called that. You got the wrong number, I'm afraid." She put down the phone. Then she turned the lounge lights back on, picked the telephone up again and replaced it so that, to the unwary eye, it looked as if the receiver was fully in the cradle.

Lights off, front door locked behind her, she got into the waiting Mondeo and was driven away.

Venetia's dreams that night were vivid and angry, full of swirling patterns and wild sounds. She thought Lucy was there somewhere in the lurid mist and she called out , *"Lucy! Lucy, help me!"*. But her friend didn't come until the next morning when it was altogether too late.

Just after half past nine, Lucy opened the front door, calling out, "Rise and shine, sleepy head!"

There was no answer. She went into the bedroom and, having pulled the curtains open, walked across to the bed and sat down next to the still and silent body beneath the crumpled sheets. As she smoothed Venetia's hair, thin, greasy strands of it came away in her hands. She walked into the kitchen and threw the hair into the bin. Then she opened the curtains in the lounge, too. Weak sunshine filled the room. She picked up the telephone receiver and placed it properly back into the cradle.

"*Oh what a beautiful morning!*" she sang. "*Oh, what a beautiful day!*" She walked into the bedroom and waltzed around the bed and the figure lying in it. "*I've got a beautiful feeling, everything's going my way.*"

"Lucy," Venetia whispered. "Lucy, help me."

"Why, sweetheart!" She stopped dancing and came to the bedside. "Whatever's wrong?"

"I can't feel my feet. Nor my hands. And I'm so cold."

"Let me help you," said Lucy. She took hold of Venetia's shoulders and pulled her upright until she was leaning against the headboard. There was a fuzz of crusted vomit on the woman's chin. "Oh, my poor darling," said Lucy. "We can't have that, can we?"

She went into the kitchen and filled a glass of water. She put it on the bedside table, dipped a handkerchief into the water and dabbed at Venetia's face, rubbing off the sick. This done, she put the hankie away, and took out a blister pack of tablets from her handbag.

"Now, I'd just like you to swallow this little pill for me. These will make you feel so much better, darling."

She popped out a white pill then opened Venetia's mouth and forced it between her teeth. "Here you go - just a sip of water to help it down."

The water was spilling over Venetia's chin and down her nightdress. "There you go, that was easy wasn't it? I am *so* pleased with you!"

She put another pill in Venetia's mouth and then another and another and another until they were all gone. Once the packet was empty, she held the woman's lips together so that she couldn't spit the tablets out. Then she forced more water into her mouth.

Venetia started to choke. "I can't," she mumbled. "I can't..."

"Sorry? A bit more water? No, it's all gone. Never mind, you don't need it."

She put the glass down and the empty blister pack, and lay Venetia back on the bed.

"You see? I told you I'd take care of you." She sat on the edge of the bed and smiled down at the woman lying there. "Everything will be fine, now. " She stood up. "Bye-bye, sweetheart." Leaning forwards, she kissed the woman's forehead. "I'm sorry - I am, really. But this was always how it was going to end for us. There was never going to be another way."

The phone rang out in the lounge but she ignored it. No urgency now, not any more. She could hear the message being recorded from where she was sitting.

"*Venetia? It's Tamara. Look, I'm probably being stupid but do you think you could ring me back when you can? I haven't seen you since your birthday - hope you had a good time - but I've been thinking and, well, I just wanted to know have you ever - it's an odd question, I know - but have you ever come across a woman called Lucy Garonne? It's not urgent but all the same, I'd love it if you could just call me when you get the chance. Byeeee!*"

Lucy frowned. Not for the first time, Tammy was getting in the way. Left to her own devices, she could de-rail the whole thing. What a pest the girl was. And there was only one way to deal with pests.

She went into the lounge and erased all the messages on the telephone recording tape. Then she went into the bathroom, opened the cabinet door and threw all the bottles and packets and jars into a black rubbish bag. Once the cupboard was empty, she carried the bag out of the room somewhat awkwardly. It was quite heavy. After putting the front door key back into the drawer, she walked out into the winter sun. Oh, what a beautiful day.

Chapter Twelve

Tamara,

That same evening

When Tamara came home from work, she found a bouquet of flowers leaning against the front door. They were wrapped in paper and tied together with a twist of twine. The blooms were simply gorgeous - roses of cerise pink, deep-red dahlias and a flower she didn't recognise that was a tremendous shade of purpley-blue. She picked the bouquet up and looked for a clue as to who they were for and who they were from. There was a little card attached to the wrapper. It had been a damp day, though, and the end of the message had soaked into the paper so that it was unreadable. Only the first nine words were legible: *"To my dear Tammy, with lots of love from..."* and the rest was a blur. She held the flowers to her nose and smelt them - they had a heady fragrance. The roses smelt like sweets. Who on earth could have sent them? What a mystery....but how very lovely.

Just at that moment, she heard a voice coming from over the picket fence between her house and next door. Her heart sank.

"Nice flowers you've got there, Tammy," said her neighbour, Mr Lynd. "Got a secret admirer, have you?"

She turned round and forced a smile onto her face. "I don't know," she said." I can't read the message."

"Let's have a look," he said. "See if I can make it out."

She walked to the fence, her feet dragging. Experience told her that what started out as a chat could easily turn into a marathon if Mr Lynd was on form.

He took the card from her. "Well, it's a bit formal, isn't it?" he said. "'*To my dear Tammy*' doesn't sound like a sweetheart, does it?" And then, as he stared at the bouquet, his face fell. "Good lord! What an error. I can't believe it!"

"What? What is it?"

"Tammy, whatever you do, *don't touch those blue flowers*!"

"What on earth?" she said to the air - because that's all there was. Mr Lynd had disappeared inside his house. When he returned, he was wearing a pair of bright yellow rubber gloves. "Right," he said. "Careful now, girl - you just give that there bouquet to me."

Astonished, she handed it over, the stem-ends just brushing the top of the fence. Taking them from her, he frowned at the flowers as if they had mortally insulted him.

"What idiot would put *that* in a bouquet?"

"What? What are you talking about?"

"I see there's no florist's mark on them - and I'm not surprised!"

"But what *is* it, Mr Lynd? What's the problem?"

"Problem?" said Mr Lynd. "It'd be more than just a problem if you were to touch one of these rascals." With his yellow rubber fingers, he extracted three long-stemmed purpley-blue flowers. "Do you see these? They're monkshood - aconite, some call them. Terrible things, they are."

"But they're so pretty." She leant forward as if to smell them and he pulled them out of her reach.

"They are - but they're also lethal. People have been known to die just from *touching* them."

There was a lot about Mr Lynd that verged on the comic. But Tamara wasn't about to laugh now. She was horrified. And, what's more, she believed him. Mr Lynd was a keen gardener. He knew what he was talking about.

"It's a proper error is that," he said. "Honestly! Putting monkshood in a bouquet - it's madness!"

This is impossible, thought Tamara, her mind in a frenzy. Who on earth would send me a bunch of poisonous flowers? It's just bizarre! It can't have been on purpose.

"I don't know who sent these, Tammy," he said, "but obviously they didn't know what they were doing. That's the danger with amateurs. It's like mushrooms - and what a minefield *they* are! I remember one time when I was about - when would it have been? 1956-ish I suppose - and there was this mad old woman who lived a few doors-"

"Tammy!" As Tamara turned round, she saw her mother standing on the doorstep. "Where are you, love? The front door's wide open - oh, hello, Barry - Mr Lynd - I didn't see you there."

"Hello, Janet, he said, smiling shyly. "I was just explaining to your Tammy here that somebody's gone and sent her a bunch of monkshood, all mixed up with roses and dahlias."

"Actually, Mr Lynd," said Tamara, " would you mind taking the bouquet for me? All of it? Can it go on your compost heap, maybe? Even the dodgy blue ones?"

"Certainly can," he said. "My Ena Harkness will love that." Then he added hurriedly. "That's a rose, of course. A scarlet climber." Which, somehow, only seemed to make him blush more. He turned as if to go indoors but instead stopped, looked around and said. "Nice to see you, both, anyway. Bye, then."

At quiet moments over the following few days, when she was at work, or on the bus, or sitting at the dining table with her mother, Tamara found herself pondering the same questions again and again. Who had sent that bouquet? Had they meant to include deadly flowers? Were they intended for someone else altogether? During the innocence of sunny afternoons, she was sure that it had been a simple mistake, whoever it was. But as evening fell, she wondered....

If they were sent to her on purpose, and with full knowledge of the likely result, then why? Had she somehow, at some time, annoyed someone? If so, it would have to have been a truly massive slight to have resulted in the sending of flowers that could kill. She couldn't think of anyone she knew, nor anything she'd done, that came close to fitting the bill. She wasn't that kind of person - she didn't go around deliberately annoying people. If anything, it was the reverse. She was quiet, self-effacing, shy, rather. It was one of the things that Keith had moaned about, that she wasn't lively enough, or outgoing enough.

She went over, in her mind, all the people she knew who might have sent this horrid bouquet, ticking them off, one by one. It couldn't have been family and it couldn't have been friends. A grateful client from the estate agents maybe? But wouldn't they have sent their gift to her work address?

When the list was empty, she wondered about strangers. Had she perhaps been involved in a road-rage incident and somehow forgotten? No, she would surely have remembered that. Okay, had she maybe had some other kind of argument with a person, previously unknown, that could have made that person so furious that they'd try to kill her? But who?

And eventually, she wondered if it could possibly have been Lucy Garonne, the woman she'd met at the hospital and whom she wanted to ask Venetia about. But Lucy would have to be insane to send poisonous flowers just because Tamara had rubbed her up the wrong way at one single meeting.

Surely not...

But then...what if, say, Lucy had been rebuffed by Arnold and somehow blamed Tamara for it? Weirder things had happened. She'd seen enough stories like that on News at Ten to believe it. There really were nutters who became fixated on strangers and wanted to kill them.

The problem was that she had no-one to discuss her anxieties with. If she had, maybe they wouldn't have intensified like they did.

Over the next few weeks, she started to lose her appetite. Soon, she began to jump at loud noises. At work, when she was arranging viewings on the telephone, there were times when she had to stop herself from trying to identify any nuances in the voice that might suggest the speaker was Lucy. Some evenings, when she came out of the office, she found herself scanning the road in case there was a brunette lurking in the shadows wearing a pale blue coat. At the slightest hint of perfume, she sniffed the air for violets. At bedtime, she took to walking round the house, checking the doors were locked. Sometimes, she lay awake in bed, listening for sounds of breaking glass. She even wondered about enrolling Poppy in training classes to make her more of a guard dog.

Occasionally, at the dead of a sleepless night, came the icy - *surely absurd?* - conviction that maybe Lucy had abducted the still missing Arnold. And that only she, Tamara, knew the name of the woman who had been at her uncle's hospital bedside. That would be a solid reason to bump a person off. It was at those moments that she recalled once again the bright blue of the monkshood and Mr Lynd's shocked face.

And that's when she also began to wonder about that night at the hospital when she had almost been killed on the zebra crossing.

Years ago, when she'd been feeling low about Keith, Alison had given her a library copy of The Alchemist by Paulo Coelho. She'd said reading it would teach Tamara to listen to her heart and to follow her dreams. That hadn't worked. But one thing that did chime was when the mysterious Englishman in the novel told the shepherd boy that everything in life was an omen and that there was no such thing as coincidence. Everything that happens to us, said the Englishman, was part of the mysterious chain that links one thing to another.

Maybe all these things – these awful things - really were linked.

She couldn't talk about it with her mum. She wouldn't understand. Moreover, she didn't want to frighten her. Anyway, these days, her mother wasn't really engaging with life. Meaningful conversation had become a thing of the past.

If Tamara couldn't discuss the situation with her mum, then she supposed she could always turn to the other members of her family for advice. But family meant her dad's cousins - none of whom she found easy company. They were of an older generation, of course, being closer to her parents' age than hers.

The one she usually felt the most comfortable with was Venetia - but the woman suddenly didn't seem interested in maintaining their relationship. She hadn't followed up on the idea of meeting for a coffee and neither was she answering her phone. Tamara didn't want to irritate her by trying again. Nobody liked a nag. With Arnold missing, that only left Karen and Alison but Tamara didn't enjoy talking to them because, although she was sure they didn't mean to, they both intimidated her.

If she couldn't speak to family, who did that leave? The people at work? Not a good idea. She was close to no-one there and, if she were to confide in any of them, she was certain that everything she said would become the gossip of the office. And speaking to friends wasn't an option, either. All of them had been joint friends, hers and Keith's. She wouldn't dream of asking them to take sides but she felt guilty in their company, as if the very act of being with her was forcing them into taking a position.

With everyone else being ruled out, Venetia, Karen and Alison it would have to be. They were the least bad option. But how to go about it?

Aware that she might sound ridiculous on the telephone, and afraid that she might just blurt it all out any-old-how, she composed a little note instead.

Hi, Karen (or Alison or Venetia),

I wondered if you might be free for a coffee and a catch-up next Saturday morning, the seventh. I've also asked Alison (or Karen or Venetia) to join us. It would be lovely to see you but also there's something I'd very much like your advice on. I'd so much appreciate your wisdom - four heads are infinitely better than one! I was thinking of Giovanni's in Market Place at half ten. Really hope you can make it!

Lots of love,

Tamara

Who would have imagined that eight short lines could take a whole day to write and a further two days to post?

Karen and Alison didn't have a problem with telephones as became clear when both of them rang her three days later, accepting the invitation. She didn't answer the phone. Instead, she sat on the stairs, biting her knuckles and listening to their messages. They sounded intrigued.

Venetia didn't contact her.

On the morning of Saturday the seventh, she dressed very carefully. The first dress she put on was her favourite, her go-to outfit when she needed to feel confident and on top of things. It used to be a snug fit but her recent lack of appetite had resulted in weight loss and now the dress hung on her like a baggy sack. She put it back in the wardrobe. The second dress was a scarlet wraparound that she had last worn when she and Keith were courting. Courting! How old-fashioned that sounded. And yet, how romantic. He'd loved her then. Perhaps he'd lost the love when she'd gained the weight that had made the red dress unwearable. But it fitted her again now. Too late.

With the dress fastened up, and court shoes on, she curled her hair and dug out some make-up, which was not always something she bothered with. There was no question of meeting Alison and Karen bare-faced. She had to cover up the skull-eyes somehow.

"Where are you off to?" asked her mother as Tamara was tweaking her hair one last time in the hall mirror. The purple and green light from the stained glass in the front door cast strange shadows onto her face. Despite all the Panstick and the blusher, and the red lipstick she'd chosen to match the dress, to her eyes she looked pale and ill.

She frowned at her reflection. "Just going out for a coffee."

"Lovely. "Her mother gazed at her. "You've got make-up on, Tammy. Are you meeting a chap?"

"No." She slicked on a little more lipstick and pouted into the mirror.

Her mother walked away and went into the lounge. "You look very nice, dear."

"Actually," Tamara said as she threaded her arms into her raincoat, "I'm meeting -"

An electronic voice blared out from the television in the lounge. "*Blobby!*" it called. *"Blobby, Blobby, Blobby!"*

She put her head around the door. "Bye, then, Mum."

"Bye, dear." Her mother didn't look away from the television screen.

She stepped outside and, to her dismay, saw Mr Lynd from next door. He was mowing the garden but when he saw her, he waved, turned off the mower, and started to walk towards her. Without pausing, she pointed at her wrist watch and shouted "Sorry, Mr Lynd! I'm rushing for a train!".

The weather was crisp and sunny and the walk up the hill, beneath the canopies of newly-fruiting trees, was a pleasant one. At Heath Halt, people gathered in random knots on the platform. She looked around to make sure that no-one else was near and then walked to the edge and gazed up the train track, looking for the first signs of the engine. She'd like to be first on so she could choose her seat.

All at once, the air became suffused with a powerful violet fragrance. Instinctively, she stepped back. In doing so, she barged straight into an elderly woman behind her who, just as the toes of her foot were being crushed, cried out "*Sorry!*' as British people instinctively do in such situations. Despite the signature perfume, it wasn't Lucy. Red-faced, Tamara offered her own apologies and moved away from the platform edge. She hadn't heard the woman walking up behind her. She was going to have to be more careful. More on her guard. She sat on the bench until the train came.

The 9.55 rumbled in and Tamara got on, almost the last passenger to do so. There weren't many free seats and she found herself being forced to sit next to the woman whose foot she'd trodden on earlier. The woman took out a novel from her bag. The sun shone through the carriage windows, dust motes caught in the air. Children in the next compartment were singing and their voices carried through to her. A couple sitting in the seats on the other side of the aisle cuddled and kissed. She caught the eye of a balding vicar who happened to look up at precisely the same moment that her gaze reached him. He smiled at her and she smiled back automatically even though his attention spooked her.

This.This was why she had to get help. Everywhere she went, Lucy, or fear of Lucy, dogged her. Even when there was nothing, absolutely nothing, to be afraid of. No-one on the train was, in reality, even remotely threatening. It should have felt so safe, so reassuring.

But it didn't. The elderly woman sitting next to her positively reeked of violets. The cloying scent saturated the air, making Tamara feel almost sick with the oiliness of it. She put a handkerchief over her mouth.

"Are you alright?" said the woman. She had put her book down and was looking at Tamara, her eyes full of concern.

"Yes," she replied. "I'm fine. Thanks, though. Thanks for asking."

The woman gazed out through the window at the fields, the grass flecked white, here and there, with the first lambs.

"I hope you don't mind," ventured Tamara, "but.. can I ask the name of your perfume? I know somebody else who wears it and, well, I love it but I've never known what it's called."

"I'd be surprised if it's exactly *this* perfume," smiled the woman. "It's actually quite rare. It's from France - Toulouse, to be precise."

"How lovely," said Tamara.

"It's made from violets. They're much celebrated there. They actually hold a violet festival every year. It's called 'Les Journées Violette' - and that's the name of my perfume."

"Les Journées Violette?"

"That's right."

"How did you come across it?"

"My sister married a Frenchman - so handsome - but then they are, aren't they, these French men? Such sophistication. Anyway, my niece brings me a bottle of it every time she visits. To tell you the truth, I've been wearing this perfume for so long now that I can't smell it any more. Not a bit. I spray loads of it on in the hope that the people around me can enjoy it even if I can't."

"It's lovely, "said Tamara. "Such a sweet smell."

"Thanks so much for telling me that. That's really kind. You've made my day."

At just before quarter past ten, Tamara arrived at Giovanni's. Two of her cousins were already there, sitting next to the window, bathed in pale sunlight. There was no sign of Venetia. A pair of half-empty cafetieres stood on the table. Karen had her back to the door and Alison was leaning forwards as if she couldn't quite hear what her cousin was saying. As Tamara walked in, Alison nudged Karen, smiled broadly and looked up.

"Hello, Tammy, dear," she said.

"Hi." Tamara tugged at the sleeves of her raincoat, trying to extricate her arms. She'd wanted to get there before them and so had run a bit and the coat fabric wasn't breathable. The lining was damp and sticky as glue and seemed fused to her dress. "How are you?"

"I'm well."

"Lovely dress, Tamara, " said Karen. "New?"

"No, I've had it for a while." She folded her coat over the back of the chair and sat down.

"Did you make it yourself, dear?" asked Alison. "Oh, Tammy, do you remember that day when the Brownies had a go at making nighties? And you accidentally sewed yours to your sleeve and we couldn't get it unpicked? Goodness me, how you cried!"

"Shall I order more coffee?" asked Tamara.

Karen raised an eyebrow at a waiter.

He was there instantly. "More coffee? And what about a few slices of cake? Or an early lunch? Our soup of the day is to die for!"

"Just a cafetiere for three. No food, thanks - unless -" she looked at Tamara - "are you hungry? No? Good. Think of your hips - they'll thank you for it." She turned her back on the waiter, order given, staff dismissed. "Now, Tammy - what's all this about?"

"Yes," said Alison. "Your letter sounded really urgent. What's wrong, dear?"

Tamara took a deep breath. This is it. Don't stuff it up, she thought. Make it sound reasonable. She'd planned this conversation carefully and had a handbag full of notes in case she got flustered. She knew what she was going to say and how she was going to say it.

"Right, well, if I could start at the beginning? It's a bit of a long story, I'm afraid. It began-"

"You know, I might have some cake, after all," said Alison. "Sorry, Tammy, for interrupting, but better now than later when you're in full flow. Where's that young man gone? Oh, here he is, with our coffee. Can I see a menu, dear? Have you any chocolate cake? Or carrot and ginger, perhaps? Is that a healthier option? Karen? What do you think? No, I've decided - I'd like the carrot cake."

The waiter nodded and walked away.

Tamara shoved the plunger down on the cafetiere and a spurt of coffee splashed out over the table.

"Tammy! You pushed it down too fast," said Alison. She mopped at the pool of liquid. "Impatience never wins the day, dear."

"And you did it way too soon," said Karen. "It won't be brewed yet."

For a moment, Tamara said nothing because the waiter had arrived with a plate of cake. He put it down in front of Alison and then, with a quick but silent smile, he whipped out a cloth from his belt, dried the table and left them to it.

"Sorry about that... I'm just a bit tense, that's all." She forced herself to smile. "Still - gorgeous day, isn't it?" She poured coffee into the three cups and pushed two of them towards the cousins. "It's so sunny."

"Fabulous," said Karen and then she looked down at her watch. "Look, I don't mean to be a party-pooper but I've got a business meeting with Mr Singh at half eleven."

"Yes," said Alison. "And I've got a Badge Challenge to prepare. Come on, dear, let's get to it. It's so funny - you were just the same in Brownies - always taking ages to get to the point in your stories. I don't know why - they were always good ones. You should have more confidence, Tammy."

"So ...let's start at the beginning." Tamara stopped, took a deep breath and then went for it. "There was a woman at my dad's funeral, at the house, later on, after the service." The two cousins looked at her encouragingly. "I saw her in the garden...coming away from the pond"... and then she heard a sudden intake of breath which was so agonised that it made her stumble over the next words. "And...she...so odd.."

"Later?" said Alison. "In the garden? By the pond? You mean when my poor Pammie..." She put a napkin to her mouth and closed her eyes.

"Oh, Tammy," whispered Karen, looking down at her coffee. "Did you have to bring that up?"

Tamara's face burned. "I'm so sorry, Alison," she mumbled. "I just wanted -"

Alison reached out a hand across the table. She took hold of Tamara's fingers and grasped them. Karen topped up Alison's cup. For a moment, there was silence.

Then Alison blew her nose, took a sip of coffee and said, "So is this what you've been so worried about, Tammy? Is it grief over your father? And over Pammie? I understand. Do you think you need counselling? I've got some excellent self-help books at the library - I've just finished "*Coming to Terms with Death*" by A.C. Hennessy. It's marvellous. Do you want to borrow it?"

Karen crossed her legs and stared at her stilettos. A fly buzzed over Alison's carrot cake.

"Thank you," said Tamara. "That's kind. But, really, my problem is that I've met this woman again, since then, and...well, I'm a bit concerned. "

"Concerned?" said Alison. "That you've met a woman? We're all very modern now, dear. You don't need to be worried about what we'd think. It's good news if you've met someone special - even if it does happen to be another woman. We just want you to be happy. "

"Especially after all you went through with that worm, Keith," said Karen. "Men really can be bastards."

"No, I don't mean.." said Tamara. "Look, it might sound stupid but she was with Uncle Arnold, too."

"What, romantically, you mean?" said Karen. "Surely not?"

"No," said Tamara. "Well, at least, I don't think so. Although, well, I don't know she did seem quite keen on him. Maybe he was just being polite."

"Well, at least Arnold's not a bastard," said Alison. "Thank God for a good one."

"He's a raging hypochondriac," said Karen. "So irritating."

"And, of course, your dad was a decent man, too," said Alison. She picked up her fork and took a mouthful of cake and chewed it, a look of concentration on her face.

Tamara put her head in her hands.

"There," said Alison, putting down her fork. "I'm sorry, love. I've gone and upset you by talking about your dad."

"And I did the same by talking about Keith," said Karen. "Sorry, sweetie."

"Tell us about this lovely woman you've met," said Alison. "When can we meet her?"

"She's not a lovely woman!" cried Tamara. "She's dangerous and loathsome!"

"Oh!" cried Alison. "Darling! How could you be so unlucky in love twice!"

"Look," said Tamara, speaking very quickly to stop them from interrupting her again. "Will you please stop talking and just listen to me! There was a woman called Lucy Garonne at Dad's funeral. I think there's a possibility - a remote one, I agree – but I think she might have kidnapped Uncle Arnold!"

There was a sudden silence at the tables surrounding them. Just for a moment. Just long enough to make it clear that everyone within ten feet of them had heard. Then conversation struck up again - in unison, forced and determined.

"Well!" said Alison.

"Well!" said Karen.

"This is pointless," Tamara stood up and took the raincoat from the back of her chair. "I'm sorry if I've embarrassed you. I didn't mean to blurt it out. I know it sounds like nonsense."

"What *on earth* have you been reading?" asked Alison.

"What utter *tosh*," said Karen.

"I'm serious," said Tamara. She looked from one cousin to the other. "And I think we should investigate it."

"Tammy dear," said Alison. "I really do think you might need help."

"But, look!" said Tamara. "Don't you think it's strange? Alison, you remember The Alchemist, that book you gave me - and what it said about coincidence!"

"Indulge me," said Karen, "What did it say?"

"That there's no such thing," said Tamara

She hesitated. A new idea – another horrifying one – had come into her mind last night in the middle of a sleepless night. In the cold light of day, it seemed even more preposterous than her suspicions over Lucy and Arnold. And yet... She decided to share it. Karen and Alison couldn't be any more incredulous that they already were.

"Don't you think it's odd that Uncle Arnold has, like, *completely* disappeared? And talking about disappearances - I hadn't really considered this until last night - but when was the last time any of us saw Venetia? I generally see her more often than you two do - and even *I* haven't managed to raise her for at least two months. She's not answering the phone or anything and I've tried her more than once."

"Oh, for God's sake," said Karen. She took a lipstick and mirror out of her bag. "You need to get a life, Tammy, and stop fantasising about everybody else's." She slicked fuchsia gloss over her lips.

How could she make them care? Maybe by personalising the threat? Potentially, there did exist, after all, a reason for someone to want the pair of *them* out of the picture, too. Something created unwittingly by Auntie Edna twenty years ago. Even if, in reality, it was nonsense, perhaps suggesting that *they* might be in danger might just make them engage.

"Look," she said, "just bear with me. There's my dad and Pammie and now Arnold ... that's 3 of our family in quick succession, all gone in one way or another. And, like I said before - maybe Venetia, too - seen as so she's gone completely incommunicado.

"And it's made me wonder...I know it might sound mad - but - couldn't it be something to do with the tontine? Because if it is - don't you see? -the ones who've gone are all in *your* generation. If it *is* because of the tontine and if this *is* all connected, then you two are in danger."

Karen stood up. "Well, much as I've loved our little conversation, I do need to get back to the land of the rational. Thanks, Tammy, for this. I hope we've put your mind at rest. You've certainly done your best to screw up mine."

Tamara felt a nudge at her elbow. "Thanks, guys," said the waiter. He handed her the bill. "Have a nice day!"

"If you're sure, Tammy," said Alison. "That's kind of you, dear. Very generous."

"Well, we *were* the guests, Alison," said Karen. "We were the ones invited. And how lovely it was."

Tamara pulled out some cash from her bag and put it on the table. This had not gone to plan at all. Not at all.

When she got home, her mother was asleep on the sofa, the tv blaring. Poppy was nestled into her ribs and Coco the cat was snoozing on top of her feet like a purring slipper. Tamara went straight upstairs to the little pink room under the eaves and lay down on her bed. She wished she could sleep so easily. She wished she could just close her eyes and dream. And dream of happy things, not of monsters in perfumed headscarves. She stared up at the ceiling, eyelids gritty and head thumping. Light played on the wall in shifting shadows. From downstairs came the jangling theme music from some game show or other. Win a prize. Change your life. Change your future. Change your destiny...

Change your destiny ....What was it that she had said to Lucy at the hospital? *'I think that too much reliance on destiny can mean you don't do anything useful to get the future you want"* She sat up. She wasn't beaten. This wasn't over yet.

Desperate times and all that. There was still someone who could help.

She got up and rifled through her dressing table drawer. At the back was a little brown book. It was full of telephone numbers.

She stood at the top of the stairs for a moment, waiting to hear any sounds of her mother's rousing from slumber. There were none. She tiptoed across the landing to her father's study. This room and the hall were the only two places in the house where there was a telephone. She was about to make a call that she didn't want overheard.

She sat down at the desk and swept her fingers over the wood. They came away coated in dust. Nobody had been in here for a long time. On the mantelpiece, framed photographs stood to attention, testament to happier days. Her as a baby, her mum as a young and pretty woman, her dad holding aloft a tiny golf trophy. One of the pictures, the big one in the middle, was of the green Jaguar that they'd had to sell not long after the funeral.

She opened the little brown book, found the right page and picked up the receiver.

Chapter Thirteen

When Keith answered the telephone, he sounded tired. For a moment, she wasn't even sure that she'd rung the right number, his voice was so different. That made the beginning of the conversation, the first they'd had since her dad's funeral three years ago, even more stilted. But she ploughed on. She'd started it and had to get it over with. Finishing the call without explaining why she'd rung in the first place would make her look even more ridiculous.

"I know you probably don't have time for this, Keith ... and I'm really sorry to ask you for help." She was glad he couldn't see her face. She knew it was scarlet.

"Don't worry," he said. "It's fine. What is it that you want me to do?"

"I was just wondering if you could come and look at my house?" She swivelled the handset upside down so that the microphone was up in the air. When she was sure of her breathing again, she swung the receiver back down. "My mum's house, I mean. Well, what I mean is where I'm living now, until I find a place of my own. And see if you think there's anything I can do to make it a bit safer...you know, the locks and doors and windows and side-gate and things." She heard a child crying in the background and she bit her lip in an agony of embarrassment. "Look, Keith, don't worry. It's fine. I'm sure you're busy."

"I'm not so busy that I can't pop round."

The child's cries were easing. A woman's voice was there, soothing, loving.

"Well, if you're sure...or I could ask someone else... the police maybe ...only..."

"When would be a good time to come over?"

"After work one evening? Or next weekend? Saturday evening after you finish football? I don't know - honestly, Keith, whenever it's best for you. "

"What about next Saturday afternoon?"

"After the game, you mean?"

"I don't play anymore, Tammy. It's ...well.. the lads still meet up but it's no good me being there one week and not there the next, so we decided.. *I* decided.. that it was wrong to keep letting people down. Best not to play at all. Then we all know where we stand. They've taken on Nobby Bannerman instead. Remember him? He's a great goalie. Got good hands."

For a moment, she said nothing while she pictured all the cheap gilt trophies that used to strut in the book case. "Right," she said eventually. "Saturday afternoon it is. Three o'clock?"

"Sounds good. See you then. Bye."

"Bye, Keith. I appreciate it."

"Don't worry. Not a problem - yes, I'm coming, Danielle, can't you hear me saying goodbye? " He put his hand over the receiver and there were muffled words. And then he returned. "See you next week at three." The last sentence was clipped, business-like, curt, even. He put the phone down before she could say anything else.

She went back to her room and put the little brown book away. Her mind was whirling. She was going to see Keith. He was going to help her. Was she pleased? She wasn't sure but the mixture of excitement and sadness felt familiar. Perhaps she'd been foolish to contact him. The problem was that she had to have help from someone and nobody else seemed prepared to step in: she could hardly accuse herself of finding excuses to get in touch. Her need was real.

But talking to him again had churned up all sorts of memories that she rarely allowed to surface. If there was one quality she had - and goodness knows she didn't have many - she was a practical woman. If a thing had to be done, she would do it.

He'd sounded unhappy. Clearly, he was making sacrifices. Maybe that was the difference being a father brought. When they'd been married, Saturday afternoon footie had been sacrosanct, untouchable. Nothing could be allowed to get in the way of it. Of course, as he'd explained to her many times, she couldn't possibly understand because there was no such thing as a female footballer. Not a good one, anyway. But women did play netball, and tennis and badminton. Why didn't she have a go at one of those? It had been one more thing to find fault with: her attitude towards keeping fit and her lack of exercise. Her lack of interest in anything physical, actually. But that was another story, or a different part of the same story.

At his insistence, she'd joined a gym but had mainly spent her time in the cafe, drinking smoothies and eating organic cookies. And the heavier she got, the harder it was to find the energy or the willingness to exercise and, soon, improving her body started to seem a futile and embarrassing task.

The thought of sharing her body, of actually letting her husband even look at it, became depressing. And once they'd decided to have a baby, it got even more complicated. How can you have a child without sex? And how can you have sex if you're ashamed of the way you look? They'd kept the lights off because she'd insisted but, in the back of her mind was the conviction that he was happy to be in the unseeing darkness. And it hadn't worked anyway, or not well enough, nor long enough, to keep their baby safe. It was just something else that her useless body couldn't do.

But this was daft talk. Hopeless talk. It didn't solve anything. People should alter what they can and accept what they can't.

Actually, while she was looking for positives, if she were to start exercising - now that Keith had stopped playing football - then she'd be the one keeping fit, not him. And, yes, it was mean and unworthy - especially as he was going to help her - but that felt like a nice plan. And she could maybe even succeed at it now that she was thinner.

How would a novice like her go about it ? Cycling, perhaps? Not a good idea. She had no balance. More to the point, she had no bike. Swimming? Not going to happen. She'd never properly mastered crawl or breaststroke and, anyway, swimming wasn't easy for a woman in glasses because she couldn't put her head under the water. A gym wasn't appealing either - for one thing, there was the cost to consider. There was nothing to stop her from jogging, though.... except that it sounded about as much fun as sticking a pin in your own head.

This was pointless. Yet another of her ludicrous fantasies.

There was a scratching at her bedroom door followed by it swinging open. Poppy stood in the threshold, wagging her tail and gazing hopefully. No doubt, she was wanting a treat. She'd become a greedy creature recently, begging for food at all times of the day. She'd taken to sitting next to Tamara at the dining table during meals, staring with imploring eyes as each forkful of food was held aloft. In fact, Poppy was starting to look rather fat.

And that, of course, was the answer, there, gazing at her from the doorway. She stood up. "Come on, girl," she said. "Come with me!"

By the time they reached the park, she had begun to wonder about the wisdom of this new plan. Her feet were hurting but, more importantly, the park was full of secluded paths and lonely tracks. To make it more difficult, Poppy, unused to the leash and the smells, was pulling and tugging, her nose desperate to investigate the aromas that beckoned in every clod of earth and clump of grass. And each time that she was pulled back, the dog had a habit of dashing around Tamara's ankles.

Halfway through their second circuit, Poppy wrapped her up like a maypole dancer and Tamara spun and tripped and fell face first into the mud. She couldn't save herself because one arm was caught up with the lead while the other was clinging to her handbag. No bones were broken but the same could not be said for her glasses. The frames bent clean in half and the right-hand lens popped out and fell into a clump of dandelions.

Two girls jumped up from a bench and helped her to her feet. Then they chased after Poppy who had effected an escape whilst her owner was floundering on the grass.

"Oh, isn't she sweet, though," they crooned when they brought her back. The dog didn't look even slightly guilty as the girls ruffled the hair on her tummy and kissed the top of her head.

"She's just gorgeous " said one of them, a blond girl in baggy trousers and a parka. "But you won't be able to wear these again - they're smashed to bits." She held up Tamara's battered glasses.

"You should ditch the specs and get a pair of contact lenses", said her dark-haired chum. "They're much better. My mum wears glasses and every time she opens the oven or comes in from the cold, they steam up and she can't see a thing. It's dead funny actually. And anyway, glasses make people look old. Not that.. I mean.. I don't mean that you-"

Tamara took the lead from the girl's hand, smiled, stuffed the ruined glasses into her handbag and limped away. The little toe on her left foot hurt and she wondered vaguely if that might be broken, too. Getting home was a slow affair. The dog was in disgrace but made it clear that she didn't care by running into the house and straight into the kitchen to her food bowl.

In the bathroom, Tamara held the broken spectacles in front of her face. It was hopeless. She bent them back into shape so they could be balanced on her nose but, although the left lens was undamaged, she couldn't see much more than a blur through the gaping hole of the empty right-hand side. The difference in vision between the two made her feel sick so she tried closing one eye. That didn't work because she couldn't keep it shut.

If she got a move on, she could just make it to the opticians in Caerphilly Road before they closed.

What followed was a revelation. She ordered more glasses but was also sent home with a trial set of contact lenses which, to her surprise, didn't hurt at all. In fact, she could hardly feel them. And what was more, she could see better than she'd ever been able to do with her specs.

In the bedroom, lenses in, she stared at herself in the mirror. Until that moment, she'd never seen what her face looked like from a distance without her glasses on. It was like stepping into another world, almost like gazing at a stranger. She pulled and tweaked at her hair and turned and swivelled to see her appearance from different angles. She wasn't a vain woman but she found herself whispering inside her own head that, maybe, just maybe, she looked.... well, quite nice. Thick waves of soft brown hair nestled on her shoulders. The contours of her face were sharper now that she had lost weight...she had cheekbones! And when she stepped back and gazed at herself full-length, she could see that her waist, nipped in by the wraparound dress, was pronounced and gave more emphasis to her hips and bust.

The next day, people in work commented on the difference her not wearing glasses made. Marilyn on the next desk said how much younger she looked and even nasty Sonia (who never said nice things to anyone) told her that she looked much less dowdy than usual.

This was the beginning of what turned out to be a happy week, the best she'd had in ages. Perhaps it was the skies brimful of sunshine and birdsong. Or perhaps it was that she was beginning to take herself in hand. Or maybe it was that good things had always been happening but she'd been too miserable to notice them. Lots of things went right. Everybody seemed to be in an upbeat mood at work. Mr Lynd had waylaid her and they'd managed an entire five minutes of conversation without her feeling the need to fake an urgent appointment. Her mother got dressed three out of the five days. And Poppy didn't pull on the lead anything like as much on the daily park walks.

All these good things meant that she very nearly forgot to worry about Lucy who might want to kill her and about Keith who was coming to see her that weekend.

Chapter Fourteen

On Saturday afternoon, when she opened the door to him, neither of them said anything for a moment. He stared at her and looked confused at what he was seeing. And she was a bit surprised by his appearance, too. His face looked lined and tired. And his hair was greyer than she remembered it being. The silence was loud and she wasn't sure how to break it so she just smiled.

He smiled back. "It's great to see you, Tammy," he said. "Just great." Poppy rushed past her and jumped up at him. "Hello, girl!" he said and he bent down to stroke the dog's head.

"Who's that?" said her mother, calling from the lounge.

"Just a friend," said Tamara. "Come on in, Keith". She didn't say the second sentence quite as loudly as the first.

She led the way into the kitchen and he followed her and she put the kettle on. "Tea?" She was amazed at how calm her voice sounded.

"I remember that dress," said Keith." I always liked you in it."

"This old thing? It's ancient!"

"And there's something else...I don't know..."

He stared at her and she began to blush. It took all of her willpower not to raise a hand and tweak her hair. She'd not long since taken out a headful of rollers and, because curls were something that neither she nor her hair was used to, she didn't know whether it looked alluring or tortured.

"I can't put my finger on it," he said, "but you look different, Tammy. Younger, somehow."

"I'd love a cuppa if you're making one," came her mother's voice above the blare of the telly. "And maybe a biscuit."

Tamara made the tea and took a cup into the lounge. "What friend was that, then, dear?" said her mother. Her eyes remained glued to the television screen.

"Nobody special. They won't stay long."

"Lovely," said her mum. "Can you bring me a couple of Digestives? Tea's too wet without them."

She took her mum a biscuit, shooed Poppy and Coco into the lounge, and closed the door on them, and on the Saturday film, which had Debbie Reynolds and Burt Lancaster in a clinch in the surf of some tropical beach.

She and Keith trooped around the house, (excluding the lounge where her mother was sitting), with cups of tea in hand. He advised window-locks on all the downstairs windows and bolts on the hinges of the French doors. Then they walked out into the garden and inspected the perimeter.

"You could put a trellis on top of that end wall," he said. "Especially with Old Folly Lane being on the other side of it. I know the lane's unmade - more of a footpath, really - and it's not used that much, either but a trellised wall would stop people from getting in from there. Trellis is flimsy stuff but, when it breaks, it splinters nastily. It's just enough to make Billy Burglar think twice."

"I've seen walls with broken glass on the top," said Tamara. "That would make *me* think twice."

"It's illegal," said Keith. "I know it sounds mad but you'd get done if someone hurt themselves breaking in." He turned and gazed at her. "What's all this about, Tammy? Why the sudden panic? I know there've been quite a few burglaries round here recently- is that it?"

She sat down at the picnic table that her dad had built the summer before he died. A froth of pink azalea nudged the back of the chair.

"And there's bad rumours going round about Old Folly Farm, as well," he said. "Of course, the place is abandoned so, by rights, nobody should be wanting to go there but, despite what I just said about it, Old Folly Lane leads to it and that's exactly what's behind all the gardens here, including yours."

"Old Folly Farm?" She put her tea down. "I hadn't heard."

"If you're really worried, then shouldn't you be talking to the police rather than to me?"

"I'm not *really* worried - I just want to take sensible precautions, that's all."

"Against anything - or anyone - specific?"

"Honestly, Keith...I don't even know if I can tell you why I've got myself into such a state. You'll probably think I'm barking."

"You're lots of things, Tammy....but you're not barking. " He sat down opposite her. "What's up?"

And this time, she was able to say it properly. This time, she managed to explain it the way she'd wanted to do with Karen and Alison. Nevertheless, it still sounded mad.

But Keith didn't seem to think so. "I don't believe in coincidence," he said when she'd finished. "Danielle was talking about it - fate and omens and stuff - just the other day. She's been reading some book called The Alchemist. Have you ever heard of it?"

She nodded and swallowed.

"If the same woman keeps popping up," said Keith, "and that coincides with what? - four different people? - all getting attacked, or dying or disappearing...well, that sounds fishy to me."

She could have kissed him. Almost. "Do you think so? It doesn't sound far-fetched?"

"It doesn't. And I'm not being funny, Tam... I don't want to spook you ...but I think you should be doing a bit more than sticking window-locks on. I reckon you need a burglar alarm."

"Really? You really don't think I'm over-reacting?"

"I don't. It's a shame that Poppy's such a useless mutt. She'd never defend you if someone broke in or jumped out at you. And that's another thing... when you're out of the house, you should be carrying one of those personal alarm things...and maybe a can of mace or pepper-spray or something."

"I'm amazed you believe me. I'm not sure that I believe it myself. It's hard to take it seriously. Things like this don't happen. Not in real life. Not to people like me, anyway. This is the sort of stuff that only happens to nutters in gangs, or to druggies, or to people who get caught up in weird love-triangles." At which, she stopped, picked up her empty cup and pretended to drink tea out of it.

"Well, you should take it seriously. You've got to be on your guard, Tammy. Honestly." He stared at her and said nothing for ages. "It's the glasses," he said at last. "That's what it is. You're not wearing glasses."

She flushed. "It was time for a change, I guess. Want another cuppa?"

He gazed at her for a moment and then looked down at his watch and grimaced. "Sorry, got to go. Jason goes to this French kindergarten group every Saturday and it's my turn to pick him up."

"French? That's nice."

"Danielle's idea. Thinks it'll give him a head-start in life." He smiled as he said this. "He's a lovely kid, Tammy. Dead smart, too. I love him to bits."

"I bet." She stood up. "Thanks for coming round, Keith. I really appreciate it. I'll get all the locks and things you said I need."

"Look, Tammy, you've got to *do* these things, not just say you will." He leaned forward and put a hand on her arm. Maybe he'd done it without thinking because the look on his face was as surprised as the one she knew was on hers. They both pulled themselves together quite quickly. But she did it first by turning her head and staring at the azalea next to her as if she'd never seen it before.

He let go of her and stood up. "Right - well, remember what I said about getting a burglar alarm, too."

"Will do." She turned back to him and nodded.

If you like," he picked up his cup and flicked the dregs of tea onto the lawn, "I could pick you one up at B&Q and fit it for you."

"Are you sure?"

"Unless...you'd rather ask someone else? I don't want to intrude - I mean, if you'd rather not have me here again... I don't want to be a pain in the arse. I just want to help."

She had the strangest sensation in her chest. "No, honestly...it would be really kind of you."

"Okay. Well, I'll buy it this week and pop round next weekend to fit it, shall I? And I'll get window-locks, too. I can do those the week after, if you like? You might as well have them, as well. Belt and braces."

She walked with him through the house, stopping off in the kitchen to put down the mugs. Poppy scratched at the lounge door in a frenzy to be let out. They both ignored her.

On the doorstep, he smiled and said, "And by the way, next time, you might want to let your mum know I'm here. I don't want to bump into her outside your bedroom door and have her scream her head off or attack me."

"She wouldn't do that! " These days, her mother hadn't the energy to attack anyone. But Keith wasn't to know how the woman had changed.

He leaned forward as if to kiss her and she stepped back at exactly the same time. This was all happening too soon. Or too late. She wasn't sure which.

That night, she lay awake staring up at the shadows above her head. It was clear that Keith was going through a rough time. He looked worn out. He obviously loved his little boy. But he still didn't seem that happy. The way he'd looked at her today - it reminded her of the way he used to look at her. He used to say sweet things to her then, things that made her feel full of love for him. And now he was giving her those same looks again. The kind that made her feel dizzy and hot. She'd forgotten how dark his eyes were.

Her mum had never liked him, of course, not from the outset. Maybe she would have been the same whoever Tamara had brought home. She'd been desperate to see her daughter married but, at the same time, no-one was good enough. God only knew what she'd say when Keith came round to fit the burglar alarm. Maybe she'd be grateful that, this time, he was there to help, not to humiliate.

A bigger deal was that she herself wasn't sure how she felt about him.

When they'd first split up, she'd had dreams, hot, panting dreams that made her writhe in her sleep. She'd wake, flushed and feverish, and remember with anguish that, in real life, he didn't want her. But in the first moments after waking, before she was ready to fully wake up and let it go, she'd lie there in the golden dawn and know what it felt like to have him full of love and lust, and she remembered how that had made her feel. Excitement, satisfaction, passion.

But she didn't feel like that right now.

Instead, the thoughts that kept intruding were mainly about the things he'd done that were irritating. Leaving the loo seat up. Never taking her out but getting crabby if she went out with the girls instead. He never cooked. He never did any of the cleaning, or the laundry, even though they were both working full-time. And the night she'd lost the baby and they couldn't get hold of him, not even down the King's Head which is where he'd said he'd be.

What was more, she wasn't sure that she fancied him anymore.

And then all of this was cut short by Poppy's furious, frantic barking.

Chapter Fifteen

Tamara sat up in bed, staring through the shadows and clutching at the sheets. She quickly considered her options. Her first plan was that she should hide in the wardrobe. That idea was instantly discarded because her hiding place would be given away by the pile of clothes she'd have to throw on the floor to make room. She didn't want to turn the lights on because it would make her easy to find - but the thought of blundering through the darkness to the study so she could ring the police was hideous. And even if she got to the study safely, she imagined herself struggling to find the desk and the phone and the dial and then being attacked as she whispered for help.

Poppy's barking sounded defiant. It made Tamara feel ashamed. Was she really less brave than Poppy? A dog, who, though much-loved, was slightly dim and hardly a warrior.

The lights were going to have to come on. It might even be enough to frighten them away. She turned on the bedside lamp, slipped her feet into a pair of soft loafers and put her dressing gown on. There was no time to put contact lenses in, so she had to make do with her damaged spectacles which were still loitering on the top of the waste paper bin. In time of war, one good eye was better than two bad ones.

She dug out a can of hairspray from the back of the dressing table, knowing from experience that this stuff stung like red ants if it landed on your eyeballs. And it could be wielded from a distance, too. From the back of the wardrobe, she plucked a tennis racquet. It had never been used in sport but it could be very useful, she hoped, if deployed in anger.

Getting downstairs was the important thing. From there, she'd ring the police and then she'd go and knock on Mr Lynd's door and come back with him and save her mother and pets.

She went onto the landing, reached out and turned on the lights. Then she stopped and listened. Poppy she could hear - but there were no human voices, nor sounds of breaking glass or splintering wood. Of her mother, there was no sign She had the most extraordinary ability to sleep through the loudest of noises.

Tamara crept down the stairs, spray and racquet in hand, her heart beating hard. She turned on every light as she came to it. Once in the hall, she stopped at the telephone table and picked up the receiver. But then she put it down again because Poppy was barking so frenziedly that she had to help her first, before anything.

She tiptoed to the kitchen and paused at the door. Grabbing her weapons, she edged the door open and ran one hand through the darkness, searching for the light switch. When she turned it on and dared to look in, she saw that Poppy was snarling at the French windows that led out into the garden. The blackness outside turned the glass into a mirror and, in it, she saw a blur of herself, white-faced and tense, and the dog, her paws almost leaving the floor as she barked, her head thrown back in fury.

Tamara edged round her, whispering, "it's okay, girl, it's okay."

Poppy turned her head and wagged her tail before turning back to the doors and resuming her growling. Tamara walked to the French windows, stood up against the glass and, shielding her face to block the light, stared out into the darkness of the garden. There was nobody there so far as she could see and no movement that she could detect. It wasn't easy with only one working eye.

And then, abruptly, Poppy fell quiet, licked her lips, and sat back on her haunches. Tamara gazed at the dog and then looked again out into the shadows. They - whoever *they* were - must have gone. But she felt pretty sure she knew who it was. She could almost smell the perfume.

She put down the spray and racquet, leant against the sink, picked up a glass from the draining board, filled it with water and gulped it down. Sitting down at the table, she put her head into her hands.

Then she felt a paw scratching at her leg. There stood her faithful hound, tongue lolling out of her mouth, and eyes full of hope. Tamara dug out a Choco-Treat from the jar and offered it to her. Poppy hoovered it up. Tamara gave her three more.

She was never going to get back to sleep now, that was for sure. But sitting in the kitchen for the rest of the night, gazing out at the garden, well, that wasn't an option, either. Going up to bed with her dog, that was the next step. She picked up the hairspray and the tennis racquet and motioned Poppy to follow her.

Just as she was passing the telephone table at the bottom of the stairs, she hesitated. Should she call the police now? And if she did, what should she tell them? The urgency had gone and the threat, too - if there had ever been one. The police were unlikely to be galvanised into action when she told them that her dog had been barking at the garden. What if it had just been a fox? Or one of the cats from next door? Poppy couldn't bear Mr Lynd's tortoiseshell and, if it had been him out there, it was absolutely possible that she would bark herself into a frenzy.

The moment was over. Using her head to stay safe, that was her best bet. Until she'd got the burglar alarm. And the window-locks. And the pepper-spray. And maybe other things, too, once she'd decided what they were.

She took Poppy with her upstairs, pulled back the duvet, crawled in, and patted the bed. Poppy jumped on and did a few circles to flatten it before she lay down and cuddled into her mistress's legs. Pretty soon, snores filled the air. But they weren't Tamara's. Eventually, she got up and pushed a chair against the door. Her broken glasses and the hairspray were on the bedside table and the racquet was balanced against it. She wouldn't go down without a fight.

After that, she slept fitfully until, just before sunrise, she eased herself out of bed, and opened her curtains. As she squinted out, she thought how bizarre the normality of the morning was, almost as if the weirdness of the last few hours had never happened. The world looked no different today than it had done yesterday. Just as at every other spring dawn, the trees stood black against the massed ochre of the sky, and the cloudbanks were underlit by the glow of the sun. It all seemed very peaceful.

But not peaceful enough for her to get back to sleep. By the time her alarm clock went off, one sleepless hour later, she had reached a decision. Or, rather, she had reached an attitude. There was no way that she was going to be terrified in her own bed, just lying there, whimpering and cowering under a duvet. That was pathetic.

Furthermore, she wasn't going to wait a week for Keith to come and help. She didn't want to delay and what was more, she didn't need a man. She was perfectly capable of looking after herself. Just because she still lived with her mother, that didn't make her a child. She was a grown woman. Whoever her enemy was, be it Lucy or anyone else, if they wanted war, then they were going to find that they had a battle, not just a skirmish, on their hands.

But no battle could be won without preparation.

In the wardrobe, next to where the neglected racquet had lain, was a crumpled stash of gym clothes. On went the jogging bottoms and tracksuit jacket. Into the hitherto untouched spaces of the trainers went her toes. She removed the chair from behind the bedroom door, roused Poppy, went downstairs, fed the dog, grabbed her lead, and flung open the front door. She could do this, after all. Enough of the tame walks around the park - they were going for a run!

By the end of the road, she had slowed to a trot and had to lean on the lamp post on the corner. Her breathing was laboured and her cheeks hot . Next time, she'd bring some water. Poppy sat down and gazed at her, her face full of trust and innocence. Deep breath and off again. If it was easy, she reasoned, everybody would be doing it. Practice was the answer, like in everything. She was exhausted after one circuit around the block but that was only to be expected. After all, she'd hardly slept so, of course, she was tired.

When she got home, she collapsed into a chair. Once she'd recovered, she went out into the garden, looking for any signs of a night-time intruder. She walked around the perimeter, poking bushes and staring for evidence at the fences and walls. There was nothing significant to see.

Until, just by the pond where Pammie had drowned three years earlier, she found what looked like a footprint. Or maybe it wasn't. It was hard to tell because it hadn't rained in a while and so the mud was rather crumbly, which meant that the print - if that's what it was - was far from obvious.

But it was enough to confirm her next plan.

It was a Sunday and that meant she couldn't hang about. She jumped into the car and drove to B&Q, a place she hadn't been to in ages. In fact, not since she and Keith had gone there to think about colours for the nursery that they were never going to need.

She put a selection of window and door locks in her trolley. She also picked out a burglar alarm. She didn't need Keith to choose one for her and what's more, she'd install it herself. How hard could it be? She was a practical and sensible person. She could follow a set of instructions as well as any man could. She also bought some sacks of sand, cement and gravel, plus a few more things she thought would be useful. She was going to make the house safer *today*.

When she got home, she took the locks and the alarm inside and put them on the kitchen table. She was ready and eager to fit all of these. Although maybe not the burglar alarm. Once she'd read the instructions on the back a bit more clearly, she realised that might need a bit more thought.

Then she brought down her dad's office chair. It made a serviceable trolley, one that was big enough, and strong enough, to carry the sand, cement and gravel even if it took several journeys.

The long fences that bordered each side of the lawn were edged by neighbours' gardens. Growing along and over them were mature bushes and, on Mr Lynd's side, there were so many spiky berberis trees that no-one could ever climb through On the third side was her house - and the alarm (probably) and all the locks should sort that out. If she could only secure the end wall, then the property would be safe from intruders coming over from Old Folly Lane. And, despite Keith's warnings about it being illegal, she knew exactly how she was going to do it. He wasn't the one that was in danger, after all.

She lay some plastic sheeting out on the grass and rustled out of her pocket the sales assistant's instructions which she'd jotted down as he'd dictated them. She frowned as she tried to read her own handwriting. They'd made perfect sense at the time. *How to make concrete.*

This honest toil was very satisfying. Here she was, an independent woman who was looking after herself. If only her arms didn't ache quite so much. But she couldn't stop now, not when it was nearly done. She gripped the shovel with extra determination and chopped at the pile, blending the water evenly throughout. There - it was finished. It looked like wet, grey playdough.

"Tammy," called her mother. She was looking out into the garden from the French windows. "What's for Sunday lunch? I'm starving!"

"Oh, for God's sake," whispered Tamara, her teeth clenched.

Sunday lunch was out of the question. By the time it had been cooked and eaten, the mortar would have dried up. She knew she had no more than ninety minutes to use it. The man in the store had been very particular about that. She was tired and hungry, though. Throwing a plastic sheet over the wet, grey mass, she walked slowly up to the house.

Her mother was in the kitchen, munching a biscuit. "You're leaving it very late to start on the food, Tammy," she said. "And you've got bits of putty and grit all over your face - what on earth have you been doing? It's in your hair and everything."

"It's going to be fish and chips for lunch," said Tamara. "If you leave now, you'll just be in time before they close."

"Me?" Her mother gaped at her. "You want *me* to go?"

"That would be great. As you so kindly pointed out, I'm looking a bit of a mess right now. I'm going to have a shower. Cod for me, please. No salt, lots of vinegar."

"But -"

"And mushy peas"

She'd hardly slept the night before and she felt almost sick with fatigue. The water woke her up a bit. She had to wash her hair three times to get all the grey dust out. She pulled on an old pair of pyjamas. Her joggers were stiff with splashes of concrete. She was going to have to throw them out.

By the time she was washed and dressed, her mother was back. In silence, she took the food out of the newspaper parcels and distributed it. She handed her daughter a plate piled high with fish, chips and peas. Tamara knew she'd never manage to eat even half of it. All she really wanted to do right now was sleep. But she had to finish work on the wall first. Her eyes, with their new lenses in, felt sore and gritty.

"Are you alright, Tammy?"

"What, now, you mean? I'm just tired"

"And there's nothing else going on that I should know about?"

At last, thought Tamara. At last, she's noticed how much strain I'm under. It'll be all the weight I've lost. She was flooded with affection as she realised how good it would be, how comforting, to have her mum's support. Finally, she could tell her all about it. She wondered how to begin.

"Well," she said, feeling her way forward, "there have been a few things recently that have been difficult."

"I knew it! I knew there had to be something."

"What made you so certain there was a problem? Mother's intuition?"

"I could just sense it. You've been so strange."

123

"Look, it's a long story. I don't want to alarm you - but I'll be glad to share it with you. It'll be a relief-"

"-I mean," said her mother, "you've always been such a considerate girl. I knew there was something wrong when you expected me - what with my heart and everything - to go out and get the lunch."

Tamara's face fell. "And that's it? That's what's bothering you?"

"Well, it was so unkind. Rude, in fact, if I'm honest. Not like you at all."

"There's nothing wrong with your heart, Mum. There never has been." She opened the fridge and took out a bottle of ketchup. "But there soon will be if you keep lying on the sofa all day, eating cake and biscuits."

"Tammy! What a horrible thing to say!"

"I'm not being horrible, I'm just exhausted." She splashed blotches of ketchup all over her chips. "And *you* might not be concerned for *me* - I mean, clearly, you're not - but I *am* worried about you. You do literally nothing all day long. And you eat too much and you've put on lots of weight. It's not healthy."

Her mother picked up her plate, opened the French windows and stepped outside. "I think I'll eat mine in the garden."

Tamara sat in the middle of the kitchen and picked at the mound of food on her plate. It was greasy and claggy. Too much batter, not enough fish. Too much oil, not enough chip. Too much mush, not enough pea. She shoved the plate away and folded her arms on the countertop. Just five minutes, she thought. I'll just put my head down here for a bit, have a really brief snooze - a power-nap - and then I'll get on with it.

It was Poppy who woke her up by nudging her as she tried to reach the abandoned food. As Tamara came to her senses, she realised that this had been no fifteen-minute doze. Instead, looking at the clock on the wall, she saw that she'd been asleep for almost an hour. She straightened and winced. The blood in her arms had almost stopped circulating because of the position she'd been in. The nap had made her feel worse, not better. Her eyes burnt like hot coals. She'd been warned by the optician not to sleep in her contact lenses and now she understood why.

But she had to get on, she had to finish the job. She put her plate on the floor and Poppy gobbled up the congealed leftovers. Then she poured herself a glass of orange juice, figuring that that might give her a burst of energy - she could certainly do with it.

Out she went into the garden, glancing towards the picnic table as she stepped through the French windows. Her mother wasn't there. She remembered their conversation and felt flooded with guilt. And yet.... maybe it was right that these things had finally been brought out into the open. There was something ludicrous about her making all this effort to keep the pair of them safe, only for her mother to eat and laze her way to permanent oblivion. But maybe she could have expressed it in a kinder way. It was too late now, anyway - what was said couldn't be unsaid.

Gloomy introspection wasn't going to get the job done. She needed to remember what a resourceful and practical woman she was and take pride in that.

She filled two buckets with glass from the recycling bin and took them down to the end wall where she put the buckets down, and lifted the plastic sheeting off the mortar. To her relief, the pile still glistened wet. Obviously, the man in the shop had been over-cautious in his warnings. The concrete had been made nearly three hours ago, double the time he'd told her it would take before it became too dry to use.

She put two bottles and a jar inside the empty gravel bag and then put her gloves back on. Next, she donned a pair of goggles, picked up a hammer, and gave the bag of glass a bash. Then she took a breath and gave it two mighty whacks. It was actually quite satisfying to feel it crunch beneath her hammer. Quite liberating.

She lodged a step-ladder against the wall, climbed up, and looked out at the view beyond. On the other side of the wall was Old Folly Lane and beyond that was a stretch of stubbly waste-ground. The houses in the cul-de-sac had been built here nearly forty years ago on unused pasture land belonging to Old Folly Farm. The agricultural outbuildings were all still there, although they were pretty derelict these days. She remembered playing in them as a child with Mandy Lynd from next door and being terrified by the rats that scampered in and out of the barns. For years, she'd had a recurrent nightmare of a rat running down a wall and onto her hand, something that had actually happened once to Mandy whilst they were playing there. God, how they'd both screamed.

When she next climbed the ladder, she was holding a trowel of gleaming grey concrete. She paused at the top, rather gingerly, her balance a little off-set because of the burden in her hand. She lay the mortar thickly on top of the bricks, humming softly while she did it. When that layer was complete, she climbed the ladder once more, holding aloft a broken glass jar of mayonnaise, label still attached. She stuck it straight into the cement, its jagged edges sticking up into the sky like the Matterhorn.

Chapter Sixteen

When Tamara woke on Monday morning, she went out into the garden in her pyjamas, intending to inspect her handiwork. She saw the wetness on the path and the beads of rain hanging on the grass but she didn't suspect the ruin that had been wrought. Not until she got to the end wall, that is, because that's when she saw that almost all of her work from the day before was gone. Some of the glass was still there, sharply serrated with sunlight caught in the chunks and blades of bottle and jar. But most of it had fallen off onto Old Folly Lane. Overnight rain had washed much of the concrete away apart from a few clots here and there, snagged under the heavier bits of glass.

She stared, aghast, her slippers gradually getting soaked through by the grass underfoot. It had all been for naught, all those hours of effort. If her dad had done this, it would have worked. If Keith had done it, the glass would have stayed on the wall where he'd put it. She could have cried. She just didn't know enough to do this on her own. She wasn't a pioneering feminist at all. She was just an idiot.

She didn't take Poppy out for a run. She had a bath but couldn't be bothered to wash her hair. Instead, she sprayed it solid with dry shampoo which made her scalp itch and her hair stick out sideways like tumbleweed. Just as she was finishing breakfast, her mother came downstairs in her dressing gown. When she saw Tamara in the kitchen, she sniffed, turned on her heel and went back up to bed.

Work was miserable. Clients were angry and rude and wanted impossible things to be done impossibly soon. Marilyn at the next desk was even more than usually dull, mainly spending the morning filing her nails and talking about her new boyfriend. Nasty Sonia told Tamara she looked old and tired - had she had a rough night?

In her lunch break, she picked up her mended glasses from the opticians. Back at the office, she went into the toilets, took out her contact lenses and threw them in the bin. She put her repaired glasses on instead and stared at herself in the mirror. Right in the middle of her chin was a big red spot. She dabbed at it with foundation and that made it look a whole lot worse. Good. She deserved it.

In the afternoon, while she was supposed to be typing up letters, she sat and imagined all the bad people who might now be able to get into her garden from Old Folly Lane. Was one of them the insane Lucy? Nothing had been solved, *nothing*. The house was as vulnerable as it had always been. Until Keith came to sort it out. Until he kissed his wife, patted his boy on the head, and came to rescue the woman he'd abandoned, the one who'd lost their baby and gone back to live with her parents. The fat ex-wife who made a mess of everything she ever attempted.

On the bus coming home, a man came and sat next to her. Why has he done that? thought Tamara. There are loads of seats. What's he up to? After a few minutes, she could bear it no longer and moved to the bench-seat at the back. The man turned his head to stare at her, as if offended, and Tamara looked away and gazed out of the window. At the end of the journey, she waited until the last possible moment to get off the bus and almost missed her stop. She didn't want to give advance warning to anyone who might be watching. She stood at the bus-stop for a few moments until the bus had moved away and then she set off for home.

On Tuesday evening, after another distracted day at work, she saw Coco walking on top of the garden wall. The animal slipped and cut her paw on the remaining glass. Tamara ran out to scoop her up but she writhed in her arms, getting blood all over Tamara's blouse. She had to coax the creature into the cat basket and take her to the vets to get the wound stitched. She didn't explain truthfully how it had happened.

The next night, Wednesday, she draped a heavy sheet of plastic over the top of the wall. It blew off into Old Folly Lane.

On Thursday, she carried the ladder down to the wall and tried to chip off the remaining bits of glass with a hammer. She was wearing goggles to protect her eyes. The heavy-duty gloves were ruined so she'd put on a pair of bright yellow Marigolds instead and they got slashed almost immediately. By now, the concrete that hadn't been washed away in the rain had become rock-hard. The hardness of the mortar meant that the jars and bottles couldn't be shifted so they were still stuck there, sharp and dangerous but, because they weren't very visible any more from the ground, they were no kind of deterrent at all.

On the Friday morning of that difficult week, she found that she'd been put on the viewings list to meet a new client at a bungalow called Cormoran, a shabby affair on the outskirts of town.

"I'm sure it's not my turn to view Cormoran," she said.

"You're the only one free," said Marilyn as she sat and gazed at her nails.

"Stop moaning, Tammy," said Sonia. "We're a team, remember?"

And then, as Tamara stood and picked out all the files for the bungalow, she suddenly realised that she didn't want to do this job any more. It was such a huge thought that she had to quickly find a chair to sit down.

"Anybody could be waiting for me out there," said Tamara. "I'd be all on my own. I could get killed and nobody would even know."

"Right," said Sonia. "Like that's obviously going to happen." She got up from her desk and strode towards the kitchen door. "I'm going to make myself a coffee while you deal with your dementia moment."

"I can't do it, Marilyn," said Tamara. "I'm sorry but I can't go to Cormoran."

"Why? You can't seriously be afraid?"

"I just can't face it. Any of it. In fact, do you know what? I've had enough."

"Had enough? What of?"

"Of everything."

"What?"

"I'm going home. And I'm not coming back. Not ever. This is it - I quit."

And she picked up her handbag, took her coat from the rack, and walked away, just as Sonia came back in, carrying a mug of coffee.

As Tamara stood in the vestibule, fighting with the sleeves of her mac, and with the agency door slightly ajar, she couldn't help but hear them discussing her dramatic exit.

"She's gone," said Marilyn.

"What do you mean, she's gone? Who's gone?"

"Tammy," said Marilyn. "She says she's had enough so she's going home - and she's never coming back. You're right - she's nuts."

"Well," said Sonia. "That's a turn-up for the books. How long's she been here?"

"Dunno," said Marilyn. "Ten years, maybe?"

"Blimey, that's longer than some of the furniture."

"Anyway, you'll have to do Cormoran now," said Marilyn. "I'm too busy." And she picked up the emery board again to deal with the nail on her little finger which had been getting on her nerves all morning.

Tamara pulled the door closed and stepped out onto the pavement. The banging shut of the door sealed her decision. She really was never coming back.

She carried on walking past the first bus stop, even though it was the one that she would normally wait at. It was crowded and she wasn't ready to face being with people. She needed space and quiet, and a place to think about what to do next.

Five minutes later, the bus sailed past. When she reached the second bus stop, there was no-one waiting. Even better, this stop was in front of a park where there was a row of benches. She sat down at one of them, figuring she had about half an hour before the next bus arrived. And in that half an hour, she was going to organise her thoughts.

She was just beginning to see that the reason the fabric of her life was so unstable was that so little of it was of her own choosing - she'd spent the last decade just doing as she was told.

She hadn't gone to university. She could have done - she had the A Levels for it. She'd wanted to go. But her mum had been distraught at the idea of her leaving, so she'd given in and she'd stayed at home. That's how she'd ended up at Metlock and Sons. *It'll be a good career for you*, said her dad. *Nice and safe. And you can stay here with us,* added her mother. *Where you belong.*

Six years later, when she was 24, she'd married Keith. Why? She'd loved him, she supposed, but she wasn't sure that she'd loved him enough to promise to stay with him forever. She'd been pushed into it because everyone else had made her feel like an old maid. All of her schoolfriends were already wives and mothers and their lives revolved around toddlers and mortgages. Her parents had been forever dropping huge hints, especially her mother, who'd made it clear that she didn't like Keith but was willing to accept him if it meant that, at last, she could wear a wedding hat and start knitting matinee coats.

And then, when the marriage didn't work, she'd held on to it, trying to win him back because it was embarrassing to be cheated on. She guessed that her friends had gossiped about what her husband was up to behind her back. They certainly got all red-faced and clumsy-tongued with her, probably because they were burdened by what they knew.

Even the baby...it was awful, dreadful, when she'd lost it, but, if she was honest, it was Keith who'd wanted to start a family, not her. And yet he soon seemed to have got over it when the child had been lost. *"It was only 12 weeks old, Tammy,"* he said when he finally came home. *"Size of a lemon. Not even a proper baby yet. We can have another one."* And that's exactly what he'd gone and done. Just not with her.

She'd always tried to be the wife Keith had needed her to be, and the daughter her parents had wanted her to be and, in reality, what that had meant was not being the person she herself would have liked to have been. Now her husband had moved on, and her dad was dead, and her mum was so caught up in her own misery that whatever kind of daughter Tamara was, it probably didn't make any difference.

She took a pen and a notepad out of her bag and wrote:

Plan of action:
Find a new home?
Find a new job?
Find a new man?

And then she scrubbed through the last one.

Looking up, she saw the bus appearing from around the corner. She felt cheerful and resolute, even though she knew that none of this would fall into place without some careful footwork. Her next step was potentially going to be the most difficult. How on earth was she going to explain it all to her mother? Her mother, who was so depressed by the death of her husband that life since then had become almost meaningless. All the woman had left was her daughter. And now, she was going to have to let *her* go, too. Oh, God.

On the bus, Tamara practised the sentences she was going to say. *'I love you very much, Mum, but I need to try and make a life for myself'.* Too callous? *'I walked out of work today and I'm never going back.'* Too abrupt?

She wanted to write down a few phrases but the bus was too jerky. None of them were any good, anyway. She needed inspiration. And then she saw it: the bakery where her mum used to work. It was on the main road between her bus stop and home. She bought two jam doughnuts. Best to go in armed with bribes. Hopefully, the words would sort themselves out when the moment came.

When she reached the house, she put her key in the lock, pushed the door open and called out, "I'm home, Mum!"

She'd expected Poppy to come rushing out to greet her but there was no sign of her dog nor, indeed, of her mother. She opened the lounge door, anticipating seeing her mum draped on the sofa, watching telly, with one, or both, pets, cuddled up to her feet. The lounge was empty and silent. She looked down at her watch and realised that it was still early afternoon and that she was home four hours earlier than normal. Would her mum maybe be napping after lunch? She called up the stairs. No response. Well, her mother was a heavy sleeper so that wasn't too much of a surprise. She was about to go up the stairs, intending to quietly go into her mum's bedroom, but suddenly had a better idea.

Take her up a cup of tea and a doughnut. *Perfect.*

She went into the kitchen and put the kettle on, whereupon she heard scrabbling at the French windows. It was Poppy. That, too, was odd. The dog spent her time eating and sleeping and didn't willingly spend much time outdoors, apart from when she was out with Tamara on their daily walks - or jogs, as it might well become. At that thought, she took her plan of action out of her handbag and added "*get fit*" to her list. Then she added "*get my hair cut*" and "*buy some new clothes*". Perhaps I should just write "*reinvent myself*", she thought and then dismissed that as unworthy and negative because what she was really going to do was to reclaim herself, not invent from scratch.

She let Poppy in and the dog danced around her ankles as if they'd been apart for months. Tea and cake on a tray, she led the way back up the stairs, trying hard not to spill anything or trip over the animal under her feet. At the top of the landing, her mother's door was wide open.

"Mum," she said softly, not wanting to wake her up too suddenly.

And as she rounded the door, she saw that her mother was, as she had suspected she would be, fast asleep. As indeed was her companion, Mr Lynd from next door, whose pink and fleshy arm lay heavy across her mother's naked breast.

Chapter Seventeen

"Why didn't you tell me?" Tamara asked, once the initial shock was over. Her mother was dressed by now and was sitting with her at the kitchen table. Mr Lynd had raced away next door, his shirt buttons done up wrongly and his shoes in his hand.

"I was embarrassed - I didn't know *how* to tell you. And the longer I left it, the harder it got." Her eyes filled. "I'm so sorry, Tammy. I've let you down."

Tamara put her hand over her mother's and squeezed it. "Of course, you haven't let me down. If Mr Lynd makes you happy, then that's all that counts."

"He does. He *does* make me happy. " She looked down. "I love him, Tammy. Oh, I know what people say about him - that he's boring and he's dull. But he's a good man, a kind man."

"I know that, Mum. "

"But if me being with him upsets you, well then, I'll stop." Her voice faltered.

"There's no need for that! Honestly, I'm not upset." She stood up. "Fancy a cuppa? And a doughnut?"

"Great idea." Her mother looked up at her with a watery grin.

Later, as Tamara was washing up, she leaned against the sink, bristlebrush in hand, and turned to gaze at her mum. "The thing is - and don't get upset - if he makes you so happy, why have you seemed so miserable?"

"Miserable? I haven't been miserable....have I?"

"Not getting dressed, spending the day on the sofa watching telly...not even really, if I'm honest, wanting to talk once I got home ...that all seems pretty miserable to me, Mum."

"But you haven't been here during the day, Tammy - you've been at work. And I was really busy while you were out."

"Were you?" Tamara was hard pushed to keep the incredulity out of her voice.

"I was. And, sweetheart, come the evening, neither of us had much energy. In fact, I thought *you* didn't want to talk to *me*. I thought you were worn out from work so I didn't press it. I thought I was doing what you wanted."

Tamara stared at her mother. Almost every evening for three years, they had sat together in near-silence, plonked in front of the telly until the end of News at Ten and bedtime. Neither of them had talked much to the other, each certain that was the quiet respite the other one needed.

"And by the weekend," said her mum, "all I wanted to do was flop on the sofa. I was exhausted by then, what with all the activity during the week."

"What activity?" said Tamara before she'd thought about it. She started to savage non-existent crumbs on a plate that was already lying in the drying rack.

"Well, Barry and I have had some lovely trips down to the seaside. Gorgeous - we took a picnic and some Asti Spumante to Eastbourne last week."

Tamara pulled off her rubber gloves, her mind racing. She hadn't seen the truth at all. She'd been so certain, so sure, that her mum was unhappy but maybe she was just looking for proof for something she was expecting to be true.

"And we've seen some smashing films at the Odeon - they've got a Matinee Special every Wednesday. Such a treat."

"That's great."

"And sometimes we just stayed home." It was almost as if her mother wasn't talking to Tamara any more. Her eyes were gazing off into the middle distance and a smile played on her lips. "And wasn't in my nightie all day, actually. It's just that I didn't always get dressed again after - ." Her face reddened. "Once I was on my own again."

Tamara didn't know what to say. How could she have read the situation so wrongly? They both had. And what might they have done differently if they'd each known the truth about the other?

134

Her mother stared down at her hands for a while. She seemed as tongue-tied as her daughter now. Coco climbed up on to her knee and she started to stroke her fur. The cat stretched and miaowed.

Eventually, she spoke. "I do still love your dad, Tammy, but ...."

"I know. He's not here anymore."

"He's not. But I am. Your dad going when he did - so young and with no warning - well, it made me realise that I've got to get on with it - life, I mean. If I want to be happy, then I've got to find happiness, not wait for it to find me."

"I get it, Mum. I understand." She rose to her feet and hugged her mother. Standing up while the other woman was sitting down made this awkward. "Honestly I do. You're right. About happiness I mean. And if you love Mr Lynd, then that's fine by me."

As she clasped her mother's head into her shoulder, she heard her mum say, her voice muffled, "Tammy, can you call him Barry? I think we're beyond formalities now."

Tamara let go and stood back. Call Mr Lynd 'Barry'? After all these years? That would be weird. "Of course." She coughed to hide her embarrassment. "No problem."

Her mother beamed, the wrinkles around her eyes scrunching up like the skin on custard.

Life was certainly much better when her mum moved in with Mr Lynd. Her childhood home felt, perhaps for the first time, like somewhere that was truly hers. Not just the little bedroom under the eaves, but all of it. She felt enveloped by affection, as if the house had been allowed to choose her, at last, as the one it most loved.

And she knew that life was better for her mother, too. These days, when she sat outside in the garden, she could hear from over the hedge the sound of her mum laughing. She couldn't remember the last time that had happened.

She had pretty much stopped worrying about Lucy and intruders. She didn't really believe in them anymore. Nevertheless, perhaps out of guilt at what she still seemed to see as parental abandonment, her mum had insisted that Mr Lynd came round and fitted the door and window-locks. Tamara had been grateful for his help even if the one-sided conversation that afternoon had rendered her almost catatonic.

She left the glass embedded on the top of the garden wall, reasoning that now that Coco knew to avoid it, it was doing no harm. She couldn't get the glass out anyway.

Keith rang her a few times to suggest dates when he could come and install the locks and burglar alarm but she'd let all his calls go straight to answerphone. She'd deal with him soon. In her own time.

Lots of things had become, at last, done according to when she felt like it. What a luxury.

For instance, she was in no hurry to find a new job. She certainly wasn't going back to her old one. There had been a few letters and some pleading telephone calls from Marilyn - there'd even been one from nasty Sonia - but her mind was made up.

The situation was made easier by the fact that, for the moment at least, she didn't need an income. She had fairly substantial savings, thanks to the sale of the bungalow she'd lived in with Keith. She also had a small inheritance from her dad. Her expenses were few, just food and the usual household bills. They weren't high. She'd offered to pay her mother rent but the suggestion had been turned down.

"Not a chance, darling. It's not as if we have a mortgage or anything - and, anyway, this is your home."

"Don't you want to sell the house? So that you and ...you and Barry... can buy something together?"

"Tammy, let's talk about it again in six months' time."

"Are you sure?"

"Honestly, this arrangement is salving my conscience."

"You absolutely don't have to feel guilty about anything."

"You're a lovely girl." Her mum leaned over and kissed her cheek. "Fancy a cuppa? And a biscuit to soak it up?"

Another reason for the lack of urgency about job-hunting was that she didn't miss working one jot. Instead, she began investigating different horizons and other ways to live her life. Maybe it wasn't too late to do a degree, after all.

She also felt fit and healthy. She dug a vegetable patch in the garden and started growing carrots and potatoes. She went back to B&Q and exchanged the burglar alarm for a little plastic greenhouse in which she planted peppers, tomatoes and courgettes. She bought new trainers and running kit. Every morning, she took Poppy for a five-mile run. When she came home, pleasingly tired, the walls of her house felt welcoming. Lack of stress and lots of exercise meant that she was sleeping well, too.

Poppy and Coco joined her in her bedroom and she woke every morning to the dog's wagging tail and the cat's indifference

The healthier she became, the greater her self-confidence. With increased self-esteem, came the inclination to spend more time and money on her appearance. These days, she felt worthy of the effort, especially as the results were so obvious and immediate. She had her hair cut into a chin-hugging bob and had honey-coloured highlights woven into it. She wore her lenses nearly all the time, but she also invested in a wacky pair of scarlet-framed glasses. She bought new clothes, including flattering dresses and shoes with high heels.

The day that she exchanged the alarm she no longer wanted for the plastic greenhouse that she did, was an important one. Because it was then that she made the call that would finally put an end to what might have been.

"So it's really kind of you to offer, Keith, but Mr Lynd has already fitted the window and door locks and, as for the burglar alarm, I don't even have it any more. I took it back."

"I could buy you another one, though... if you'd like? Or if you change your mind?"

"Honestly, there's no need. I won't change my mind."

"Are you sure, Tammy?"

"I absolutely am. Really, I appreciate it and everything but .. well, I think I just got things out of proportion."

"What about your mum - what does she think? Isn't she a bit anxious?"

"Why should she be anxious?"

"Well, she might have heard the same stuff I've been hearing. You remember I warned you about it - about Old Folly Farm and the break-ins."

"Keith, without giving too much away, that's the last thing on my mother's mind, right now"

"What's going on, Tammy?"

"Nothing's going on, Keith." There was silence for a moment and then she said, "Look, I just wanted to say sorry for bothering you, and thanks for all the things you've offered to do. And also that I'm fine now and I don't need any help, after all."

"What about the weird woman with the brown eyes and the perfume?"

"Well, that was me being silly"

"So you don't need me?"

"No."

"Okay, I get it. I hear you. But you know, if you still fancy meeting up for a coffee or something? That would be good, you know, for old times' sake."

She thought about it for a brief moment. She pictured him smiling at her. She imagined him kissing her.

And then she said, "honestly, Keith, that's a lovely idea - but I don't think so."

After which, she put the phone down and decided to open a bottle of wine. It wasn't just about Keith. It wasn't just about closing doors on the past. It was more that life was good and the future was beckoning. There was so much to look forward to.

Until the letter arrived.

Chapter Eighteen

She read it three times to make sure that she understood what he was trying to say. In truth, she'd grasped it the first time but hoped that she'd misread it.

Dear Tammy,

I know you'll be relieved to hear that all is well, and that I'm in a safe and happy place. I'm sorry I haven't been in touch earlier. I was afraid to share my location. I still am. That's why I haven't put a return address on this letter. It's not that I don't trust you. It's more that I can't be sure it won't end up in the wrong hands.

I would have rung you but there are no telephones here and, anyway, I don't know anybody's number. And yours is the only address I've got - and I'm not even entirely sure about that - so I hope this has got to you safely. I do know where Venetia lives but, as I'm sure you'd know, I wouldn't write to her anyway.

I'm writing to warn you all.

I don't do this without personal cost. Even thinking about home gets my asthma going. In fact, I might never come home again. I love where I am. I might sell everything and stay right here forever. If I do, I might need your help in selling my house - but that's for another letter, another time.

I just hope that this current letter doesn't somehow lead to me being found. But you and the family need to know the danger you're in, so I'm being stoic.

And here it is. Do you remember Lucy, that woman at the hospital? I know you'll find it hard to believe but bear with me. Tammy, she tried to kill me - not once but twice.

First of all, she forced a poisoned mint on me. Luckily, I'm sugar-averse so I spat it out. I didn't know at the time what a close shave that was. I still ended up in hospital.

But later, after she'd brought me home, I overheard her speaking on the telephone. She said - and she was practically boasting - that she was going to "finish me off" the following morning. Can you imagine the shock of hearing those words? Being said on my own telephone in my own lounge? (Well, she was in the lounge. I was standing in the hall, listening to her and trying not to black out). That was just before I escaped the house. I left in a tearing hurry, I can tell you.

Now look, Tammy - don't just rip this letter up and decide I've lost my marbles. Read it until the end and then make your mind up. If you decide after that to ignore what I'm saying, well, that's up to you. I will have done my duty and won't need to feel guilty anymore.

The thing is, all of you are in danger. I know this because the other thing I heard that woman say was that there were "three down and three to go."

Now, she could have been talking about the price of fish, but I don't think so. I think she was talking about people or, more specifically, us - our family. Clearly, your dad and poor Pammie were two of the three that were already 'down'. I think we both know that they must have been murdered. A hit-and-run? An accidental drowning? I don't think so. And I think she meant that I was the last of the three. Well, she was wrong there. The beast.

The important thing to understand, though, is that Alison, Karen and Venetia are surely next on her list. And my name must have gone back on it, I suspect.

And possibly yours, as well. I heard Lucy call you "a problem" - and, what's more, she knows where you live. Fool that I am, I pointed your house out to her on the way back from the hospital. Sorry, Tammy. I didn't know that I was in a car with a psychopath.

It must, I suppose, be because of the tontine. I can't think what else it could be about. It can't be a personal grudge. What have I ever done to make someone want to kill me? Money, they say, is the root of all evil and I suspect that will turn out to be the case here, too. Although quite how Lucy would benefit from the tontine, I don't know.

Nor do I know who she was on the telephone to when she said these horrible things. Clearly, she's not working alone. So, dear Tammy, do be on your guard, not just against Lucy, but against virtually everybody you know.

To survive, you're going to have to rely on the family and your own wit, I'm afraid. I don't think there's any point in going to the police. What proof do we have? Nothing. And, sorry, but I can't come home and give any kind of help. I'd have to be mad.

You need to warn the others. Make them believe you. Show them this letter if you need to.

Please don't try to find me. I quite like staying alive.

With love,

Uncle Arnold.

She had another look at the outside of the envelope. Her uncle had got her address wrong and it had been re-directed several times. He'd actually written it many months before.

Arnold could be wrong but it was a risk that she couldn't take. The three cousins already thought she was an idiot. She had nothing to lose by trying again to persuade them that there was a madwoman on the loose who might be trying to kill them. She had a duty to warn them one more time and she needed to do it straightaway.

She got out the little brown book and dialled Karen's number. "*Hi,*" crooned the answerphone. "*Sorry, darling caller, whoever you are, I can't speak to you right now. Leave your number and I'll probably get back to you.*"

Then she tried Alison. "*Hello,*" came a deep voice. She sounded rather stern. "*I'm afraid I can't answer the telephone at the moment. Please leave your name, number and a short message and I will return your call as soon as possible. Thank you.*"

And, finally, she rang Venetia. There was no personally recorded message on this number, just the long ringing out of a phone call ignored or unheard. After what seemed an age, a robotic voice invited her to leave her name and number.

She put down the phone without leaving a message for any of them. What on earth could she say?

And then it struck her. They weren't answering the telephone because they were all at work - Karen would be at the boutique, Alison at the library and Venetia at the pharmacy. She'd almost forgotten that other people still had jobs to go to.

If Arnold was right, then any further delay might be lethal.

She'd have to visit them at work. She looked at her watch. It was almost lunchtime - maybe she could persuade them to come outside with her for an hour. She wanted to tell them all together, not one at a time, because, if they were going to ridicule her again, she'd like to get it over with quickly. She wondered if she could do a kind of Pied Piper and get the first one on the list - say, Venetia - to come with her to the next place - say, Alison's - and then, finally, they could go on together to get Karen. Then they could all go to the park, or somewhere else where they couldn't be overheard, and where she could show them the letter.

She dressed carefully and wore high heels. She put on lots of make-up, finishing with a swish of scarlet lipstick. It made her feel braver.

The pharmacy had two windows, one on each side of the door. The one on the left was decorated with posters of beautiful women smiling enigmatically and holding creams and elixirs. The other window offered hot water bottles, patent medicines and tubs of vitamins. Clearly, the shop was covering all eventualities and a variety of neuroses.

Tamara pushed open the door and a bell rang somewhere behind the counter. A tall, rather rotund man in a white coat came out to greet her. His ginger hair was a mass of curls and his eyes, behind the rimless glasses, were blue as cornflowers.

"How can I help?" he said.

"I was wondering if I could speak to Venetia?"

"I'm afraid she's not here. Can anybody else help?"

"Has she gone to lunch already?" Her heart sank. "When will she be back?"

"Sorry, can I ask - this is a bit awkward - are you a friend of hers?"

"She's my dad's cousin. Is there something wrong?"

"If I'm honest, I don't really know. I wonder if I could have a confidential word - seeing as you're Venetia's family..."

"Of course," she said, wondering what on earth she was letting herself in for.

"Celia!" he called through the doorway behind the counter. "Can you come out onto the shop floor, please?"

"The only thing is," said Tamara, "I've got to get to the library by half twelve."

"My name's Douglas Conway," he held out his hand. "I don't want to delay you - but the thing is, I'm a bit worried about Venetia."

He led her behind the counter and into a little lounge cum kitchen. They passed a harassed-looking woman on their way in. "Thanks, Celia," said Douglas. "I'll be out in five minutes."

"Well, I hope so," said Celia, her brows knotted and tight, "I've got a whole box of that new acne cream to unpack. You said you wanted it out first thing but you've given me so much else to do this morning, I haven't had a chance."

She scowled at Tamara, who hesitated and then smiled. That seemed to make the woman even crosser. The bell from the door rang out.

"I suppose you want me to deal with that, too?" said Celia.

"If you don't mind," said Douglas, calmly, his face expressionless.

The woman huffed, and sucked her teeth, and walked out of the room . "I'll never get that box unpacked at this rate."

He turned to Tamara. "Take a seat, Miss...? "

"Benson," she heard herself say. Somewhat to her surprise, for the first time in years, she'd introduced herself using her maiden name. She sat down on an ugly mustard sofa. "Tamara Benson."

"Tamara? As in the ancient goddess of rivers and streams?"

She stared. "I'm amazed that you've heard of her. Most people haven't."

"Your parents and mine," he grinned, taking a seat at the table, "they were clearly on the same pagan wavelength. Except mine got me on both halves of the name. Douglas means 'dark river'. Conway means 'holy water'."

"Neat." She smiled but wished he'd get on with it. If Venetia wasn't here, then so be it but she needed to warn the others.

"I got away lightly," he said. "My gran wanted to call me Jesus."

"Was she besotted?" She'd go round to Venetia's house straight after she'd seen Karen and Alison. God, she hoped they'd believe her this time. She looked down at her watch.

"No, just Spanish." The bell rang again and he got up and looked into the shop. "Call me if you need me, Celia."

When he came back, he didn't sit down. "Look, Tamara. I'm really concerned. Venetia hasn't come to work for almost four weeks now."

"*Four weeks*? Have you heard anything from her?"

"Not a dicky bird. I've rung and rung. Nobody answers. I've left messages too - but she never comes back to me."

Tamara didn't like the sound of this. Not one little bit.

"I've even been round to her house - twice," said Douglas. "I hesitated for a while. Venetia's pretty hot on the 'non-invasion of personal space' thing. But I'm genuinely worried."

"I'm not surprised," said Tamara. "So am I."

"I haven't a clue where she is," said Douglas, "I mean, it might turn out that she's won the lottery and doesn't need to work anymore. Or had enough and moved on. She was always threatening to leave. But she should have let me know. I've got Celia in as a temporary replacement but she's nagging me to death to make it permanent." He frowned. "Not sure if I could cope with that, if I'm honest. But I need to know what's happening with Venetia before I make a decision either way."

"What happened when you went round to her house?"

"I knocked on the door and rang the bell - nobody answered."

"Oh, my god...."

"And I've written to her, too. She hasn't replied."

Tamara got to her feet. It was a struggle. The mustard sofa was so soft it seemed to suck her back in. "I need to go round there."

Douglas helped her to her feet. "You don't think she's just had a better offer? Not simply run off into the sunset? She was always threatening to do exactly that."

"I'm certain she hasn't. I think she's in trouble. Big trouble."

"Then I'm coming with you."

"That's nice of you, but, honestly, you don't need to. After all, she's *my* family, not yours."

"But also after all, she works for *me*, not for you."

"Dougie!" shouted Celia from the shop. "Mr Harrison wants to talk to you about his haemorrhoids."

"I know it's a cheek," said Tamara, "but do you think I could use your phone?"

"To ring Venetia? Of course"

"Actually, it's to ring Venetia's cousins."

"Ah, I see. Yes, if you've got family who can go round to her house with you, that makes sense."

"Have you got a Yellow Pages, too? Sorry, but they're both at work and I don't know their numbers."

Celia poked her head into the room, one hand leaning on the door jamb. "Dougie, for the love of God, can you *please* come and help? "

"Sorry, Celia, yes, I'm coming. Tamara, the directory's over there, in the corner on the middle shelf and the directory is right next to it. I shouldn't be more than five minutes. "

Celia frowned. "Not if Mr Harrison has anything to do with it, you won't. He's got some long and interesting stories for you about his bowel movements."

She disappeared from the room and, with an apologetic smile to Tamara, Douglas followed her out.

Tamara sat down in the chair in the corner of the room and rifled through the phone directory. She rang Karen first.

"Tammy, what do you want? I can't just leave the shop floor like this, you know. It's unprofessional to take personal calls in work time."

"Sorry, Karen, but I need your help. Venetia's disappeared and I -"

"Oh, for God's sake, not that nonsense again!"

"It's not nonsense. I'm being deadly serious."

"So am I. It's half-day closing today and I'm really busy getting everything done so that I can leave on time."

"Could you meet me when the shop closes?"

"Not a chance. In exactly half an hour, Mr Singh is coming round to pick me up and we're going out for lunch."

"Could we meet after that? Honestly, I wouldn't ask if it wasn't important."

"Look, darling, much as I'm fascinated by your paranoia, straight after lunch, he and I are off to the Glamorgan Fashion Awards. And that really IS important."

"But Uncle Arnold's sent me a letter and-"

"I have to go - I've got customers. Ring me tomorrow if you still need help." And with that, Karen put the phone down.

Then Tamara rang Alison.

"Sorry, dear, I'm on my own in the library today. Poor old Gordon's gone down with a nasty tummy bug."

"But Alison, I'm so worried about Venetia. She's disappeared."

"Ten to one, she's gone and taken an impromptu holiday."

"For four weeks?"

"Well maybe she's started another job and not let the chemists know. That would be typical, I'm afraid."

"Hmmm..maybe...."

"You're a lovely girl to worry - but I know that this will turn out to be Venetia being Venetia. Maddening and unreliable."

"Is she? I mean, is she unreliable?"

Alison sniffed and then said, "she's actually a *very* irresponsible person."

For a moment, Tamara said nothing and then she reconsidered. Reliable or not, Venetia was family and she might need help. "Could you come with me to her house after work then? Just to make sure that she's ok?"

"Honestly, I would if I could but I've got Brownies tonight."

Tamara bit her lip to stop herself from saying something rude. What 's wrong with these people? Don't they care?

"I'll have to go now, dear," said Alison. "I've got a toddler group coming at any moment and I need to get the room monster-proof. Look, if you're still concerned about Venetia, ring me again tomorrow and we'll see what we can sort out, ok?"

"Alison, there's something more. Uncle Arnold has sent me a letter and he says that I've got to-"

"Oh, God, sorry, dear! Two of the monsters are here early and there's me without the room ready. Look, ring me tomorrow and tell me all about it. Glad to hear that Arnold's okay. I always thought he would be and, you wait and see, Venetia will be too. Bye, Tammy."

Tamara put down the phone. Fine. She would go round to Venetia's house alone. Unlike them, she couldn't be so certain that there was nothing to worry about. She turned to leave the room and bumped into Douglas just as he was walking back in.

He looked at her downcast face. "No good?"

"They can't come with me. They want to, obviously, and they're really concerned but...."

"I should hope so. Why aren't they going with you?"

"They can't get away from work right now. It's okay. I'll go there on my own."

"There's no need for that, " said Douglas. "Honestly, just go to the cafe across the road and wait for me. It's half-day closing today. I'll be with you in twenty minutes and we can go together to Venetia's house."

"I haven't got my car in town - I came in by train."

"I'll drive."

"Are you sure?"

"Dougie!" shouted Celia. "You're needed!"

"On my way, Celia! Look, Tamara, I don't want you going there on your own. This is my responsibility, too."

Ten minutes later, she was sitting in the cafe with a toasted sandwich in front of her. She nibbled at the edges of it. The morning's panic had numbed her appetite somewhat.

She poured herself another cup of coffee and listened idly to the radio playing in the background. Now that she had time to think about it calmly, it seemed probable that she'd over-reacted. Alison had hit the nail on the head. After all, she knew Venetia well and if she thought that the woman had simply run off to do more exciting things, then she was probably right. It was pretty thoughtless not to let anyone know, though, even if she was only doing something she'd often threatened to do. Rude, in fact.

She thought back to the last time she'd seen Venetia, nearly three months ago, on her birthday. The woman obviously couldn't wait to get rid of her. She'd clearly been expecting to spend the evening with someone altogether more exciting. Maybe that's what this is about, she thought. Venetia's run off with some chap.

Which meant that there was little point in going to Venetia's house today with Douglas. When he arrived, she'd have to tell him that she'd reconsidered the situation. Puzzled at the sudden flash of disappointment that caused, she sipped her coffee and considered her next steps.

Most importantly, she'd go and see Alison and Karen tomorrow and insist that they listened to her. Even if her worries about Venetia were nonsense, they should definitely see Arnold's letter.

She wondered if Douglas would still like to have a coffee with her today even if they didn't need to drive to Venetia's after all.

On the other hand, maybe they should still go? At least then she definitely wouldn't need to worry any more. She would have done all she could.

As she was gazing out of the window, Keith walked past. She froze. Don't let him look in, she thought, not *now*. At that precise moment, a sharp gust of wind blew along the pavement and he turned his head aside, presumably to avoid the worst of it. His eyes met hers and he smiled and waved. And opened the cafe door.

Chapter Nineteen

Keith slid onto the bench seat opposite her and yanked his arms out of the sleeves of his coat. His face was creased by a huge smile but, as he opened his mouth, a blast of sour breath washed across the space between them. He smelt of whiskey and old cigarettes. She tried not to let her surprise show.

"Hi, Tam," he said. "This is a lucky break, seeing you like this." He picked up the menu from the table and scanned it. "Anything you'd care to recommend?"

He leaned the menu on the table and looked straight at her, his eyes, it seemed, trying to fix onto hers. And then he broke his gaze and did a double-take as he took in the whole of her appearance. He whistled and the man at the next table gazed at them.

"You look amazing, Tammy! More fanciable than ever!" He winked. "What've you done to your hair?"

The man at the next table laughed out loud.

She felt her face reddening and picked up her sandwich. "These are pretty good." *Was he drunk?*

"So, what've you got there? Cheese and ham toastie on brown bread? And, let me guess, a decaf cafetiere with cold milk on the side."

"Am I so predictable?"

He grinned and placed a hand on her arm. "Not predictable, Tammy - just reliable."

Just at that moment, the waitress arrived at the table. "What can I get you?"

Tamara pulled her arm away from his grasp.

"The same as the lady," said Keith." I don't think I can improve on what she's got."

"Righto, my duck," said the woman. "Good choice."

"I like to think so," said Keith. He grinned at Tamara.

She ignored him and looked out through the window. The lights were being turned off in the chemists across the road. Douglas was going to be here soon. From nowhere, a surge of irritation against Keith pulsed through her.

"Actually," she said, taking a tiny bite of her sandwich, "I don't mean to be rude but I'm not going to be here long. I've got somewhere to go."

"Somewhere interesting? Somewhere you'd like company?"

She chewed slowly. Finally, she swallowed and said, "Just Venetia's house - so not especially interesting."

"So you're mates again, you and her? "

"Not exactly."

He didn't say anything more for a moment. He ran his finger through the steam that had built up on the window. Without looking at her, he said, "So the woman with the perfume - she's disappeared from view, has she?"

"God, I hope so," she said before she could stop herself.

He turned to look at her. "I thought all this scary stuff was over - you said on the phone that you weren't worried anymore."

"I'm not. And I thought all the scary stuff was over, too...and maybe it is...Oh, look, I don't know, Keith. It's just that Venetia's missing - or she might be missing."

His face dropped. "You're joking!"

"I'm thinking of going round to check that she's ok. I mean, I'm sure she is. It's just that my uncle wrote to me and stirred everything up again." Stop *babbling,* she thought to herself. "But I'm sure everything's fine."

"Wow, " he said. "Sounds like exciting times."

"Not sure about exciting. More stressful than -"

"-so shall I come with you?"

"No need. I haven't decided yet if I'm definitely going to go."

"So you don't have to dash off, after all?" He smiled. "Great."

Tamara, you idiot, she thought. "It's more likely that I will go than that I won't - but anyway another friend has offered to come with me."

"Another friend? Is that all I am now? Just a friend?"

He leaned across the table and tried to grasp her hands but she pulled them away and folded them in her lap. This is horrendous. What's *wrong* with him?

"I'd hoped for more," he said.

"I hope that's what you'll always be, Keith. A good friend."

For a while, neither of them said anything. Keith gazed across the room and drummed his fingers on the table. Tamara pushed the remaining bits of her sandwich around on the plate and picked up her coffee and pretended to drink it even though the cup was empty.

Eventually she said, "So how are things with you? All ok?"

He turned his head and stared out of the window. A slight drizzle was beginning to fall. Finally he looked at her.

"Do you really want to know, Tam? About how things are with me?" The intensity of his gaze made her feel even more uncomfortable. "Are *you* a good friend? The same good friend you say I am to you?"

"Yes... of course I am." The fug of his breath was loathsome.

"This thing with your dad's cousin? It'll turn out to be nothing - she just doesn't want to talk to her family anymore."

"Let's hope you're right."

"But the thing that's happened to me? It's doing my head in."

Okay, give in. "Keith, what's happened?"

He ran his fingers through his hair. The grease on it shone dully under the light. "Actually, you're the only one I can tell. The only one who'll get it."

"Really ? What about Danielle? Can't you tell her?"

He snorted. "I don't think so."

Oh, God, she thought. Have they split up?

"What about all your football mates?" she said. "Or the guys at work?" She put the cup back down on the saucer and pushed it away from her. "I've said I'm your friend, Keith - and I am - but, honestly -"

"I haven't got any friends these days. And work? Well, right now, I guess I'm on - what do they call it? - Gardening Leave. Only I've got no garden."

"Oh.... I see...." What does he mean? Has he lost his job? "Well, that's a shame." She knew that was a lame response but she didn't want to sound too interested in case it made him think that she had more to give him.

"I was going to ring you," he said, " and then I saw you through the window and realised it was meant to be."

"Realised *what* was meant to be?"

"That I should see you and tell you what's going on."

"Okay....." She stole a glance at her watch.

"I'm in a mess, Tammy, a real shithole mess."

I don't want to hear this, she thought. I know there's something really wrong and that I should care and that I should help - but I just don't feel that way. He put his head in his hands and, as she looked at him, she caught sight again of the balding spots at his temples. Suddenly, she felt an urge to slap him hard right across the top of his greasy head. She took a deep breath. What was wrong with her? I'm stressed, she thought. That's what it is. I need to get away and find Venetia. I need to warn Karen and Alison. I need this man to be gone before Douglas gets here.

"He's not mine." Keith looked up at her. "Jason - my boy - he's *not* my boy."

"What?"

"I'm gonna lose him." He ran his hand across his face, brushing against his eyes with the palm. "She's taking him away."

Tamara stared at him in astonishment. "What do you mean? Of course he's yours. Who's taking him away?"

"Danielle."

"But why?"

"She says he isn't my son."

"She can't be serious!"

"She's totally serious." He stared at her, a frown contorting his face.

"Well, whose is he then?" she said. "Who *is* his father?"

"That bastard, Paddy McGloughlin - the landlord down The King's Head. Where Danielle used to work."

She thought back to her dad's frantic search for Keith on the night she'd had the miscarriage, when their baby was dying inside her and she'd needed him to comfort her. "*It was only 12 weeks old, Tammy. Size of a lemon. Not even a proper baby yet. We can have another one.*"

"One cheese and ham toastie on white, my duck," said the waitress, plonking the plate down on the table. "And a latte."

Keith said nothing.

"Thanks," said Tamara." That's great." She pushed the plate and cup towards him.

He ignored it. "When Danielle knew she was up the duff, Paddy didn't want her. He didn't want the baby either. So she told me it was mine and, fool that I am, I believed her. And then I left you and - God forgive me - I married her."

"And you really thought the baby was yours? " Her eyebrows were raised so high they almost hurt. Keith had left her for nothing. He'd ruined everything for a lie.

"Of course I did!"

As she looked through the window, she saw Douglas closing up the shop.

"But now Paddy's changed his mind. He wants Danielle back ... and he wants Jason too."

"Oh, Keith - I don't know what to say."

"So she's leaving me - and she's taking Jason with her." He looked furious, his lips white and tight, his eyes staring.

"God, I'm so sorry - this is awful!" Douglas was at the crossing now; she could see him standing there, waiting patiently in the drizzle for the lights to change.

"I haven't slept since she told me. I can't eat, I can't think straight." He thumped the table and the cutlery jumped and banged on the table top. "That fucking bitch!"

The man at the next table said to Tamara , "is everything ok?" He leaned back into his chair and pushed up the sleeves of his jumper as if to prepare for a scrap. In fact, he looked quite hopeful for one.

The waitress began to walk across to them.

Oh, my god, thought Tamara. Swallow me up. "Thanks," she said to the man, " but I'm fine."

And then the door opened and Douglas walked in. His glasses steamed up as the heat of the cafe hit the lenses.

"We'll have no trouble in here, if you don't mind," said the waitress to Keith.

Douglas took off his glasses and rubbed them with a handkerchief. As he looked towards the table, a puzzled frown spread across his face.

Tamara stood up and turned towards him. "Hi," she said. "I'll just pay my bill and we can go." She picked up her bag and coat.

"This isn't what I ordered," said Keith to the waitress. He pointed to the food. "I don't want it. I'm not paying."

The man at the next table stood up. "Oh, I think you are, buddy."

Douglas walked across and stood next to Tamara. She couldn't look at him. She knew that her face was scarlet.

The waitress smiled at Keith, crossed her arms and looked firm. "That'll be £7.50, my duck - unless you want to leave a tip as well."

"Is there a problem here?" Douglas said under his breath to Tamara.

"Yes, here's a tip," said Keith. "Stop calling people 'my duck'."

"No, no problem," said Tamara. "None at all." She pulled two notes out of her purse and thrust them into the waitress's grasp. "Here you go," she said. "That's for the both of us. Keep the change."

Keith stood up and pulled on his coat. "I'm sorry," he said to the waitress. "I shouldn't have said that - I'm having a bad time right now." He leaned across, took a single note out of the woman's hand and replaced it with one of his own. "I can pay for my own food."

"I should think so," said the waitress.

"The order's still wrong, though. Just saying. Everything's wrong, actually."

"He's drunk," muttered the man at the next table, sitting down. He looked disappointed.

As Keith walked past Tamara, he leaned in and took her arm. "I thought *you'd* get it," he said. "I've already lost one child - now I'm gonna lose another one."

Douglas took a step backwards.

"I thought *you'd* remember what it feels like," said Keith. "But, no - it looks like you're over it." He pointed to his chest. "But me? I'm *dying* in here."

He pushed between her and Douglas, opened the door and walked out onto the pavement. A squall of rain and wind blew and the folds of his coat ballooned around his body. He pulled the fabric tight and then strode away into the gloom.

"*Well!*" said the waitress. She put Tamara and Keith's money into the pocket of her apron.

"What a dick," said the man at the next table. "A *dick* - that's what you should have called him," he said to the waitress. "Not a *duck*."

Tamara was silent. How could Keith imagine, imagine *for a second*, that she'd forgotten the agony of losing their child?

"Shall we go?" said Douglas.

"You want my advice," said the waitress, "I wouldn't bother with that one." She jerked her thumb toward the window. "He's mad. Stick with this fella instead."

This time it was Douglas who blushed.

Chapter Twenty

They were silent in the car. The man was a complete stranger who'd just been plunged into the most intimate of her secrets. He seemed to understand how she felt because he didn't ask her anything, nor initiate any kind of conversation. Or maybe he's not sensitive, she thought. Perhaps he's just wishing he'd never met me. Maybe he's regretting offering to help and can't wait to get away.

They pulled up outside the house and he looked at her. "Ready?"

She nodded. Might as well get it over with.

She rang the doorbell and waited a few moments before ringing it again. Nobody answered. She tried to peer through the windows but it was too dark inside to see anything. She banged on the door with her fists. Nothing. This reminded her of trying to get into her uncle Arnold's house last year.

"I don't know what to do," she said.

"I don't know either," he said, gloomily. "But it looks like Celia's going to get Venetia's job, after all. Joy of joys."

"Just a thought," she said, "and it's almost certainly a stupid one...but do you think we should report this?"

"Who to? The police?"

"Well, Venetia's a missing person ... .isn't she?. "She rang the doorbell one last time. "As in, she's a person who's definitely missing. We don't know where she is."

"What will you say to them?"

"I'll tell them that I have a relative who's...well, that she's...that she has..." She bit her lip. What *would* she tell them? They hadn't been interested when she'd gone to them about Arnold. She might look like some whacko who got her kicks from being a serial reporter of absent relations.

"Isn't it simply," said Douglas, " that this middle-aged, unmarried, lonely woman got distraught at the mundanity of her dead-end job in a downtown pharmacy? And that she decided to leave it all behind and try her luck somewhere else? Like she'd often threatened to do?"

Tamara said nothing. It was true that people did sometimes have a crisis and changed their existence utterly.

"You don't *seriously* think that she's fallen into the river?" continued Douglas. "Or crashed down some motorway embankment? Or been mown down by a madman on a motorbike?"

"If you're wondering what's currently on my mind," she said, "you're closer than you might imagine with that last one".

"*What?*" He half sniggered, and then coughed loudly as if to disguise it.

"It's not a laughing matter, Douglas."

"I'm sorry - that was rude of me."

She began to walk away from the house. The rain was falling lightly from a pewter sky. She shivered and pulled up the collar of her coat.

He knocked on the door again.

"You're wasting your time," she said, calling the words over her shoulder. "She's not there."

"You don't actually think she's been done away with?" he said, as he caught up with her. "You can't mean it?"

They stood shivering underneath a lamppost and a canopy of wet branches. Just at that moment, the streetlamp burst into light. The heavy sky and the shadow of the trees must have cast sufficient darkness for the lamp to think that night had fallen. Raindrops glittered like opals on the curls of Douglas's hair.

"Do you fancy a cup of tea?" she asked.

Poppy went mad. Perhaps it was the excitement of having a guest but she wouldn't leave Douglas alone. She clambered up on the sofa and pawed at his knee. Even Coco came and gave his trouser leg a sniff.

"I'm so sorry," said Tamara, shushing the animals away. "They're badly trained - it's my fault. Poppy! You are a very naughty girl!"

The dog's tail thumped on the carpet. The cat stalked away.

"No, it's fine," said Douglas and then he sneezed.

"Can I offer you another cuppa?"

"No, two's enough for any man."

"Another biscuit? To make up for the ones that Poppy ate?"

"Honestly, no." He sneezed again, apologised and pulled an enormous white handkerchief out of his pocket.

She picked up his empty cup and took it into the kitchen. Whilst she was in there, she heard him talking. "No, there's a good girl, Poppy, don't climb on me again, No, you're very sweet but -." And then she heard three explosive sneezes.

"Was it the rain?" she said. "Do you think you've caught a cold?"

"No, it's ..." Another volcanic explosion followed." ...an allergy - I'm pretty allergic to cats - but even more so to dogs. I love them but they totally incapacitate me. I don't suppose you have any antihistamines in the house?"

"I'm sorry," she said. "I don't, not these days. I used to get hay fever but I grew out of it."

"And I grew *into* it - it's maddening."

"Just cats and dogs?"

"And willow trees. It drives me nuts."

"So you wouldn't be up for a dog-walk along a tree-lined river bank?"

"Have you got any old antihistamines knocking about? I shouldn't tell you this but they last for years and years beyond the Best Before date."

"There's nothing in my medicine cabinet newer than 5 years old so it's absolutely possible. I'll check."

"What you need," said Douglas, "is a good local pharmacist." And then he sneezed so loudly that even Poppy jumped.

Ten minutes later, over a glass of water and a battered blister pack, order was restored.

"I'm sorry about earlier - in the cafe," she said.

"That chap looked a bit heated - the one you were with." He picked up the glass and drained it. "Was he... was he a close friend?"

"His name is Keith and he's my ex-husband."

"Sorry - I don't mean to pry."

"You're not prying. It's not a secret or anything."

He ruffled Poppy's ears. No sneezing. The tablets might have been a bit yellow but clearly they still worked. "So - Venetia: what do you think we should do? What about these cousins of hers? Are they going to be any help?"

He looked at her and his gaze was so steady and so calm.

"Okay," she said. "It's a bit complicated."

156

Could she trust him? She knew nothing about the man. Except he had nice eyes and a lovely smile and it was sweet the way his hair curled round in crazy soft ringlets around his ears. And her pets liked him. That had to count for something, surely?

"Well - I'm a good listener," he said. " And I already feel involved because of my link with Venetia."

"Yes, I suppose so." She hardly dared confide in him. He'd run a mile.

"Honestly, Tamara - if it would help to tell me, then I'm here to listen. If you'd prefer not to - then that's fine, too."

"How long have you got?" Where should she start? Where was the beginning?

"All the time in the world. I'm in no hurry to be anywhere else." He sat back against the cushions and cuddled Poppy into his side. Coco miaowed and climbed up onto his knee and began to knead his legs. His face altered as the cat's claws cut into the flesh of his thighs but he didn't push her off and he didn't shriek.

Wow, thought, Tamara. *Just wow.*

Half an hour later, he sat on the sofa, pets still firmly planted, and said, "I don't know how you've coped with all this. It must have been a nightmare."

"Let me show you my uncle's letter. It's why I was in such a panic this afternoon." She dug it out of the bureau and handed it to him.

He read it quickly and then put it down. "Your cousins must be mad not to listen to you. It sounds as if they're really in danger."

"I know - but they just won't give me a chance to explain."

"Tell me more about them?"

"They're really my dad's cousins not mine."

"And your dad died...?"

"Three years ago. He got run over. No-one was ever charged. This Lucy woman was at his funeral. I'd never met her before. Never even heard of her. And then she was at the hospital sitting next to my Uncle Arnold's bed. I don't think she liked it when I recognised her."

"Lucy...that's the woman with the perfume? The dangerous one?"

"Yes.."

"What about.. what are their names? Alison and Karen?"

"Okay, so Alison works at Heathgrove Library."

"And what's she like?"

" She's a very kind, middle-aged spinster."

"And that's it? That's her in total?"

"Well, she's also a super-dedicated Brownie leader. It's really all she's got in her life."

"Is she lonely, do you think?"

"If I'm honest, I think she might secretly be a bit in love with Gordon, the guy she works with."

"Intriguing."

"It was her twin sister who died in the pond at my dad's funeral."

"Right..." he looked down, as if he was trying to digest the information, as if he was trying to store it somewhere safe, ready for retrieval at a later date. Nowhere in his face did it register what a peculiar thing, in the normal run of things, Tamara's sentence would have been. "And the other cousin?"

"That's Karen. She works in a boutique in Queen Street - well, she just about runs it, I suppose."

"And what's she like?"

"She's gorgeous and madly sophisticated and completely terrifying."

"Really? What makes her so scary?"

"Oh, I don't know - she's just so polished. She never looks like I do."

"What's that supposed to mean?"

"She's never flummoxed. She always seems on top of things. She doesn't ever get herself into a crazy panic."

"And you do?"

She smiled. "All the time."

"I think you're being a bit hard on yourself"

"Maybe."

"And does Karen have a husband?"

"She's had several. But no current one."

"Any kids?"

"She's got one daughter - Isabelle. But she lives in France with her dad – someone we didn't actually know still existed. There was a huge bust-up about it five years ago and now they don't seem to get on so well."

"And do you believe your uncle? All this stuff about Lucy trying to kill him? And this *three down and three to go* business?"

"I think so."

"You're not sure?"

"It's just that ... I love my uncle to bits but..."

"Yes?"

"He exaggerates."

"What do you mean?"

"He's a complete hypochondriac, always ready to die of one thing or another. Actually, though, he's as fit as a fiddle - nothing at all wrong with him except loneliness and being in the wrong job."

"And he's a teacher?"

"He was. God knows where he is or what he's doing right now. "

"Well, it looks like he's not planning on coming back any time soon." He rubbed his chin with his hand and Poppy raised her head to look at him. "But if he's right about all this, then Venetia's disappearance looks bad."

"I know....."

"Shall we go back to her house again? Tonight? But this time, if no-one answers the door, what do you say to trying to get inside anyway? For clues."

"You mean break in?" She looked at him in disbelief.

"I don't want to give you the wrong impression - but tampering with front door locks happens to be one of my specialities. It's a long story."

She gazed out through the window. Night had fallen. "Are you free tomorrow?" she said. "In daylight hours? For a spot of house-breaking?"

"I can be," he said. "I'm sure that Celia will be delighted to man the pharmaceutical fort yet again. Briefly."

He stood up and stretched. Poppy jumped off the sofa and stared at him hopefully. Her tail wagged slowly. Coco carried on snoring.

Once he'd gone, she went to put Arnold's letter back into the bureau. Before she tucked it away, she re-read it. This was a mistake now that she was alone in a dark and echoing house.

She turned on every light, bolted every door, and double-checked every window. That done, and somewhat comforted, she sat on the sofa and cuddled Poppy, just like Douglas had done earlier. For the first time in ages, she wished that her mum was there but she and Barry had gone away on an off-peak break to Mablethorpe. There was no point in ringing Karen, nor Alison either. She wasn't about to call Keith, that was for sure. She was on her own.

The last time she'd been so scared, she'd decided it was paranoia. This time, she had Arnold's letter to make her think that she'd every reason to worry. If he was right, it wasn't only the cousins who needed to take care. And staying safe was even harder when you didn't really know where the danger might come from. She thought back to the letter and her uncle's warning: *Clearly, she's not working alone. So, dear Tammy, do be on your guard, not just against Lucy, but against virtually everybody you know.*

She poured herself a glass of wine and sipped it slowly. Then she had another. By the third glass, the more she thought about the situation, the less afraid and the more furious she felt. She put on some Led Zeppelin really loudly and engaged in some serious head-banging and air guitar.

How dare they - whoever *they* were - how dare they make her feel frightened in her own home? How *dare* they make her feel scared? It was so disrespectful, so demeaning, so bloody *arrogant* of them. What a ludicrous dilemma to be in, a grown woman, sitting there afraid.

But then she realised, of course she *wasn't* totally alone. There were people out there, official people who were paid a salary and whose job it was to offer help when danger threatened. And that was surely now. Whatever Arnold said.

She picked up the phone and dialled the police. She couldn't be sure they'd do much but she hoped they'd at least come and visit Venetia's house – something they agreed to do although they didn't identify when that would be. Today, this week, next week, they hadn't sounded as if it would be a priority. *I'll pass this query on to the Duty Sergeant, Miss Benson...we'll definitely be sending an officer round to investigate...*

She'd expected to lie awake that night but, in fact, she quickly fell into a deep sleep. The wine probably helped plus the fact that she'd kept the bedside lamp lit so that there were no shadows to brood on. And a part of her knew that, these days, she would actually make quite a hard target. She was fit and she was young and she was strong and, what's more, she was crossly defiant.

By morning, although the Pinot Grigio bravado had worn off, her attitude remained bullish. Maybe this was what war felt like, she thought: energy fed by anger.

After breakfast and a paracetamol, she wondered about ringing Douglas and telling him that she'd spoken to the police. But if she did, maybe he wouldn't think there was any point in going back to Venetia's today - or any day. Maybe he'd wash his hands of it, consider his role in the drama over. And maybe he'd be right - maybe there was no point in going there. But she couldn't just sit on her hands and wait for the police to get involved. Who knew when that would be?.

Well, fine, she could go to Venetia's place on her own.

A little more thought persuaded her that going without Douglas would be a waste of time. She hadn't the slightest idea how to break into a person's house. No-one was going to answer that door, she was certain of it. She didn't truly believe that they'd go inside and find the worst possible scenario - but surely they'd find some clues as to what Venetia was up to?

But was she safe with this stranger, despite his sweet smile?

So, dear Tammy, do be on your guard, not just against Lucy, but against virtually everybody you know.

And, what's more, after all those questions about the cousins, why hadn't Douglas asked what a tontine was?

He rang the doorbell at half past eight, as promised, and Poppy went bananas. When he came into the hall, she leapt all over him as if her favourite person in all the world had come home after a year-long absence. She yelped when Tamara locked her in the kitchen.

They walked down the path together and when they reached the pavement, Douglas opened the passenger door of his car for her.

"Actually," she said, "Are you okay if I drive myself and meet you there?"

He looked surprised . "Of course, absolutely."

She strode to her car, got in and set off, with him following. Her mind was so full that she drove badly, unable to concentrate on what she was doing. She ground the gears and revved the engine and almost drove through a red light. She pulled up outside Venetia's house ten minutes before Douglas, who, she'd noticed the day before, was quite a sedate driver, quite measured and careful.

"Are you okay?" he said.

"Never felt better. Why?"

"Nothing." He looked concerned, though. "It was just the way you were - it doesn't matter."

They walked together up to Venetia's front door.

"One last time?" said Douglas, as he rang the doorbell. No-one answered. "Okay," he said, "here goes." He put his hand inside his jacket and pulled out his wallet. "And now for the old credit card in the lock trick."

Tamara took his arm. "You really don't think she's in there, do you?"

"I don't. Like I said, Venetia regularly announced that, one day, when the stars were aligned and she'd had enough of customers, or sales reps - or me - that she'd up and go. And now it looks like that's exactly what she's done."

Tamara walked across to a window and peered through the glass.

"See anything?" He folded his arms and leant against the wall.

"No.

He looked down at his watch. "I'm really sorry, Tamara, but, unless we're going in there soon, I'm going to have to shoot off. I can't leave Celia on her own for too much longer. I'll never hear the end of it."

"Aren't you even a *little bit* scared about going inside?" She walked back to him and gazed at the door.

"Nope. All we're going to find is empty wardrobes, a lonely fridge and lots of dust. But, who knows? Maybe we'll also find a clue as to where she's gone - *'flying to Torremolinos'* written on a wall calendar or something."

Tamara still looked troubled.

"Look," he said, "I know this might seem a bit unorthodox but, after all, this is a family home that we're going into - not one belonging to some stranger."

"No... I suppose not."

"And, anyway, I've opened doors without a key more times than I can remember - it's really no big deal."

"How do you know how to do it?"

"Remember my Spanish granny? She was always - and I mean all the time - losing her house keys. We got fed up of replacing them. By the end, me, my brothers and my sister, even my mum and dad, none of us had a key to Granny's. But we all had credit cards. This actually feels normal to me"

"It still feels pretty weird to me, though."

He smiled. "Are you ready?"

She nodded. Wide-eyed with anxiety.

He pushed the door away from him, thrusting it as far back as it would go and plunged a card into the gap between the door and frame. He slid it downwards, at an angle, pushing until it stopped. Then he tilted the card so that it was facing him before wiggling it back and forth. Suddenly, there was a click and the door inched open.

It was when they stepped into the hall that the smell hit them.

Chapter Twenty One

Tamara rang the hotel in Mablethorpe, asked Reception to put her through to her mother and sobbed out her distress over the telephone. By lunchtime, Janet and Barry were home. Barry didn't want to stay. Instead, he mumbled his sympathies, patted Tamara on the back, and escaped next door, his arms garlanded with carrier bags and holdalls.

Ten minutes later, mother and daughter sat at the table in the kitchen and Janet dispensed tea and biscuits and comfort.

"Tell me again, Tammy, if you can bear it, love...it was hard to follow what you were saying earlier. What exactly went on at Venetia's?"

Immediately, Tamara had a flashback to the moment when she and Douglas had stood in the hall and that vile stench had filled the air around them and filled her head and her nose with the certainty of what had happened, what must have happened, to Venetia. Douglas had stared at her, his eyes round with horror. And she had run out, unable to take another step into that miasma.

"I couldn't go in, Mum." She covered her face with her hands and her mother got up, walked around the table and wrapped her arms around her. "The smell was..."

"There, there..." Janet crooned as she rocked her daughter from side to side. Then she let go and handed her a box of paper hankies.

Tamara took a handful and blew her nose. "God, it was awful."

"Sweetheart, I'm sure it was. It must have been a nightmare." Janet filled a glass with water and gave her that too. "So you didn't go inside the house at all?"

"I went as far as the hall - but then I had to come outside again."

"And your friend - the chemist man - what did he do?"

"He's not my friend, Mum. Venetia works for him - worked for him. " She picked up the glass of water and drank several mouthfuls. "Oh, God. I just can't believe it."

"And did he come back outside with you?"

"Not straightaway - he was braver than me. I was so afraid I could hardly stand up straight."

"Darling, this wasn't about bravery. It must have been a nightmare."

"I stood in the porch and I saw him open the door of Venetia's bedroom and go inside ...and then he came running out past me, his hand over his mouth. He was sick in the grass."

"And is that when the police arrived?" said Janet. "How did they know about it so quickly ?"

"They didn't. I rang them last night. I was worried about Venetia. I thought she was missing. I never, though, not for a moment, truly believed that she could be dead." A lump came into her throat and she closed her eyes.

"Oh, you poor love," said her mother.

"When I explained last night that Venetia had disappeared, they told me they'd send an officer round to her house. They said they'd talk to the neighbours and that sort of thing."

"Well, they were a bit late for that."

Poppy suddenly lifted her head, her ears cocked. Then she jumped up from her basket and trotted into the hall.

"Anyway," said Janet, "I suppose it's a case of better late than never. What did the policeman do?"

"I was outside, leaning on the wall, and the officer came up to me and said, 'what's going on here?' but I couldn't answer him," said Tamara. "I couldn't speak."

"I'm not surprised, love."

"And then Douglas - he was outside again by now - he looked at me and hesitated a bit - and then he told the policeman that there was a dead woman in the house." She shook her head as if to throw away the memory.

"Oh, darling," said Janet. "I wish I could have been there to help you. I'm so, so sorry. I should have been here, not gallivanting about in Mablethorpe with Barry. I should have gone to Venetia's with you, not this Desmond chap."

"It's Douglas," whispered Tamara. "Not Desmond."

The doorbell rang and Poppy jumped up at the glass, her tail wagging from side to side.

"Who can that be?" said Janet. "I'll send them away whoever it is. You stay here, love." She got up from her chair and walked into the hall.

From the kitchen, Tamara heard her mother say that she was sorry but this was not a good time for visitors and please to leave and come back another day.

"I understand completely," said Douglas. "Could you tell her that I've brought back her car? She left it at Venetia's. She wasn't quite up to driving it when...here are her keys."

"Mum," called Tamara. "Let him in - it's fine."

Douglas came into the kitchen with Poppy jumping up at his legs, trying to lick his hands. Her mother fussed for a bit, too, and only calmed down once she'd thought of putting the kettle on again. Douglas sat down next to Tamara and smiled sadly at her. And then sneezed. Twice.

Tamara got up and pulled out the antihistamines from the cupboard

.

They sat outside in the garden for a while, looking at the daffodils dancing in a yellow, frothy wave.

"They're so cheerful, aren't they," said Tamara. "Such a bright colour. Makes you believe that spring is really here at last. Makes you feel hopeful." She gave a weak smile and sipped her tea. "Hope is a good thing, isn't it? Hope that things will be better."

Nobody said anything for a while after that, until eventually Janet turned to Douglas and said, "I'd like to thank you for helping Tammy today. It must have been awful for you both, just awful."

"It was," he replied. "But you don't need to thank me. I didn't do much to help anybody. I was pretty hopeless, in fact."

"Well, I'm still glad you were there, " said Tamara.

"Can I just ask - ." He stopped, looked down at the table for a bit and then ploughed on. "Look, do you know whether Venetia - I know this sounds bizarre - but is there any chance she might have been in contact with someone who could have supplied her with illegal drugs?"

"Drugs!" repeated Janet in a tone of incredulity. "What on earth are you talking about? "

Tamara stared at him. "What kind of drugs? " she said. "I can't believe that Venetia was an addict if that's what you mean. I'm sure we would have known. I'm sure *you* would have known. Wouldn't she look glazed or something? Or gaunt and thin?"

"Well, that's the point right there," said Douglas. "She was pretty plump. Hardly your stereotypical user."

"I'm sorry," said Janet, "but what does Venetia's weight problem have to do with her being a drug addict? Which, let me tell you right now, I don't believe for a moment. We're not that sort of family."

"On Venetia's bedside table," he said, "was a packet of pills - don't worry, I didn't touch it - I couldn't bring myself to get close enough for one thing. But I could read quite clearly what they were."

"Well," said Tamara. "What were they?"

"Subatramine tablets," he said. "They're banned in the UK but they're still available if you know the right - or actually, the wrong - sort of people."

"What do they do? " said Tamara. "And why are they banned?"

"They're diet pills, " he said. "They suppress the appetite. And they do work. But they can also kill you."

"Oh, good lord, no, " whispered Janet. "That poor, poor girl. " She fumbled for her daughter's hand across the table and grasped it.

"How do they kill you?" said Tamara. "Do people starve to death or something?"

"No. But there are cases - documented cases - of fatal heart attacks in susceptible people who have taken too high a dose."

"And that's what you think happened to Venetia?" said Tamara. "She had a heart attack?"

"That would be my guess," he said.

"So wanting to be thin is what killed her?" said Janet.

"Somebody supplying her with Subatramine is what killed her," he said.

"She was always chubby," said Janet, "even as a child."

That evening, after Douglas had gone, her mum asked her to come round and eat with them next door. Barry was such a good cook but he always made too much so they could take their pick of all the left-over meals he'd frozen. And maybe have a little glass of wine, too, to calm their nerves. She knew how much Barry would like to have her there.

"You know that Venetia wouldn't have wanted us to mope," said Janet. "And grieving won't bring her back. Nothing will." And then she stopped and looked anxiously at her daughter. "And, anyway, darling, I don't want you here all alone tonight. You've been through too much already today. So, what do you say? About six? Half past? Tammy? Did you hear me, darling?"

"We have to tell the others," said Tamara. "I've just realised - they don't know."

"Alison and Karen, you mean? Lordy lord, I suppose you're right."

How will I tell them? thought Tamara. I only rang them yesterday to say I was worried that Venetia had disappeared - and now this.

"I can't face it," she said. "Would it be too awful to wait until tomorrow to let them know?"

"I don't think it will matter one jot, " said Janet. "It's not as if they were that close to her. None of us were."

"I used to be," said Tamara. "When I was a kid. She used to buy me toys and sweets and little treats. Every Christmas, she bought me a Tammy Annual. She called it my special book and told me that it had been written just for me. It was only later, once I was a teenager, that she seemed to lose interest, get less friendly. " At the recollection, she stopped and covered her face. "I should have tried harder to stay in touch."

"I know it was a terrible experience for you today but it would have been awful to find *anyone* like that, even a stranger."

"I've been trying to get hold of her since her birthday. It's weighed on me. And all the time, it was leading up to today."

"You don't think she's been dead all this time, surely? "

"No," said Tamara. "She can't have been. Douglas told me she was at work four weeks ago. He's been trying to contact her ever since."

"He seems like a decent chap," said Janet. "Nice hair. Nice eyes."

"And a lovely smile, too, don't you think?"

"I bet Venetia ran him ragged," said Janet. "Poor man." She stood up and tapped her daughter's knee. "Anyway, I'd better go home now and see what Barry's been up to, see if he's unpacked and everything. He's good like that, is Barry. Nothing is too much trouble. I'll see you in an hour or so?"

Tamara nodded. "Will do. Thanks for inviting me. I've got to say, the last thing I feel like doing right now is cooking."

She didn't feel like dressing up either but she put on a bit of make-up and pulled out a navy trouser suit that she'd bought the week before. Just as she was putting a pair of pearl studs into her ear lobes, the doorbell rang.

She began to walk down the stairs and, from the middle step, she looked down through the stained glass panes in the door to see who it was. It was Keith. Her heart sank. *Not him, not now,* she thought. He glanced up at just that moment and, through the pane of clear glass that was at the top of the door, he looked straight at her and smiled.

She had no choice but to open it. He'd clearly made an effort since the day before. His hair shone, he'd shaved and he was wearing a suit. She could smell his aftershave from where she was standing. It used to do strange things to her, that woody-limey fragrance; it used to give her butterflies.

It left her feeling pretty much unmoved right now, though.

He was also bearing a bunch of flowers which he rather shyly handed to her across the threshold. "These are for you," he said. "To make up - if I can - for what an arse I was yesterday."

"They're beautiful, " she said, tucking them under her arm. "Thank you - there was no need, though, no need at all."

"I'm really sorry, Tammy. I was totally out of order."

"That's ok. Don't worry. I can see that you're going through awful times right now."

"It's no excuse. But look - do you think I could come in? There's something more I'd like to say - and I don't want to do it standing out here on the doorstep." He put one foot forward.

She didn't move, though and he had to step back again. His face fell.

"Sorry, Keith - but now isn't a good time. I'm about to go out."

"Again? To Venetia's house? With your new friend?"

Her lip wobbled and he took her arm. "Are you okay? Tammy, what's happened? Tell me!"

She let him lead her into the lounge, closing the front door behind them. He eased her onto the sofa and then he took the flowers into the kitchen, put them in the sink and brought her a glass of water.

"Here you go," he said. "Drink this. Take it slowly, deep breaths, and tell me why you're so upset."

Over the next few minutes, slowly and falteringly, she told him about the horror of discovering Venetia, dead for a month, and about her fatal consumption of diet pills.

"Where would she have got them from?" he said.

"I don't know. I guess there's always someone out there willing to make money out of people like Venetia."

"So...this new friend of yours - sorry, what's he called again?"

She hesitated a moment, unsure about the word '*friend*. "He's called Douglas," she said, eventually. "Venetia worked for him. At the chemists."

"I remember her talking about that. She hated it there, didn't she?"

"She hated lots of things. She was family and I loved her - but she was that kind of person."

"And he said that these pills can kill people? But only if they're '*susceptible*' - like if they've got a weak heart?"

"I suppose so," she said. "And they end up having a heart attack. Like she did."

"Did she have a weak heart, then?"

"I'd never heard her say so."

She sat and thought for a moment, recalling all the times Venetia had boasted about being strong as an ox, how she'd never had a day ill: about how hard she found it to sympathise with all the hypochondriacs at the chemist, and what an irritation she found Arnold with all his imaginary complaints.

"Has anybody else in the family ever had a heart attack?" he said.

She shook her head.

"I don't trust this guy, this Douglas," he said.

"What? Why? What do you mean?"

"I think you should stay away from him," he said and then added, "no, honestly, I do, Tam. I don't want you to go near him."

"Keith - we're not married any more. It's sweet of you to be concerned - but please - don't try and tell me what to do. It's not helpful."

"I get that, I do. But think about it. This is the fella that doesn't get in touch with the police even though Venetia's been missing for a month. Then he breaks in - *breaks in*! - to Venetia's house. Even when you said you didn't want him to."

"That's not quite how it happ- "

"-this doesn't hold together for me, Tammy. He went into her bedroom alone - he could have put those pills in there himself, couldn't he? And he's a chemist - who better to know what can kill people ? And who's better placed to get hold of stuff like that in the first place?"

"But why? Why would he do that?"

Keith shrugged. "Why would someone run your dad over? Why would your cousin drown in a pond? And your uncle disappearing? What was that about? And then you, on the zebra crossing? And those flowers? You could have been killed, too." He took both of her hands in his and stared into her eyes. "If that had happened, Tammy, I swear I don't know what I would have done." She tried to pull her hands away but he wouldn't let go. "No, let me finish," he said. "I've been an idiot, Tammy. A complete twat. But I know that now. Please - please - will you give me another chance?"

Chapter Twenty Two

Karen,

Two weeks later

Karen was feeling glum. Funerals could have that effect on a person. But Venetia's send-off had been even worse than the norm.

It had not been a well-attended affair. Of the Bensons, there had been just herself, Alison, Janet and Tammy. Not Arnold, of course. Even though he must have known. It was in the papers, for god's sake. Typically selfish.

There had been a few new faces, too. Janet had brought along some chap called Barry. Apparently, he'd been the next door neighbour for years. And what else has been going on for years? Karen wondered. Meanwhile, Alison had arrived with some bloke in tow, a huge, lumbering, clumsy fella that she apparently 'worked with'. Well, that was probably a euphemism.

Mr Singh had accompanied Karen to the church. He was such a rock. And so gorgeous, with his gleaming white teeth and his beautiful smile and big, brown eyes. Just thinking about him made her feel warm.

It was clear that Venetia hadn't had many friends. Her boss from the pharmacy had been there. It must have been a surreal experience for him, she mused, because he'd been the one to discover the body. Well, him and Tammy.

And talking about Tammy, what a transformation that was. The girl had somehow become svelte. Attractive even. She had good hair, no glasses and was wearing make-up *and* it was carefully applied. What's more, she'd walked down the aisle, with apparent ease, in a pair of towering stilettos. She was a million miles away from the lumpy woman she used to be. Maybe it was all done for the benefit of the ex-husband, Keith. He'd been there, lurking at the back of the church. Karen had seen him staring at Tammy, and he was looking anxious. He'd obviously noticed the difference in his ex-wife, too.

Lots of lucky things seemed to have happened to that girl recently. To the surprise of all, even - or so she claimed - of Tammy herself, in her will Venetia had left everything to her. Not to know such a huge thing? Very unlikely. Meanwhile, Arnold - that waster - had apparently been back in touch with Tammy and had instructed her to sell his house for him. It seemed that he was never coming back from whichever bolthole he'd found. And no doubt, Tammy would be paid handsomely for her efforts.

It was so unfair.

Janet wasn't a blood relation, so she wouldn't expect to get a mention in Venetia's will. And Karen could understand why she and Alison might not feature in it. The cousins were hardly close and missing out a generation might appeal to those who held grudges. But it didn't seem right for Tammy to be given so much and for Karen's daughter, Isabelle, to get nothing.

Thankfully, her own money situation was looking rather less bleak than it had done. For one thing, her income from the tontine was about to go up again, this time because of Venetia's fatal romance with dodgy dieting pills. It wasn't surprising what the woman had done; she'd always been distressed by her weight. Although clearly, not so upset that she'd consider eating fewer pies. Karen found it difficult to understand people who didn't look after their bodies. You only got the one, after all. And although she'd been blessed with hers, it wasn't something she took for granted. Especially now that the dreaded menopause was trying to wreck all her efforts. She frowned and smoothed one hand tentatively over her face.

Now that Karen's finances were on a more even keel, she hoped she was one step nearer to persuading her daughter to forgive her and to come home again from France. Maybe she could tempt her back by offering a partnership in the fashion house that, with Mr Singh's backing, she felt sure she would be able to set up soon.

In her heart, she knew that thinking about Isabelle was the real reason she had felt so miserable at the funeral. The day had been a reminder that her daughter was far away, not just physically but emotionally, too. And, worse, it had brought back memories of her own hopeless efforts to keep Isabelle close.

In particular, she regretted the lies she'd told Isabelle about her father. Or at least she regretted being caught out - and she definitely regretted their lasting repercussions.

For years, Karen had told Isabelle that her dad had died before the girl had even been born. In fact, the man was alive and well in some sleepy French hamlet. What's more he knew about Isabelle and, for years, he had been trying to track his daughter down in order to reclaim her.

Like most falsehoods, this one, too, had been uncovered: one unlucky day, Isabelle had happened to get to the mail just ahead of her mother.

Karen had then transformed a bad situation into a terrible one. She'd produced a letter which she'd sworn, hand on heart, was from Isabelle's father. It said that he'd be willing to give his daughter up if Karen were to pay him off with £1,000. It was not, of course, a genuine letter. Isabelle had seen straight through it immediately. She hadn't even been angry. She'd looked at the letter and then at her mother in incredulous pity.

The truth was that Karen had kept the man secret in case Isabelle had chosen her dad - a wealthy French hotelier - over her mum - a debt-ridden, serially-divorced Welshwoman with far too much dependence on alcohol and love.

And that's exactly what Isabelle had done.

But that wasn't all. There was something else – something that occasionally caused Karen a sleepless night. The man Karen had paid to write this letter was the husband of a woman who worked with her at the boutique. A man who made his living through petty thieving and forgeries. He was also a woman-hater who regularly caused his wife to wear heavy make up to cover the bruises he'd given her the night before. He'd made clear that he'd love the opportunity to do the same to Karen, given the chance..

So not only not had she failed to keep her daughter but she had also managed to make a dangerous enemy, It was as if she had caught the eye of a mad man in the street and forced him to notice her.

A few days after Venetia's funeral, a letter arrived. When Karen heard the plop of the envelope, she'd run downstairs, hoping, as she always did, that it was from Isabelle. It wasn't. She realised instantly from the handwriting who'd written this. With a sigh, she opened it

Dear Karen,

I know you think I'm mad, banging on about the danger the family might be in. The problem is that I've never really had the chance to explain myself. And also, although I've mentioned it, you haven't seen the letter from Uncle Arnold. If you were to read that, I'm sure you'd understand my concerns a bit more.

I'd genuinely appreciate the chance to talk to you about the situation (and to Alison, too - I've sent the same letter to her).

Consequently, I'd like to invite you both to my house next week for dinner, plus maybe a glass or two of wine and, most important of all, a proper discussion. If, at the end of the evening, you've convinced me that I'm wrong, I promise that will be the end of it - you'll never hear another word from me on the matter. But if, on the other hand, I've convinced you, then maybe we can work out a plan of action.

There's one more thing - or two, if I'm being precise.

As you know, Venetia was kind enough to leave me her house in her will. It was a complete surprise. She was always very kind to me when I was a child and I suppose that explains it. Anyway, I am very grateful.

I haven't been able to face going there, though, as you can imagine. But my mum said - and she was right - that there was no point in the house just sitting there. So, last week, she found a professional cleaning company who were willing to come and totally blitz the place. At least then it will be in a fit state to sell. I could certainly never live in it myself.

Mum went to the house early the day the cleaners were arriving. The bathroom was one of the first rooms she looked at and she was astonished at what she discovered in the cabinets - that being precisely nothing. They'd all been emptied. And that, frankly, is astonishing.

Do you remember all the fancy beauty products Venetia used to bring home from the chemists? Those bathroom cupboards were always full - they groaned under the weight of pots and jars and bottles. I can't believe she'd stopped using this stuff. And I can't believe she'd

175

throw it all away, either. It was too important to her. But if she didn't, then who did? It's probably nothing but, still, it puzzles me.

And there's something else. After they'd finished the job, the cleaners mentioned that, rather weirdly, they'd found a load of what looked like human hair in the bins. Apparently, it was brown and it didn't look like it had been cut. Presumably this was Venetia's. I've been trying to find out what I can about these sibutramine tablets and nowhere does it say in the list of possible side-effects that your hair would fall out in handfuls. So now I'm wondering - was there something else wrong with her?

Anyway, I thought I would mention it.

I really hope you're both able to accept my invitation - perhaps you can let me know? I'm thinking of this coming Saturday at, say, eight o'clock.

Lots of love,
Tamara

Karen was tempted to crush the letter up into a ball and throw it away. What was wrong with the woman? Why couldn't she just leave things as they were? Why did she have to keep stirring things up?

Instead of binning it immediately, she decided to ring Alison. She was sure to agree that all this stuff was nonsense. However, to her huge surprise, her cousin seemed keen to go to Tammy's that weekend.

"But why, Alison?" she said. "Surely you don't believe all this guff?"

"It's just..." said Alison and then she stopped.

"What?"

"There's a curious thing in her letter - something that intrigues me."

"Oh, for goodness sake. You're as bad as Tammy. It's not healthy, all this determination to see murder and mayhem everywhere."

"Well, Karen, you know, you don't *have* to go on Saturday if you don't want to. I can tell you all about it later."

Karen thought for a moment. Did she really not want to be there? What if something important was said?

"What's this 'curious thing' that you're talking about, Alison?"

" I don't want to talk about it yet. I still need to think it through. It's just that she said something that reminded me of something else."

"Well, that sounds cryptic."

"It's probably nothing - I mean, I'm sure it's nothing - but I want to do a little research before I decide. And before I share it with you both. I don't want to sound mad."

"Nobody could sound madder than Tammy."

"So you're not coming then?"

"Are you joking? I'm intrigued now. I wouldn't miss it for the world."

At half past seven on Saturday night, the doorbell rang. Karen checked her face in the hall mirror and wiped a slick of scarlet lipstick off her front teeth. Then she practised smiling at her reflection, gazing anxiously at the wrinkles that this cast on her forehead. When she stared impassively, they went a bit flatter- but she looked so serious then. With a sigh, she plumped up her hair, running her fingers through the thick bob - still artfully blond - and opened the door. Mr Singh stood in the porch. He had no wrinkles.

"Your carriage awaits, madame," he said, sweeping through the air with a long and elegant arm.

"Amandeep," she said," this is so kind of you. Are you sure you don't mind?"

"I do not mind at all," he said. "It is my pleasure to be of service to you."

"I should get my licence back soon," she said. "Any day now. It's so tiresome."

"Shall we go?" he said, proffering his arm. "And may I say how lovely you look tonight?"

She grabbed her handbag, turned off the light and closed the door. Taking his arm, they walked together towards the waiting car.

Tamara had prepared a pot of spaghetti bolognese which she served with a salad and a slab of garlic bread. There was a trifle for pudding. Karen left the carbohydrates virtually untouched apart from the wine. Alison, meanwhile, ate everything put in front of her with gusto and then had seconds. The meal was a happy, even jovial, affair. The women had agreed that all talk of murderers and accidents, the hand of fate and that of killers, could wait until after they'd eaten.

And so, after chatting about the weather, the books most in-demand at the library, and the latest fashion range at the boutique, they trooped into the lounge. Tamara brought in a tray with coffee and After Eights.

They sat on the sofa and shooshed away the dog. And then it couldn't be put off any longer.

Tamara dug out Arnold's letter and passed it round. The two women read it in turn. Alison became upset at the mention of her sister, Pammie, dying. She put the letter down, blew her nose, drank a slug of coffee, and ate an After Eight mint.

The moment that made Karen bite her lip was when she read that Arnold had refused to write to Venetia. She wasn't surprised by that. All the cousins knew that he'd hated Venetia since they were children. And, like them, Karen knew why. It was because, all those years ago, Venetia had called Arnold a liar when he said he'd seen his brother, Gerald - that bullying bastard - push Pammie into Pond Hill Lake. He'd been telling the truth, of course. The girl had teased Gerald about something or other and, as usual, Gerald had over-reacted. But the water was deep and cold and the lake was full of reeds. Pammie had been under the surface for many minutes and had very nearly died. She might as well have done - she was a moron after it. There was no point in beating about the bush.

.And yet here they both were, sitting in that bastard's lounge, listening to his stupid daughter peddling lunacy.

She threw the letter down on the table and picked up her coffee cup. "I'm sorry, Tammy," she said. "I know you're only doing what Arnold asked you to do - but this really isn't helpful."

"So you still don't believe any of it?"

"I don't. I think it's nonsense."

"I don't know how you can be so adamant."

"Maybe because I'm older and wiser?"

"Is danger easier to identify just because a person has lived for longer?"

"Bullshit certainly is. Have you asked your mum what she thinks? I'm surprised not to see her here tonight as well."

"I would have invited her, of course I would, but she's gone away. She and Barry are on a cruise in the Caribbean."

Well, well, the Merry Widow, thought Karen. And how has she afforded that?

"So, Alison," said Tamara. "Do you think it's nonsense, too?"

"Well..." said Alison.

"Of course, she does," said Karen. "We both do."

"The thing is, Tammy," said Alison, "how can we look out for this Lucy woman? You and Arnold are the only ones who've met her."

"Exactly," said Karen.

"We don't even know what she looks like," said Alison. "We can't be on guard with everyone we meet, can we?"

"It's a bonkers idea," said Karen.

"After all," said Alison, " we both work with the general public. Am I supposed to fear every customer who wants to borrow a book from my library?"

"Or who buys a dress from my boutique?" said Karen. "You need to remember that those of us who still have to earn a living can't just hide away." She went to pick up a mint and then stopped, glaring at her hand as if it had let her down. "Unlike you, we have to work."

Right," said Tamara. "I get that totally - about what Lucy looks like, I mean. Not about working, though. I don't mean to be rude but I really think that it's not for anybody else to pass judgement on what I do or don't do."

"Gosh, Tammy, " said Alison, "You sound so fierce. Good for you."

Karen was taken aback. "So go on, then," she said to Tamara. "Describe this mysterious woman for us. I've just about got time to listen to it. Mr Singh won't be here for another..." she looked at her watch, "half an hour."

Tamara bent down and ruffled Poppy's ears. What did Lucy look like? She tried to picture her in her mind's eye. "She's pretty," she said, finally. "Although no, that's probably not the right word. She's more handsome than pretty."

"How old is she, would you say?" said Alison "Does she look the same sort of age as me and Karen?"

Karen frowned. Clearly there was a gulf between the way she and Alison looked, even though they were born only five years apart.

"Hmmm," said Tamara, "I reckon she's probably in her late thirties. But she's in very good shape, she's got a great figure. She's elegant, I would say."

"Is she blond?" said Karen. "Like me?"

"No," said Tamara and then coughed.

Karen raised an eyebrow.

"She's got dark hair, " the younger woman continued quickly, "and rather beautiful brown eyes. Oh, and she's got a little heart-shaped

179

birthmark on her face just here." She pointed to her cheekbone. "She often seems to wear an eau-de nil coat."

Alison began to choke on the After Eight she was chewing. She heaved and spluttered and Karen beat her on the back.

"Are you okay?" said Tamara. "Shall I get you some water?"

"She's fine," said Karen. She looked again at her watch, picked up her handbag, extracted a lipstick from it and slicked scarlet gloss over her lips. "And is that it? Nothing more? She sounds too perfect to be true."

"Well," said Tamara, "she might not be entirely perfect. When I saw her the second time - at the hospital - she had a bit of a limp. From a fall maybe? It wasn't obvious but it was there."

"Thank heavens for small mercies," said Karen. "Alison, will you stop coughing, for goodness sake!"

" I suppose there is one more thing," said Tamara, "but it's not so much the way she looks, it's more-"

"-does she wear very strong perfume?" interrupted Alison, her voice still hoarse from her coughing fit . "Tammy, does this woman ... does she smell of violets?"

"Yes!" said Tamara. "That's exactly what I was going to say but - how did you know?"

"I'm absolutely positive it must be a coincidence," said Alison, "but two years ago, Gordon - you know, my assistant at the library -" Karen chuckled and Alison stopped speaking.

"Yes," said Tamara. "What about him?"

"As I was saying," Alison sat up a little straighter on the sofa. "Two years ago, Gordon had a girlfriend called Lucy."

"It's hardly an uncommon name," said Karen. "I personally know at least three women called Lucy."

"But it's not just that," said Alison." She really was a beautiful, elegant woman. She had dark hair and dark eyes, too, and she had a little mark on her cheekbone, just like Tammy said. *And* she wore a coat that was eau de nil. Regularly."

"I'm still not convinced," said Karen. "In fact, this is sounding more and more like astrology."

"Astrology?" said Tamara. "I don't follow."

"Vague descriptions to convince those who want to believe," said Karen. "But I'm not that naive. If you want to convince me, you'll have to come up with proof, Tammy, not just scare stories."

"She wore violet perfume, too," said Alison. "She reeked of it. I hated it. It made me feel sick."

"And don't tell me," said Karen, her voice mocking, " she was a Cancerian and a home-maker and loved being by the sea."

"I don't know about that," said Alison, "but I can tell you that she probably does walk with a limp now."

"You mean you don't actually know?" said Karen, with a laugh. "What did I tell you? It's just guess-work and supposition."

"Why might she walk with a limp?" said Tamara.

"Because she fell down the stairs," said Alison. "At Gordon's place. It should have been me who fell - but he caught hold of me. He saved me. So she tumbled all the way down instead. She broke her leg really badly. It was horrible."

"And is she still Gordon's girlfriend?" said Tamara.

Alison blushed. "No, she isn't," she said.

"That, I think we knew," said Karen, smiling. "Judging by his presence in church last week with you hanging on his arm." She winked at Tamara, who immediately looked away.

"I did *not* hang on his arm," said Alison. "If you must know, I found that whole ceremony very upsetting, and Gordon was there - as a *friend* - to give me his support."

"But Alison, going back to Lucy," said Tamara. "Is she still around? Think hard about this. It could be important."

Karen snorted. The way the two of them were egging each other on was comical.

"No," said Alison. "She disappeared after that. I never saw her again. And I hope it stays that way."

"Why?" said Tamara.

"Because she was horrible," said Alison." And what's more, she was all wrong for Gordon. They weren't suited."

"I wonder if she was *the* Lucy?"

"They sound similar."

"If you think about it ," said Tamara, "she's actually been on the scene for a while - and she just keeps turning up. I first saw her three years ago at my dad's funeral. You knew her two years ago. And then I met her again at the hospital with Uncle Arnold last year."

"So you really do think it's her?"

"I'm afraid so. It sounds to me like you had a lucky escape."

"Oh, for goodness sake," said Karen. "If this was *the* Lucy - as you so dramatically put it - and if she really *was* the psychopath that you're describing - then why isn't Alison dead?"

"Karen! " said Alison, her eyes wide. "How can you say that in such a matter of fact way? You sound almost irritated that I'm still here!"

"Let's have another cuppa," said Tamara, "and we can all calm down and think about this logically."

"So what happened to this wicked Lucy after she fell down the stairs?" said Karen. "How come your Gordon didn't stick around after her injury? He must be a fickle type. Is he just a fair-weather kind of friend?"

"He isn't *my* Gordon," said Alison. "He is his own man. And he is far from fickle. He has always been a solid and reliable friend to me."

"Would anybody like an After Eight?" said Tamara, holding the plate out between them.

"And where is Lucy now then?" said Karen. "Now that she and your friend are no longer an item?"

"They stopped being 'an item' as you call it, some time ago. From what I understand, the woman's leg was broken really badly. It needed pins and all sorts. I think she probably went home to her own people to recuperate. And then clearly she decided not to come back."

"She doesn't sound like a master assassin to me," said Karen. "Not got the focus."

"I'll put the kettle on," said Tamara.

When she came back with fresh drinks, and the little box of truffles that Alison had brought as a gift, both women were sitting stiffly on the sofa, not looking at each other, and not speaking.

"Thank you, dear," said Alison, taking a cup. "That's kind."

"And thank *you* for the chocolates."

"Not at all. Money's tight - it always is! - but if you can't afford a little luxury now and again, then where would we be?"

"Have you got skimmed milk?" said Karen

"I haven't. I'm sorry."

"No coffee for me, then. Nor truffles, thank you. Remember, a moment on the lips-"

"-yes, we know," said Alison. She sipped her drink and then, almost as if she'd remembered something, she put the cup down with such force that liquid slopped out onto the saucer. "There's something more," she said. "Something else I should tell you both."

"Oh, god," murmured Karen. Was this the 'curious thing' in Tammy's letter? And would it explain why Alison was being so prickly this evening?

"What is it?" said Tamara. "Something more that you've remembered about Lucy?"

"No," said Alison. "It's about her hair - *Venetia's* hair - falling out."

"We don't know that it did," said Karen.

"Weird, isn't it?" said Tamara, ignoring her. "Why would that happen to a person? Do you think she secretly had cancer and didn't tell people?"

Karen reached out to the box of truffles. She chose one and nibbled the corners of it slowly as if eating the entire thing would be too much.

"No," said Alison. "I think she might have been deliberately poisoned."

"Are you completely off your rocker?" said Karen, her voice slightly thick with chocolate.

"No," said Alison. "Not even slightly."

"Mr Singh is going to be here any minute," said Karen. "Shall we wait for him to arrive? Then he can listen to this bedtime story too."

"Just hear me out, will you?" said Alison. "I've hardly slept thinking about this."

"Yes, let's just listen to her, shall we?" said Tamara.

"It was when I realised the connection," said Alison. "That's what's been worrying me."

"The connection?" scoffed Karen. "What connection?" She took a handkerchief out of her bag and used it to wipe smears of melted truffle off her fingers and lips.

"The connection between what happened to Venetia and what happened to Thomasina Tuckerton in '*The Pale Horse*'."

"Who's she? " said Tamara, looking puzzled. "And what's the pale horse?"

"It's an Agatha Christie book. It's brilliant."

Karen rolled her eyes and sighed loudly.

"Look," said Alison. "I'm a mad keen Agatha Christie fan - you both know that. I've read everything she ever wrote. And Christie really knew her stuff."

"Knew her stuff about what exactly?" said Tamara.

"Poisons," said Alison.

"Oh, here we go," sighed Karen. "And did she kill anyone off using illegal dieting pills? Because I've read a few Christies myself and that's not ringing any bells."

"She didn't," said Alison. "But here's the thing: in '*The Pale Horse*', Thomasina Tuckerton's hair falls out."

"Because of poison?" said Tamara.

"Yes," said Alison. "Because she's been given something called thallium. That's what it does to you - it makes you go bald. And it kills you as well, obviously. And when I read your letter, Tammy, it reminded me so strongly of that story."

"But that's all it is," said Karen. "A story."

"So yesterday," said Alison, "I went into the Science section at the library and dug out a book on poisons. I read the section about thallium last night and it's given me the heebie-jeebies."

"All this talk of murder and intrigue has made me thirsty," said Karen. "I've changed my mind about that coffee," she held out her cup. "Provided it's not laced with arsenic, of course. I'll even have another truffle, while I'm at it. Just to show how much I trust you both." And this time, she popped the entire chocolate into her mouth.

Tamara picked up the cafetiere and filled Karen's cup.

"It can't be a coincidence." Alison's face was flushed. "I tell you, I'm actually scared. I wasn't before - but now I am."

"I'm not surprised, " said Karen. "It's no wonder you're scared after listening to all this hokum."

"It's not hokum, Karen. I believe Arnold and Tammy. I think we *are* in danger. And it's not a nice feeling."

"You're right there," said Tamara. "It's horrible."

"I've brought the poisons book with me," said Alison, "if you want to read the bit that matters." She bent down and took a thick hardback out of her handbag. She flicked through it until she found the page with a bookmark in it, at which point, she handed the book to Tamara ."Here you go. Read it out loud to us, Tammy."

Tamara held it at an angle so that the light from the lamp behind her spilled onto the page. Then she cleared her throat and began to read:

"*Thallium is colourless and tasteless, dissolves in water, and has a slow onset of vague symptoms. The first signs are usually vomiting then diarrhoea, followed by a range of neurological symptoms. Fatal cardiac toxicity occurs some three weeks after adequate exposure. Hair loss is also very common. Being tasteless and odourless, it has been used by murderers, both literary and factual, as a difficult to detect poison."*

She put the book down and looked expectantly at the two women.

"There," said Alison. "Do you see what I mean?"

"Venetia died from eating diet pills," said Karen. "We know that. Why bring in anything else? We know how she died."

"But do we, though?" said Tamara. "Everything I've read about these pills suggests that you have to be quite fragile for them to kill you. Venetia wasn't weak. She was strong as an ox. I don't ever, *ever* remember her being ill."

"Then why leave a packet of pills on her bedside table?" said Karen. "What was the point of that?"

"To disguise what she'd really died of? " suggested Tamara. "By giving us something we'd believe? Or did they weaken her body first with thallium and then finish the job with the diet pills? It's just so cruel. And the worst thing is that we might never know the truth."

"Worse than Venetia dying, you mean?" said Karen. "Nice."

"What do you mean, Tammy?" said Alison. "Why might we never know?"

"Because she was cremated," said Tamara. "And the only other way we might have confirmed it would have been through analysing the hair in her bin - but that was thrown out."

"I can't believe I'm hearing this rot," said Karen.

"Well, how else do you explain her hair falling out ?" replied Alison.

"It *must* have been thallium," said Tamara. "it must have been."

"Listen to you, " said Karen. "The pair of you, Sherlock Holmes and Dr Watson. You sound ridiculous."

"Well, I'm sorry," said Alison. "But I've come round to Tamara's point of view. And I think we should all be careful."

"Okay," said Karen, "let's just assume for a moment that there is a nutcase out there trying to polish us off, one by one - why would they do that?"

"I don't know," said Tamara. "Uncle Arnold thinks it's because of the tontine."

"The tontine," said Alison slowly.

"Good god," said Karen. Somewhere in her brain, doubt was just beginning to stir. But was then extinguished. "Nonsense."

The two cousins looked at each other, their expressions unfathomable.

When the doorbell rang, the three of them nearly jumped out of their seats. Poppy barked.

"I'll get it," cried Tamara, running into the hall.

She brought back Mr Singh, who stood towering above them, tall and composed, safe and strong. He gazed down at them, a gentle smile on his handsome face. He brought a calmness into the room and Karen immediately felt herself begin to relax. He had to get her out of there quickly, away from the madness.

"How lovely it is to see everybody ," he said. "I do hope that you have had a splendid evening together."

"Can I offer you a coffee?" said Tamara. "Or a truffle maybe?" She handed the box to him. "Do take one - they're delicious."

"Thank you," he said, smiling. "You are most kind. Unfortunately, I do not drink coffee - but I am a great fan of chocolate." He took one and popped it into his mouth. Then he saw Karen's face and quickly swallowed the truffle in what looked like a single gulp.

Tamara offered the open box to Alison and Karen but neither of them took her up on it.

Instead, Karen picked up her bag and stood up. "Thanks, ladies, " she said. "Sorry to rush off like this but - well, there you go. It is getting late, after all. Bye, both."

Alison stood too. "Yes, I must be getting home, too, I suppose. Thank you, Tammy, dear, for a ... for a lovely night. "

"It wasn't a lovely night, " said Tamara. "It wasn't lovely at all. I'm more worried now than ever. "

Mr Singh looked concerned. "Has something happened?" he said. "Is everything ok?"

"Oh, it's nothing," said Karen. "We all got a bit silly, that's all. Some kind of group hysteria."

"Silly?" repeated Mr Singh. "Hysteria? What do you mean?"

"Would you mind - I'm sorry to ask," said Alison, "but would you mind just coming out with me to my car? And could you just check that it's.... well, that it's safe before I get in?"

"My dear lady," said Mr Singh. "Of course, I will do that. But why are you so afraid?"

"She's being ridiculous," said Karen.

"That would be very kind of you," said Tamara. "Thank you. And while you're out there, if you wouldn't mind just checking the bushes in the front garden?"

The man looked bewildered. "I am happy to do that, of course. What am I looking for?"

"The bogey man!" said Karen, pulling a comic face. "He's out to get us all. Or maybe he's just out for me. Or maybe he's just out to get you, Alison." She took hold of Mr Singh's arm. "Which one of us is it, I wonder? Which one is dangerous? And which one is in danger?"

"Don't," said Alison. "Don't, Karen. That's just mean."

"*I'm* mean?" said Karen. "You're the one that brought scary stories about poison and psychotic girlfriends. You're the one that's made everything worse than it already was."

"Well I didn't intend to," said Alison. "I just needed to share what I knew. I thought that if I talked about it, I'd be less afraid. But I'm not."

Karen turned to Mr Singh. "She can check her own car," she said. "And Tammy doesn't need to worry about lunatics hiding in the bushes. Nobody's out to get her. She's not even in the tontine. Let's go."

He looked confused but he took her arm and steered her out of the house. Tamara waved goodbye to them from the doorway, her face troubled.

"What happened tonight, Karen?" he said, as they walked down the path. "Was there some kind of argument?"

"I don't want to talk about it," she said.

He opened the car door for her and she got in. He went around to the driver's side.

"What do you think is the most important, Amandeep?" she said, as he climbed into the seat beside her. "Family? Or money?"

"Oh," he said, the light from the streetlamps making his turban glow like a white halo. "That is a most interesting question. Very interesting indeed." He pulled away from the kerb and they drove for almost the whole of the journey in silence. But just as they reached the river and Karen's house, he said, almost as if there had been no break in the conversation. "I believe that money and family - and love - all three are equally important."

She undid her seatbelt. "So money isn't the main thing in life?"

"We are all different, " he said. He took his keys out of the ignition. "But for many people, money affects how a man is judged," he said. "For some, it can be a measure of importance."

"Really? Do you think so?"

"I *don't* think so. It is not the Sikh way."

"It isn't supposed to be the Christian way, either."

"Let me tell you a Punjabi proverb: *when a rich man's dog died, everyone commiserated. When a poor man lost his mother, no one noticed.*"

"And what about you, Amandeep? What do *you* think is the most important?"

"Why do you ask me these questions, Karen? Why are you so anxious?"

"I don't know what to do."

"I can see that you are troubled." He turned and looked at her.

"I am."

"I have lived my whole life guided by the wisdom of those who have gone before me." He put his hand on hers and she felt her skin tingle. "Let me tell you another Punjabi saying, one that I hope will help: '*a man should listen to everyone but do what he considers right.*' Or a lady, of course. Same advice. Do what you think is right, Karen. That is the way forward. "

"Do what I think is right," she repeated. "What I think is right." She looked thoughtful as she considered the implications of doing what he suggested.

But it didn't help at all. Not one tiny bit.

Chapter Twenty Three

Mr Singh didn't usually come into the house when he brought her home. Traditionally, he would escort her to the door, smile, say goodbye and leave. But tonight, she didn't want to be alone, or not just yet anyway. She felt tired but apprehensive too. He didn't need to stay with her for long. She was unlikely to be good company. But she needed to be with someone friendly for a little while, to talk to them of light, bright things. Only then would she be able to sleep without nightmares, she was sure of it.

He seemed a little taken aback when she invited him to come inside but, after a momentary hesitation, he nodded and agreed. She was glad but not surprised. He never said no, not to anything. He never let her down.

Over the years, she had got used to people letting her down. Isabelle, who had abandoned her to live in France. Her cousins whom she didn't really understand and who clearly didn't love her. And Aunt Edna who had left her an insurance scheme instead of money.

Her luck with friends was no better. There was always an agenda. No man had ever hung around for long without wanting to bed or wed her. And mission accomplished, they didn't stick around. She nursed a long list of lovers who had promised much but given little. And as for the more committed ones, the ones who had married her, they were off once the money and the romance had faded.

She had never really had female friends, either. Her boss, Patrice, was the closest and even she had become a little cold since last year, when she had finally confessed to Karen how she really felt and Karen had had to explain that she wasn't that way inclined.

But with Amandeep Singh, she had managed to achieve a friendship that was above the physical. He cared for her, looked after her, helped her and never attempted anything more intimate than a chaste peck on the cheek and the occasional non-threatening hug. Plus he approved of all her business schemes and was willing to provide financial backing. Despite all the differences in their backgrounds, over the four years since their first meeting - in a supermarket, of all places! - she had grown close to him. They shared more than they differed. This was a relationship to nurture, one that she must never spoil. It was special.

Once they were inside her house, she knew it was pointless offering him a drink. He always avoided everything but juice and water. He was still handy with a corkscrew, though. Sitting on the sofa in the lounge, she could hear from the kitchen the squeak and pop of the cork followed by the splash of the wine as it hit the inside of the glass. They were such welcome sounds, symbols of time off, pleasure, entertainment, all those things that had nothing to do with work or duty or bills. Or with threats from mad women. Not that she really believed in those.

"I'm going to ask you another question," she said, when he came back from the kitchen, and handed her a glass of wine.

"Tonight, you are asking many things," he said. "You are being very curious." He sat down at the opposite end of the sofa and, leaning back against the cushions, crossed his legs and balanced his hands on his stomach, fingers interlaced, steeple-like. He often sat like that, almost as if he were interviewing her.

"It's this," she said. "Be honest with me - do you think I'm a mean person?" She sipped the wine. It was delicious. Cold and crisp and slightly honeyed.

"Mean? Are we still talking about money? There is so much else that we could discuss. Let us leave this subject behind."

"No, I meant, am I unkind?" She drank a little more wine, hesitated briefly and then swallowed two more deep, fragrant mouthfuls. "Am I a bitch, Amandeep?"

"You are not unkind, Karen. Far from it."

"Yet everybody leaves me. Always." She drank a little more and then put her almost empty glass down on the coffee table. Her hand was unsteady. "Eventually."

"I am sure this is not true. You are just upset. You have had a difficult evening."

"I have," she said." It was horrible." Her head was beginning to pound and, as she looked at Amandeep, she found it hard to maintain her gaze. Her eyes felt so heavy. But she wanted to look at him. His face was so beautiful. "You'll leave me, too, one day."

He leaned across the space between them, took her hand and kissed it gently. "My friend, I will never leave you." Then he placed it gently back against the cushions and sat upright again. He gazed down at the carpet as if there was something of great interest there.

"You are the only one I can trust," she whispered. How odd she felt. She tried to calculate how much wine she had drunk over the evening. Three or four glasses in Tammy's house. Or more? It was hard to keep track when a person kept having their glass re-filled. And on top of that, she'd just about finished a full glass here, sitting on the sofa with Amandeep. Amandeep. He was so good to her. Such a good friend.

"What does it mean?" she said.

"What does *what* mean?" He looked up. "That I will never leave you?"

He smiled and her heart leapt a little, tired as she was. "No, your name - Amandeep. What does it mean?"

"In Punjabi, my name means lamp of peace."

"That's good - that's what you are. You make me feel calm."

She leaned sideways until she lay flat on the sofa, her head close to his legs. She could smell him. He smelt of soap and clean linen and something else - he smelt like a man. She hesitated just a moment longer before lifting her head and then laying it on top of the hard muscle of his thigh. She gazed up at him. He looked down at her face, seemingly astonished, and raised his hands as if he didn't know what to do.

"You don't mind, do you?" she said. "I just feel so tired. I think I've drunk too much." And then she closed her eyes.

There was such a lot of birdsong and it was very loud. That was the first thing she noticed when she woke up. Then she became aware of how badly her head hurt and that her mouth felt dry as talcum powder. She tried to swallow and the leaden thing that was her tongue almost made her choke. Other things quickly became apparent. Like the fact that her cheek was not lying against a pillow. It wasn't on any kind of fabric at all. Indisputably, her face was lying on warm skin. Someone else's skin. And a nest of soft curly hair that tickled her nose. Slowly she opened her eyes.

The room was flooded with early morning sunshine. She was in bed, naked. And her head lay on top of Amandeep's bare chest, which was lifting gently up and down with the rhythmic rise and fall of his breathing. Her right arm was draped across his stomach. Gingerly, she lifted herself up onto her elbow and looked with horrified eyes at his sleeping face.

*Oh...my...god...*she fell back onto the pillows and stared, unseeing, at the ceiling. She lay there, trying to piece together how on earth this could have happened. Amandeep... and her... *surely not...*

Snatches of the night before suddenly came to her, jumbled and incoherent like some crazed dream. She had been sitting downstairs with him. She had drunk too much. She remembered that. And then she recalled other moments: of her pulling him into bed, of her grabbing at his clothes and wrenching them off. And still more pictures, of her astride him, of him on top of her, of unimaginable pleasure coursing through her body...

She sat up very slowly and stared, aghast, at the man at her side. What the hell had she done? Had she ruined this too? The only pure relationship she had left?

The throbbing in her head made her feel sick. How much had she had to drink? She would never have done this sober. She had an awful track record to stop her. Sleep with them and they go. And she didn't want this man to go. She wanted him to stay.

She pulled the sheet up around her breasts. And then she looked desperately around the room. Where were her clothes? She had a horrible feeling that they might be on the lounge floor. If she could only slide out of bed without waking him, she might make it unobserved to her dressing room. Then she could pull on a robe, go downstairs and wait in the kitchen, cup of coffee in hand. When he came down, she could pretend that nothing had happened. Perhaps she could even put on yesterday's clothes and mess up the sofa a bit to make it look like she'd fallen asleep and stayed the night down there. Alone.

As she lowered one foot onto the carpet, he coughed and rolled onto his side and she froze, her toes suspended. Now he was facing away from her. By the sudden stiffening of his body, she guessed that he, too, was now awake.

Whilst he was looking towards the wall, she stumbled, not to her dressing room as per her first plan, but to the tiny ensuite bathroom instead. Not only was it closer but it suddenly felt a more urgent place to visit. Closing the door behind her, she snatched at the light-pull and looked in the mirror above the sink. Her hair was all over the place, her face was flushed and there were mascara spiders littering the skin below her eyes. Leaning on the basin brought her even closer to the trainwreck. A white rash of dried saliva crusted around one side of her mouth. She must have been dribbling onto his chest while she slept. Hideous.

And what the hell was that? She squinted at the glass, trying to focus on the raspberry bloom that tattooed her right breast. Horrified, she slowly glanced downwards and there, staring back up at her, was an enormous love-bite.

She suddenly felt nauseous and she collapsed backwards onto the closed toilet lid. Gripping the edge of the seat, she tried to take deep breaths. Please don't let me be sick, she prayed, please don't. I can't have him hear that too. I've tried so hard to make him respect me and now I'm losing everything. All dignity. *Everything.*

After a few moments, the room stopped spinning and she was able to stand. She pulled a silk dressing gown off the back of the door and put it on so that she could no longer see the purple badge of lust from the night before. Then, desperate to remove the trash-can sourness from her mouth, she quietly brushed her teeth. That made her feel a little better but did nothing to improve the way she looked. God, she'd have to deal with that, however horrible she felt. She grabbed a bottle of cleanser and removed her makeup, rubbed moisturiser into her face, brushed her hair and spritzed herself with Chanel. The smell of the perfume was so strong it nearly made her gag and she had to sit quietly again until the moment passed.

She opened the ensuite door slowly and saw that he wasn't in the room. Now she really didn't know what to do. Should she look for him? Or was there any chance she could take a shower first? The thought of being clean and fresh appealed hugely. But it would take at least an hour to bathe, wash her hair, style it (if she could bear the roar of the dryer), to get dressed and then put makeup on.

Which meant she was going to have to face him now, just as she was. There was an urgency about this because, although a large part of her was aghast at the damage she might have wrought, there was still a bit of her that wanted to know - wanted to *ask* him - how he felt about what had happened. Or, more specifically, whether he had enjoyed it as much as she knew she had done, disjointed though her recollection was, and much as she knew she shouldn't have.

A quick fix was needed. She tousled her hair to make it look a little more Bardot and pinched her cheeks to get a bit more colour into them. She put on a pair of slippers and then, deciding they were too homely, yanked them off and slid her feet into a pair of kitten-heeled black ones with feathers on the toes. Tying the belt of the silk gown tightly around her waist, she walked slowly down the stairs.

She found him in the lounge, standing almost on alert, as if he had been waiting to hear her footsteps. But her slippers were very quiet. As she rounded the corner, he jumped into action.

"Thank you for allowing me to sleep down here last night," he said, picking up the sofa cushions. He began to zip and unzip them and to rather theatrically beat them. "I must have been too tired to drive home. This was indeed a most comfortable bed." He replaced the cushions on the sofa and patted and smoothed them as if they were pets, keeping his head averted from her the whole time he was talking.

She was nonplussed, not knowing whether to go along with the charade or denounce it.

"Would you like a coffee?" she said, finally, and then kicked herself because it made it look as if she didn't know him well enough to be aware that he didn't drink it.

"Perhaps you have some juice?" he said.

She walked past him and into the kitchen. First of all, she poured herself a large glass of chilled water which she downed in one, swallowing two paracetamols at the same time. Then she poured two glasses of orange juice, before putting the kettle on to hide any ugly retching noise she might suddenly be unable to stop herself from making. She leaned on the sink and tried to concentrate on the view through the window, focusing on the bench at the bottom of the garden and on her breathing. She was trying hard to dam the headachey sickness which kept returning.

She walked unsteadily back into the lounge and handed him the juice.

He took a sip and then abruptly put the glass down on the coffee table. He clamped one hand over his mouth and his eyes bulged. "I am very sorry," he said. "I am not feeling myself. It might be best if I leave."

Before she could say anything, he dashed out of the house, calling goodbye over his shoulder.

The moment he was gone, she raced to the bathroom getting there just in time to be sick.

Chapter Twenty Four

She spent the rest of the morning in bed, intermittently snoozing, stretching and sipping water. By lunchtime, she felt sufficiently improved to lie there weakly, nibbling digestive biscuits. All this time in bed gave her plenty of time to think. About Isabelle. About Venetia's lost hair and about her death. About Alison and about Lucy who might have pushed her down the stairs. About Gerald and Pammie and the missing Arnold. About the tontine.

But although these were worthy of proper concentrated thought, the pictures that kept coming back into her mind were of her and Amandeep Singh, writhing in naked, passionate, *incredible* embrace. And how, despite all her misgivings, and her certainty that it was a mistake, she longed to do it again.

At two o'clock, she felt able to face the shower and the hairdryer. She got dressed and sat quietly on the sofa. And wondered if she should ring him. And didn't dare to.

At three o'clock, he arrived at her house.

When she opened the door, he hesitated a moment and then thrust into her hand a bouquet of red roses. "These are for you." He smiled tentatively and turned to go.

Before he stepped away from her front door, she said, just as she had done the night before, "Would you like to come in?"

Ten minutes later, they sat side by side on the sofa, silent and distant, as if they were strangers at a bus stop. The roses were on the coffee table in a crystal vase.

"They're very beautiful," she said at last. She had already said this at least twice before.

"Thank you. It is my pleasure to give them to you."

"You are very kind"

"Not at all"

"Would you like some water? Or cordial perhaps? I think I have some."

"Thank you, no."

There was another stretch of silence.

"Have you read the papers today?" she said, eventually.

"I have not. Has anything exciting happened?"

"Not really."

They both stared at the flowers again for a few minutes.

He got to his feet. "I think I should be going, Karen. I have ... there is a lot I must do today."

"Right. Yes, I see. Well, thanks for coming and thanks again for the roses. They really are very beautiful." She leaned forward to smell them. "And they are so fragrant."

She walked with him to the door. Say something, she thought, don't let him leave. *Make him stay.* She shook her head to clear it of all the voices. She would say nothing. It was for the best. Maybe this way they could stay friends.

On the doorstep, she stood, one hand in her pocket and the other holding the door-frame. "Goodbye, then."

"Goodbye, Karen." He hesitated just for a moment and she stared at him, waiting, wondering, if he would say anything more.

He walked past her.

And, in the next heartbeat, she grabbed the back of his jacket. As he turned, she said, her voice trembling, pleading, like a child's. "Don't go...please, Amandeep, don't leave me."

He smiled instantly and she felt a wave of joy sweep through her.

"My darling," he whispered, taking both of her hands in his and bringing them to his lips. "Leave you? Don't you remember what I promised last night?" He gazed into her eyes and seemed to have found an answer, because he led her inside, closed the door behind them, wrapped her in his arms and kissed her.

And kissing is where it stopped.

She tried to take him in the direction of the stairs but he resisted. Pulling her around to face him, he said, "When I told you that I would never abandon you, I meant it but... Karen, we need to talk. It's ....it's complicated."

They sat down on the sofa just as they had the night before but, this time, they were close together rather than at opposite ends. She stared into his eyes, her mouth trembling, though she tried to keep it firm. She was waiting to hear, yet dreading to hear, that he had changed his mind, that it was all the most terrible mistake, that, despite what he'd promised, he was leaving her forever. *Complicated.* What an ominous word that was.

"Last night," he began, "with you, it was wonderful. Magical. Like nothing else I have ever known." He took her hand and held it tightly.

Despite herself, she began to smile. Perhaps she had been wrong, after all. He was glad. As glad as she was.

Which he clearly saw because he rushed to his next sentence. "But...I am so sorry, my dear, dear love...it cannot ever, ever happen again." A nerve began to twitch on his forehead, just above his eyebrow. "Karen?" His face looked tortured.

She took her hand away and stared down at her knees. So her first instinct, her fail-safe, gut instinct, had been right. He regretted it. She had lost him. She had thought she was prepared for this but the truth was, she wasn't.

"You had better leave, I think," she said.

"You are right," he said. "I should go. But I hope that you can forgive me. Please tell me that we can still be friends. You are so precious to me."

"Am I?" she said, her voice breaking. "Am I really?" She picked up the roses from the crystal vase, the water dripping from their stems over the coffee table. She walked into the kitchen, opened the bin and threw them in.

He followed her and took hold of her shoulders.

"You don't understand," he said. "I must try and make you understand." His lips were tight.

"Oh, I completely understand," she said. "I've had a lifetime's experience of this exact same moment, many, many times over."

"I don't know if that is true," he said, "I hope it isn't because, if it is, then you have suffered pain - and I hate to think of you suffering."

"Don't tell me these lies!" she cried. "Don't make it sound as if you care - because I know that you don't!"

"But I do!"

"Then why are you doing this?" she said. "How can you hurt me like this? If you don't want me to be in pain? Don't you see that it's you who's making me suffer?"

She pushed him away and covered her face with her hands.

He sat down on a kitchen chair. She heard the scrape of the wooden legs against the tiled floor. "Why?" She opened her eyes and looked at him. "Just tell me why."

He gazed at the centre of the table as if he were thinking about what to do next, what to say, next. He looked like a man caught in a terrible dilemma. And then he spoke. "It is because of kama," he said. "That is why."

He looked so wretched that, despite herself, she felt a rush of anguish for him. She took one of his hands again in hers and held it tightly. "Oh, Amandeep," she said.

"Kama is a Thief," he said. He released his hand from her grip, stood up and pulled out a chair for her. She sat down.

"Tell me," she said. "Tell me. I promise I will try to understand."

"Sex outside marriage is completely forbidden in my religion," he said. "Apart from my beloved wife, may her departed soul rest well, you are the only woman that I have known in this way."

"So, what are you saying? That you've committed some sort of sin by sleeping with me? That you regret it? "

"I said to you, just now, the word '*kama*'."

"What does it mean?"

"It is one of the Five Thieves that I have tried hard to avoid all my life."

"A thief? What do you mean? You need to make this simpler for me. I just don't follow."

"My faith warns me to avoid the Thieves which steal a man away from the right path. They are anger, greed, love of worldly things, ego and ...kama - which you know as 'lust'. I want to be a good man. And last night I failed."

"You *are* a good man," she said. "You are the best, the absolute best, of men. You are kind and good and true. You are modest and decent. I have never known anyone like you."

He put up his hand as if to ward off the things she was saying.

"Amandeep," she said, "You haven't failed. You haven't suddenly become a bad person because of what happened last night."

"I have tried so hard not to love you," he said. "It has been difficult to resist." He smiled. "But last night.. I know that it was ..." he hesitated for a moment, as if embarrassed or suddenly shy, "...it was wonderful."

"It was," she said. "It was fantastic."

"And yet - it is so strange - there is also a lot that I just can't remember." He gazed at her, his face troubled. "And I want to remember everything, all of it, that whole beautiful night with you."

"What can't you remember?"

"I don't know how it happened," he said. "I don't even remember going upstairs."

She recalled her own disorientation, her nausea and that strange feeling of detachment from the world. "I felt the same," she said. "But that was because I drank too much wine."

"Yes, but me? I felt intoxicated, too. And that is impossible."

"Intoxicated? You mean you felt drunk?"

"Yet I drank nothing at all. I do not drink alcohol. You know that. So why did I feel so strange?"

"In what way, strange?"

"As if I had no inhibitions, as if nothing else mattered. I try always to be so controlled, to behave modestly - and then, this morning, I woke up in your bed and I was astonished. I could remember some of it and, yes, it was very beautiful - but it was also so, so wrong."

She knew she should be hurt at this, yet could not be because, at the time, she had felt exactly the same: that their night of love had been beautiful but wrong.

But she was willing to repeat it and he was not.

"And when I came downstairs," he said, "I thought I was going to be ill. Really ill. I had to leave you quickly before I embarrassed myself. Otherwise I would have spoken to you about these things then. But I could not stay. I did not dare."

For a moment, neither of them said anything.

Eventually, she said, "well if you didn't drink anything, maybe it was something you ate."

"Maybe." He looked thoughtful. "Last night, before I came to get you, I dined with my cousin, Ikbir, in his home. We both ate the same meal - saag and naan."

"And was he ill?"

"He was not. He rang me this afternoon about a business matter and I had to tell him of my sickness. He was astonished and very sympathetic."

"So you don't think it was food poisoning?"

"No." He shook his head. "Ikbir apologised but I told him that it was not his fault - because if he had done something wrong, or if the food was bad - then he too would have suffered. But, as I say, he was well."

"And you ate nothing else? No lunch?"

"I eat in moderation always, Karen. I had no lunch yesterday because I knew that Ikbir would prepare a very large meal for us in the evening."

She opened the kitchen door and late afternoon sunshine streamed in from the garden. She stood on the path for a moment, taking deep breaths of green healthy air. Despite the bright sky, it was cold and she shivered. He came and stood next to her and wrapped his arm around her shoulders. She leaned in to him. How could something that felt so natural, and so obvious, be forbidden to them?

"Maybe it was just some bug," he said. "It must be because the only other thing I ate was that chocolate your relative gave me...Tammy, is it? But that was so small, it cannot be that."

She looked out at the bench at the bottom of the garden. On the wall behind it, a climbing rose whispered in the breeze, its blossom full and soft as pink sherbet. How beautiful it was.

"And also," he said, "if it was that, then everybody else who had a chocolate would have been ill, too. "

All this talk of sickness was reminding her of her own nausea that morning. And that was when she had the thought. It was just a small thought at first but it soon grew...there *was* only one other person who ate a chocolate. And there *was* someone else who felt ill.

Alison had brought those truffles to Tammy's house. But she hadn't eaten any. And Tammy hadn't eaten one, either. It was only she, Karen, and Amandeep who had. Tamara had almost forced the chocolates on him.

Money - or lack of it - could drive people to do terrible things. Even to other family members. Alison was always complaining about how tight things were. Although less so now that Pammie was gone - Pammie, whose constant needs had ruled her life. A situation she'd been put in because of Gerald, the man who had ruined everything for both of them. And he'd been helped in that by Venetia when she'd lied for him and covered up what he'd done to Pammie.

Well, all three were dead now.

And Tammy? Could she be caught up in this? What was in it for her? Nothing except that Alison wouldn't be able to do this on her own.

Her misgivings grew.

There was only Tammy and Alison's word that the murderous Lucy even existed. In fact, there was only Tammy's say-so that this mad warning letter was from Arnold. After all, she herself had commissioned a fake letter. She knew how easy they were to buy, if you knew the right people.

Which might actually mean that Arnold, too, might be dead. In which case, there was just her and Alison left.

Winner takes all.

"Shall we go inside?" said Amandeep. "It's getting a little cold, I think."

She stared at him, a fresh dilemma having reared its head. Should she ask his advice? Two heads were better than one. Sometimes.

"You know, thinking about it," she said, "I'm sure you're right. It must have been some horrible bug that made you sick. Still, things are on the mend, now." She looked up at him and smiled. "For both of us."

A tiny fly landed on her arm and she squashed it flat before flicking it off onto the path.

Chapter Twenty Five

They went back into the kitchen and he retrieved the flowers from the bin and put them back into the crystal vase, topping it up with fresh water. She realised that, in some way, this might be symbolic.

He stayed for a little while longer, holding her hand and soothing her but when he said that, this time, he really was going, she was content to let him leave. She needed to be on her own so that she could attempt to digest the events of the last twenty four hours. Having him there next to her was distracting. In so many ways.

The truth was that she felt utterly drained, both emotionally and physically. She was no superwoman. In real life, no-one was. Being sick was tiring. Wondering if your relatives were intent on murder, well, that certainly took it out of you. And she was dealing with both..

After he'd gone, she still couldn't settle. She didn't want to eat anything and, for once, she couldn't face a drink. She watched a pathetic TV soap without seeing any of it. At half past ten, restless and anxious, she went to bed. The next day was her day off. She had no idea how she was going to spend it. She supposed she should make some kind of plan but there was so much to think about, she didn't know how to begin.

She turned the lamp off and lay sleepless in bed, watching the light from the street playing across the ceiling. Her mind was full. Names kept driving through it. Repetitive lists of names and questions but no answers, no solutions... *Isabelle...Gerald...Pammie...Venetia...*

Eventually, she rose, got a glass of water, came back to bed and read a book for a while. None of the words reached her brain. Eventually, she turned the light off and tried once more to capture the sleep that she desperately needed. And there they were again, intrusive and disturbing. *...Arnold.... Alison.... Tammy...Lucy...*

At several points in the night, and through the early hours of the morning, she looked at her bedside clock and watched the time crawl past. And weaving in amongst the thoughts that wouldn't leave her in peace there came, again and again, the most significant name of all. *Amandeep.*

Until, at half past four, just as the first birds were beginning to stir, she heard a noise coming from downstairs. She couldn't be sure if she'd imagined it so she sat up in the shadows and strained her ears, trying to identify whether she had heard something - or nothing. There it was again. A loud creak as if somebody was treading the polished boards of her lounge. Was it the man she'd got to forge that letter five years ago? That vicious wife-beater? He'd threatened her often enough, the thug.

She got up and tiptoed to her bedroom door. As quietly as she could, she turned the key in the lock. She put her ear to the jamb and listened again.

And then she was certain she could smell violets.

She leaned back against the locked door in horror. It wasn't the forger – it must be her! It was *Lucy!* She had finally come to get her....was she with Alison? And Tammy? Was it to be all three of them against her?

She dragged a Windsor chair from the corner of the room and tried to get it under the door handle but it wouldn't fit. Then she ran to her window and looked out. Beyond the road, the waters of the river gleamed in the starlight and the first traces of dawn. The street itself was deserted - there was no-one to call out to for help. If she were to jump out of the window, she would definitely break at least a leg and then she couldn't even run away.

Should she ring the police? But what if she were wrong and there was nobody downstairs? What if she was just overwrought and over-tired and had imagined the noise ? They'd laugh if she mentioned perfume as a reason for calling. She had never rung the police in her whole life, not about anything, and despite her distress, to do so now felt embarrassing and dramatic, an almost theatrical overreaction to a panic she wasn't even sure had substance.

But she was still scared. She turned on the light and dialled the number of the only person she could trust.

She was watching out for him through her bedroom window. When he pulled up outside, she felt like sobbing with relief. As he got out of the car, she called to him and when he was standing beneath her window, she threw him a key to her front door.

"Be careful!" she said. "I don't know if they're still here."

And then she heard his footsteps on the stairs and she unlocked her bedroom door, wrenched it open and threw herself into his embrace. It was over. He had rescued her, not just from intruders - if there were any - but from so much more than that. She sobbed into his chest and he mumbled soft, shy, comforting noises and held her tight and, when she was all cried out, he put her back to bed and pulled the covers gently over her.

As he walked out through the bedroom door, she called to him. "Don't leave me!"

He stopped and came back in.

She stared at him, her eyes heavy with fatigue. She was more exhausted than ever but she still feared the nightmares that sleep would bring were he to go.

"There's no-one here, Karen - just you and me. Don't be afraid. The house is all locked up. You're safe. "

"I don't want to be on my own. I need you to stay here with me."

He came and sat on the edge of her bed. "Do you have a spare room?"

"No."

"Would it help you feel safe if I slept in the lounge?" He looked at her with such tenderness but she knew that he would not do what she really wanted him to do. Not after their talk earlier.

"I'd feel safe if you slept there." She pointed to the wall opposite, to a brocade chaise longue which she had bought last year at hideous expense. "There are spare blankets in the cupboard in the corner. Please? "

He squeezed her hand. "Of course."

And as she heard him making up his makeshift bed, she fell quickly into peaceful, dreamless sleep. When she was terrified and alone, his was the name she had called. And he had come to save her.

Several hours later, she woke up to a room drenched with golden light. She stretched and yawned and then remembered who else was there. At this thought came such joy that what she had to do next became instantly obvious. Blindingly so. Maybe it had always been the answer but she hadn't always understood what the question was.

She sat up and looked at his sleeping frame and smiled. He looked so absurd on the chaise longue. His legs were hanging off the end because he was too tall to fit on it. The blanket he had taken out of the cupboard had slipped off. He had made few concessions to the fact that he was supposed to be sleeping, having merely unbuttoned the top of his shirt and removed the belt from his trousers. His shoes were underneath his brocade bed, the tips facing out like a pair of shiny black noses. His jacket was on the floor, neatly folded. His tie and belt lay on top of it.

She went downstairs and made herself a coffee and drank it. Then she poured two glasses of orange juice and put two frozen croissants in the microwave. When they pinged ready, she placed them, a cafetiere, two cups, the juice, napkins, two plates, two knives and a pot of jam on a silver salver. Finally, she pulled out a red rose from the bouquet he had bought her the day before and added that to the tray. All loaded up, she walked back up the stairs.

As she walked in to the bedroom, he was just waking. He lay on his side and smiled a lazy smile and her heart jumped like a firecracker.

"Good morning," he said. "Did you sleep well?"

"I did," she said. "Because of you. "

"And do I see breakfast?"

She put the tray down on her dressing table. Plucking the rose from the little vase into which she had put it, she walked over to where he lay.

"You do," she said. "But there is something else that I would like to give you."

Just for a moment, a shadow crossed his face and she saw it and knelt down by his side. "No, no that. Or at least, yes, that - but not that alone."

He propped himself up on one elbow and stared down at her.

"I offer you my heart, too, and my life, as well, if you'll take it." She gazed at him, trying to gauge his reaction. She was sure - but was he? She handed him the rose and he took it from her, his eyes never leaving her face.

"My darling, darling man," she whispered, "I adore you."

"And I you," he said.

"I want to be with you always."

"We will. Always."

"Till death?"

"Till death. I promise you."

"I've never felt like this before," she said, "and I feel shy. But I have to ask you to do one more thing, just one last thing, for me."

"Anything," he said. "Just ask."

"Here goes." She closed her eyes, took a deep breath, opened them again and said, before nerves got the better of her, "Amandeep Singh, will you marry me?"

And as ever, without pause or hesitation, he said yes.

Chapter Twenty Six

Alison,

After the dinner party

After Karen and Mr Singh had left Tamara's house, Alison didn't feel up to leaving straightaway. She sat on the sofa for ten minutes, glass of water in hand, with Tamara there next to her, as they tried to make sense of what had happened. Both of them felt in a state of shock.

She looked at Tamara and saw how sad her face was. "I'm sorry, dear...you must be disappointed. You tried so hard to have a sensible discussion with us both." She took a gulp of water and put the glass down on the table. "It all went a bit to pot, didn't it?"

"It wasn't a complete waste of effort," said Tamara. "We did learn some new things."

"Whatever Karen says, I'm convinced that Venetia was killed by a mixture of thallium and diet pills – not the diet pills alone."

"Me, too. It makes complete sense."

"And that hateful woman who tried to push me down the stairs - Tammy, she's *got* to be the same creature that Arnold's talking about. "

"I agree."

"In the meantime, we've got to stop this Lucy woman before she kills anyone else - and by anyone else, I suppose I mean *us*. We have to find a way to protect ourselves."

"*Us?* You mean *me* too?"

"I haven't forgotten that bouquet someone sent you. Nor what happened at the hospital when you visited Arnold."

"I wondered if I was just being neurotic thinking I was in danger." Tamara thought back to that night when she had lain on the wet pavement, nursing her crushed handbag and bloodied knee. It could so easily have been a crushed head. And then those beautiful but deadly flowers. If she'd touched them, who knows what might have happened? "It's a horrible thought. It's just so frightening."

"Maybe we should go to the police, Tammy."

"About my dad? Or about Pammie? It's too long ago - and we've no proof whatsoever."

" I suppose not. Till now, we thought that your dad had been run over - a tragic accident. Who knows, maybe it was. There were no witnesses, no CCTV. And my poor Pammie died in a crowded family garden."

"We could tell them what we think happened to Venetia."

"But what would we say? They've already decided how she died. We can hardly prove that it was anything else, can we?"

"I suppose not," said Alison, picking up her water glass and draining it. She looked thoughtful.

"We'd just sound ridiculous."

"I'm inclined to agree with you, dear."

"And Uncle Arnold clearly thinks the same," said Tamara. She picked up the letter discarded on the table and read aloud. " *I don't think there's any point in going to the police. What proof do we have? Nothing. And, sorry, but I can't come home and give any kind of help. I'd have to be mad.*"

Alison took the letter from her. "He does tell us what we *should* do, though, doesn't he? " And then she read a different sentence. "*To survive, you're going to have to rely on the family and your own wit.*"

A few nights later, home again and having locked all the doors, Alison settled down to read her latest library book - "*Self-Defence for Women*".

By the end of Chapter Two, she felt able to have a go. She got her car keys out, pushed the sharp bits through the side of her closed fist and practised the Hammer Strike. She decided that she could add to the element of surprise by yelling defiant slogans at the same time. At first, she shouted, "*get off!*" and "*leave me alone!*" but these seemed a bit tame. Once she'd got the hang of it, she became ruder and ruder. She reached the apex when the upswing with the keys was accompanied by her calling out "*take that, you.... bastard ... motherfucker!*" At which point, she stopped, red-faced, and gazed in horror at the thin wall which divided her domain from that of her neighbours. Time for a calming cup of tea.

After that, she made a pyramid of cushions and had a go at repeatedly kicking them over with an attack called the Groin Strike. This seemed to be the final gambit in most escapes from Grabbing by Strangers.

Escaping was harder to practise than attacking. She went through the manoeuvres, saying the steps aloud while she rehearsed the motions with an imaginary aggressor. Bend forward if bear-hugged and then follow that up with a confident Groin Strike. If bear-hugged plus hands grabbed, shift sideways to off-balance them. Then fell the bastard with a Groin Strike. When escaping from a headlock, shove your body into the assailant's side, pull backwards and then deliver a Groin Strike. It was all going very well.

Shortly after having dispatched and disabled a baker's dozen of hapless attackers, the phone rang and interrupted her exertions. Rather breathlessly, she answered it.

"Alison," said Tamara. "Something's happened. Something bad."

"What is it? Are you okay?"

"I'm fine - but next door's been burgled - Barry and mum's house. Someone's broken in."

"You're joking! When?"

"It must have been sometime today. It was fine last night."

"Oh, my god, Tammy! "

"I know."

"How did you find out?"

"I went round to water the plants and saw that the French windows had been kicked in - there's glass everywhere."

"Oh, of course, I forgot - they're not back till next month, are they? Oh, you poor girl! Have you called the police?"

"Yes, they're here now."

"And what's been stolen?"

"Just the telly. From what I can see, anyway."

"Right, what can I do to help?"

"Could you come over? I'd really appreciate it. I'm a bit unnerved."

"I'm on my way."

She rang the doorbell and Tamara answered it and ushered her into the lounge. A policeman was sitting on the sofa, notebook in one hand, cup of tea in the other.

"Police Constable Trevor Danvers," he said, standing up as she walked in.

"Alison Benson."

She knew it was middle-aged of her but this policeman looked incredibly young. How much experience of crime-fighting could he possibly have had? But then he smiled as he shook her hand and it was such a warm and sympathetic response that she cast away the thought as an unkind one and smiled back widely as if to make up for it.

She took one of Tamara's hands in hers. "Are you okay, dear?"

"I am," said Tamara. "It's just a bit of a shock." She sat down on the sofa and Alison sat on the chair opposite.

"I bet. You poor thing." Poppy put her paw on her lap but she brushed it off. "Shooh, Poppy, sit."

Turning to the policeman, she said, "Well, this is a terrible business, isn't it, Officer?"

He frowned ruefully. "I'm really sorry it's happened. I know how worrying burglary can be."

"Were there any fingerprints or anything? "

"It's been dusted. It's something we'll be investigating."

"And is next door safe now?"

"We've called out an emergency locksmith and a glazier. They're here as we speak, securing the back doors of the property. And I've checked the house and garden to make sure that there's nobody there who shouldn't be."

"They must have known that your mum and Barry were away, Tammy," said Alison.

"I hope not," said Tamara, "because that would mean they've been watching the place. And I don't like that idea at all."

"Me neither," said Alison.

"I'd just like to say three things if I may," said the policeman. "Firstly, I know this might be hard advice to take - but try not to panic. There's been a spate of break-ins locally and I know that that's worrying- "

"-It certainly is," said Tamara.

" - but, nevertheless, burglary remains quite rare. In fact, it may reassure you to know that, nationally, it's on the decrease."

"Not that helpful at the moment, I'm afraid," said Alison. "But I know you mean well."

"Secondly," he said, addressing Tamara, "your mum and step-dad's house -"

"-My mum and *partner's* house," she interrupted.

"Apologies. But my point is that it's unlikely they were targeted. All the recent local burglaries appear to have been opportunistic ones of houses that were vulnerable."

"Tammy," said Alison, "I think you should pack a bag and come home with me."

"Do you think I should? But what about Poppy and Coco? You're not keen on animals - and I can't just leave them."

"Try to keep this in proportion," said the policeman. "Because my third point is that this property is less vulnerable than most."

"Really?"

"Let me be clear - ultimately, all houses are vulnerable to the determined burglar. And some things actually make it that little bit easier for them. For instance, you've got Old Folly Lane running along behind the gardens here. The perpetrators almost certainly gained access over the walls at the back of the premises at each and every one of the houses burgled over the last twelve weeks."

"Tammy, I still think that you should pack a bag," said Alison. "I can put up with the pets for a while. Or there's always boarding kennels."

"Remember, though" said PC Danvers, "that burglars tend to avoid premises with dogs."

Tamara thought back to that night four months earlier when she had found Poppy standing guard at the French windows and she rubbed the dog's head.

"In addition," said the policeman, "because you don't, at present, leave the premises to go to a place of work, your movements during the day have no pattern to them, so you're not advertising a safe time for them to break in."

"Well, that's lucky," said Alison. The man's face looked so calm and serious, she thought. Despite his youth, there was something about his demeanour which inspired trust, as if he knew what he was talking about. He reminded her of somebody but she couldn't quite remember who.

"I suppose it *is* lucky," said Tamara.

"And," said PC Danvers, "looking around the property, I can see that you've installed window and door locks and they definitely make a difference. Furthermore, I see that your French windows have been fitted with a double-cylinder locking bolt. Very wise."

Tamara felt a wave of appreciation for Mr Lynd's DIY efforts. She was also grateful to Keith for persuading her to buy the locks in the first place. She still wished he'd stop calling her though.

"What's more," continued the policeman, "I've checked your garden and I can see that access to it from either side is well-nigh impossible because of the thick hedging between your house and theirs, especially the berberis and thorn trees. "

"I'm feeling a bit less anxious now," said Alison. "And I can see your cup is empty, Constable. I'll just put the kettle on, shall I?" She stood up and walked to the lounge door. The dog immediately got up and followed her. "Shoosh, Poppy," she said. "Go away, go and sit down, there's a good girl."

"There's one more thing," said the policeman, " and this is rather less positive, I'm afraid."

"Oh," said Alison. "I'd better sit down again then, I suppose."

"What is it?" said Tamara. "I don't like the sound of this."

"At the back of your property, you've got broken glass on top of the wall. That's illegal. It needs to go, I'm afraid."

"I have tried to get it off," said Tamara. "But it won't budge. I only put it there because I found footprints around the pond in my garden. I was scared someone was trying to break in."

"Footprints? Did you call us?"

"No...I didn't...I wasn't sure. I didn't want to make a fool of myself."

"Never worry about that. It's our job to help. It's what we're here for." He stood up and then hesitated before saying the next thing. "However...it might interest you to know that, while checking the perimeter earlier today, I discovered traces of blood on that glass."

"So someone *did* try to break in after all!" exclaimed Tamara.

"Possibly," said PC Danvers.

"Despite everything you've told us about the house being unattractive to burglars."

"Getting into the garden isn't the same thing as getting into the house. Can I assume the blood isn't yours?"

"It's not mine."

"And will that help you trace whoever tried to break in?" said Alison.

"It will be one line of inquiry."

"Well, that's good news, isn't it?" said Alison.

"It's also possible that whoever tried to climb that wall cut themselves badly. We'll be checking the hospitals."

"Brilliant!" said Alison. She knew now who the policeman reminded her of. It was Gordon. Gordon as he might have been as a young man. She found herself smiling at the thought. Just like PC Danvers, Gordon was kind and reassuring and absolutely capable.

"In the meantime, Miss Benson, do remember - and be reassured by - everything I've said about the security of your property." He looked at her with genuine sympathy and an encouraging smile. "And, of course, we will be keeping you informed of the progress of our inquiries."

"That's kind," said Tamara. "Thanks. I appreciate it. And I will remember what you've said. It does help."

"In the meantime, I've given you a crime number. Tell your mum to quote that to the insurance company." He moved towards the door. "And remember, any worries, call us straightaway."

"Thank you, Officer," said Alison. "But I hope we won't need to."

" Before I leave, I'll just check one last time that next door is safe and secure."

"Actually," said Tamara. "There is just one more thing."

Alison looked at Tamara in apprehension. She knew instinctively what this 'one more thing' was that she wanted to discuss. Despite their chat the week before.

"Yes?" he said.

"This is a coincidence but - do you remember coming here before? Three years ago?"

"Yes," he said. "I do. It was to tell you the sad news about your father. I recall it well."

"Would it surprise you to know that there have been two more family deaths since then?" said Tamara.

"I'm sorry to hear that."

"But they've all been suspicious deaths."

"Suspicious? " He got his notebook and pen back out of his pocket. "Your dad got run over, didn't he? At Oakfield Country Park."

"That's right. Well remembered. That was the first death. Then there was another one-" She looked at Alison in mute appeal.

"-my sister," said Alison, somewhat reluctantly. "My twin, Pamela."

"She drowned," said Tamara. "In the pond in our garden on the day of my dad's funeral."

"I see." But he didn't look as if he did see. "That's awful."

"And then two months ago," said Tamara, "another cousin died. *Apparently* from taking illegal diet pills."

"This is all terrible, of course, and I extend you every sympathy - but how can we help you?"

"We think that all three of them were murdered," said Tamara.

"*Murdered?*" he looked genuinely astonished. "And the motive for that would be...?"

"It's complicated," said Alison. This was going exactly as they had predicted it would.

"Because of a family insurance scheme," said Tamara. "The last one alive inherits everything."

"Hmmm," said the officer.

Was it her imagination, wondered Alison, or had some of his earlier sympathy evaporated? He looked rather distant now.

"And which family member do you suspect of carrying out these murders?" he said.

"Oh, she's not a relative, " said Tamara. "She couldn't *actually* inherit anything."

He looked puzzled. "Then why...?"

"It's a woman called Lucy. We don't know why yet. But we're sure - well, we think - it might be her."

"And what's her full name?" he said, flicking his notebook open. "Lucy what?"

"I can't remember," said Tamara. Her face was red. "It was a French name, though, I think."

"And where does she live?"

"We don't know that either," said Alison. Oh my god, she thought. We sound insane.

"Well, do you have proof of any of this?"

"Not exactly," said Alison. She tried not to squirm.

"So, in a nutshell, you believe a woman - whose name and address you don't know - is killing members of your family for an inheritance that she can't touch?"

"She just keeps popping up and, when she does, people die," said Tamara. She looked very dismal.

"Look, do you know what," said Alison, "never mind. It doesn't matter."

"No, it does matter. I can see you're both genuinely anxious." He frowned. "I think the best thing you can do is to write all this down - dates, times, places - and come into the station with it so that your concerns can be properly logged."

"Yes," said Alison. "That's a great idea."

"Perhaps you should ring ahead and make an appointment first," he said. "So that we can make sure we give you enough time to explain everything properly."

"Will do," said Alison. "Thank you so much for your interest, Police Constable Danvers. Anyway, look at the time - you should probably be going now. I'm sure you're very busy." She almost propelled him along the hall to the front door. "Goodbye."

As she closed the door behind him, she turned round. "Oh, my god," she said.

"That was awful."

"We really are on our own, aren't we?"

They sat down on the sofa, in silence, thinking about burglars and mad women and kind policemen.

"You know, Tammy," said Alison at last. "I've had a thought. We *are* on our own - but we're also in it *together.*"

"Right," said Tamara but it was a long-drawn out word as if she didn't really know what else to say.

"Look, Gerald died while he was on his own. And Pammie must have wandered to the end of the garden on her own - otherwise someone would have helped her. Someone would have *saved* her."

"I guess so."

"And Venetia was on her own, too. Don't you see? The answer to our problem is that we have to stick together, you and me. We mustn't be alone. Not ever. That way, we can be safe."

"What, constantly together? The whole time?"

"Well, whenever reasonable, yes."

"Do you mean that we should move in together?"

"I do. And as that lovely young constable just told us, your house is as safe as.. well, as safe as houses. And I don't think my flat is a good place for Poppy and Coco - so what do you say to your gaining a lodger? As in, me." She smiled nervously.

Tamara didn't need to think about it for long. "I'd love one."

"Really? Are you sure?" It will be safer, thought Alison. But also what a relief to not be so alone. Thank god.

"Totally sure," said Tamara. "I think it's a great idea."

"And just you wait, it'll be fun, not just safe. I've been learning lots of new things that I can teach you."

"You have? "

"Tell me, Tammy, have you ever heard of the Groin Strike?"

Chapter Twenty Seven

Living together worked well. The two women enjoyed each other's company, despite the age difference. In fact, it helped them to fill the empty gaps. Tamara missed her mother. Alison missed her sister. And when they needed time and space to be alone, there was enough room for that, too.

They agreed that safety was paramount and that meant locking up at night and sticking together whenever possible. In addition, every other evening, they practised the self-defence manoeuvres in Alison's book. They'd got up to Chapter Six and felt confident that they could fight off any but the most determined of attackers. Indeed, Tamara had become positively terrifying.

Leaving the house occasionally was, of course, inevitable.

The two women went shopping together once a week and stayed side by side in the supermarket aisles. Neither of them hung around alone at the chiller cabinets and they parked close to the entrance where there were lots of other people. Alison still had to go to work but, whereas before she had gone to work by bus, now she drove there so that she didn't have to hang around at lonely bus stops. She also avoided staying late at the library and only parked in well-lit spaces, preferably right outside. Tamara stopped her daily run - there were too many shadowy corners and too much shrubbery for that - but she joined a gym and got to know, and trust, the staff.

If a proposed outing sounded too difficult, they chose options that could be enjoyed at home instead. The cinema was out of the question but a good film, sitting on the sofa in the lounge with popcorn and soda, well, that was great. Restaurants might not be sensible but a thoughtfully prepared meal, eaten safely in the dining room, made for a great alternative.

So while cohabitation might not be a forever solution, for now it was a great success.

The one role that Alison didn't enjoy was that of fielding the regular phone calls from Keith. It had started to become embarrassing.

"Can't you just tell him, dear?" she said, one night over dinner.

"I have told him. He doesn't believe me. He thinks I'll come round."

"And will you?"

"No."

"How can you be certain? Is there someone else?"

Tamara hesitated. "Not exactly."

"What does that mean?"

Tamara started to clear the table.

"Not so fast," said Alison. "Firstly, there's still some cake left on my plate and secondly, don't avoid my question."

Tamara put the plate back in front of her cousin. "Sorry, Alison. That was rude of me. I thought you'd finished."

"So what does '*not exactly* 'mean?" Alison picked up her fork and chased the last remaining crumbs. "Poppy, get down, there's none for you!" She pushed the dog away. "Why does she always *do* that to me?"

"It's because she's trying to win you round. She's like Keith - she won't take no for an answer."

"I don't see her doing it to anybody else. She won't leave me alone."

"Well, actually, she's like it with Douglas, too." Tamara smiled. "She adores him but he's so allergic. She clambers all over him. Makes him sneeze like mad."

"Douglas? Is that the chap from the chemist?"

"Yes. You met him at the funeral, I think."

"I remember him - largish man, auburn hair, glasses, winning smile?"

"That's him. He was with me when ....at Venetia's house. I don't know what I would have done without him if I'm honest."

"Have you seen him since?"

"He's come round for coffee once or twice and we've had lots of phone calls. I like his company. He's funny and wise. In fact, Douglas is a really nice person."

"That's it, isn't it?" said Alison. "I can tell from your face when you say his name. It's Douglas - he's the '*not exactly*'."

"I'll take the plates now, shall I?" said Tamara. "Only Fools and Horses' is on in ten minutes."

The first awkward moment came some three weeks after Alison had moved in. She was distracted at the breakfast table, pushing her cereal around the bowl before finally thrusting it away, unfinished. She repeatedly picked up her teacup, without drinking from it. Several times, Tamara asked her a question but had to ask it again before the woman registered that she was being addressed. Finally, although she didn't want to pry, Tamara felt that she had to ask.

"Is there something wrong, Alison?"

Alison was staring out into the distance. She didn't even flinch when Poppy, ever hopeful, put her paw on the woman's lap.

Tamara sat down at the table. Then she leaned forward and touched her hand. "Alison?"

"Yes?" She looked at Tamara as if she'd only just realised she was there.

"Are you okay? You don't seem yourself."

"Me? No, I'm fine, sorry, just got lots on my mind. And I'm a bit tired - I didn't sleep well last night." Abruptly, she stood up, pushing the dog away. She took her bowl and cup to the sink and rinsed them, leaving Tamara sitting there, feeling rather foolish.

When Alison turned around and saw her cousin's face, she hesitated for a moment. Then she sat down again.

"You've a right to the truth, Tammy dear - and you're spot -on. I'm *not* myself today." She gazed down at her hands which she was twisting clumsily in her lap. "I knew you'd see it but I didn't want to say anything. I don't like to make a fuss. But I just can't help myself. It's such a difficult day for me every year, not just this one."

"Why? What's happened?"

"It's the date, you see. It's the anniversary."

"But what of?"

"It was thirty six years ago today that my Pammie..." she hesitated. "That she went into the water at Pond Hill."

"Oh....." Tamara flushed bright red and the words of sympathy, though they were sincere, stayed lodged in her throat. She'd grown up with the guilt of what her father had done. As a child, she'd recognised that her dad's cousin was 'a bit simple'. Her mother had given her a version of the accident but Karen had told her the truth one terrible summer's day after Pammie had thrown a tantrum at a family barbecue.

"It's not her fault, Tammy," she'd said. "She can't help it. If anyone's to blame, it's your dad. Don't look at me like that, with those huge sheep eyes. I know what they will have told you - and it's not true. Pammie didn't fall. Your dad *pushed* her into the water. It's his fault that Pammie's like she is. HIS fault."

"It's not that I'm morbid," said Alison. "I don't do anything different when the day arrives - but I'm aware of it. I feel a heaviness. It's worse than when she actually *died* because, if I'm honest, she'd been long lost by then. She left us thirty years ago, not three."

"I'm really sorry," said Tamara. "It's kind of you to try and save my feelings - but I know what my dad did. I'm so, so sorry."

Alison took her hand. "Tammy, dear, it's not your fault. I don't blame your dad anymore. He was only a child himself. It's all in the past. Let's not talk about it. It does no good. It certainly won't bring her back." She stood up and brushed hair off her skirt. "That damned dog."

Tamara gave her a hug. "I'm so glad you suggested moving in, I really am."

Alison blushed. "You're a very kind girl." She looked down at her watch. "Goodness, I'd better be going. "

She walked out into the hall, from where she called, "Oh, before I forget - I've found a little something for you at the library. " She came back into the kitchen with her coat on. "Like I say, it's nothing extravagant - but I think you'll like it."

"That sounds intriguing. Thank you!"

"I found it when I was weeding the archive stacks and I thought of you immediately. When you see it, you'll know why."

"How long can I keep it?"

"It's forever. I've purchased it for you."

"You've bought it? I didn't know you could do that with library books."

"Indeed you can. Selling withdrawn books is a small but steady income stream for us. I'll bring it home tonight. Which reminds me, dear, I know we agreed that I wouldn't stay out late but I've got no option this evening, I'm afraid - so don't worry when I'm not back at six."

"Out on a date?" said Tamara, smiling.

"Yes," said Alison. "In the library with twenty Brownies and assorted parents."

"But it's not a Brownie night. How come?"

"I'm participating in a cunning scheme."

"Cunning? That doesn't sound like you at all."

"Well, needs must. We've got a new Brownie, Chloe Marshall. Very shy, very awkward. Her mum's come up with an idea to help her make friends. I don't suppose you've ever heard of a woman called Charmiane Belinda?"

"I don't think so - should I have done?"

"As you're post-pubertal, no, not really."

"So who is she?"

"Charmiane Belinda is a fantastically popular author - God knows how. As chance would have it, she's also related to little Chloe Marshall. I've been persuaded by the family to host an interview at the library tonight where I'll be putting questions to the author. I use the term loosely."

"Is she so bad?"

"Well, her main character is a ten year old girl who also happens to be a crime-fighting werewolf. I'll leave you to imagine the rest. But God help us, the kids love it."

"So all the little Brownies swooning in the audience will want to be Chloe's friend?"

"That's the plan."

"Good luck! Hope it works."

Alison smiled and left. Five minutes later, she was back.

"You'll never believe it, Tammy - my car won't start. I've tried everything - well, more specifically, I've revved it to death and now I think I've flooded the engine. I thought I'd better let you know that I'll be going to work on the bus. Which means I'll be late - Hell and damnation!"

"Don't even think of it," said Tamara. "I'll take you there in my car. Give me five minutes to get dressed."

"Really? That would be great! Of course, I'll get the bus back home again tonight."

"Not a chance," said Tamara. "After all our commitment to not being alone? Standing at a bus stop in the dark? No way. What time shall I come and get you?"

"Are you sure, dear?"

"I'm entirely sure."

"Well, the interview finishes at half seven. By the time I've tidied and locked the place up, I guess I'll be ready to leave at about eight. "

"I'll be outside the library at quarter to."

"You really are marvellous!" she said as she kissed her on the cheek.

They had both forgotten that the best-laid of plans don't always work out as they should.

Chapter Twenty Eight

At half past five, the last reader left the library and Alison breathed a sigh of relief. Peace at last. It hadn't been an easy day. This year, as every year, she'd tried not to dwell on her sister and those cataclysmic moments of thirty years before, but it wasn't easy. *If only.* That was the constant phrase. If only she hadn't left her sister at the water's edge. If only Pammie hadn't teased Gerald. If only he'd been less vindictive. How different, then, Pammie's life might have been. And how different her own. At which point, she felt a wave of irritation with herself. Get a grip, Alison, she thought. When will you learn? This maudlin nonsense helps nobody. She repeated the words, slowly and calmly. It's the past. It's unalterable and it's merciless. You've got to move on, or you'll just go mad.

She forced herself to concentrate on sensible, practical matters. The upcoming author interview, yes, that was it. She had just under an hour before it was due to start - leaving plenty of time for a cup of tea with Gordon and perhaps a biscuit or two. She also had a bit of Brownie admin to do - badge sorting mainly. After that, they'd lay out the chairs and move a few book racks to create a space for where she and Charmiane Belinda would sit later on. If the evening was a success, this was an area that she might explore further - getting in guest speakers was a great way to advertise the library and to increase membership. It would also advertise the Brownie pack and that could only be a good thing.

She wouldn't be able to manage any of this without Gordon, though. It was hefty physical work, laying out the room. She appreciated the way that he'd offered to help, rather than waited to be asked. He was always like this. Smiling and kind and thoughtful. His willingness made everything so much easier. He was a godsend.

Thinking about his easy manner reminded her of PC Danvers and thinking of him reminded her of Tamara. And that, in turn, reminded her of the book that she'd bought for her cousin. Despite her intention to put it straight into her bag as soon as she got to work, she'd forgotten. She'd do it now. It was quite big and would only just fit inside - she was pretty sure she wouldn't be able to zip the bag up again. No matter.

She went into the office and pulled the book out of the top drawer of her desk. With a smile, she opened the cover. But when she had a proper look at the contents page, she almost fell off her chair. She couldn't believe the hideous coincidence of the first story. Not only that, but someone, at some time, had committed the cardinal sin of folding over the page the story was on, thereby drawing still more attention to it. Today of all days. She closed it slowly.

She heard Gordon calling and so she opened her handbag and slid the book inside. A handful of detritus was displaced by it and sprawled out over her desk - hankies, Brownie badges, a packet of chewing gum. She shovelled it all back in and struggled in vain to close the zip. Eventually, she gave in and hung it by the strap over her chair where it gaped open, the spine of the book facing upwards.

"Ready to do the chairs, boss?" he said, poking his head round the door. "Time for a cuppa first?"

"Definitely. And don't even *think* of giving me a chipped mug."

At half past six, Charmiane Belinda sat next to her, all perma-curl hair and lip gloss. In front of them, two dozen beaming little girls and their mums were ranged in three concentric rows. There were no dads available to attend the talk, it seemed.

"Good evening, everybody," said Alison, standing and smiling at them. "I'd like to thank you all for coming to the library tonight and, in particular, I would like to extend a warm welcome to our guest, Charmiane Belinda, creator of the extraordinary young heroine, Lupa WhiteFang."

An hour later, as the last answer to the final question came to an end, Alison clapped her hands and encouraged the audience to do the same. Their applause was rapturous. Charmiane Belinda stood up and smiled graciously, the book from which she had read aloud clasped under her arm. The Brownies jumped from their seats and gathered around her skirts, little Chloe Marshall in particular. The child was now guaranteed an endless supply of playdates. Their task was done.

Gordon escorted the chattering children and their families off the premises. She could hear the called goodbyes and thank yous and smiled. He was so effortlessly popular with the girls and their mums. He had the knack of making people like him. He was a lucky man. And she was a lucky woman to work with him.

He came back in through the swing doors just as she had started to move the chairs back to their rightful places. Two years ago, she would have known that he was there because of the rather fetid smell that he would have brought in with him. If Lucy had done anything positive in her life, it was this. Well, that and putting an end to her own snooping days.

"Well done," said Gordon, as he slid the first book rack back. "That was a really successful evening. Lots of happy little girls."

"Yes, it went well, I think."

"It was great," he said. "Actually, boss, *you* were great. I didn't know you could do this sort of thing. You were dead impressive."

"Didn't know I could do *what* sort of thing?"

"Public speaking - I thought you'd be shy. But you nailed it."

"Well, a little girl's happiness was at stake. It was important."

In silence, they lifted and moved the chairs and racks until the room looked like it should do. It was almost quarter to eight. Time for her to lock up and meet Tamara outside. How kind the girl was, she thought, and how lucky it was that they got on so easily.

Living with any other family member wouldn't have worked half so well. Well, in fact, of course, the only other relative was Karen and living with her would have been a nightmare. She was such a difficult person.

They'd heard nothing from her since that awful dinner in Tamara's house. Still, she supposed they should get in touch with her and make the peace. After all, they were family and they should pull together right now.

Musing on this thought, she was rather careless about where she placed her feet and thus it was that she managed to trip over a carpet edge and fall. And this made it possible for Gordon to catch her. They stared at each other for a moment and she felt so warm and aroused by him that she was shocked. She gazed into his eyes, her heart pounding, her breath shallow. He didn't immediately let her go.

"Gordon," she said, "I think that I'm in love with you."

He released her gently and stepped back. Gazing down at the carpet, his face flamed red. Even his ears were scarlet. She gazed awkwardly over his shoulder.

"Alison," he said at last, "you're such a wonderful person but-"

"I know - you don't have to say anything more. I get it. I'm no Charmiane Belinda. And I'm certainly no Lucy."

"*Lucy?*" He looked at her then. "What has *she* got to do with it?"

"Gordon...." Long pause. He didn't fill it, so she had to. "It's quite simple."

This was a make or break moment - she had to take her courage in her hands. It was not in her character to be forward - but neither was she a coward. She'd started this so she'd have to finish it and deal with the consequences whatever they were.

"Look," she continued, "I'm under no illusions. I'm a middle-aged woman with sciatica and thick ankles. I love books, I love the library, I love my Brownies and, yes, I love you. I've tried not to say it, but now I have and I can't take it back. I thought - it was foolish of me - but I thought - I hoped - that maybe you felt the same."

For a moment, there was silence and then, eventually, he said, "I never slept with her, you know."

"With who?"

"With Lucy. I wanted to but I just couldn't bring myself to touch her. God knows why, but she was mad keen to move in with me. And I agreed to it because, I don't know, I was flattered, I suppose. And I guess, too, that maybe I thought it would help me be different."

"Different?"

"Different to what I really am."

"I don't understand," said Alison. "What are you trying to say?"

"Alison, I've never had sex with a woman - not ever. I'm not capable." His face looked tortured. "Please don't make me say it. You've no idea how difficult this is for me."

"Gordon, do you mean...are you *impotent?*"

"No, Alison, for god's sake! Can't you see? Do I have to spell it out? I'm *gay.*"

She turned her back to him and gripped the nearest chair. Her dreams, all of them, ones she hadn't even properly put into words, they were tumbling and ruined. She was never going to find a future with Gordon, love him desperately though she did. She would never live in a sweet cottage, with its laden bookshelves and its candles gleaming on polished wood, with Gordon working in the vegetable garden and waving to her through the window, while she sat inside and peeled potatoes for tea. And there could be no-one else. She was always and forever going to be alone.

Without turning around, she said, "I'm truly sorry, Gordon. I can't apologise enough for embarrassing you."

"Boss, I-"

"You should go." She turned around and faced him, forcing a smile to her lips. "Honestly, we're just about done with the tidying here. I'll lock up."

He stepped forward and held out his hand. "I know this has been an awful moment - for both of us. But please - can we still be friends?"

"Of course. Of course, we're still friends. It was just a mistake, that's all, a silly mistake." She took his hand and held it for a moment. "Can we try and forget it ever happened?"

"Absolutely. I've forgotten it already!" He tried to laugh but it sounded hollow.

"I could do with a moment on my own, if that's ok," she said. "Just to re-group."

He started to say something more - she couldn't guess what - what was there left to say? - and then he closed his mouth, turned and walked away through the double swing doors.

She sat alone in the quiet, her eyes closed while she breathed in the calming smell of the books. There was no point in crying. Being with Gordon was not to be her destiny. She could deal with that. She would accept the new path she was on because the old one, the one she'd hoped for, was never going to be hers. It was sad - *so sad* - but on this day, of *all* days, she should see how precious life was, even without the man by her side that she'd hoped was going to be her companion forever. She must move on. Be resolute.

Five minutes later, she followed in Gordon's footsteps, her coat on, her gaping bag slung heavily over one shoulder. She felt very old. Very old and very tired. She pushed open the swing doors and stepped into the lobby.

Just as she put her hand on the main door, all the lights went out.

Chapter Twenty Nine

She almost gasped aloud at the sudden gloom and then quickly got a grip of herself. Don't panic, Alison, she thought. You're fine. It's just a blown fuse. Stay steady. It's hardly pitch-black in here. There was still evening light coming in from the windows cut high into the front of the library building.

She felt along the wall until she came to the fuse box but, though she repeatedly flicked the switches, the lights wouldn't come back on. Part of the problem was that it was too dark to see the box properly. This was a job for another day. She'd lock up and go home and get the lights sorted tomorrow. She'd get somebody in.

She pulled at the latch on the main front door. To her astonishment, it wouldn't budge. She couldn't really see it very well and so she was forced to fumble with it but, pull as she might, the door remained stubbornly closed. She was locked in. Soon, there would be no light at all. Would she have to spend the night here? Alone in the dark?

That was no way to think. Mindless fear got a person nowhere. What she *should* do was consider her options. The telephone. She would find her way to the library office and call Tammy. No, that was no good - by now , the girl would be outside, in the car, waiting for her. What an irony - so close but utterly unreachable. Right, this was an emergency and she was going to call the police - 999 was an easy number to dial in the darkness. How astonished Tammy would be to see police cars arriving.

What a hideous end to a horrible day.

She stumbled back into the building, her hands outstretched into the murk and edged her way into the library proper. It was a lot darker in there. Pulsating shadows seemed to dance around her. She could barely see enough to walk safely from rack to rack of books. And then, just as she reached Dewey Decimal Classification 500 (Natural‧Science and

Mathematics), she smelt - how could she not have noticed it before? - the oily tang of violets.

Instantly, she dropped to the floor. She waited for no more than a second and then, crawling on all fours, she set off again, in a tearing hurry through the darkness towards the office door. Her heart was thumping wildly, lit by a thrilling mixture of adrenaline and fear. She'd been preparing for this moment for a while now. If Lucy - for surely it was her - if *that woman* tried to grab her, Alison knew exactly what to do.

Back up against the wall, she sat down and felt inside her handbag for her house-keys. She pushed the sharp bits through the side of her closed right fist. "Right, you bitch," she whispered, hesitating only slightly over the last word. "I'm ready for you."

She slid up the wall until she was standing. Hitching her bag securely over her shoulder, she stepped crab-like sideways until the closed office door was behind her. Facing outwards into the library, her eyes searching for shapes in the shadows, she felt with her left hand for the door handle. Her right hand, meanwhile, was tensed and held in front of her, the keys sticking out, ready to stab and thrust.

When she found the handle, she couldn't get the leverage to open it. The angles were all wrong. She bit her lip in frustration. If she wanted to get to the telephone, she was going to have to turn her back to the library. It would make her vulnerable but it was the only way.

The instant she turned away, she heard running footsteps. Just as she put her hand on the door handle, there was a rush of air and then an arm snaking past her spine. It quickly wound itself around her neck, pulling her roughly backwards. She knew immediately who it was, even though she couldn't see.

"It's so lovely to meet you again," whispered Lucy. "After all this time."

Lucy swivelled the two of them around so that they were both facing into the darkness of the library. Alison could hardly breathe. She dropped her bag and the keys and scrabbled at the arm around her neck - to no avail. After that, she tried to thrust her jaw down to her chest. But she couldn't do it. The woman was too strong, her arm too thick. Her next thought was that she'd bend forward, taking Lucy with her. Then she'd step sideways to off-balance her. She'd follow that up with a swift and satisfying Groin Strike.

Just as she was tensing herself to lean, she realised that there was another figure standing in front of her. Lucy hadn't come to the library alone. Through the gloom, she could just about see who the other person was. She could hardly believe her eyes.

"We're going to go for a little trip into the countryside," Lucy said. "Just the three of us. It's going to be lovely. You'll see."

"When we get into the street," said the figure in the shadows, turning on a torch, "I want you to consider very carefully the terrible consequences of you making a fuss." They picked up Alison's bag. The torchlight fell onto the keys - which were instantly pocketed. "You won't be needing these, I think."

Alison stared. By the light of the torch, she could see perfectly clearly now. This made no sense *at all*.

"Considering how much you love Tammy," said Lucy. "It would be a shame for her to get hurt because of you behaving stupidly." She propelled Alison towards the swing doors. "We know where she lives. Don't forget that. We can get to her quicker than you can imagine and then-"

"-and then," her accomplice continued, holding the swing doors open, "it'll be curtains for poor Tamara."

They don't know, thought Alison, her mind whirling. They don't know that she's waiting outside. She'll see me being bundled out of here. Please God, Tammy, don't try and intervene! Please just go and get help!

"I'm going to release you, now," said Lucy. "But you'd better remember what we said." She let go and Alison rubbed her throat and swallowed. It was sore. But she was still not free because, having released her neck, Lucy grabbed her arm instead. "Don't even think of trying to make a run for it. Remember how selfish that would be."

Thank God Tammy's outside, thought Alison. Thank God.

By torchlight in the lobby Lucy's accomplice knelt down and fiddled inside the fuse box. Instantly, the library lit up and the big front door could be seen. Out came the heavy pin that had been preventing it from opening: with a screech, the bar slid back into its housings. Lucy flicked all the lights off again, one by one, and they were cast back once more into darkness. "Don't want to waste electricity, do we?" she said, smiling.

Alison saw the warning hand being held out as the door into the street was slowly opened. After that, came the quick check outside, presumably to make sure that there were no busybodies around.

232

But Tamara's going to be a busybody, thought Alison. She'll see this pair kidnapping me and she'll know what to do.

The three of them emerged outside. How absolutely normal it all looks, thought Alison, how just the same as always. And yet, it was also utterly different. How beautiful the world suddenly seemed beneath the glow of the lamps. How dear the Georgian buildings next door. How elegant the park gates opposite. How awful to think she might never see any of it again.

That's no way to think, she remonstrated with herself. You will see this street again. Of course you will. Tammy will save you. And there, underneath the street lamp, with a spurt of joy in her heart, she saw the car waiting, just as she'd known it would be.

But the car wasn't Tammy's.

Her shoulders sagged. There was no hope now, no escape. She'd lost. They'd won.

"We'll need to take her handbag with us," said Lucy. "Have you still got it?"

"Yes, but what the hell's in it?" The heavy book was pulled out. "This can't stay in her bag. She'd hardly take a massive book like that with her - not on the trip she's supposed to be on."

"You're right." Lucy reached across, took the book and threw it onto the ground. "We'll just leave it here. And turn off that damned torch, will you? It'll attract attention. You don't need it anymore anyway. It's not that dark outside yet. Now come on, let's get her into the car."

Oh, thought Alison, if only I'd read Chapter 8, 'How to fight off two attackers'. Then she would have shown them what for. But then - if she *did* try to fight back - which was her natural instinct - she might put Tammy in danger. She still had *words* though.

"Look," she said, trying to sound firm and reasonable. "You must see you're making a huge mistake. People will come looking for me, you know that."

"Alison," said Lucy. "Get real. No-one cares what happens to you. You've got no parents and no loopy sister anymore." She smirked. "Not even a gay boyfriend to come searching - hah! That was a sad moment, wasn't it?"

Alison wrenched her arm away from Lucy's grip and slapped her across the face.

"You old bitch!" Lucy cried . She rubbed her cheek. A dark handprint blazed across it. In fury, she pulled her own hand back, clearly about to reciprocate.

Her partner grabbed her wrist. "Get a hold of yourself, will you? What would they make of a mark like that on her skin?"

Lucy pulled her arm away. "Don't you *ever* tell me what to do again," she said. And then she turned to Alison. "I'm looking forward to the next hour or so. I don't think you'll be able to say the same. And you can't imagine what pleasure that thought brings me."

Alison felt sick. Her legs trembled. But she didn't fall to the floor because they didn't allow that to happen. They had grabbed an elbow each, just as if she were an old lady wanting to cross the road and they were benign Boy Scouts.

Chapter Thirty

Tamara,

Earlier that evening

Just before seven, Tamara set off to pick up Alison. She had given herself more time than was needed but she intended to savour the journey. She had chosen a longer, pretty route to get maximum enjoyment from what remained of the evening light and stared happily out of her window at the lanes and fields and trees she passed on the way.

She still made good progress, especially as the traffic in town, once she got there, was light. She turned the radio on and hummed along. Undoubtedly, there were lots of reasons to be anxious right now - but there were also lots of reasons to be cheerful if a person just looked for them.

At a junction only two blocks away from the library, the car immediately in front of hers stalled when the traffic lights turned green. They changed all the way back to red and returned to green again and still the car wouldn't start, despite the chorus of car-horns behind it. Regardless of the driver's frantic and repeated turning of the key, plus all the advice from well-meaning passers-by, that car wasn't going to go anywhere apart from, perhaps, on the back of a pick-up truck. All the vehicles behind, including Tamara's, were forced to reverse and find an alternative route.

The delay meant that she was unlikely to get to the library until after eight but she didn't think that would matter too much. Alison would be fine about it. And when they got home again, they could sit in the garden with a glass of wine and maybe a bowl of Twiglets.

Once she reached the library, she was disappointed to see that Alison wasn't waiting for her on the pavement. What was worse, the solitary parking space outside the building had already been taken. Damn. Now she'd have to park at the multistorey. The thought did not thrill her.

And then she took a closer look at the car that had taken the library parking spot. It was a vehicle that she recognised. A vehicle that surprised her by its presence there.

What on earth? she said to herself. What are they doing here?

Still puzzling over this, she drove away. Luckily, just before she reached the multistorey - a place of frightening silences and scary dark corners - she spotted an on-road space which she took gratefully. She walked back at speed. She was now half an hour later than she'd said she'd be. Alison would think her rude.

When she reached the library, she noticed, with a flash of irritation, that the car was gone from outside. Maybe if she'd hovered a bit, she could have nabbed that space herself.

She was a bit surprised to see that there was still no sign of anyone waiting. Alison must have gone back inside to wait, she thought. Well, that was sensible. No point in hanging about on a deserted pavement when you could wait indoors in safety. Except that, as she looked at the library windows, the building appeared to be in darkness. Perhaps any lights that were on inside couldn't be seen from the road.

She tried to push open the library door but, as she had expected, it was locked. She was pleased that Alison had taken this precaution. Then she banged on it. There was no answer. She banged on it again and, this time, she yelled *Alison!* through the letter-box.

It was then that she began to become afraid.

She tried to think a little more clearly. Maybe Alison had waited for her at the library but had got anxious at the delay. That was understandable. Maybe she'd phoned around looking for a lift from someone else. Maybe that was why that familiar car had been here earlier on. That was it. *They'd* taken Alison home instead. The thing to do was to ring home and check she was okay. Which, of course, she would be.

She walked to the telephone box on the corner. The home number dialled, she held the receiver close to her ear, her hand tense. When the phone peeped to show the call had been answered, she could have laughed in relief. She thrust a ten-pence piece into the slot, ready to apologise and to laugh with Alison at how foolish she'd been.

Hi, this is Tamara. Sorry, I'm not here to answer your call. Please leave your number and I'll get back to you as soon as I can. Thanks.

Her heart sank.

Maybe Alison was still enroute? She should leave a message. Alison would walk into the hall and see the answerphone flashing and she'd listen to it and understand instantly what had happened and so wouldn't worry about the empty house she was standing in.

"Hi, Alison," she said, "it's me... Look, I'm so sorry I wasn't there to pick you up after work like I'd promised. There was this car that broke down in front of me and....look, never mind, I'll tell you all about it later. It's a long story... Anyway, I'm in the call box outside the library and - of course - you're not here - because you're at home!... So I'm on my way back right now - or I will be the moment I put down the phone! Hope you're not too cross with me...Huge apologies for letting you down ... .I'll see you very soon ...."

She wondered if there was anything more she should add. The phone peeped for more money. She didn't put another coin in. The message she'd left was garbled enough.

She looked at her watch - almost half past eight. Then she opened her purse and gazed at the contents. She had two more ten-pence pieces. She knew that she'd just promised to come straight home but there was one more person she thought she should ring. Just in case.

Karen answered straightaway, almost as if she'd been waiting for it to ring. "Oh," she said, "it's you."

"Hi," said Tamara, "sorry, but I had to call. I don't suppose Alison is with you?"

"No - should she be?"

"Well, I just thought I'd ask. It's just that - well, this is really urgent."

"Isn't it always?"

"It's a long story and I don't have time right now to go through it all. But I could do with your help - or at least some advice. I don't know what to do."

"Let me guess - there's been another disaster? Or a death... .or wicked Lucy's hiding in your garden..."

"Look, none of those things... I hope....No, I'm sure everything's fine."

"Well that's a first. So what's happened that's so urgent?"

237

"Alison and I are living together right now and-"

"Living together? Why?"

"We just are, okay?" Tamara knew she sounded exasperated so she tried again. "We thought it would be safer - considering."

"Oh, Lord...." Karen sighed deeply. "Here we go."

Tamara couldn't answer. Why did Karen always have to be so horrible? Why couldn't she, just for once, say something kind?

And maybe Karen heard this unspoken thought. "Sorry, Tammy," she said, "don't mind me. I'm just a bit tired and peevish tonight. What's happened? Why have you *actually* rung?"

"Alison's car wouldn't start this morning so I took her to work. The thing is, I was supposed to pick her up again tonight and I was really late getting to the library - and she's not here. It's all locked up and in darkness. I don't know what to do. I'm really worried."

For a moment there was silence. Oh, lord, thought Tamara. If she's concerned too, then there really must be a problem.

But apparently not because, a heartbeat later, Karen said, "Well, it's obvious, isn't it? She got fed up with waiting for you and caught a bus home instead. That sounds like her. She's hardly the most patient of people."

"I've rung home and she's not there."

"Try again.. Give it more time. Ring again in ten minutes. Or just drive there now and see. You're making a mountain out of a molehill."

"Do you really think so?"

"Certain of it. If you get there and you still can't find her, ring me again and we'll talk about what to do next." She paused. "Anyway, Tammy, while I've got you - I think I should tell you that something big has happened."

More money! shrieked the phone. Tamara hesitated. This was her last coin but she had to know what it was that Karen wanted to tell her. There was also a slightly awkward question that she herself would like to ask, if she only knew how to phrase it. She plunged the ten-pence into the slot.

"You're not the only one who's changed their domestic arrangements," said Karen. "As of last week, I am officially Mrs Amandeep Singh."

"Wow! I mean, congratulations! That's great! "

"When the phone rang, that's who I thought it was going to be - my lovely new husband."

"So he's away then?"

"He's in Wolverhampton at a trade fair. Back tomorrow."

"I'm so pleased for you both. It's super news."

"I'm thinking of having a little celebration - say, the Saturday after next. Ask Alison, for me, will you? I think I probably need to mend some fences with her - might as well get it over with. And ask your mum, too, of course, and Larry."

"It's Barry."

"Whatever."

And in the silence that followed, the money ran out again .That awkward question would have to wait.

She closed the kiosk door and leaned against it miserably. What to do? Perhaps Karen was right. She should drive home and see if Alison was there. She *must* be there. The alternative was too horrible to contemplate.

She got in her car and set off. Her mind was so tied in knots that she left the car to find its own way home and thus it was that she took a wrong turning. Not much of one but sufficient to take her along the High Street rather than bypass it. As she drove past the chemist that Venetia used to work in and where Douglas still did, she looked at the flat above it and saw that the lights were on. And that was when she decided that there was someone else who might be able to help.

Provided he could answer one question, something that had really been troubling her.

When he answered the door, she couldn't make up her mind whether he was pleased. Certainly, his face changed when he saw her. He raised his eyebrows and his lips altered shape - but was it a grin? Or a grimace?

"Hi," she said. "I'm really sorry to bother you."

"Not at all," he said. "It's no bother. None at all. It's lovely to see you."

She tried to smile but couldn't quite manage it. He took her arm, "Are you ok? Tamara, what's happened?" Without waiting for an answer, he ushered her in and up the stairs. "Come on, come in. I was just about to open a bottle."

"Thanks, but I'd better not." She sat down on the sofa. "I need to be able to drive. The thing is, Douglas, I'm scared that something bad - I mean, *really* bad - might have happened to Alison."

He sat down next to her. "Tell me everything," he said. "Tell me how I can help."

"Before I do, I need to ask you something."

"That sounds serious!" But when he saw that she did not respond with a smile, he squeezed her hand and said, "Ok, I can see you're anxious. Ask me - fire away."

"When I told you about the tontine, you didn't ask me what that meant. And I have to know why."

"Because I already knew what a tontine was - that's why."

"Sorry - *really* sorry to press you - but how do you know?"

"Because I used to live in Richmond."

She looked at him, utterly confused. The reference meant nothing to her. As he must have quickly realised because he explained.

"The building of Richmond Bridge was financed by a tontine. When it was finished, people had to pay to cross it. The toll-money was shared between the investors. Every time one of them died, the share values went up and the last guy standing got the lot. So it's not quite the same as the tontine your auntie dreamed up - but it was close enough for me to get the gist."

She had to try really hard not to cry. It wasn't fear, it wasn't distress, she knew that. It was relief. It was going to be all right.

Chapter Thirty One

Ten minutes later, they got into Tamara's car. Their plan was to try the library one more time. If it remained clear that Alison was not there, then they would go back to the house where they sincerely hoped that they would find her, sitting in the garden, looking up at the stars, with a cup of tea in her hand. They had rung the home number again from Douglas's flat but there had still been no answer. Maybe she was in the bathroom, Tamara reasoned. Maybe she hadn't heard the telephone from the garden, suggested Douglas. Maybe, she'd ...and then they ran out of all the maybes they were willing to consider.

Tamara pulled in to the parking space outside the library. They both got out and walked in silence to the darkened building.

"Well, she's definitely not here," said Douglas, peering through the letterbox. "But it was still worth trying. Let's drive home now. And if she's not there, we're calling the police."

They got back into the car and, for a moment, Tamara gazed at the windscreen and then down at the gear stick as if she'd never seen them before and didn't know what to do with them.

Douglas looked at her. "Try not to worry too much," he said. "I know that's easy for me to say - but I honestly do think it will be all right. We *will* find her and she *will* be safe."

"Oh, if only certainty and hope were enough," she said. "But thank you - I literally don't know what I'd do if you weren't here. I'm beginning to feel numbed by it all."

"Do you want me to drive?"

"No, honestly - it's fine. It gives me something to concentrate on."

She turned the key and the engine burst into life. Immediately, her headlamps lit up the front wall of the library. She stared at it, unseeing, because a new possibility had just occurred to her. What if Alison was locked inside but had fallen ill? In that case they'd need to get a key.

Who else would have one? Gordon? Perhaps, but where did he live? She felt sure that Alison had told her but she couldn't quite recall it.

It was while she was thinking about this that her brain finally registered what it was that her eyes were seeing.

"There's something on the ground," she said. "Just to the side of the library door. Look, do you see? It's lying half on the pavement, half in the hedge."

Leaving the headlamps on, she turned the engine off and got out of the car. Douglas followed her. At the library door, she bent down and picked up a large book. It was a Tammy Annual from 1986.

"I think this belongs to Alison," she said.

"Really? How can you know?"

"She told me about it this morning - or, at least, dropped massive hints. She said she'd found a special surprise for me, something that was a perfect gift."

"My sister used to get these," said Douglas, "every Christmas. But her name is Liz. I can see why Alison would think you'd like it. There was never a Douglas Annual, sadly."

"Venetia used to give these annuals to me every year but she stopped when I was about twelve. I've been on a hunt ever since, trying to track them all down. I've got every single one except for this, the 1986 edition. It was the last annual they ever published. Alison knows I've been looking for it. I'm certain she planned to give it to me tonight."

"What on earth is it doing out here?"

"I don't know." She flicked through the pages.

Douglas peered over her shoulder. "Isn't there a page turned over? Bit surprising in a library book."

"There is." Tamara opened the book at the page that had a folded-down corner. "I need to get this into some proper light - I'm not sure I've read the words right. It seems too much of a coincidence."

They walked back to the car, Tamara carrying the book out in front of her as if it were a tea-tray. Once inside, she turned on the interior light and looked again at the turned-down page.

"No," she said, "I was right. And it *is* a coincidence, a big one. I think Alison will have been really upset to read this." She held the book open and tilted it to face Douglas "Do you see? It's called '*Pamela at Pond Hill*."

"Sorry," he said, "but I'm not sure I get it. I know that was her sister's name - but the Pond Hill bit? Why is that significant?"

"It's the name of the nature reserve just outside town - do you know it? "

He nodded. "I do."

"It's where Pammie nearly drowned when she was twelve. It left her brain-damaged. Ruined her life. And Alison's too, probably. And that happened exactly thirty six years ago today."

He took the book from her. "Today? So it's an anniversary of sorts. Was Alison upset this morning?"

"Big time."

He started to read the story. It didn't appear to be about water. Maybe it was all just chance.

"Douglas, do you think Alison left it here on purpose? I don't know, as some kind of sign? A message?"

"Hang on," he said, staring into the darkness of the footwell, "I think something just dropped out of it." He bent down and then turned to Tamara, his palm open. "What on earth is this?"

In the middle of his outstretched hand lay a triangular brown patch of cotton. Embroidered in yellow across the centre was a picture of a fish hovering over three bubbles of water. Across the top were stitched the words *BROWNIE GUIDES*.

"Well, that clinches it," said Tamara. She took it from him and held it up in the light. "This is definitely Alison's. It's a Brownie Swimmer Badge."

"I suppose you got loads of these things when you were a kid?"

"This was the only one I failed. I was hopeless. Sank like a stone. I still do. I just can't get the hang of swimming."

Tamara stared at the annual and at the little triangle of brown cotton and tried to make sense of it.

"I think we should set off for your house pronto," said Douglas. "We can take these things with us. They must have just fallen out of her bag or something." He reached up to turn off the light and then fastened his seat belt. "And then we can sit and star-gaze in the garden - which is what I bet Alison is already doing."

Tamara put the book and badge on the back seat, pulled out into the road and drove away. God, she wished she could share his confidence. What was stopping her was the nagging certainty that she was missing something. Her mind was in such a fog of overload, it prevented her from thinking clearly. She forced herself to concentrate on the mechanics of the journey. Listen to the engine. Change gear. Check in the mirror, indicate, make the manoeuvre.

But in the background, her brain was quietly putting all of the pieces together. And when it had finished making the connections – wrong though they were it shouted them to her so fast and so urgently that she slammed on the brakes and Douglas lurched forward and nearly snapped his collarbone on the seatbelt.

"What the hell?" Douglas said, rubbing his shoulder. "What did you do *that* for?"

"I've got it," she said, gripping the steering wheel and staring out through the glass. "I understand everything."

"Not about the Highway Code you don't." He swivelled round and looked in horror through the back window. "For Christ's sake, Tamara, there's a load of cars coming up right behind us - and we're just sitting here in the middle of the road. Get going again, will you? Lucy won't need to polish us off - you're going to do it for her."

"Alison did leave that book and badge for me to find," she said, swinging the car across the carriageway into the beginnings of a three-point turn. "And we're going the wrong way."

As she reversed into the second part of the manoeuvre, a car swept up from behind and dodged past them, its horn blaring. Another one appeared at speed from the other direction. "*Sorry,*" mouthed Douglas. The car went around them, the man sticking his fingers up in a very unfriendly fashion.

Tamara took the car into the final part of the turn just as an articulated lorry appeared on the horizon. And then she stalled.

"I am a man not given to exaggeration," said Douglas in a tight, controlled voice. "But I am about to soil my pants. A three-point turn? On a blind corner? And now you've stalled the car. We are going to die."

"Just bear with me a second." She put the handbrake on and turned the key several times. The engine coughed and sputtered and then burst into life. They sped off, a whisker away from annihilation by 32 tonnes of road-haulage. This near-miss caused Tamara's focus to crumple and the car lurched to the right into the face of the oncoming traffic. And then back to the left as Douglas grabbed the steering wheel.

"Let go! " she shouted, batting at his hands.

"Jesus, Mary and Joseph!" shouted Douglas. "Stop this car straightaway. Pull over!"

She pulled into a lay-by and looked at him. Beneath the glare of the sodium lights, his face had taken on a greenish, sweaty tinge.

"Right," he said. "Get out. I'm driving. You've lost your mind."

"I'm sorry, Douglas. I know that was all a bit mad - I panicked. But I understand now where we have to go - and we don't have much time to get there."

He sighed. "That was the single most terrifying experience of my life - but I know you must have had a good reason to drive like a lunatic. So what is it?"

"Look, Alison deliberately arranged for me to come to the library tonight. She left that book outside so that I would find it - it's a message." She pointed to the back seat. "It's a Tammy - that's my name. There's a turned-down page about a girl called Pamela and what happened to her at a place called Pond Hill. Pond Hill is where Pammie nearly drowned thirty years ago today. And what's more, there's a swimming badge inside the book."

"And...?"

"For God's sake - don't you see?"

"Tamara, my brain is currently inaccessible on account of its recent brush with death. What exactly am I supposed to see?"

"I think ..." she was hardly able to force out the words. "Douglas, I really believe that Alison's gone to Pond Hill to drown herself. We've got to get there - fast - and stop her."

They set off from the layby, Douglas at the wheel and Tamara sitting next to him, her face drawn and white. At a deserted junction on the fringes of the town, just before the final signpost for Pond Hill Nature Reserve, he pulled in beneath the shadow of the trees.

"Wait here," he said.

He opened the door. She leaned across and put a hand on his arm. "What will you say?"

"It'll come to me," he said, turning his head to face her.

She watched him cross the empty road. The lights inside the telephone booth glared yellow above his head. Five minutes later, he was back. He sat in silence for a second then did up his seat belt and started the engine. He looked across at her, took her hand and clasped it tightly.

"Don't worry," he said. "Everything will be okay. Trust me."

She nodded.

They took the turning to the Nature Reserve and drove along the ancient sunken lane. The canopy of trees met overhead like black lace on navy satin. Exposed roots, gnarled as witches' fingers, reached out from the banks to either side. Tamara stared ahead through the windscreen and imagined dark figures rearing up from the shadows or, even worse, transporting themselves into the back seat of the car. She didn't dare look behind her just in case.

"I hate the countryside," said Douglas. "It's so unreliable... cosy one moment, bat-shit scary the next."

I like it," said Tamara. "Not this, obviously - not these black lanes and creepy trees. But I love thatched cottages and rose gardens and dappled orchards. I'd like to live in the countryside one day."

"Give me the city any day - fewer surprises."

"Or just less variety."

"Should we head for the car park?" he said. "That's got to be down here somewhere."

"She must have come by taxi. She could have been dropped off anywhere."

"Well, how do we get to the water? Hang on - just ahead - there's a road on the left. That's the right direction, I think." He stopped. "Isn't there a sign on that post?" He screwed up his eyes. "I can't make it out."

"It says..." she leaned forward, "...'*Entrance to lakes*'."

Douglas took the turning and drove along it cautiously And then he stopped the car altogether. Barring the way was a pair of padlocked gates.

"This is it then," he said. "Journey's end. By car at least."

He turned off the headlamps. Without them, the sky didn't seem quite as dark nor the shadows quite so dense. They both got out. Beyond the locked gates, there appeared to be nothing but a solid wall of dense dark forest.

She put one hand on the car roof and tried to quell her fear by forcing herself to concentrate on the metal beneath her fingers and on the smells in the air. The earthy, mushroomy fragrance of the trees was pungent and rich. She breathed it in, straightened her shoulders, closed the car door and took a step away from it. From the blackness of the woods, an owl hooted and an animal shrieked. She grabbed Douglas's hand.

"Come on, old girl," he said. "There's nothing to be afraid of." He didn't sound convinced, though.

They walked together around the gateposts and set off into the gloom. After a few yards, they reached what appeared to be a quivering barricade of bush and shrub. Douglas began to lead the way forward, one step at a time. Abruptly, the path veered to the left and suddenly the way ahead was wide and moon-lit, a white glow slanting across the trees along the path edge. She grasped his hand still tighter.

Please God, let me be in time, she thought. Please let me save her. And then she had another idea: maybe Alison has just come to *look* at the lake? Just to remember it, to honour her sister with her presence on this significant day. After all, surely a person can't force themselves to drown? Especially as Alison is an excellent swimmer. But maybe she's weighted down her dress? Wasn't that what Virginia Woolf did? Put stones in her pocket and walked out into the water?

Horrible images burst into her mind of Alison, cold and weeping, and drifting down into the black lake, her dress heavy with rocks. Or perhaps even now, she was lying back amongst the bulrushes and gazing up at the same moon that Tamara was looking at.

"Can we go a bit faster?" She quickened her step until she was almost running. It began to feel as if she were dragging Douglas along behind her, his hand slipping out of hers.

And that was when they heard the voices. Or rather, it was laughter.

Tamara heard it first. For Douglas, it might have been masked by the wheeze of his lungs. When she suddenly stopped, he almost ran into the back of her.

"Thank God," he panted. "I thought I was going to have the embarrassment of asking you to slow-" And then he stopped. "What's that?"

And there it was again. The laughter of a woman who didn't care who heard. It came from the left of the path. They tiptoed together to the edge of the trees and listened.

And then they heard a voice. A woman's voice.

"We'll have to go into the forest," said Tamara. "That's definitely where it's coming from. It doesn't sound like Alison, but whoever it is might have seen her, you never know."

He nodded. "Okay. Let me just get my breath back."

Tamara didn't wait. She plunged into the woods and he had no choice but to follow. In her wake, tree branches thrashed into his face and one of them thwacked him straight in the glasses. The bridge snapped and he had to grab it to stop both halves of his spectacles from falling into the undergrowth. He held them onto his nose with one hand and pushed the branches aside with the other. Presently, he found himself in a little hollow, all alone in the darkness amidst the rustling leaves and waving branches.

"Tamara, where are you?" he whispered. "Tamara?"

And then Tamara came sliding back through the trees to get him. She took his hand. "I've found her," she said. "But she's not alone. You won't believe it."

She led him by the hand until the trees thinned out and they reached the water's edge. Here, she stopped and hid behind the trunk of a weeping willow. She motioned him to stand behind her. Then she put one finger across her lips, mouthed, "sshh...." and pointed.

Perhaps twenty feet to the other side of the willow, three figures stood at the lakeside, drenched in moonlight. One of them was a slim brunette whose chiselled cheekbones were cast into even greater relief by the silver wash. Next to her was a dumpy, middle-aged woman, who stood erect and upright like a sergeant major. The person furthest away was tall and elegant. His turban glowed like a beacon beneath the glitter and glow of the night sky.

Chapter Thirty Two

For a while, the pair of them stared in silence at the three people by the lake. Finally, Tamara broke the silence. "It was his car I saw outside the library tonight," she whispered. "He's supposed to be in Wolverhampton."

"Quiet, he's saying something," said Douglas.

"So this here, Alison," said Mr Singh, brandishing a piece of paper, "is your suicide note. Would you like to read it? You're very sad about your sister. It's very moving."

"Don't be ridiculous," said Alison. "People will see straightaway that that's not my writing. You're mad."

"On the contrary," said Lucy. "Everyone will believe it's yours. The writing is identical."

"That's not possible," said Alison. "My handwriting is very distinctive."

"Ah," said Mr Singh, "but my mate Spenser is an excellent forger. All he needed was something to copy - like, for instance, that postcard you sent to Karen last year. Bingo!"

"We're just going to pop this note into your handbag," said Lucy, taking it from him, "and leave it here to be found on this nice big rock. We would have liked to put it on the dashboard of your car, but seeing as you didn't drive to work today, we're having to think on our feet a bit."

"On the contrary," said Alison, "you're not thinking at all. I can't imagine how you started with this lunacy, I really can't."

"Well," said Mr Singh, "that's down to Spenser, too, funnily enough. "

"I've never heard of him," said Alison.

"That's hardly surprising," said Mr Singh. "He was my cell-mate in Wormwood Scrubs."

Alison stared at him and he laughed. "Oh, I haven't always been the upright citizen you see before you."

"Upright? Clearly you're thinking of someone else."

"About four years ago," continued Mr Singh, "Spenser told me all about some woman who worked with his wife in that boutique place." He picked up a stone and skimmed it into the water. "He was talking about Karen, of course. That day was when my life changed. When it got good."

"Not good - just better," said Lucy. "Our life was already good."

"Of course it was." He nodded. Then he picked up another stone and swung his arm back. "So, anyway, a while back, Karen did a really stupid thing. She knew what line of work Spenser was in and she got him to write this letter that looked like it came from her ex-husband. Well, Spenser sometimes takes weird dislikes to people – especially women." There was a loud splosh as the stone hit the water. "He'd like to see her suffer, I think."

"So would I," said Lucy.

"You've a right to know this stuff, Alison, don't you think?" In the moonlight, they saw the gleam of his huge smile. "Considering."

"I think you should be ashamed of yourselves," said Alison. "You disgust me." She folded her arms.

"But what Spenser *really* wanted me to know was that Karen was about to come into a fortune," said Mr Singh. "He knew I'd be interested. And that she'd be easy pickings. They love me, these middle-aged women. It's the gallantry. They can't get enough of it."

"It's your arse they can't get enough of," said Lucy. She leaned forward and grabbed his buttocks. "It's not your manners. Don't kid yourself, babe."

"You will never ever get away with it," said Alison. "Not ever. I don't even see the point. What's in it for you? This fortune of Karen's that your friend told you about? Well, he was wrong. You can forget that. It didn't happen."

"Oh, but it did," said Lucy. "Big time. Even better than we'd thought."

"We're not rich. All we have is the tontine money. Wait - *is that it?*"

Lucy looked at Mr Singh and they both smiled.

"You'll never get it - you can't. You're not family."

And then Tamara and Douglas heard again the laughter that had brought them to the water's edge in the first place.

"They're married, you old fool!" said Lucy.

"Married?" said Alison. "Who is? What are you talking about?"

"As of last week," said Mr Singh, "Karen became my lovely wedded wife."

"You're lying!" Alison looked at him, incredulous.

"Nope, 'fraid not. All it took was one glass of drugged wine at bedtime and *bingo*! She was all over me. And when she inherits the tontine - courtesy of you drowning yourself tonight - all that lovely money will be mine."

"*Ours*," said Lucy. She leaned across, grabbed hold of the man's coat and pulled him towards her. She kissed him passionately on the mouth.

"But I'm not *going* to drown," said Alison. "Not on this night nor on any other. It'll take more than you pair to kill me. I'm an excellent swimmer."

"Well," said Lucy. "I'm looking forward to the challenge. I owe you a broken leg, plus a year as a cripple."

They moved towards her, one each side.

From behind the willows, Tamara gasped so loudly that Douglas glanced at her in dismay. "We've got to stop them," she whispered.

"I know," he whispered back. "I'm just waiting for the right moment."

"How will we know when that is?"

He said nothing, his eyes fixed on the hideous spectacle opening up in front of them. "Soon."

Meanwhile, Alison's heart was beating fast as a metronome. Calm down, woman! she thought. Come on, girl, you're smarter than these two put together. *Think of something...use your brains*!

"Aren't you forgetting Arnold?" she said.

Lucy smiled, as if amused. It wasn't a nice smile.

"Don't you think it's sad that postmen are paid so badly?" She laid a hand on Alison's wrist. "Including the guy who delivers mail to Tammy."

"What on earth are you talking about?" Alison pulled her arm away. "*Postmen?* This is gibberish."

"Really? Well, thanks to that bent postie, we've been reading all of Arnold's letters to Tammy - which is more than *she's* managed to do recently. The last one had a return address on it and so now we know exactly where he is - he's tucked away in some crazy religious commune in Wiltshire." She chuckled. "For the moment."

She took Alison's arm again and Mr Singh took the other. They stepped in a line towards the lake. Or tried to. Alison refused to budge. She wasn't taking one single pace closer to the water's edge.

"Karen is the single most selfish person I know," she said. "You won't get a penny."

"Not while she's alive, maybe," said Lucy. "But alcohol dramatically shortens a person's life expectancy."

"It will all be left to her daughter," said Alison. "Karen may be a difficult person - but she's a devoted mother."

"I hear that Isabelle loves riding her bike," said Mr Singh. "And they're so dangerous. It really wouldn't surprise me if Karen outlived her."

"What on earth makes you think that you'll manage to kill -" Alison stopped speaking while she counted. "Seven - for god's sake, *seven!* - people without the police realising?"

"Trust me, they won't," said Lucy. "Have they believed you so far?"

Alison didn't reply.

"It's not as if I'm in a hurry," said Mr Singh. "And it'll be worth it. It's an awful lot of money I'm talking about."

"It can't take too long, though, babe," said Lucy, gazing at him. "We want to get on with the rest of our lives, don't we? And follow our dreams. Together."

"Of course we do. And we will. " He leaned past their captive, took Lucy's free hand with his and kissed the back of it. "Babe."

My God, they're ghastly, thought Alison. "I happen to know something of the Sikh religion," she said. "And a very fine one it is, too. Aren't you scared of being judged and punished by God?"

"I'm no more Sikh than you are," said Mr Singh. "There wasn't much sign of God - *any* god - in the children's home where Lucy and I grew up."

"He's not even Indian," said Lucy. "His mum and dad were Portuguese - and *he* was born in Blackpool."

"I bet if I'd really been Indian," said Mr Singh, "there would have been an army of aunties to take me in when I got orphaned."

They attempted another step forward which was again aborted by the woman imprisoned between them. "But how can you be called Singh?" she said .

"Oh, Alison," he said, sighing. "I've had lots of names. Singh's as good as any other."

"So the rest of it," she said, "the way you dress and everything - it's all just for show?"

"Let's say two paths collided."

"Really?" she said. "How so?

Lucy tutted in irritation.

"Karen wanted cheap fashion production in India," he said. "And at the same time, I urgently needed to disappear. *Bingo!*"

"I see," said Alison, nodding as if in admiration of his forward planning.

"And you know what?" He didn't wait for her reply. "A European guy becomes unrecognisable once he grows a beard and puts a turban on."

"Look, let's get on with it," said Lucy. "It's freezing here."

"Yes," said Alison, "I'd hate for you to catch cold."

And it was at this point that Douglas started to sneeze.

"It's the trees," he gasped. "The willows!" And then he sneezed again . And again. Explosively. "I can't help it," he wheezed. "Allergies!"

Tamara stared at him in horror.

"What the fuck?" said Lucy, gazing through the trees. "Who's there?"

Alison tried to move away and Mr Singh seized her arm and pulled her back. "You stay right here."

"Come on, Tamara!" said Douglas, hoarsely. "This is it - *this* is the right moment!"

Chapter Thirty Three

Putting his broken glasses in his pocket, Douglas took Tamara's hand and they rushed towards the waterside, both roaring like banshees.

Things happened very fast after that.

"No!" said Lucy, letting go of Alison and taking a step towards them. "I don't believe it - what's the *matter* with you? Why are you *always* everywhere you shouldn't be?"

"Just shut up," said Tamara. "You've said more than enough already." Then she grabbed Alison's arm. "We got your secret message! We've come to save you!"

"Thank you, dear," said Alison, "but I believe I have this covered." She pulled herself out of both Tamara's and Mr Singh's grasp and then turned and booted Lucy straight in the groin. Lucy doubled up in pained surprise and fell to the ground.

Alison dusted off her hands as if to clean them. "You cannot believe how long I have wanted to do that - what an immense satisfaction."

At that exact moment, Mr Singh yelled, rushed forward and pulled back his fist, ready to punch Douglas straight in the head. To Tamara's astonishment, Douglas blocked the attack and jabbed a quick one-two of his own. The man shrieked and put his hands over his face. Blood poured between his fingers and ran down his beard and wrists as he sank back against the boulder where Lucy had put Alison's bag earlier. He slid to the ground, moaning. "My nose - you've broken my nose!"

Tamara stared at Douglas.

"I was an amateur boxer in school," he said, trying to look modest. "Useful for when people wanted to smash my ginger nerdy head in." He shrugged his shoulders. "Never thought I'd-"

"How *dare* you?" screamed Lucy, rushing towards him. "How dare you even *touch* him? I'll kill you!"

"Douglas, look out!" shrieked Tamara.

He gazed around blindly and Tamara pulled him towards her but not quickly enough to stop Lucy from cuffing the side of his head. She must have been clenching a sharp-edged stone because Douglas grabbed his head and when he pulled his hand away there was blood on his fingers.

As Lucy pulled back her hand to hit him again, Tamara grabbed her wrist. "No, you *don't*, you mad bitch!" she said. "Don't you even *think* about it."

The two women struggled furiously, spinning around and around for a handful of feverish seconds, their arms flailing, until, with a resounding splash, they both fell straight into the lake.

"*Help!*" screamed Lucy, spitting out black water, and clawing at the reeds. "*Help me!*"

"*Help!*" called Tamara. "I can't swim!"

Alison pulled off her cardigan and threw it onto the ground. "I'm coming, Tammy," she shouted. "I'll save you."

Douglas ran forward and put a hand on her arm. "No," he said. "It has to be me. Hold these, will you?" He took his broken glasses out of his pocket and handed them to her. "Keep calling, Tamara!" he shouted as he jumped into the water. "I'll find you, darling!"

Alison rushed across to her handbag and took a packet of chewing gum out of it. She unwrapped a piece of bright pink gum and used it to glue Douglas's glasses back together again. She did this almost entirely by feel because her eyes were on the women retching and floundering in the lake.

Meanwhile, Mr Singh didn't move from where he was, sitting on the mud, one hand to his nose, his back against the rock. He stared, as if bemused, at the two writhing figures.

"*Save me!*" called Lucy. "The water's freezing. I ...I can't feel my legs... I..." she was gasping now. "I can't move..."

"For god's sake," Alison cried to Mr Singh. "Jump in and help!"

Mr Singh touched his bloodied nose gingerly.

"Mr Singh!" cried Alison. "Get in the water right now and save that ghastly woman."

"I'm not sure I will, actually."

"Can't you swim?" said Alison.

He didn't reply.

"Oh, for goodness sake." She put the repaired glasses on top of her bag, made for the water's edge and prepared to jump in herself.

"Hang on," he said, standing up and grabbing her arm. "You know, this might all be for the best."

"I'm drowning..." Lucy's voice was no more than a whisper now. "Help...me..." She sank beneath the water and then came gasping back up again.

At that precise moment, Douglas climbed out onto the shore, cradling Tamara as tenderly as if she were a baby. Once on dry land, he kissed the top of her head. She held on tightly, her arms encircling his neck.

And that was when Mr Singh decided to make a run for it through the trees.

Alison picked up Douglas's chewing-gummed glasses and handed them to him. "Here you are!" she said. "Now go after him!"

He lowered Tamara to the ground and put his spectacles on. It looked as if he had a giant pink snail on the bridge of his nose. Then he raced off into the forest in pursuit.

Despite being soaking wet and very cold, Tamara couldn't stop herself from grinning.

"He's a good man," said Alison. "And I very much approve. Now excuse me a moment, there's something I need to do." And she raced to the edge of the lake and jumped in.

But it was too late. Where Lucy had been, there were only moonbeams dancing on the water. Alison parted the reeds, dived under them, came up gasping for air and dived again. Eventually, she had to admit defeat. Slowly, she swam back to the bank and pulled herself out.

At that moment, with a crashing of branches and hideous cursing, Douglas appeared. He had Mr Singh in a headlock which meant that the man was forced to stumble along, his gaze facing downwards as he was dragged through the undergrowth.

"Well done, Douglas!" called Tamara. "You're amazing!"

Douglas grinned. If he'd had a tail, he would have wagged it. "It was nothing. He hadn't gone far."

"We need something to tie him up," said Alison. "Or he'll be off again."

Douglas forced Mr Singh upright.

Alison strode towards them. "You don't have the right to wear this turban," she said as she began to unravel it from Mr Singh's head. "I, on the other hand, have need of it."

Metres and metres of white cloth spooled in loops on the mud. He certainly looked very strange denuded of his headgear, his shorn head gleaming black.

"Well," said Alison. "What do you have to say for yourself now?".

"I never killed *anyone*," he said. "It was Lucy - all the deaths, all the accidents."

"Really? And you expect us to believe that?"

"She was blackmailing me. She's friends with some really shitty people - all the ones that want to know where I am. I had no choice - don't you see! *I'm* a victim, too."

"Mr Singh, I loathed that woman but nevertheless-"

"-even when we were kids, she was weird. She always liked killing things - insects, birds. She killed a cat once. She laughed."

"We still shouldn't have let her drown. I wanted her punished in a prison cell, not in this godawful lake."

"She'd never have lasted a day in prison. Not a day. She couldn't stand being locked up. That's what they used to do to her, you know? At the Home - lock her up in a cupboard."

"Well, I hope you're proud of yourself," said Alison. "Because, thanks to you, she's dead."

"She would never have given up," said Mr Singh. "She would never have let me stay with Karen- the woman I really love. She's my life – she means everything to me. I've had to pretend-"

"-I've had enough of this whining nonsense," said Alison as she pulled back her hand and slapped him across the face. "That's for my cousin Gerald," she said. Then she slapped his face on the other side. "And that's for my cousin Venetia."

Douglas braced himself, ready to intervene, but Mr Singh appeared too exhausted and demoralised to protest. And then Alison pulled back her foot and executed her second Groin Strike of the day. "And *that*, you bastard, is for my sister."

He collapsed in agony onto the ground whereupon Douglas dragged him to the base of a slender birch tree and tied him to it with the fabric from his own turban.

While all this rough trussing was being implemented, Alison walked to the water's edge. She stared up at the glistening moon. "Goodbye, my

Pammie," she whispered. "Goodbye, sweet girl. We made them pay, didn't we? Did you see?"

And that was when the first police car arrived.

Chapter Thirty Four

Very soon, sirens and flashing blue lights heralded the arrival of two more police cars plus an ambulance. Mr Singh was untied from the tree. A paramedic wrapped them in foil blankets. Mr Singh's nose was patched up and he was bundled into the back of a panda car. Alison, Tamara and Douglas sat on the rock at the waterside and answered what felt like hundreds of questions. Eventually, the police let them leave the forest with instructions not to leave the town. They were to expect further contact and interviews the following day.

Lucy's body was yet to be retrieved.

The walk back to the car did not require further battle with the trees. It turned out there was a short, gravelled footpath that led all the way there. When they reached the barred gates, they found them open, the padlock hanging uselessly. They saw Mr Singh's Mondeo, hidden in the trees. They hadn't noticed it earlier.

Douglas drove them home in silence. Tamara was not fazed this time by the lane with its phantom figures and witches' fingers. She'd seen too much real-life horror that evening for fantasy creatures to scare her.

They got home and collapsed onto the sofa. After Douglas had been prepped with Tamara's ancient antihistamines, he was able to handle Poppy and Coco's slobbering attention without sneezing. He cuddled both animals tightly and they soon settled down into his embrace. Tamara held onto his arm and rested her head against his shoulder. Alison lay back and thought of her dead sister and of how close she had come to joining her.

"Should we eat something?" said Tamara eventually. "Is anyone hungry?"

"Not even slightly," said Alison. "I feel a bit sick, if I'm honest."

"Something small?" said Douglas. "Something light, maybe?" He smiled at her and, tired though she was, her heart skipped.

Ten minutes later, she called them both into the kitchen where, despite their earlier indifference to the idea, they wolfed down the omelettes that she'd prepared. She offered a glass of wine, too, but no-one could face it. Alison made a pot of tea instead. They sat almost in silence, too exhausted and traumatised to talk.

However, once they had eaten, they had more energy. Sitting back down again on the sofa, they began to discuss all they had learnt and seen that evening, slowly at first and more volubly as midnight approached.

"One thing still puzzles me," said Alison. "What did you mean earlier about my leaving you a secret message?"

"You know," said Tamara, "the Tammy Annual and the Brownie swimming badge - that you left for me to find outside the library."

"Oh, my dear, dear girl," said Alison. "That wasn't me - that was Mr Singh. The annual was in my handbag - he took it out, no doubt thinking that a person intent on suicide wouldn't bother taking *that* on their final journey. And it was Lucy who threw it on the floor. As for the badge - it must have been stuck inside the pages of the book."

"Oh, my god." Tamara stared. "If it hadn't been for us finding it then..." but she couldn't finish the sentence.

"Then I might be dead."

"When I read the title of the first story," said Tamara, "and saw it was on a page with a turned-down corner - well, that seemed to clinch it." Her face was white and her eyes huge with tiredness and strain. "I was so certain you were trying to tell me where you'd gone - and why you were going there."

"And I'm *glad* you were so certain. You saved my life." Alison took her hand. "But there, that's fate, isn't it? It just wasn't my time."

"Well, thank god for fate," said Douglas.

They wondered, too, about Karen and how she had been so cruelly duped. What had Mr Singh said about drugging her? Had she been tricked into marrying him? Poor woman. Should they ring her? Were they even allowed? But what would they say? Where to even start?

"There's absolutely no point in getting in touch with her tonight," said Alison finally. "It's much too late, for one thing. She's not expecting him home until tomorrow anyway. If we ring her now, we'll terrify her. I bet tiredness will make us say all the wrong things."

"I'm sure the police will already have contacted her," said Tamara.

"I don't know what the protocol is," said Douglas. "This is my first murder."

"And what about Arnold?" said Alison. "He can come home now. If he wants to."

"I can't tell him what's happened," said Tamara. "I don't know where he is. Like Lucy said, she intercepted the one letter which had his address on."

"Hasn't he become a monk or something?" said Douglas. "Hasn't he found God?"

Eventually, there was nothing more to be said. They had exhausted all that they knew or could guess at. Douglas was persuaded to stay overnight. He slept on the couch. And above him, in the little pink bedroom under the eaves, Tamara remembered their embrace at the waterside and smiled. There had been wonderful things too that night. Not everything had been terrible.

When she got up the next day and tiptoed into the lounge, he was snoring. Poppy lay across his feet, Coco was purring in the crook of his elbow. Tamara kissed her fingertips and then lay them gently across his cheek. He didn't stir.

She made coffee and toasted some bread. Alison came downstairs five minutes later, still in her dressing gown, and sat next to her at the table. The two women sat in silence for a while, gazing out at the garden and at the breakfast litter in front of them.

"Thank God it's a Saturday," said Alison, eventually, as she buttered a slice of toast. "Half-day for me."

"Half-day? You mean you're actually going into work? After last night?"

"Of course," she said, ramming her knife into a pot of marmalade. "Why wouldn't I?"

"And this is why you're a Brown Owl," said Tamara. "You're amazing." She washed her plate in the sink. Then she put a cup of coffee, a glass of orange juice and the battered pack of antihistamines on a tray. "Breakfast in bed for my very own Prince Charming."

"Great idea. He deserves it."

When Tamara went into the lounge and called his name, Douglas slowly sat up, looking dazed. Poppy and Coco appeared affronted at the intrusion. When he saw her, his face brightened and he looked altogether more awake. Taking the tray, he set it down on the table and then pulled her into his arms. It was a little while before he drank his coffee.

Showered, dressed and almost ready for the day, Alison went out to the garage. Sitting in the car, she turned the key in some apprehension but, to her great relief, the engine started first time. Clearly, it had just needed some time off. That was a feeling she could recognise. She patted the dashboard. "Well done, trusty friend."

The car's recovery had saved her from some awkward decisions. She didn't fancy catching the bus and certainly didn't want to ask Tammy to take her to work again. She closed her eyes, involuntarily remembering the events of the day before, which, though vivid, felt like a million years ago.

Despite her earlier assumed breeziness in the kitchen, she was exhausted. She could understand Tammy's amazement that she would want to be in work today but what the girl didn't realise was that the library was her safe space and it had been violated. Going back would exorcise the demons and make the place hers again. She yearned for the old familiar calm of the library stacks; she wanted to be sitting at peace in the stockroom, breathing in the musty comforting smell of the pages. It would bring her some respite from the turmoil in her mind. And returning couldn't be put off. She had to go back and the longer she left it, the harder it would be to face it.

And to face him.

When she arrived at the library, Gordon was already in the kitchen, kettle in hand. "Fancy a coffee, boss?" His tentative smile asked so much more.

"You betcha," she said." But don't even think of giving me a chipped mug."

She didn't tell him what had happened over the previous 24 hours. It was pointless.

When she got home again that afternoon, there was a note on the kitchen table.

Hi, Alison,
I've gone out for a jog with Poppy.
Douglas has gone to work.
Also, the police rang. They're coming round to speak to us at four.
Be back soon!
Tamara XX

She sat down at the kitchen table and gazed out into the garden. It had helped, going into work, just as she had known it would ...but still. She was still coming to terms with it all, not least the loss of her dreams with Gordon. He had been so kind today, the first day of their new understanding.

The doorbell rang, the jarring noise making her jump.

To her surprise, and somewhat to her embarrassment, it was Karen.

Ten minutes later, as they sat in the kitchen, sipping tea, Alison tried not to stare at her cousin's red-rimmed eyes. How foolish she must feel, she thought. How taken in. At least all I missed in Gordon was that he was gay. Small beer, I guess, in the scheme of things.

"Have they let you see him yet?" she said, finally, "your new husband?"

"No." Karen put her cup down and stared at her hands.

Alison said nothing, unsure what to add that wouldn't make her cousin feel even worse. Silently, she passed her a plate of custard creams.

"How did Tammy and Douglas know to go to Pond Hill last night?" asked Karen eventually.

"It's a long story. Let's just say it was because of something they'd read."

Karen didn't enquire further. Instead, she said, "and what about the police - how did *they* end up going to the lake?"

"Douglas had rung them - anonymously - from the telephone box just outside the Nature Reserve. He thought he was on his way to prevent a suicide - mine, as it happens."

She tried to smile but couldn't. It just wasn't funny. She gave up on it and took hold of her cup of tea. Her hands were shaking and she grasped the smooth china to keep them still.

"He wasn't sure a suicide would be enough to make them come quickly," she continued. "So instead he told them there was a dangerous lunatic rampaging in the woods. Which turned out to be rather closer to the truth."

She got up and opened the French windows. "Stuffy in here, isn't it?" Standing in the doorway, she breathed in the fragrant air from the garden. The jasmine just outside the door had a heady scent.

"One thing I don't understand," she said," is why Lucy always wore such strong perfume. It was a mad thing to do. She must have known the smell would give her away long before we could see her."

"Oh, she couldn't smell it anymore," said Karen. "She'd been wearing it too long."

For a moment, Alison said nothing. She gripped the edge of the door, her knuckles white. Eventually, she turned round and faced her cousin.

"How could you possibly have known that?"

Chapter Thirty Five

For a moment, there was silence. "Well, I just assumed it, obviously." Karen said at last. "Everybody knows that's what happens with perfume eventually. Why does it matter, anyway?" She smiled but her glance remained wary. "The woman's dead."

There was a moment of silence which Alison eventually broke. "You knew, didn't you?"

"Knew what?"

"That they were in it together."

"Of course I didn't!" A nerve started to jump in Karen's cheek, just below her right eye. "It must be the menopause, Alison. It's sending you loopy."

"It horrifies me to even contemplate it but you *must* have known. And not only that they were working together - which would be bad enough - but also that they were going to try and kill me. And you didn't stop them. You didn't even try and *warn* me. What is *wrong* with you?" She shut the French windows and came and sat next to Karen. "I've known you all my life. You're my cousin - for god's sake, *we're family!*"

"You're being ridiculous. You've had a difficult twenty four hours and you're tired."

"I need to hear the truth. All of it. You must have been aware of at least *some* of this - I realise now that it's the only thing that makes sense."

Karen said nothing. Her eyes were focused downwards, her lips were tight, and she appeared to be deep in thought. It seemed then that she had come to some conclusion because it was with a new steeliness that she opened her bag and took out a cigarette. She flicked her lighter again and again but the spark refused to ignite the flame.

"How else would you have known about Lucy and her perfume?" persisted Alison. "And the short hair under your husband's turban -

265

Sikhs don't cut their hair, you must know that, it must have made you suspicious. And you've already told us that you've never met any of his family, nor any of his friends, nor even gone to his house or place of work... Come *on*! You're not a stupid woman. You must have smelt a rat."

Karen took the unlit cigarette from her lips and dropped it onto the table where she slowly began to crumble it into bits.

"Karen - tell me now or, I swear to God, I'll call the police and you can do the explaining in a prison cell."

Silence.

Alison stood up, pushing her chair back as she did so, the legs making an ugly scraping noise against the floor. "Right," she said, "the police it is. My patience with you is exhausted."

"Wait," said Karen, her eyes still fixed on the shredded tobacco flakes and cigarette paper in front of her.

"Well?"

"You have to understand something." Finally Karen looked at her cousin. "I swear to God I did not know they would try and kill you." The nonchalance of a moment ago had gone. "I promise you I did not know that!"

Alison put her head in her hands.

"Do you really think I'd just stand by?" She wrapped her hands over Alison's. "My own flesh and blood?"

Alison shook off her embrace. "Have you been in on it right from the start?"

"Are you seriously asking me if I had anything to do with Gerald's death? And Pammie's? And Venetia's?"

"Yes," said Alison. "I am. Did you?"

"Of course not - what do you take me for?"

"Did you know they were going to take me to the lake?"

Karen swallowed. "Yes."

"How could you!"

"Amandeep said they could persuade you to sign a waiver - forfeiting all rights to the tontine." She looked at her cousin's face, so white, so dismayed. "You don't need the money, Alison!" she said. "But I do, I really, really do! It's the only way I can set up my business and make a career for my daughter. Don't you see? It's the only way I can get Isabelle back!"

"And you believed him when he said that was all they were going to ask me to do? To sign a waiver?"

"He said he'd talked to a lawyer. They took you to the lake to - to add pressure."

"To try and drown me, more like!"

"You're wrong!"

"That's why you were so jumpy when Tammy rang you last night - you were expecting *him* to call and tell you they'd done it - that they'd killed me!"

"I swear that's not true!"

Alison turned her head away. This was even more horrible than the revelations of the night before. "When did you know that he wasn't who he'd said he was?"

"A few days before we got married. I saw him with a man called Spenser....and I knew something was up. Why would he be with him? How did he even *know* him? Spenser is - "

" - I know, he's a forger. And an expert one apparently. So why *was* he with him?"

"He needed ID - for our wedding. He had to have something with the name Singh on it."

"And you still went ahead with it? You still married him? Knowing he wasn't who he said he was....what the hell were you thinking of?"

"Alison, my husband is not a murderer!"

Her cousin shook her head in obvious despair. "This is dreadful."

"It was all Lucy!" cried Karen.

"Well, how very convenient."

"He explained everything to me - she was mad. She'd never have stopped killing - she enjoyed it. She...." Karen stopped and gazed down at the table top. Then she looked up defiantly. "And, anyway - I love him. I absolutely adore him. You've never been in love so you don't know what it's like."

Alison thought of Gordon and her face flushed. "What about Tammy nearly being killed at the hospital?" she said. "That was him, wasn't it? He tried to run her over. He's not the innocent he's pretending to be, Karen. Why can't you see that?"

"Lucy rang him from the hospital and *told* him to do it - but he didn't hit her, though, did he? I told you, he's not like that. He couldn't kill anybody!"

"And the poisonous flowers Tammy was sent?"

"That was Lucy!"

"Oh, Karen, for god's sake! What's wrong with you!"

"Nothing is wrong with me - I know the truth, that's all. I love him...and he loves me back."

"Well if he loves you, once I was out of the way, he would have had to defy Lucy to keep you alive ....And if she's such a maniac, that wouldn't be easy. So what was he going to do? Was he going to kill *her*?"

Karen didn't reply. She started to twist her wedding ring around her finger.

"You know, he stopped me from saving her last night," said Alison. "It's his fault she died."

"He accepted what he might have to do. For me. For Isabelle."

"For money, you mean. You didn't hear the things he said last night. He's got you convinced - but it's all a lie. Did you know that he drugged you? You've been conned."

"He doesn't want the money. He just wants me."

"You're kidding yourself."

At that moment, the sound of voices came to them from the pavement outside. Karen looked out through the window. "It's Tammy," she said. "I suppose you're going to tell her everything?"

For a moment, Alison said nothing. Eventually, she said, "I'll have to think about that. It depends on whether her knowing the truth about you might keep her safe."

"Oh, for god's sake!"

Poppy came thundering in with Tamara behind her.

"Look who's home!" she said. "Mum and Barry! I just bumped into them outside. They're a day early." And then she saw who else was in the kitchen and came to a halt.

"Karen," she said. "Hi."

"Hello, everybody," said Alison. "Karen was just leaving."

"Yes, must dash." Karen stood up. "Poor timing. Love you and leave you."

"Well, it was nice to see you, dear," said Janet. "However briefly. You're looking well."

Actually, Karen looked rather ashen. Janet, on the other hand, was very tanned and happily plump.

"There was food poisoning on the ship," she said, "so the cruise finished a bit early. I was fine. But we've had the time of our lives, haven't we, Barry?"

"Yes," he said, "It was lovely. Once I stopped being sick, we had a grand time. Saw all the sights. The best place was probably-"

"-they don't want to hear all our holiday stories, love," said Janet, shaking her head. "You'll bore them to death." She pulled out a chair and sat down. "We would have popped round to see you sooner, Tammy, but we've just had that nice policeman in."

"Policeman?" said Karen. "Is he still there?"

"I thought they were coming round this afternoon," said Alison. "Why did they come early? And why didn't they come here?"

"Oh, it wasn't about the murderers," said Janet. "This chap - Danvers, is it? - he came to speak to us about the break-in. He says that we're not to worry - they've caught the burglars red-handed."

"That's great," said Alison.

"Good news," said Karen.

"They've found everything that was stolen," said Janet. "Including our telly. It was all stashed away in the old farmhouse at the end of Old Folly Lane."

"You remember that place, don't you, Tammy?" said Barry. "Where that rat ran down our Mandy's arm? I'll never forget-"

"-she doesn't want to remember that, do you, Tammy?" interrupted Janet.

"I do remember it, though," said Tamara. "It was horrible."

"What about the blood they found?" said Alison. "Did he mention that at all? You know, on the broken glass on the bottom wall of the garden."

"God, yes," said Tamara. "I haven't removed that yet - I'd better get on with it, I suppose."

"It wasn't human," said Barry, grinning. "It was cat's blood, apparently."

Tamara had a sudden memory of taking Coco to the vets to get a stitch in her paw.

"I remember the time my old tortoiseshell, Mickey, cut himself," said Barry. "It was on a flint if I recall rightly. You've never seen such blood-"And then catching sight of Janet's frown, he stopped and coughed.

Karen picked up her handbag and walked past them all on her way to the doorway. "Great to have a happy ending," she said. "Isn't it?"

Alison stood up. "I'll see you out," she said.

In the hallway, the two women stopped. "This isn't over," said Alison quietly. "You must know that."

"Oh, I think it is," said Karen. "While that lot were babbling on about burglars and cat's blood, I was thinking. And I've reached a conclusion. One that I can live with."

"Really? Enlighten me."

"We're finished, you and me."

Alison stared at her, the lights from the stained glass window casting purple and green shadows over their faces.

"If you made me choose," said Karen, "between my husband and you, I'd struggle, I really would - but I'd still pick him in the end. That's love."

"Oh," said Alison. "Well, that's very touching."

"But it's not a choice between you and him," said Karen. "I *need* the tontine money. I need it to get my daughter back. So actually this is a choice between you and *her*. And you're not even in the same league as Isabelle. Not even close."

"Karen - what exactly are you saying?"

"I'm saying that I intend to get that money. I'm going to live longer than you and longer than Arnold - if he's still alive. Whatever it takes."

"I think you'd better go," said Alison. "Before I act out some new self-defence moves I've been reading about."

Chapter Thirty Six

A few days later, a letter arrived from Arnold. It seemed that Tamara's postman had refound his vocation now that he wasn't being bribed any more.

Dear Tammy,

Stop press! Don't sell my house!

I'm coming home.

I don't believe the retreat is the right path for me, after all. I have too much to offer the world. I'm going to write a poetry book instead, all about man's existential struggles with the universe. I've already made a start on it. I might write a novel, too. I've always wanted to.

Before I pack my bags and set off, I just need you to confirm that nobody else in the family has died or been attacked. I'm assuming that's the case or you would have told me. Which means that my ideas about Lucy weren't right. I must have been suffering from a mental disorder brought on by stress. It's hard work being an academic.

Also, I think I might have diabetes. Or possibly anaemia. I'm exhausted all the time and they just don't seem to understand here that I need to rest. Also, they're vegetarians.

Love,

Uncle Arnold.

To mark the end of those long and anxious days, Tamara proposed hosting a dinner party. Janet would be there and Barry and, of course, Douglas. She would have liked to invite Karen, too, but Alison was insistent that she shouldn't.

"Just think about it," she said. "What does *she* have to celebrate?"

271

"No-one trying to kill her anymore?" said Tamara. "Isn't that a good thing?"

"And a husband locked up?" said Alison. "That's not quite so great, is it?"

"But doesn't that make this *exactly* the time that family should pull together?"

"Do you remember me trying to teach you to swim, Tammy?"

"Indelibly," said Tamara, groaning. "It was awful."

"And did you listen to me? Did you pretend to reach down into an imaginary pocket when you were learning front crawl? Did you breathe out into the water when you were learning breaststroke?"

"No...."

"And can you now swim?"

"I cannot."

"So it's time you listened. Karen must not come to this house. Not on Saturday - perhaps not ever again. Trust me on this."

As the five of them sat around the table that weekend, feeling rather shiny and very full, Tamara filled their glasses with champagne.

"This is, after all, a celebration," she said. "It's the beginning of all the good things that are yet to come. And, god, it's such a relief to be able to say that!"

"It certainly is," said Alison, taking a glass. "By the way, did you hear that Mr Singh - I really can't get used to ever calling him anything else - did you know that he's revealed the poisons that he and Lucy used?"

"No," said Tamara, "I hadn't. And were you right? Was it thallium that they gave Venetia? Like in The Pale Horse?"

"Yes," said Alison. "Hollow victory though it is." She took a sip of her champagne. "Unbelievably, it turns out that Lucy was an Agatha Christie fan."

"Well, that's a bit disappointing," said Janet. "It upsets me to hear anything positive about that horrible woman."

"But when Lucy tried to kill Arnold," said Alison, "she gave him a mint covered in a different poison - taxine. Thank god he spat it out."

"Taxine?" said Douglas. "That's made from crushed yew berries. Absolutely lethal. It has a horrible taste, too. I guess that's why Lucy put it on a mint - another strong flavour."

"Dame Agatha used it to kill off Rex Fortescue in *'A Pocketful of Rye'*," said Alison. "It's a favourite book of mine. Or it used to be. And do you remember that awful bouquet that you were sent, Tammy?"

Tamara shuddered. "How could I forget?"

"Those blue flowers were monkshood - as used to murder Harold Crackenthorpe in "*4.50 to Paddington*". Bizarrely, that's a novel that actually includes a tontine scheme, too. *"*

"Impressive in fiction," said Tamara. "But rather less so when it's real life. *"*

For a moment, everybody sat in silence, thinking back over the tumultuous events of the last year. And they remembered, particularly, the three who had not survived it.

Eventually, Alison said, "I know we've had some sad times. And I know that we miss those whom we've loved and lost. But they would not want us to be made so bereft by their passing that our lives stop, too. For us to be sad is almost to say Lucy's won. Which she most certainly has not."

"Hear, hear," said Barry, and then he looked around shyly, as if worried that he'd said too much again or spoken out of turn. He clearly hadn't because Janet beamed at him.

"Well said, Barry! " she said. "And well said, Alison. That's exactly right. Gerald wouldn't want me to grieve for ever. He knows that I loved him."

"And my Pammie," said Alison, "despite everything that happened to her, she had hardly a low moment. She was always happy! She certainly wouldn't want me to be depressed now."

Nobody commented on the third person who had died until finally, Tamara said, "Venetia was a kind person. Things just went wrong for her. She was..." she stumbled then.

"Venetia was a very genuine woman," said Douglas, coming to her rescue. "She never left you in any doubt as to how she felt - and she absolutely wouldn't understand any of us sitting round being depressed because she's no longer here."

"No," said Alison. "Poor woman - empathy wasn't her strong suit."

"I should say," said Janet.

"Look," said Tamara, "I know this isn't New Year - but it does feel rather like a fresh start. So I'd like to suggest that we all take a minute to think of what plans we might have for the future. And then maybe we can share our resolutions - now that the nightmare is behind us. And we should offer up a toast to our success!"

"What a lovely idea, Tammy," said Janet. She looked at Barry, her eyes full of meaning. "We have plans to share, don't we, dear?"

He coughed and went rather pink.

"So," said Janet, plunging on, "what Barry and I would like to say is that..." She looked at him again as if waiting for him to finish the sentence. For once, he didn't seem to want to speak.

They're going to get married, thought Tamara. I think I'm pleased - at least, I want to be pleased.

"Don't you think that Tammy should go first, Janet?" said Barry. "As it's her idea? And her dinner party?"

"Of course, Barry. You're absolutely right." She picked up her champagne and took a sip. "What's your resolution, dear?" She smiled and rubbed the back of her daughter's hand. "Tell us all about it."

"Well," said Tamara. "Having recently found myself utterly helpless in the water - " she smiled at Douglas and he grinned back " - and having been reminded by Alison a few days ago how useless I am, I've decided to learn to swim."

"That's nice," said Alison. "And it's a hugely useful skill. But I was expecting a resolution that was a little more substantial if I'm honest."

"Well, It's not the whole story, " said Tamara, looking around the table, "because I've also been accepted by Cardiff University to do a Bachelor of Education degree. I have to learn to swim because I'm going to train to be a P.E. teacher. Starting in September. It's a four-year course. And I'm so excited!"

"Congratulations!" said Douglas. "That's great!"

"Cheers!" said Tamara and lifted her glass.

Cheers! Was the chorus.

"And now, Mum," said Tamara. "Tell us - what's your resolution?" She braced herself. It wasn't that she didn't like Barry. He was a very nice, if very dull, man. It was just hard to think of her mum being married to him - as if it meant her dad really was being replaced. Somehow that was much more real than them simply living together. She knew that was an unworthy thought and completely selfish and so she smiled an extra-large smile at both of them.

"We're buying a timeshare in the Caribbean!" said Janet. "Aren't we, Barry?"

His face flushed bright red.

"That's lovely," said Alison. "Fantastic!"

"Wonderful!" cried Tamara.

"Congratulations" said Douglas and raised his glass.

Congratulations! Was the chorus.

"The only thing is," said Janet, putting down her champagne. "The tiny problem is-"

"-You'll need to sell this house," said Tamara. "To pay for it. I understand. That's absolutely fine. I'm so pleased for you." And relieved, she thought, picking up her champagne glass again. Thank God. She took a big mouthful.

"Yes," said Janet. "We're so sorry, dear. But not to worry, we've talked about it and Barry says that you can come and live with us next door."

At which Tamara choked so savagely that champagne came gushing out of her nostrils and Douglas had to bang her on the back.

"Well," he said, as he stood and rubbed Tamara's shoulder blades in comforting circles. "Perhaps I can tell you *my* resolution?"

"Please do," said Alison. "Although you've got a hard act to follow. Glasses raised, everyone and drum roll!"

"I'm going to get married," he said, sitting down again. "Or at least, that's what I'd *like* to do. I'm going to propose anyway. Wish me luck, everybody!"

At which there was a moment of stunned silence.

Tamara was the first to respond. "Good luck...".She picked up her glass and looked at him. Or tried to. Her vision had gone all blurry.

"There's only one snag," he said, gazing at her, his eyes bright as cornflowers.

How can he look at me like that? she thought, her heart in agony. How could he have embraced me and kissed me while, all the time, he was planning on spending his life with someone else, some other woman. Her eyes spilled over. She wondered if she could leave the room without making too much fuss. And then she could go upstairs and weep till her eyes were dry and swollen as gob-stoppers. She tried to smile at him but her lips wouldn't stay still.

"What's the snag?" said Barry.

"What if my P.E. teacher wife hated living in the city?" He took Tamara's hand. "What if she wanted to live in the countryside instead? In a thatched cottage with a rose garden and an orchard and, who knows, a clutch of red-haired kids?"

Tamara gasped aloud and, energised by this, Poppy jumped up at the table and knocked Douglas's champagne glass over. Alison reached forward to stop it and in her flying grasp, managed to ensure that the fizz cascaded even further.

"Yes," said Tamara. "Yes, Douglas, I will. And I'll live anywhere, so long as it's with you. The chemists, the countryside, the city, anywhere."

Alison re-filled his glass and looked up, ready to congratulate them both. But she had to look away again because they were embracing with such loving intensity that it was painful to watch. Oh, Gordon, she thought. If only you could have been my resolution. Or one of them, at least.

"I'm delighted for you," she said. "Here's to the happy couple!" She raised her glass.

The happy couple! Was the chorus.

"What's your resolution, Alison?" said Janet. "What do *you* plan to do?"

"I need a change," she said. "A big one. It's been on my mind for ages. And now that Pammie's not here - well, I can do more or less what I want. And this evening's talk has crystallised it for me."

"What on earth do you mean, Alison?" said Janet.

"I've been reading a book called '*How you can Help'.*"

"Do you mean you want to work in a Citizens Advice Bureau?" said Janet. "That could be interesting. I suppose."

"The book was about *international* volunteering. Reading it has made me decide to have a go at living abroad for a while - somewhere I can put my skills to use. And, you know - cliché alert! - try and make a difference."

"Oh, how exciting," said Tamara. "Where?"

"I've applied to become a mobile librarian visiting orphanage schools. In the Cook Islands - they need people like me there. And I'm not sure - but I think I might need people like them!"

"I think that's a fantastic idea," said Douglas. "Just wonderful."

"But that's not all," she said. "If you'll allow me, Tamara, I'd like to have *two* resolutions."

"I don't see why not," said Tamara.

"I'm going to challenge the tontine." Alison looked around the room, registering the look of surprise on every face.

"But if you do that, it will be cancelled," said Tamara. "You do realise? That you'll lose everything?"

"I know," said Alison.

"Won't it all go to some kind of animal charity?" said Janet. "To a bunch of dogs, or donkeys or something?"

"Arnold will go mad," said Douglas. "And as for Karen...." he looked at Tamara, his eyebrow raised.

"I don't care," said Alison.

"But it's a potentially *huge* amount you're giving up," said Tamara. "It could be millions."

"I can't spend the rest of my life looking over my shoulder," said Alison. "I've done my research and, honestly, I'm not sure the tontine was legal in the first place. In fact, I'm sure it's not. Aunt Edna must have been gaga to have suggested it - and that ancient solicitor, Mr Merryweather, he must have been besotted with her to have gone along with it."

"It's a fortune you're giving away, you know," said Janet. "To homes for aged alsatians. Sounds crackers to me."

"It's brought us nothing but trouble," said Alison, "and I don't want it. And I don't want anybody else to want it, either. So I'm going to put it out of reach - forever."

"Unless you're an aged alsatian," said Barry. He looked so serious that Tamara didn't know whether to agree with him or to laugh.

"Ladies and gentlemen," said Alison. "Raise your glasses to - " she hesitated.

Surely not to alsatians, thought Tamara.

"To family," said Alison.

To family! Was the chorus.

And for the first time in a long time, this meant something wonderful.

They could not know it but, at the precise moment that their champagne glasses chinked against each other, a beautiful brunette was sitting alone in a south London bar. All around her, the air was suffused with the oily perfume of violets. She was gazing at herself in the mirror on the opposite wall and, as she sipped a glass of creme de cassis, she smiled at her reflection.

She had been given a second chance at life and this time she wasn't going to waste it on people who were going to let her down.

She was busy making resolutions, too. And she could hardly wait to make a start on them.

.

Printed in Great Britain
by Amazon

30179842R00156